Russell L. Greer is a former U.S. Air Force B-52 pilot and T-37 instructor pilot. He is a native Georgian and holds a bachelor's degree in business administration from the University of Georgia and a master's degree in secondary history education from Columbus State University. Mr. Greer is retired from teaching history in Georgia public high schools and colleges. He currently resides in Woodstock, Georgia with his wife, Karen. *Pale Horse 3* is his second novel.

This tale is dedicated to the 'crew dogs,' maintainers, force protectors, and everyone who honorably wore the blue uniform and raised the Strategic Air Command's 'Iron Fist' to hold the line of nuclear deterrence against the Soviet Union.

Russell L. Greer

PALE HORSE 3

A TALE OF COLD WAR GONE HOT

AUSTIN MACAULEY PUBLISHERS™

LONDON • CAMBRIDGE • NEW YORK • SHARJAH

Ordering Information:
Quantity sales: special discounts are available on quantity purchases by corporations, associations, and others. For details, contact the publisher at the address below.

Publisher's Cataloging-in-Publication data
Greer, Russell L.
Pale Horse 3

ISBN 9781647501419 (Paperback)
ISBN 9781647501402 (Hardback)
ISBN 9781647501426 (ePub e-book)

Library of Congress Control Number: 2020904919

www.austinmacauley.com/us

First Published (2020)
Austin Macauley Publishers LLC
40 Wall Street, 28th Floor
New York, NY 10005
USA

mail-usa@austinmacauley.com
+1 (646) 5125767

I wish to thank the following individuals who helped bring this yarn to life: the late Darwin G. Edwards, for convincing me that sweltering September day back in 1977, that I just might have what it takes to make it through USAF Undergraduate Pilot Training; Steve Beals, for finessing the paperwork to get me commissioned and into pilot training; '2Dogs,' for his knowledge of fighter tactics and air-intercept radars; David English, for refreshing me on details of B-52G operations that had dimmed somewhat in my memory over the course of 34 years; William Bregar and Roger Roley, for their knowledge of the overall U.S. Army force structure in Cold War era Germany; Glenn Kenney, for his assistance with matters pertaining to submarine warfare and naval operations; Albert Sauter, Thomas Keck, and Douglas Hime, my three B-52 squadron-commanders, for their superb, inspirational leadership; Michael Loughran, for his wisdom and the example he set as the best B-52 squadron operations officer in the business; Phillip Litts, for nearly four decades of friendship; David Collett, Todd Hubbard, Steve Joy, J.B. Timmer, Grady Harbour, Chuck Sandwick, Steve Weilbrenner, Bernie Daigle, Greg Crittenden, Kurtis Sutley, Ted Cornell, Don Schumacher, Rob Ball, the late Jim York, Andy Hriz, Rickey Box, and Jerry Maxwell, all first-rate instructor pilots who taught me in the T-37, T-38, and B-52G; Bill Evanoff, Greg Finan, Don Kluk, and Bob Heim, for steering a young co-pilot in the right direction; Bruce David, for his knowledge of USAF security forces; Oley Olsen, Jerry Valentini, Glenn Palazza, and Richard Barnes, for being the best radar navigators I ever had on my airplane; Joe Collins, Steve Danforth, and John Parsons, for always getting me there; Bill Wentworth, Wes Carter, Chris Parsons, Ralph Hager, and Beau Howard, for faithfully manning the tail guns and their superb scrounging abilities; Svetlana Lewis, for her insights into Russian language, culture, and customs; and my wife, Karen, for her unconditional love, support, and the wonderful life we have together.

To avoid confusion, all Soviet military equipment is referred to by its NATO code designations, e.g. "MiG-25" or "Foxbat." Actual Soviet designations of their own weapons and equipment differed from the NATO nomenclature. The author has also taken some liberties with temporal and spatial distortion, in the interests of storytelling.

A brief glossary of terms is included at the end of this story to assist the reader who may not be familiar with the labyrinth of Air Force acronyms and terminology.

"We will not prematurely or unnecessarily risk the costs of a worldwide nuclear war, in which even the fruits of victory would be ashes in our mouth, but neither shall we shrink from that risk any time it must be faced."

John F. Kennedy

"In a fight, you do not stop to choose your cudgels."

Nikita Khrushchev

"And I looked, and behold a pale horse: and his name that sat upon him was 'Death,' and Hell followed with him."

Revelations 6:8

The Crew of "Pale Horse 3"
December 4, 1982

609th Bombardment Squadron 423rd Bombardment Wing (Heavy)

Spurlin Air Force Base, Maine

Pilot/Aircraft Commander: *Captain Spaulding R. McQuagg.* As Aircraft Commander, he was also the commander of the crew assigned to him. As the left-seat pilot in command, all aviation-related decisions rested on his shoulders.

CoPilot/Deputy Aircraft Commander: *First Lieutenant Dillon J. "Outlaw" Lawless.* His duties included assisting the pilot with all flight deck-related tasks. His duties as "flight engineer" included fuel system management, monitoring of electrical systems, fuel usage computations, as well as computation of weight and balance, takeoff and landing data.

Radar Navigator: *Captain Hannes T. "Stumpy" Stumpfegger III.* A navigator whose primary function was weapons delivery, whether gravity bombs or missiles. He also assisted the navigator in appropriate positioning of the aircraft along its route of flight. In previous times, his title would have been, "bombardier."

Navigator: *First Lieutenant Jeffrey L. "Banjo" Coley.* Primary duties were to ensure appropriate positioning of the aircraft along its route of flight. He also assisted the radar navigator with accurate weapons delivery.

Electronic Warfare Officer: *First Lieutenant Enrique "Henry" Chinchilla-Raldirez.* Responsible for employment of all electronic counter measures, to include "jamming" of hostile radars and communications systems, as well as employment of thermal flares to defend against infrared, "heat-seeking" missiles. He also assisted the pilot and copilot in communicating with various command posts and other agencies/entities, ground or airborne, as well as taking sextant shots to aid the navigator with celestial navigation, if and when the need arose.

Defensive Aerial Gunner: *Senior Airman Montel G. "Burnt-the-Fuck-Up" Stokes.* He was primarily responsible for defense against enemy fighter-interceptor aircraft. In the B-52G, he sat in the main crew compartment, as opposed to older models, where the gunner actually sat behind the vertical stabilizer in the rear of the aircraft. His equipment consisted of a fire-control radar system and a remotely operated turret consisting of four .50-caliber Browning machine guns and 2,400 rounds of ammunition. He also assisted the crew with operation of the Air Force Satellite Communication System (AFSATCOM) by monitoring, receiving, and sending communications to and from various command agencies.

Things never happened this way, but they could have…

1. "An Unsustainable Reality"

423rd Bombardment Wing (Heavy) B-52G, Tail #57-0258

Radio Call-Sign: "Pale Horse 3"

Overhead Greenland-Iceland-United Kingdom (GIUK)

Gap, North Atlantic

December 4, 1982

First Lieutenant Dillon "Outlaw" Lawless felt his pulse pounding in his temples, thinking of what he'd just done, as well as the hellstorm he and his crew were about to unleash upon East Germany. He was now in command of the huge B-52, which would soon be the first aircraft to release a nuclear weapon in anger since 1945. In his moment of consternation, Outlaw wondered if history would remember him as a hero or a villain. "Villain" seemed the likely label, yet, unlike the stateside training sorties, returning from this one was about as far from a certainty as one cared to surmise. So, should he not survive, his fretting was pointless. All of the soul-searching and hand-wringing would have to wait until later, if "later" was to become reality.

Two days previously, Soviet ground and air forces, along with some very reluctant Warsaw Pact allies, had attacked through the Fulda Gap into Germany. They seemed to be getting a hell of a bloody nose, according to the briefings, but had yet shown no inclination to call the whole thing off and return to their side of the fence. Despite appalling losses, which they seemed perfectly willing to incur, they were still pushing overstretched and outnumbered NATO forces westward toward France, forcing U.S. President Basil Harvey to order this trans-Atlantic nuclear strike.

Lawless began the mission as the crew's copilot, but was now commanding the mission and responsible for enough destructive force to rank as a second-tier nuclear power. Glancing back over his left shoulder, he saw the lifeless form of his aircraft commander, Captain Spaulding McQuagg, dead of a gunshot to the head. Outlaw had fired the shot himself, less than an hour ago. Even in his most bizarre of nightmares, he would've never thought it would be necessary to do anything of the sort. He was a bomber pilot and that meant flying airplanes and killing, if need be, but he wasn't supposed to *shoot* anyone; least of all, one of his own.

As horrific as things were, Outlaw was glad of the fact that McQuagg had been wearing his helmet, which slowed the bullet and altered its trajectory enough for it to lodge in his ejection seat headrest. Had its trajectory remained straight and true, a shattered window or punctured airframe would've likely led to a decompression in the crew compartment; a problem that would've complicated matters enormously, possibly to the point of aborting the mission.

Aside from the raw act of taking a human life in such a manner and in such a confined space, Outlaw regretted shooting his boss mainly from the standpoint of the widow and three children he left behind. He'd developed a rapport with McQuagg's younger, precocious son, Beasley, though not with the other two children, and had also grown quite fond of Martha, his standoffish, albeit pleasant wife. At this point, he couldn't be sure whether or not the magnitude of what he'd just done wouldn't completely consume him.

McQuagg had been an insufferable, strutting, self-promoter, who meticulously clung to a worldview heavily tilted toward the hubris of reactionary political thought and railed incessantly to anyone who would listen about the need to "fight the good fight" of preventing the Communists from spreading their malignant atheism and draconian human rights violations around the globe. It was this, among a host of other "evils" that clouded his perceptions of the world foisted upon him, he felt, by people with whom he happened to disagree, both politically and theologically.

To many, a little bit of McQuagg went a long way and he'd recently fallen into a pattern of making some very questionable decisions, taking unnecessary risks with the aircraft and the lives of his crew. Outlaw and his fellow R-13 crewmembers had grown increasingly alarmed and were beginning to have some somber, late-night discussions concerning how to rein in Spaulding McQuagg. Despite their concerns, none of them ever gave voice to the idea that McQuagg would've attempted to undermine the mission.

Sometimes, Outlaw had liked McQuagg, but most times, he hadn't, because McQuagg was difficult to like in ways that often seemed contrived. He had a proclivity for sowing seeds of strife with those around him when none needed to be.

For some months, Outlaw had sniffed the essence of a mutual dislike, even though McQuagg had recently written him a glowing Officer Effectiveness Report. Keeping that "OER" in mind, Outlaw played the game and did what was necessary to stay in McQuagg's good graces, even when it meant biting his tongue to keep from overstepping lines with his boss. They had the lives of the other four crewmembers in their hands, and persistent tension between the two pilots would undoubtedly make the others more uncomfortable than McQuagg's recent antics already had.

Despite his belligerent blather, when the time came for Captain Spaulding McQuagg of the Strategic Air Command to strike a nuclear blow against the heathen Red Menace, he couldn't bring himself to do it. He simply didn't have the stomach for it. All hat and no cattle. His self-image had turned out to be simply an unsustainable reality, replete with unrealistic expectations and fingers of blame always pointed outward.

This mission wasn't a full-spasm, SIOP nuclear strike deep into the bowels of the Soviet Union to destroy industry, infrastructure, military targets, and civilian population centers. Instead, it was a "shot across the bow" of Soviet and East German forces, now very close to overwhelming NATO in West Germany and the Low Countries. By launching seven nuclear-tipped PALM-7B Precision Air-Launched Missiles, known as "PALMs," against targets in East Germany, the Soviets, so the logic went, would get the message and cease hostilities, lest the full nuclear fury of the Single Integrated Operational Plan be unleashed against them.

Outlaw's thoughts wandered briefly back to what Captain Hannes "Stumpy" Stumpfegger, the radar navigator, had said during his portion of the mission briefing, prior to launch, "Gentlemen, we'll be launching all seven of our PALMs from high altitude on a semi-ballistic trajectory. Remember, this is the newer version of the PALM-7A, with an increased range on the order of two-hundred and fifty miles. We'll be right on the ragged edge of that range, but they'll fly to their targets at speeds approaching Mach-3. Two-thousand miles per hour. That'll make 'em very difficult for the Warsaw Pact forces to intercept."

Outlaw had expressed his concern, "Even two-hundred and fifty miles from our targets at 37,000 feet is a little too close for my comfort, Stump. At that altitude, we'll just be lumberin' along by ourselves and totally exposed to fighters or SAMs because we got no place to hide; no hills or high terrain for us to duck and dodge their radars or missiles."

Captain Enrique Chinchilla, the electronic warfare officer, known to his squadron mates as "Henry Chinchilla" and always called by both names, nodded his agreement with Outlaw's threat assessment, then added, "Our only alternative would be to go in at low altitude, below 500 feet, which reduces the PALM's range to a mere fifty or so miles, but there isn't any substantial, defensive advantage in that over water; that, plus the fuel penalty we'll pay for going in on the deck. The main benefit of us going in low is the no-launch 'footprint' it provides. That'll make our missiles even more difficult to detect and intercept. So, it's basically a trade-off, but not one I'm totally comfortable with."

"You're right," Outlaw said. "We're gonna need to save every molecule of gas we can, since we have no way of knowin' what we'll be comin' home to. A divert is a big possibility, if we make it all the way back. Does that square with you, boss?"

To this point, McQuagg had said nothing in the briefing, other than the obligatory items for the aircraft commander in the briefing checklist. Beyond that, he had remained silent and simply nodded his affirmation. Given the alternative, Outlaw was now resigned to the high-altitude launch profile and hoped that NATO tactical fighters could handle the threats from enemy aircraft and SAMs. Two-hundred miles was a damned sight better than fifty in the big, green monster he was piloting.

When the valid execution order had been received over the radio, decoded, and authenticated by Stumpy and the navigator, First Lieutenant Jeffrey "Banjo" Coley, McQuagg had insisted that it be given to Henry Chinchilla, who, in addition to being the electronic warfare officer, was an aeronautically rated navigator and thus another of the "positive control" crew members, to decode and verify once more. Henry Chinchilla confirmed the nav team's findings, informed the crew, and then turned his attention back to his myriad electronic warfare screens and gauges. They had a valid "go" order on the PALM strike, but that wasn't the news McQuagg wanted to hear. At that point, he disengaged the autopilot, banked the huge bomber into a steep, right turn, and rolled wings-level on a heading he estimated would return them to Spurlin Air Force Base, Maine.

"Pilot, what the hell are you doin'?" Banjo asked over the interphone.

"Takin' us home," McQuagg responded. "We're gonna start World War III if I don't."

"Pilot, I have the aircraft," said Outlaw, putting his hands on the control yoke and throttles and his feet on the rudder pedals.

"Negative, Co," McQuagg said, refusing to relinquish control. "I have the aircraft and we're goin' home."

"Spaulding, you gimme control of this aircraft, right now," Outlaw responded in a frosty tone. "We have a valid execution order! We've got a chance to stop this war, assumin' Ivan or our side hasn't already lit the big fuse!"

"Negative, Co. I'm takin' us home."

"Spaulding, screw yourself over if you want, but you don't have the authority to take us down with you! I got no intention of doin' time in Leavenworth on account of this! Now, gimme control of this aircraft!"

"No!" McQuagg shouted into the interphone microphone inside his oxygen-mask, now in a sweaty, confused panic.

Trying to diffuse the argument, Outlaw demanded another oxygen-and-station check from the crew. When he queried them, they all reported their stations, "Good," signifying no problems at all.

He then told McQuagg, "Pilot, both offense and defense are Code One. We're Code One up here on the flight deck, too, and there's no system-related reason at all for us to abort."

The radar navigator and the navigator comprised the "offensive" crew component and the electronic warfare officer and defensive aerial gunner made up the defensive component.

"Doesn't matter, Co. *I* signed for this aircraft, *I'm* in command of it, and we're goin' home," McQuagg insisted.

Over the interphone, Stumpy and Banjo then angrily demanded McQuagg give Outlaw control of the aircraft, as a heated argument resumed between the two pilots.

Senior Airman Montel "Burnt-the-Fuck-Up" Stokes, the gunner, asked over the interphone, "Co, Gunner; you need some help up there?"

"Negative, Gunner. Everybody stay put," Outlaw replied.

Despite McQuagg's size of six feet three inches and two hundred and twenty pounds, Outlaw knew Stokes could handle McQuagg physically because McQuagg was soft and Stokes, raised on the mean streets of South Chicago, and by his own admission, was mean enough to "burn down Hell" and go "full-tilt thug" when circumstances dictated. Stokes had reached a turning point and began walking a different path at the age of seventeen, on the heels of rescuing a 90-year-old woman and her three great-grandchildren from a burning apartment building. For his trouble, he received several deep, third-degree burns on his arms and had a large part of his scalp burned away above his left ear, where hair never again grew. Hailed as a hero in his neighborhood, his friends began calling him "Burnt-the-Fuck-Up" because, as he would subsequently explain to anyone brazen enough to ask, "That's just what happened: I got *burnt-the-fuck-up.*"

"Pilot," said Outlaw in a slow, deliberate tone, "turn this aircraft around and get us headed back toward our launch point. We don't have the gas for you to go pissin' it away like this."

"Don't talk to me that way, Lieutenant," McQuagg responded in a haughtily. "I'll have you brought up on insubordination charges when we get back!"

"Insubordination? When you're refusin' to obey a lawful order; *this* order? Not gonna happen, Spaulding, and you know it," Outlaw insisted.

The argument between McQuagg and the rest of the crew persisted for another ten minutes.

Exasperated, Outlaw keyed his interphone switch and announced, "Copilot clearin' off for the urinal."

He disconnected his oxygen hose and communications cord, draped them around the back of his neck, unlatched his lap belt, and left his seat. The urinal was downstairs behind Stumpy and Banjo, but Outlaw didn't need to relieve himself. He needed to talk to them about McQuagg. When he got to the bottom of the crew ladder, he didn't plug his communications-cord into the instructor navigator communication's panel behind Stumpy, to talk to him and Banjo on private interphone, just in case McQuagg happened to be listening. Outlaw just tapped Stumpy and Banjo on the shoulders and shouted at them over the considerable, ambient aircraft noise. McQuagg wouldn't have been able to overhear them, upstairs on the flight deck.

"Whaddya think?" Outlaw asked Stumpy.

"We have a valid order," Stumpy responded. "The tickets match and it's a legitimate strike order. Banjo, Henry Chinchilla, and I are in complete agreement."

"I don't know the consequences of disobeyin' an order that comes from this high up and I sure don't wanna find out," Banjo shouted over the noise.

Stumpy continued, "How does he think he's gonna explain this cock-up when we get back to Spurlin'? If we allow Spaulding to do this, our careers are almost certainly over, man. His will *definitely* be over and we might all end up in federal prison, along with the very real possibility of us bearing the blame for losin' the whole damned war. I don't want that fallin' on any of us.

"You're just gonna have to shoot him, Co," Stumpy added, "and if *you* don't, *I* will."

Outlaw recoiled, went weak in the knees, and stammered, "I...don't think I can do that, Stump."

The very thought horrified Outlaw. If he had to do it himself, he knew he would regret it for the rest of his life, regardless of how long that might be and, at present, longevity wasn't up for wager.

Stumpy pressed his argument, "Just listen to him, Co. He's scared out of his mind and I don't see any way to talk him down from that ledge. If you've got any ideas, tell us, but I'm not seein' it."

"I…just…don't know," was all Outlaw could manage to say.

"Look, Dillon," Stumpy said, pressing his argument, "it's gotta be done. It's unwritten, but it's accepted protocol, under these circumstances."

Outlaw attempted to counter, "Yeah, but I never thought it'd actually happen."

Stumpy's facial expression hinted at exasperation and he responded, "Well, it *did* and here we are. He's gotta be factored out of the equation. We let this slide and we could be responsible for well north of ten thousand more casualties on the ground in Germany; maybe a hundred grand or more. Who knows how many? Weigh Spaulding against that."

Stumpy stabbed the air with an emphatic index finger and continued to make his point, "None of us are obligated to help him shit the bed! Orders are orders!"

Outlaw voiced his grudging agreement, "Alright, I'm the one up on the flight deck with him. I'll do it."

Banjo gave only a reluctant, sour nod and turned back to his charts and radarscope to update the aircraft's position. He turned his oxygen regulator to "OFF" and lit a cigarette, shaking his head in a state of utter disbelief.

Outlaw then looked up at Stokes and Henry Chinchilla, who sat upstairs, aft of the crew ladder, facing rearward at their defense stations. Both were looking down at him. With his index finger and thumb, he made a gesture imitating the shooting of a pistol. Realizing what he was telling them, Stokes and Henry Chinchilla nodded their concurrence. Chinchilla appeared on the verge of tears and again turned his attention to his electronic countermeasures displays. Stokes had temporarily disregarded his fire control radar system and looked forward toward the flight deck, staring daggers through the back of McQuagg's head.

Outlaw then said to Stumpy, "Defense is on board."

"Alright," Stumpy replied, "but you know you're gonna have to help me out with some switch settings on the PALM-7 consent panel that you can't reach from your seat; that, and you're gonna have to turn off the IFF on Banjo's call. You know what you gotta do to release a nuke from the aircraft, under these circumstances."

Outlaw had momentarily forgotten that detail; turning off the Identification Friend-or-Foe transponder northwest of the British Isles and thus, ending the "peacetime" portion of the flight plan. He would have to leave his seat for that, as well.

Outlaw's previous aircraft commander had been a unit instructor pilot and he'd gotten enough time flying in the left seat to feel comfortable with it, although he was now beginning to sense the difference of flying from the left seat on training sorties, as opposed to actual command responsibility in a combat situation; a whole universe of difference. They'd discussed just this scenario quite a few times on alert and in target study: *dead pilot,* which could certainly occur during a combat mission, though not the way this scenario was about to unfold. Outlaw quickly determined he would fly the remainder of the mission in his own seat, due to the fact he was also the flight-engineer, and would need ready access to the fuel-panel and the AC generator switch-panel, both of which could be time-critical in emergency situations. He would just have Stokes drag McQuagg's corpse out of the pilot's seat, when the time came. That way, he could unstrap from his own seat and move to McQuagg's fairly quickly, as circumstances warranted. He'd done it enough times with an instructor pilot and a second copilot on board to get either in or out of his parachute harness in a matter of seconds.

"I'll have Montel come up and drag him to the aisle," he told Stumpy, over the roar of the ambient crew compartment noise.

He climbed back up the ladder to the flight deck, with the seeming weight of the world on his shoulders, and into his living episode of "The Twilight Zone."

Once he returned to his seat, strapped in, plugged in, and then said over the interphone, "Okay, Spaulding, last chance to give me control of this aircraft."

He seemed disconnected from his own voice as he said it, as if divorced from his own thought processes. It seemed to him as if someone else had said it.

"Negative, Co," McQuagg replied, "We're goin' home."

Outlaw knew he had to act quickly. McQuagg was sweating profusely and had his hands in a death-grip on both horns of his control yoke. He wasn't going to relinquish control of the aircraft without force or a fight. Given that the autopilot wasn't engaged and McQuagg was "hand-flying" the aircraft, Outlaw knew that a struggle between the two pilots might well result in the aircraft departing controlled flight and crashing into the ocean. Uncontrolled flight might well distort the airframe to the point of hatches not firing and ejection seats not clearing the aircraft and, even if they did, none of them would live more than a half-hour in the freezing North Atlantic. He reached across his body with his right hand and drew his revolver. He then twisted and leaned to his left as far as he could. McQuagg watched him do it and quickly found himself staring into the muzzle of a .38-caliber revolver.

"One last time, Spaulding…gimme control of this airplane," Outlaw shouted over the cabin noise.

McQuagg's hands didn't budge from his yoke and he screamed, "Nooooo!"

Outlaw squeezed the trigger. The B-52 had no noise insulation inside the crew-compartment, and with the entire crew wearing helmets, the shot sounded no louder than a dull pop. Nevertheless, everyone reacted with instant alarm.

"Everything okay up there, Co," Stumpy wanted to know.

"Yeah, it's done," said Outlaw, who found it now suddenly difficult to breathe with a crushing sensation in his chest.

"You didn't miss, did ya?" said Stumpy with his "Mona Lisa" smile, as he reached over and nudged Banjo with this right elbow.

Banjo simply shook his head and betrayed no emotion, other than disgust with Stumpy's making light of the situation. He felt sick to his stomach and reached for his airsickness bag, although he could only manage a dry heave. Banjo had agreed with the decision out of necessity, given the "big stakes" nature of this mission.

"Gunner clearin' off and comin' forward on your call, Co," said Stokes over the interphone.

"Roger, Gunner. Everybody, stay put. Oxygen-and-station checks, crew, until I get this sorted out and see if we're gonna have pressurization problems," said Outlaw, as he recovered his breath.

Composing himself, Outlaw added, "Everybody go to one hundred percent oxygen until I say otherwise. Once you check in on oxygen-and-station, come on up, Gunner."

The crew immediately clipped their oxygen masks to their faces and selected "100%" on their oxygen regulator-diluter panels.

Outlaw looked across McQuagg's body at the hydraulic panel, literally choking back vomit, as he did so. All the gauge needles looked to be "in the green," within normal limits, and no yellow lights were glowing on the panel. He next glanced up at the eight oil pressure gauges on the eyebrow panel overhead. The needles were all where they were supposed to be.

Next, he checked the cabin altimeter, which was also overhead on the "eyebrow" panel. It showed a normal, cabin pressure altitude of eight thousand feet. If the skin of the crew compartment or the windows had been pierced, the cabin pressure would have bled off rapidly, requiring the whole crew to don oxygen masks to remain conscious. Outlaw next shifted his gaze to the eight sets of engine instruments in front of him. Everything was normal.

After reaching for his checklist, he scanned the fuel-panel directly in front of him. The fuel-feed sequence he had selected fit current fuel load and weapons configuration. The appropriate valves were open, allowing the selected tanks to feed the engines in a sequenced manner and maintain the appropriate center of gravity.

Finally, he pressed his oxygen mask to his face and checked his oxygen regulator. He had a good "blinker" on his panel, indicating the system was feeding oxygen to his mask when he inhaled, and the oxygen quantity on the indicator was well within the normal zone.

After he had allowed sufficient time for the four remaining crewmembers to similarly look over their stations, he told them, "Crew, check in with oxygen-and-station."

"Offense, good," Banjo answered for the nav-team downstairs.

After checking with the Chinchilla, stokes answered for the defense team, "Defense, good."

Outlaw concluded the checks by stating, "Copilot, good. Cabin altimeter is eight thousand."

Stokes added, "Pilot deceased."

"Jesus, Montel. That ain't funny…at all," Banjo replied from downstairs.

"Nav, Co," Outlaw said, disregarding Burnt-the-Fuck-Up's remark and Banjo's rebuke, "Gimme a headin'. Let's get back on track to the launch point."

"Roger, Co. Go ahead and start a left turn back to your previous heading. I'll give you corrections of that. Gimme four-five-zero true airspeed. We can make up some time, at least until the jet stream shifts northward, which its forecast to do."

"Roger, Nav. Startin' left turn," Outlaw acknowledged.

Outlaw noticed the shaky timbre of Banjo's voice and wondered if he sounded the same, but dared not ask the others. Everyone acquainted with Banjo knew he could make a pot of coffee nervous, but let it go because Banjo was a top-notch navigator. It was Stokes who'd begun calling him, "Banjo," referring to the fact that he was always "tight, like a human banjo string."

Outlaw's father, a P-51 Mustang pilot who'd flown bomber escort missions over Germany during World War II, had several times quipped, "Sometimes, the way forward is best seen by the light of a burning bridge."

In an instant of road-to-Damascus clarity, Outlaw now fully comprehended his father's enigmatic statement. The "bridge" with McQuagg had been burned. It was a bullet that couldn't be un-shot and there would doubtless be consequences for it, should he and his crew survive to tell the tale. Yet, orders originating from the President of the United States had to be followed. His way forward was now crystal clear and McQuagg could no longer stand in the way. Outlaw rolled the aircraft out onto the correct heading, set the throttles to hold four-hundred-and-fifty knots of true airspeed, and then re-engaged the autopilot.

"Crew," he said over the interphone, "we're back on track and George is flyin' the jet."

After Outlaw had performed another hourly fuel check, he looked at the fuel totalizer gauge and marked the reading on his fuel curve chart. Things looked okay, for the time being.

Outlaw looked back over his left shoulder and saw that Stokes had secured McQuagg's body to the electronic equipment racks, with several bungee cords he normally carried in his A-4 bag. This would prevent the corpse from tumbling around when the aircraft maneuvered. It seemed harsh, but Outlaw decided it was the most dignified thing to do, given these perfectly horrid circumstances. To have McQuagg's body bouncing and flailing seemed disrespectful, and McQuagg deserved at least that consideration.

"Crew, Co; we're about eight grand low on the fuel curve. It shouldn't be a problem. We can slurp a little extra off the tanker, on the way home," Outlaw reassured them.

Pale Horse 3 was now eight thousand pounds below planned fuel weight; twelve hundred gallons or so. No great worry, aside from the fact that those lost gallons cut into what fuel reserve they would need to divert, should Spurlin weather be below weather landing minimums when they returned, or should Spurlin no longer exist, which was a frightening possibility.

"Roger, Co," said Banjo. "Heading and course are good. True airspeed's good. Time's still pretty good. We've got some jet stream tailwind that'll help us make-up a little of what we lost."

Outlaw figured that the command authorities stateside needed to have some idea of what had occurred, albeit in the vaguest terms possible, and told Stokes, "Guns, send an AFSATCOM message to the effect that Pale Horse Three is proceedin' with its assigned mission, as ordered and authenticated by emergency action message traffic."

The Air Force Satellite Communication System allowed the B-52 to communicate with Headquarters Strategic Air Command, HQ SAC, literally from any place on the globe. It was controlled by the gunner and transmitted messages via data uplink to orbiting satellites, which in turn downlinked them to whichever Air Force or national command agency needed the information.

Stokes replied immediately, "Roger, Co. I already had it formatted. Want me to tell 'em about Spaulding?"

Outlaw answered tersely, angry at the tone Stumpy and Stokes had taken, "Negative, Gunner. We'll have plenty of time to get our story straight before we have to explain it all to the Wing-Brass, OSI, and God-Knows-Who-Else. None of us wants to end up swinging a sledgehammer on the big rock pile at Leavenworth. We'll tell 'em about the onboard fatality when we contact command post on our way back."

"Roger, Co. Sendin' it now."

As the mission progressed, the name "Outlaw" had begun to weigh heavily on the mind of Dillon Lawless. He'd first been tagged with that cognomen on the schoolyard by a friend in the fourth grade. Until now, he hadn't given it much thought. Killing McQuagg just might have pushed him from the point of having a jaunty "call sign" to the real thing, in the eyes of Air Force brass, the Judge Advocate General, and the Uniform Code of Military Justice.

Things were tense and uncomfortable for the next half-hour of high-level cruise, until Stumpy broke the silence on the interphone, "Co, Radar; you up to this, man?"

"Affirmative, Radar. It ain't like we've got a choice. I ain't turnin' around."

"Yeah," Stokes added. "He got us on the ground without a hitch a coupla months ago when Spaulding had the bends."

Outlaw replied, "In the land of the blind, the one-eyed man is king. We can do this, guys."

A bit more at ease, now, Outlaw sought to find a way to break the tension caused by McQuagg's diversion and the enormity of what had just transpired the flight deck.

"Radar, Co," he said to Stumpy. "Just so I'll have a war story to tell, *if* I can tell it to anybody, what kind of targets are we hittin'?"

"Wait one, Co. Lemme look in the strike folder," Stumpy answered.

"Okay." Stumpy said after a short pause, "I have the target list, Co."

"I'm all ears, Radar," Outlaw replied.

"Let's see. Garden-variety fighter-bomber airfields; four of 'em. Then, there's a regional STASI/KGB headquarters; you know, East German Secret Police and their Russian friends. We got a railroad marshalling yard and a MiG-25 base at a place called 'Wolfhorn.'"

"Foxbats?"

"Affirmative."

"I didn't know they had any MiG-25s stationed outside Russia. That could be trouble. They'll be lookin' for somethin' *exactly* like us; kinda like the bastards are expectin' us," Outlaw responded.

"Sure sounds like it," Banjo answered dourly.

"No surprise, here, Co," Stumpy interjected. "They've had a MiG-25 base stationed right along the East German-Polish border, for some time, to intercept SR-71s transiting into and out of the Baltic Sea. This Wolfhorn is closer to *our* flightpath. It's right along the Baltic coast, nestled right up against the East German border with the West German state of Schleswig-Holstein."

"Radar, how could you possibly know that?" Outlaw asked.

Stumpy responded, "My first assignment was as an intelligence officer with the 9th Strategic Reconnaissance Wing, before I applied to and got accepted into nav school."

"Roger that," was all Outlaw could muster, by way of reply.

Outside of this perfectly wretched circumstance, Outlaw would've chuckled to himself at the thought of Stumpy, who always played his personal cards very close to the vest, revealing something of his past. None of the crew, up until this point, had any idea of Stumpy's "past life" as an intelligence officer.

By design, the MiG-25 was a high-altitude, high-speed interceptor and Outlaw knew their presence in East Germany, that close to the border, with West Germany and Denmark was a portent of bad news.

"Roger that, Co," Stumpy responded. "This looks like a fairly recent change to the strike folder. Yep, 15 July 1982 appears to be when this strike folder was updated."

"Thanks, Stump," replied Outlaw. "I don't know if what we throw at 'em will cause 'em to cease fire, but it sure should take some of the heat off our ground forces."

"One's about as good as the other, I suppose," interjected Banjo.

"Yeah, assumin' both sides ain't started throwin' the big stuff at each other, by the time we get there," added Stokes.

"Roger that," Outlawed replied. "Gunner, no more of your silly bullshit about Spaulding. The same goes for you, Stumpy. It ain't like it's the most pleasant thing I've ever had to do, and I'll prob'ly rot in Leavenworth or in Hell for it. Prob'ly both. We *all* might, come to think of it."

"Roger, Co," answered Stokes.

Stumpy didn't respond.

Outlaw only glanced back the corpse when he absolutely needed to. McQuagg's right eye was bulging out of the socket. The sight of that and the blood that had trickled out of his nose and mouth sickened him. The right side of his neck was covered in blood, as well, indicating he had bled out from the ear. Outlaw didn't bother to tell the crew that he'd vomited into

25

each of the two airsickness bags he carried in his lower, right leg flight suit pocket.

2. "Feathers"

"Lieutenant, wake up, sir!?"

Outlaw stirred from his sleep, nauseated and disoriented, as the Security Police airman jostled him awake by a shoulder.

"Sir, you okay?" the airman asked.

"Uh...yeah. I'm good...I think," was all Outlaw could get out of his dry, pasty mouth.

He then sat up and took stock of his surroundings. He squinted into a brilliant, pink sun creeping up over the eastern horizon which, with the seismic hangover roaring inside his skull, made him feel as if he'd been stabbed in the forehead with an icepick. He was in the middle of a field he knew to be between the Officers' Club and the old, World War II-era barracks building he called "home" and was still in his flight suit. When he sat up, his first action was to try and spit dirt out of his mouth. Struggling onto all fours, he spewed last night's mix of *hors d'ourves,* beer, and tequila into the dewy grass.

"Damn. I've been out here all night," he sputtered, trying to get the taste of vomit out of his mouth.

"Looks like it, sir," said the security police airman. "You need us to give you a ride to quarters, Lieutenant?"

"No, thanks. I'll walk."

"Whatever you say, sir. A little too much to fun last night?"

"That's an understatement. Assignment Night," Outlaw said as he put his fingertips against his throbbing temples.

"What'd you get, sir?"

"F-16 to Luke," Outlaw answered.

"Congratulations, sir! Brand new bird! I'm guessin' you'll be a top grad in your class, huh? Sounds like it'll be fun."

"Compared to this hangover, having my face eaten off by rats sounds fun, right now," Outlaw said.

"Anyway, I got the only F-16 in this assignment drop and, from what I'm able to remember, a good time was had by one and all."

"Well, you look pretty rough, after sleepin' in this field all night, sir. It's Saturday, so why don't you just go back to your quarters, take a shower, and get in the rack for the rest of the day?"

"Sounds like a good idea, but I'll skip the shower. Even my *shadow* hurts. I'm cuttin' back on the booze; *way* back, as of right now."

Although he was completely unaware of it, Outlaw had gained a bit of a reputation through his time in Undergraduate Pilot Training, referred to commonly as "UPT," as a clown in the Officers' Club Bar, and a "good stick" and top performer in both the T-37 and T-38 trainer aircraft. The fighter pilot IPs loved it and actively encouraged his Friday night antics and word had quickly spread through the T-38 squadron about this kid's talents. The fighter pilots in the T-37 and T-38 instructor cadre knew he would be a top graduate and receive a plumb fighter assignment. Thus, they began drawing him into their circle.

While no one else seemed concerned about Outlaw's O-Club shenanigans with the fighter pilot IPs, Marble Man was, because he was the Student Squadron, or "STURON," commanding officer and an arrogant, humorless martinet. He had earned the nickname, "Marble Man," for his propensity to stand in the STURON hallway from time to time, arms folded, aristocratic nose held high with not a single, prematurely-silver hair out of place and watch the comings and goings of students and instructor pilots in the building. Occasionally, he would acknowledge greetings with a slight nod of his patrician head, but otherwise, remained silent and almost still. After one such encounter, two of the T-37 academic instructors stepped outside for a cigarette break and one remarked, "Get a load of that guy, just a statue standin' there, like he was made of marble or somethin'. *Marble Man.*" The new moniker quickly spread through both flying squadrons on base, as well as throughout the STURON.

To Marble Man's way of thinking, this punk, Lieutenant Lawless, didn't deserve assignment to the F-16. There was just something about the kid he couldn't stomach. Perhaps it was because he was better looking and had no gray hair, or that women seemed drawn to him in the O-Club bar. Perhaps it was also because everything the kid touched turned to gold, as far as his performance in both the T-37 and T-38 was concerned. Marble Man simply didn't like him and the reasons why weren't important.

He sank his first hook into Outlaw by way of a failed room inspection. Outlaw had committed the unforgivable sin of forgetting to clean the oven in his on-base quarters, prior to it being inspected by his class commander. The other shoe dropped a week later when Outlaw squealed tires in his Mustang on base one night, after which he was stopped by the Security Police and blew a .02 on the breathalyzer. It was not enough to be considered legally drunk, but enough to warrant a citation. That was all Marble Man needed, but being the thorough-going bastard he was, he decided he would examine Outlaw's T-38 gradebook and personnel folder, get his assignment changed from the F-16 to a B-52, and then spring the news on him after he made the announcement at the Wednesday afternoon STURON staff meeting. Marble Man was enough of an administrative chickenshit artist to get his way and wanted this Lieutenant Lawless to serve as an example.

Outlaw went weak in the knees and almost fell over from the position of attention, right there in front of the desk, as Marble Man told him the news, two days later. He'd seen how the Assignment Night crowd reacted to the three B-52 assignments that came down to buddies in his class. While the crowd had roared its approval at the F-16, F-15, F-4, C-141, and C-5 assignments that were handed out, the B-52 assignments were met something akin to the silence of the tomb. Being a top graduate, he had trouped up to the podium and received his F-16 assignment to raucous cheers. Even in his moment of euphoria, he found it disconcerting that three of his classmates were not accorded the respect and enthusiastic applause he and others received. Instead of remaining at the top of the heap, Outlaw was immediately awarded what seemed to him second-class-citizen status, based on what he'd heard on Assignment Night. Supposedly, the bottom graduates of each class were assigned to the likes of the B-52 and KC-135, at least to hear the fighter and cargo pilots doing their tours in the Air Training Command tell it.

The change of assignment, in and of itself, would be bearable. It was simply a bite of the fabled "Big Shit Sandwich" he'd be forced to take. He'd still graduate with his class, get his wings, the vaunted "feathers," and be able to call himself a U.S. Air Force pilot. He knew that the ROTC detachment staff back at the university would be proud of him, as would his parents and friends. The multi-engine, "heavy" time would, of course, set him up for an airline job, should he choose to leave the Air Force when his seven-year

29

obligation was up. But what really angered him was the smug expression on Marble Man's face as he'd broken the news. The bastard had actually seemed to be enjoying himself.

After graduation and temporary assignments to both the water and land survival courses, the first month of B-52G/H academic course was intense and involved a great deal of off-duty study time, as the aircraft was large and complex. However, Outlaw didn't consider his initial hands-on experiences in the B-52 especially challenging. While a large and complex aircraft, it was basically flown straight-and-level all of the time. No "yank and bank" under high g-loads, like in the trainers he had flown and certainly not like what he would've experienced in the tactical fighter world. He did, however, find the paperwork load of a copilot challenging. And boring. He spent laborious hours hand-computing fuel curves, the night before mission planning days, and was constantly computing and re-computing of takeoff data, which had to be updated with changes in temperature, wind, pressure altitude, and a host of other factors. Sometimes, he felt like an accountant doing tax returns.

The extreme "down" side to this new world of the B-52 was his realization that, once he arrived at his unit, there was not going to be much "stick and rudder" time for him, as a copilot. If his aircraft commander, or AC, wasn't a squadron IP, he was going to be relegated to sitting with his hands in his lap as the AC flew takeoffs, air refueling, and landings. At most, Outlaw was going to get to fly some high-level cruise, usually with the autopilot engaged, and some occasional low-level terrain-avoidance flying, absent an IP on board. He found that realization a bit disheartening, but steeled himself to make up for that lack of "stick time" as part of the Accelerated Copilot Enrichment, or "ACE," program, in which he would be able to fly the T-37 when not flying the bomber, mission planning, or sitting nuclear alert.

Outlaw arrived at his first operational duty station, Spurlin Air Force Base, Maine, at 2300 hours on July 1, 1981, after a two-day drive up from visiting his family in Georgia. The morning after his arrival, he put on his duty uniform, tugged on his "woolly pully" sweater to cope with the forty-degree *summer* morning and reported to the 609th Bombardment Squadron.

After meeting the instructor cadre in Training Flight and handing over his training records from UPT and the Combat Crew Training Squadron, CCTS, to the Chief of Training Flight, he was told to report to the squadron commander, Lieutenant Colonel Alvin Spraggins, known in military parlance as the "Old Man." After the Old Man had welcomed him to the squadron, Outlaw asked, "Sir, is there some sort of exercise goin' on around here?"

"Why do you ask? Oh, you wanna know why everybody's in flight suits?"

"Yes, sir."

"Lieutenant, as I like to say, and I said it the first day I took command of this unit: the 609th Bombardment Squadron is a *flyin'* outfit. Therefore, we wear flyin' clothes to work. *My* decision.

"I've already heard the word that you were a top performer in UPT and CCTS and I need you in the air, every chance you get; that means in the bomber *and* the ACE program. Once you've been mission certified in the bomber six months, you'll get checked out in the T-37 and you can fly with other copilots. I need to the best sticks in the air I can get. Take advantage of every flyin' hour you can log.

"Keep your blues pressed and dusted off, just in case we need 'em for the odd ceremony or somethin', but the 'green bag' is the 'uniform of the day,' unless I say otherwise."

"Thanks, Colonel. I'm startin' to like this place, already."

3. "Bergen"

423rd Security Police Squadron
Small Arms Qualification Range
Spurlin AFB, Maine
July 18, 1981

The sight of her took his breath away, just as it always had. Without question, Bergen Cyr was the most beautiful woman he'd ever known, as well as the brightest. Although he knew she was from nearby Upton, he'd never given thought to the idea that she might be stationed at Spurlin and the surprise was total.

Outlaw arrived for his initial small arms qualification training a half-hour early. He walked inside at 0730 hours and the security police staff sergeant, who was carrying boxes of ammunition to the firing line area, told him to help himself to the coffee and doughnuts in the break room. She was sitting on the end of an old, cracked, vinyl sofa, smoking a Virginia Slim, and staring out a window. He noticed the expression on her face, which was in profile to him. Over the years, he had learned that when she smoked or looked like that, she could be deep in thought or thinking about nothing at all, just letting her mind wander.

Outlaw had first met Bergen Cyr shortly after enrolling the Air Force ROTC program, in the fall of 1976. He'd noticed her the first day he'd walked into the ROTC building. It was difficult not to and it was those piercing, ice-blue eyes that had initially caught his eye. At first, she seemed a bit aloof, but not in an arrogant way. It was just *her* way, he would learn.

The day after he had gotten his hair cut to Air Force grooming standards, he entered the ROTC building and literally bumped into Bergen at the base of the stairs leading up to the administrative office.

He'd seen her only once, the day before, but she quickly ran a hand through his hair and said quite matter of factly, "That's a great cut. You're really a nice-looking man."

Without even telling him her name, she hurried up the stairs to the administrative office. To his memory, that was the first time a woman had ever referred to him as such; a "man," not "boy."

Their first lengthy conversation happened on their way to class, one morning shortly after the student body returned from Christmas break. She met him walking down the hill from her dormitory, as he crossed the street to the sidewalk. She was absolutely stunning, squinting into a brilliant, morning sun with a million-watt smile and a very short, tapered hairstyle few other women could wear well. Her angular face retained a softness about it that defied description. Her neck was slender and the tapered brown hair in back always seemed to rest perfectly on it. There was a slight upturn to her nose that added a touch of "cute" to her smoldering elegance. Bergen Cyr was slender of build, tall, and moved with a feline grace. Whatever she wore, she did so with a strong sense of style and, although Outlaw never bothered to ask her the name of her fragrance, she always smelled exquisite.

She smiled and said, "Hi, Dillon! Are you going to the party, tonight?"

The warmth in her voice almost made him weak in the knees. She was referring to a ROTC detachment kegger the cadets had planned and to which the detachment officers and staff had been invited.

Outlaw answered that he indeed was going and she responded, "Well, I was certainly hoping you'd be there. Do I get first dance?"

As they continued their small talk, he noticed the measured rhythm and soft, round tones of her voice, which he found almost musical and soothing. Outlaw was completely overwhelmed by Bergen Cyr as she stood before him in light blue slacks and an attractive light-blue and white turtleneck sweater. He knew immediately, though he did not know in what capacity, that this woman would be a special one in his life.

As gorgeous as she was, looks didn't complete the package by any measure. She had a quick, keen mind, the result of her upbringing the remote area of northern Maine. She seemed independent and tough and he would soon learn to like the "Mainer" in her a great deal. Early on, he knew she would be more than able to navigate her way through a career in a testosterone-fueled, largely male Air Force.

Not only did Lawless spend his entire time at the party talking to and dancing with Bergen Cyr, she rode with him back to his apartment. Beyond that, the entire "romantic" phase of their relationship lasted two weeks and encompassed four dates. Then, Bergen inexplicably pulled away. She wouldn't return his calls or engage him in conversation. After three attempts, he quit trying, though she softened a bit after two weeks and began talking to him, again.

While perplexed, Outlaw was not overly distraught by Bergen's change of heart. He assumed he'd done or said something to warrant being pushed away and, furthermore, he still had a crumbling relationship with his high school sweetheart he needed to help finish destroying. Besides, Bergen was four years older and Outlaw considered himself "fighting out of his weight class" with her. She seemed classier and much more refined than he could ever hope to be and thus things had worked-out the way they were supposed to.

Beyond that brief, awkward period of strain, he and Bergen remained fast friends; so much so that wherever she found her happiness, he was glad to see her find it. She and her boyfriends attended parties at Outlaw's apartment, went out to eat with him in groups, and generally took part in all of the social hell-raising that went on outside of the ROTC detachment and off campus, and Bergen Cyr could raise hell with the best of them.

Periodically, she would arrive at Outlaw's apartment on a Saturday or Sunday afternoon with a bottle of tequila and a cigar or two. The two of them would sit on his small patio, weather permitting, drinking shots, smoking, and talking for hours. Occasionally, Bergen would join him with a cigar, though she mostly stuck with her Virginia Slims. These visits would inevitably end with Outlaw pouring her into his bed while he slept it off on his couch, followed the next morning by varying degrees of hangovers and visits to the nearby pancake restaurant.

In the early stages of their friendship, Outlaw sought to reconcile himself with her sometimes enigmatic nature. She could run hot and cold. When she complimented someone, it was warm and sincere and she was always deliberate with her words and a master of the art of well-placed, well-intentioned flattery. Yet, she could also be an "ice princess" to those she deemed trifling.

Two years later, by the time the long-distance relationship with his high school sweetheart had completely crumbled to dust, Bergen graduated and was commissioned as a second lieutenant. He never understood why she left campus without even stopping by to say goodbye, or for one more bottle of tequila, and that puzzled him. He found the next year at school quite a bit emptier without her.

She was, at first, unaware of his presence in the break room. He stood there, watching her smoke, until she mashed the cigarette out in the sand-filled butt can beside the sofa.

"Hi, Berg," he said, in a subdued tone.

Her eyes flew open wide upon recognizing him and she squealed, "Dilly!"

34

Other than his little sister, who coined the name, Bergen Cyr was the only other person on the planet allowed to call him that, and then not in front of other people.

She seemed to literally fly across the room into his arms.

As she hugged him tightly, she gushed, "I've never been so glad to see anyone in my life!"

"Hey, it's just me," he replied, "Nothin' to get that excited about, Berg."

"Are you kidding me?" she asked in her familiar, sparkling tone, pulling back and looking him in the eye, "When I graduated, I thought I'd never see you, again, silly!"

"Yeah," he said, "I've always meant to ask, if I ever ran into you, why didn't you come by the apartment, or at least call to say goodbye. That, plus I never heard from you, until now."

Her tone softened and she took a step back.

"I didn't know how to do it, Dillon. I pushed you away at a time when maybe I shouldn't have. I always thought you held that against me; at least, on some level, even though you were always a special friend."

"I just figured 'easy come, easy go,' Berg," he answered, "I was a little disappointed, but I still had to hold funeral rites for another relationship. Besides, I wasn't much of a catch, then, and I didn't want or need for you to be my rebound girl."

She replied in a more hushed tone, "Don't be ridiculous."

She then lightly touched the black leather name tag on his flight suit, on which stamped in silver were his name and pilot wings.

"So, you made it; earned your wings. I never doubted you would. I see by the shoulder patch you're flyin' the BUFF."

"Yep. So, you're in civilian clothes. OSI?"

"Sure am," she said, perking back up. "Office of Special Investigations. I'm here for my annual weapons qualification with the .38. I'm guessing you are, too."

"Yep."

"Okay, *Flyboy,*" she said, poking a very well-manicured index finger into his chest. "Worst score buys the tequila and cigars. You up for it?"

"Get ready to lose, girl!"

"We'll see, Flyboy," she said with a laugh. "Do you have a place, yet?"

"Yep. Got moved in a couple of weeks ago and just bought some new furniture."

"Good. I'll be smoking your cigars, drinking your tequila, and probably passing-out in your bed, this evening," she said in a delighted tone, as she headed out the door to the firing range.

Bergen didn't have it entirely correct. Outlaw out-shot her by two rounds and she bought the tequila and two cigars. She did, however, pass out in his bed, per her prediction. When it came to drinking with the boys *or* the girls, she could hold her own. True to his vow made the morning after his UPT assignment night, Outlaw kept his tequila consumption to a mere two shots.

She woke up just before noon that Sunday. He was sitting on the sofa, watching TV.

She walked out of the bedroom and whined, "Dilly, you let me sleep in my clothes, again. I look like one massive wrinkle. I *hate* it when you do that! Plus, I smell like cigar smoke."

She sat on the couch beside him and punched him lightly on the arm.

"Hey, that falls on *your* back, Bergen Cyr. Nobody held a gun on you and made you drink all that tequila! And what are you complainin' about, anyway? You got to hang out with the *Outlaw*, God's gift to military aviation and womankind!"

"Oh, so now you're the 'Cool Hand Luke' of Air Force pilots," she teased through a white-hot headache.

"Cool Hand Luke? Nah, he's a loser."

"How could you possibly say that about Paul Newman? He's *gorgeous,*" she cooed.

"Think about it, Berg," he said. "First of all, Cool Hand Luke is a fictitious character; nothin' more'n a white-trash fairy tale. Second, at the end of the movie, he got shot and killed for all his trouble. *Loser,* like I said. I'd rather be the *Joe Namath* of Air Force pilots."

"Why Joe Namath?"

"He drank up all the booze, dated all the babes, and won the Super Bowl. He's a real cat; coolest cat alive. I might rank a close second," he added with a comical, raised eyebrow.

She punched him on the arm, again; this time, a little bit harder.

"Well, as pathetic as you look, right now, I s'pose I'll buy lunch. You bought the tequila and the smokes," he said.

They crowded next to each other in the bathroom, jockeying for mirror space, while Outlaw brushed his teeth and Bergen tried to tame a stubborn, pillow-induced cowlick.

"Berg, I need a favor," he told her.

"Sure. What?"

"I had my annual dental, yesterday. I've been havin' trouble with my right-side molars and the Doc said it was because my wisdom teeth grew in crooked; all that, after two years of braces.

"Anyway, he said to come in tomorrow mornin' and he'll pull all four. Can you shake loose during the day to drive me home?"

"I'll be there. What time'll you need me?"

"Doc said I'll be done by about 1100."

"Roger that, Flyboy."

"Agent Cyr, he's had a rough morning," the dentist told her.

"He sat through two extractions essentially without any anesthesia. Infection on the right side kept neutralizing the anesthetic. He's probably going to experience some serious pain over the next couple of days. I nearly had to *stand* in his mouth to get those two right wisdom teeth out. He's about ready to jump out of his skin, right now."

He handed her a bottle of opioid pain medication.

"Get him home and get him in bed. Hide his car keys. If he gets hungry, he can have some soup, or only very soft food, like mashed potatoes. I want to see him again, first thing Thursday morning."

On the drive to his apartment, Outlaw leaned his head against the cool glass of the window and didn't say anything. Bergen remained quiet, realizing how traumatized he was, and just plugged in an Eagles cassette and let it play at low volume. Once in the apartment, she suggested he get in bed, but he insisted through a mouthful of gauze that he wanted to use the foldout sofa-bed because there was no television in the bedroom.

She countered, "Dilly, it's only daytime TV. There's really not that much to watch and you need to rest."

He insisted, stating he had enough movies and cartoons recorded on videocassettes to keep him entertained.

"Cartoons, huh? Well, knock yourself out, Flyboy," she said. "I need to run to the store and get you some gauze. You *do* have soup, don't you?"

He shook his head.

"That's what I thought. I'll be back shortly."

She had intended to make the sofa-bed for him when she returned, but he had done it himself by the time she got back. She found him sprawled diagonally across the bed, sound asleep without a pillow. She brought two from the bedroom, and tugged him out of his boots and flight suit, then covered him with a comforter. Realizing his pain pills were still in her purse, she placed bottle on the end table beside the sofa-bed and left a note explaining the dosing schedule.

She stood and took stock of his apartment, which she found charming. It was essentially the attic of a grand old three-story house on High Street, which had a Romanesque tower running up one side. Everything else smacked of heavy wooden beams and rustic charm and she liked it a great deal. Even more than the intrinsic charm of the place, she liked the way it smelled. He had been in it long enough for the place to smell like "Dillon," just the way she remembered him.

Before she left to handle some loan paperwork at the base credit union, Bergen looked in his refrigerator and cabinets to see if he had any groceries at all. In the freezer, she found half a bag of pizza rolls, a box containing exactly one fish stick, and a half-eaten Snickers bar. In the refrigerator below, she found two Cokes, half a bottle of ketchup, and a partially wrapped, half-eaten, petrified Big Mac. In the cabinet beside the refrigerator, she found a quarter of a loaf of bread that had already grown enough penicillin to cure a statewide clap epidemic and wondered aloud why anyone would leave just one fish stick in the box, instead of just heating and eating the damned thing when he'd eaten the rest.

Shaking her head, she asked herself, "Do men *ever* quit being boys?"

After completing her errands, she returned early in the evening to find him sprawled on his back across the sofa-bed, completely naked, with one leg under the comforter and a videocassette of Bugs Bunny cartoons playing in the VCR. The TV sound was turned completely down and a Buck Owens album was playing on the turntable. She laughed at the delivery pizza box on the end table, with which he had knocked the bottle of pain pills onto the floor.

"They *never* quit being boys," she said under her breath, as he helped herself to a cold slice, then put the box in the refrigerator.

Bergen put away the groceries and switched off the TV and VCR with the remote control, before taking off her clothes, pulling the comforter up over him, and getting into bed beside him. She put her head on his shoulder and gently ran her fingernails over his chest and shoulders. He murmured through his warm, opiate-fueled, half-sleep about how nice it felt and she fell asleep doing it. Before drifting off herself, she thought to herself how wonderful it was to have him in her life, once again.

They slept until 6:00 a.m., when she awoke to the smell of eggs and bacon frying, and coffee brewing in the kitchen. When she walked into the kitchen his back was to her, but she could see a comical case of "bed-head" sticking up all over. She walked up behind him, put her arms around his waist and rested her chin on his shoulder as he flipped the bacon.

"Mornin', Flyboy," she said, "How're you feelin'?"

"Like a bag fulla assholes," he said through a mouthful of gauze, "Pain pills pretty much kill the pain and give me a nice buzz, but they make it hard for me to shut down my mind completely. Hard to sleep for more than a few minutes at a time. I flipped and flopped most of the night."

"I know."

He turned to face her and she laughed sympathetically as she gently cradled his swollen cheeks in her palms.

"Oh, man, you look like a chipmunk with a mouthful of nuts. You storin' 'em away for the winter, Flyboy?"

She could tell from the expression on his face that he was amused and that it hurt him to smile. She untied the sash on his robe, allowing it to fall open. He was naked underneath and she still was, as well. Placing her arms inside his robe, she stepped in and hugged him, again. Aside from sleeping through the night like that, it was the first time they had been so intimate, yet they both acted as if things had been that way for years.

"Glad to see the drugs haven't dulled your mind enough for you to fry bacon naked, Flyboy," she teased.

"It only takes one bad experience to learn that lesson," he said.

He found the sensation of being skin-to-skin with her electrifying, yet he also found the current dose of Vicodin overpowering it. As always, he found her scent intoxicating.

"I made you breakfast. Eggs're just the way you like 'em: scrambled hard, with cheese. Thanks for pickin' up the groceries," he mumbled through the gauze.

"You're welcome, Flyboy. You gonna join me?" she asked.

"No. Shouldn't-a tried to eat that pizza yesterday."

"That's right. You shouldn't have. The dentist told you so, but none of that seemed to seep into that thick skull of yours. You didn't wanna hear it from me, either."

"Thanks for takin' care of me, Berg," he managed to say, as he rolled his eyes and crawled back into bed.

"You would've done the same for me," she replied.

"You know I would," he said, before nodding off.

She ate her breakfast at the table and watched him settle down.

When she returned to bed, he was sleeping on his left side. She spooned in behind him and draped her right leg and arm over him.

"You still sleepy?" he asked, stirring awake.

"Nope. That wouldn't describe the feeling. I want you."

"Berg," he said, "could it wait 'til I feel a little better? We've gotta talk, first."

"You're right, Flyboy," she answered, a bit disappointed. "Meanwhile, let's just lie here for a few minutes and just *be*. I have to get to work, but I like the way this feels."

"Me, too," he said, before drifting off.

By Friday, the dentist cleared him off "quarters" restriction. He returned to work and began his classroom instruction course in Emergency War Orders, which would lead him to mission-certification status. After a Friday afternoon happy-hour drink in the O-Club bar, they went for lobster at Pierre's, literally the only "nice" restaurant in town.

After they had ordered, Bergen said, "Okay, Dilly, I guess we gotta talk, huh?"

"You have my undivided attention," he replied.

"Dillon, I've always been attracted to you; much more than you know and much more than I ever let on."

"Really? You seemed to lose interest in me, at least as far as the two of us being an item. I'm not sayin' that to be a smartass."

"I know you aren't, but if you were, I'd sit here and take it. I owe you that."

"No, you don't owe me anything, Berg. I've always known you were special and I've always known I wanted you in my life, but I was happy to just be your friend. Bein' around you has always put me in a pleasant place."

"You never held it against me, the way I turned you away?" she asked.

"No, I never did. I knew that bein' your friend would have to be enough. At the time, we didn't have very much invested in each other, emotionally. Besides, I was on the tail end of a dyin', goin'-nowhere relationship."

She nodded her understanding and said, "Tell me about it."

"Long story short, she was my high school sweetheart," he said. "We'd been together since I asked her to our junior prom, and I was convinced she was the woman I'd be with for the rest of my life. I had no reason to think otherwise. Maybe I was *too* comfortable with that thought. But, it just wasn't gonna work out and we were both reluctant to admit that to ourselves and each other."

She waited for more, but he didn't seem to have more to offer.

Breaking the brief, awkward silence, she said to him, "Dillon, I never told you this: I married a soldier when I was eighteen. My parents tried to talk me out of it, but I wouldn't listen. I went to Germany with him and stayed behind in Upton with my parents, when he was sent to Korea.

"I loved him, or at least thought I did, and was willing to wait for him. When he came back from Korea, he'd changed a great deal. He didn't seem interested in me anymore, and I had strong suspicions that he was cheating on me. Those suspicions were confirmed by a mutual friend.

"We moved to Georgia, so he could attend the university on the Bootstrap program and earn a commission. I kept convincing myself that things would settle back down to the way they'd been before, but they didn't. He left me when I found out I couldn't have children, and by 'left,' I mean he got right up off the sofa and walked out of the apartment, slamming the door behind him. I didn't see him again until divorce court, six months later. I haven't seen him or heard from him, since.

"I was devastated, not from the fact that children weren't an option for me, but by the fact he was screwing everything in a skirt and didn't seem to care whether I knew it or not. I'm convinced he was trying to rub my nose in it."

"I knew you were married, before, Berg, but I had no idea about all that," he said.

"What I'm trying to say, Dilly, is this: I'm terrified of anything like that happening, again. I've hurt a few men, since I first met you. Once, I overheard myself referred to as a 'man eater.' I didn't like it, but looking back on it, maybe that shoe fits."

"Well, sometimes things just work out the way they're supposed to, my dad used to say," he responded.

Without acknowledging his comment, she continued, "But I do know, Dillon Lawless, that you are a special man and I didn't do right by you, and it's something I regret. I'm very sorry."

"You have nothin' to apologize for, Berg," he answered. "I just always assumed the timin' wasn't right, and I believe everything in life is a matter of timin'. I'm here now, right?"

"That, Dilly, is just one of the reasons you scare the hell out of me. I don't know how I would handle being rejected by *you.*"

Outlaw shifted back in his chair with a look of mild surprise showing on his brow.

"Wow. I didn't see that comin'. So, what is it you see in me, anyway?" he asked.

"There's a depth to you that you can't see, Flyboy. But, I can. You sell yourself short when you really shouldn't."

"Whaddaya mean?" he asked.

"Remember that time your buddy, Joe, came to visit you; the musician with that four-track recording system?"

"Yeah, I remember that. Joe and I learned to play guitar together in the seventh grade. We were gonna be the next Lennon and McCartney. Why?"

"You guys set that recorder up and played around with it all day, one Saturday. When I stopped by, the next day, you two were playing over it. It sounded like you had a whole band in there. When you sang, you weren't just singing from your throat. You were singing from your *soul*. I could see it and I could hear it. It wasn't a superficial talent; it was much deeper and it seemed effortless to you. There is a natural smoke, a spice in your voice that very few singers have; at least, those *I've* heard.

"Though you weren't really looking at me, when you sang 'Stand by Me.' I hoped you were singing it for me, Dillon. I wanted to be the girl in that song."

"You were."

"It was beautiful; not only the musicianship, but the way your voices blended into one. Your guitar solo was wonderful. Like I said, it was effortless. You were fabulous, that day, even though you only had an audience of one," she said.

"Glad you thought so."

"One Sunday morning, after one of our tequila drunks, I woke up and you were still passed-out on your couch. There was a binder of songs and poetry on the floor beside your bed; stuff you had either started or completed. I read through it. It was really wonderful, amazing stuff.

"I also looked at the books stacked on your closet shelf; nine hundred-or-so-page works of history, all sorts of philosophy, classics, all of them things you read simply because you wanted to know. You, Flyboy, are quite the Renaissance Man," she said.

He blushed.

"You're an amazing case study, Dillon Lawless."

"You see more in me than I see in myself. I do have a question, Berg," he replied.

"Shoot."

"That morning, after weapons qual, you came out of my bedroom gripin' about how you hated it when I put you to bed with your clothes on. What did you mean by that?"

"Isn't it obvious? I meant I was always disappointed that I didn't wake up naked beside you."

"Oh, I see," he responded. "Well, I was under the impression that sex with you wasn't a consideration and I would've never risked violatin' your trust by pushin' the issue. Besides, if we had woken up that way, I seriously doubt either of us would have remembered anything, as drunk as we used to get, and I would have wanted to remember everything about you," he concluded.

"Another reason I'm piss-in-my-panties scared of you. Some parts of you are just too good to be true."

"There've been times I missed you, Dilly, more than you can imagine."

The server arrived with dinner and Bergen made a grand show of teaching Outlaw, who had never done so, how to eat a Maine lobster.

As he gleefully cracked a large claw, she said, "When you get done with that lobster, Dillon Lawless, I'm gonna be your dessert and you're gonna be mine."

"You don't say," he responded.

"Yep. You're gonna have to fuck, fight, or go for your guns, Flyboy," she said with a seductive grin.

The two parents sitting in the booth across from them didn't care much for Bergen's choice of words, but their two school-age children did and literally fell out of their side of the booth giggling.

4. "Tactics"

Spurlin Air Force Base, Maine
1981

While some considered a seven-day confinement to the 423rd Bombardment Wing Alert Facility, "alert shack" in crew dog parlance, tantamount to a week in prison, Outlaw didn't mind it too much. There was time to bone up on both his B-52 and T-37 flight manuals, late night guitar-pulls with other crew dogs and ground crews who also played, watch movies in the recliner-laden theater, read selections from the surprisingly diverse library, and the entertainment of the antics, the unpredictable and bizarre Stumpy would uncork to piss off nearly everyone, particularly the KC-135 tanker crew dogs, who Stumpy referred to as, "stankers." Stumpy had a firmly established reputation as a miser and claimed to live on only two thousand dollars a year, while investing the rest, and projected the cryptic aura of a cowboy movie undertaker.

Burnt-the-Fuck-Up once remarked, "Stumpy's so tight with money, when he picks up a quarter, he can squeeze a booger out of George Washington's nose."

No one had ever been invited to his apartment, but some only guessed it would be very Spartan, with minimal furniture and no comforts. Stumpy admitted to having no TV and only a record-player with a collection of jazz albums.

Stumpy owned enough clothing to last him between alert tours and would bring two duffel bags full of dirty clothes to wash in the alert shack laundry room to save on his utility bills at home. Late at night, he would stalk the laundry room and wait until a tanker crew dog had put a load in a washer and, assuming all of the other machines were in use, lift the lid, plop the stanker's load of wet laundry on the floor, and "play through," as he termed it. In predawn hours, he would shower in the tanker crew dogs' latrine, then dry himself off with paper towels, scattering them all over the floor as he used them. Tanker crew dogs absolutely hated him. Frequently, threats to beat his skinny ass were issued, though nothing ever came of them.

The alert shack "chow hall" was also fair game for Stumpfegger, who filched packets of mustard, ketchup, and mayonnaise, as well as the small packets of salt and pepper. All made their way back to his kitchen table. Additionally, rolls of toilet paper from the latrine were known to sprout legs and walk away, finding their way very quickly into Stumpy's apartment bathroom. It was all just more money he could invest in whatever mutual funds and stock opportunities he thought prudent. Outlaw wondered if perhaps the word, "miser," might've been too generous a term. "Kooky bastard," he decided, described him best. Stumpy's behavior, he'd quickly learned, often bordered on the obsessive, not to mention "strange."

Stumpy could make himself difficult to be around and most crew dogs patently didn't like him, nor he them. Most simply avoided him or kept interactions with him to a minimum. But, he seemed to like Outlaw, right away, ostensibly because Outlaw brought a set of piloting skills with him that few other copilots had. Plus, he knew Outlaw to have a well-defined perceptive sense about him and Outlaw would call him on his bullshit. Outlaw would always fight back effectively and thus, the two of them conversed a great deal over the large, contraband Cuban cigars, which Stumpy brought back from each of his visits to Canada. He steadfastly refused to share with anyone but Outlaw, *his* copilot, who, he maintained, he'd "raised since a pup." Outlaw was amused by him for no other reason than the eccentricities and Stumpy was brimming-full of them.

Realizing McQuagg's flinty nature and the personality quirks that came with it, Stumpy quickly learned there was great delight to be found in pulling his chain. Outlaw realized that Stumpy could take the concept of giving Spaulding McQuagg a case of the red-ass to heights and extremes that no one else would dare to try. Most times, Outlaw would simply roll his eyes or shrug his shoulders at McQuagg, when Stumpy was so inclined and McQuagg's patience was wearing thin. It was primarily out of earshot of McQuagg that Outlaw would chuckle at the antics, either by himself or with others. He tried his best never to laugh in McQuagg's presence, though it was sometimes impossible.

During one mission-planning day in the bomb squadron, Stumpy calmly removed his flying boots and socks, then began clipping his toenails.

Banjo simply intoned, "That's gross, man," and turned away to light a cigarette.

McQuagg was incensed, became red in the face, and screeched, "Stumpfegger, what the hell do you think you're doing?"

Stumpy didn't even look up to make eye contact with him. He just kept clipping. When the last, crusty toenail flew across the room, he looked up and said, "There's a drive! This one could be outta here! It's going…going…*gone!* Home run!"

McQuagg grabbed his coffee mug, spilled a bit on his flight suit and his mission briefing guide, then stomped out of the room for the coffee urn upstairs in the lounge. Stumpy simply flashed his mortician smile at Outlaw, put his socks and boots back on, and resumed his portion of planning the next day's mission.

Eccentricities aside, Stumpy was an excellent radar navigator; so good, in fact, he confided to Outlaw that he could control his bomb scores enough to keep them from becoming *too* good and thus being put on *instructor* radar navigator orders. He eschewed the added aggravation of it all and preferred to just do his job, go home, and not be bothered by crew dogs or anyone else.

After a week-long nuclear alert cycle, bomber and tankers crews had four days off; a program known as "C-Square," a convoluted abbreviation of "Combat Crew Rest and Recuperation." After being released from the alert shack on Thursday mornings, Outlaw usually made a beeline for the ACE Detachment, which was manned by a cadre of three T-37 instructor pilots from Garriott Air Force Base and a maintenance staff of civilians who maintained the unit's three T-37 trainers.

When he could get away from the bomb squadron, he practically lived at the ACE detachment, asking a million questions and soaking up whatever knowledge the ACE IPs had to impart. They loved flying with him, because he always arrived prepared, regardless of whether they were going to fly a formation sortie, simple contact work to "beat up" the traffic pattern, or some serious, under-the-hood instrument training. Other copilots enjoyed flying with him, as well, due mainly to his sense of situational awareness and superb judgment.

Sometimes, Outlaw and another copilot, or one of the ACE IPs, would fly cross-country, leaving on a Thursday and coming back Saturday. Sometimes, they would just fly locally, but Outlaw enjoyed it all and began to stack up hours in his log book and quickly earned a reputation as an excellent pilot. He seemed to be hyper-aware of what was going on around him and his knowledge of Air Force and FAA regulations was encyclopedic.

If he chose to fly the T-37 locally, Outlaw managed to stack up his share of party hours, as well, often joined by Bergen, when she wasn't working.

Mostly, he fell into the mission-plan-fly, mission-plan-fly cycle between alert tours, as did the other crews.

During the target study portion of his fourth alert tour, after the crew had stowed their gear aboard and performed the necessary "assumption of alert" checklists and nuclear weapons inspections, Outlaw took the time to look through a booklet he had seen in the mission package on his first tour. It was entitled, *Fighter-Interceptor Tactics*. From the looks of its pristine condition, he guessed it had never even been opened.

From his earliest days in UPT, he'd heard fighter pilots boast, "There's two kinds of aircraft: fighters and targets."

Apparently, the bomber pilot world was also infected with that type of thinking, though Outlaw refused to think that was always the case. Yet, fighter-interceptor tactics weren't taught or studied at CCTS or during follow-on training in the operational units, nor were they much discussed during mission planning when fighter-intercept training was planned. These exercises were rarely even debriefed with the fighter pilots. The bombers were expected to just bore along, mostly straight and level, and come under repeated, simulated attacks by the fighters.

The idea that bombers were merely "targets" was not the totality of it all, as much as fighter pilots liked to think to the contrary. In the jet age, at least two North Vietnamese MiG-21 pilots learned a fatal lesson in the hostile skies over Hanoi and Haiphong in December of 1972. The bombers couldn't maneuver with them, but they could bite back, even with their limited capabilities.

Outlaw implicitly understood the logic in "bombers as targets" and saw, once he became mission certified, that his fellow crew dogs all assumed the same thing and that was precisely the reason that little publication was completely overlooked in the mission packages. The crew dogs, pilots in particular, seemed to be conceding that idea to precisely the wrong group of fighter-interceptor pilots: *Soviet* fighter-interceptor pilots. During every subsequent target study session, Outlaw made it a point to read through and take mental notes on what he read in *Fighter-Interceptor Tactics*.

Once back at the alert shack, Buffy Gardner would inevitably come by his room and talk air combat. Gardner was a B-52 pilot who had just returned from a four-year exchange tour in the Tactical Air Command, TAC, during which he had flown the F-4E Phantom, a two-seat fighter-bomber. Because of his being a "BUFF" pilot, "Big, Ugly, Fat Fucker," and only on loan to TAC, his fighter pilot contemporaries had tagged him with the name, "Buffy."

While Buffy was a top-notch bomber pilot, he'd earned the respect of his fighter pilot peers as well. He and Outlaw talked a great deal about the concept of "energy maneuvering," which had been a necessary part of completing the T-38 portion of UPT, though not to the extent it was hammered home in the "real" fighter world.

"We did somethin' similar to what that little book calls the 'high-low split.' For the bomber, it presents two problems," Buffy explained. "The first is this: the guy who goes high is gonna keep his energy up. If he doesn't launch a missile or fire his cannon at you durin' the head-on portion of the intercept, he's gotta maneuver to get behind you.

"He'll fly past like a bat outta hell and, to get on your 'six,' he's gonna have to do somethin' akin to the 'slice back' we were all taught in the T-38. If he's smart, he'll use his speed brakes to keep from gainin' too much airspeed while divin' in the turn. If he don't, he'll likely overshoot. You may be able to sucker him into gun range or spit him out of the turn with airbrakes or lowerin' the landin' gear. If he's goin' too fast, he's not gonna be able to turn with you durin' a stern attack at interception speed.

"On the rare times, when the rules of engagement were changed to allow the bombers to maneuver, I saw a couple of my F-4 buddies get embarrassed, but I never did, 'because I understood what the BUFF can and can't do."

"So, how do we counter the high guy?" Outlaw asked.

"Just let the gunner know where he is. Count him down by clock position."

"Got it, I think. So, what's the other problem?"

"If you can sucker-punch the guy who goes high, the other problem is that the guy who went low is still gonna be out there, slinkin' like a snake in the grass. To get himself spun around, he's gonna have to execute something akin to a chandelle, a climbin' turn, because he and the high guy are gonna offset themselves to either side of you before they fly past. He's gonna lose energy climbin' in the turn, so it's gonna take a little longer for him to unload the '*g*' off his jet and get enough smash back to line up either a gun or missile attack from astern.

"He'll eventually get that smash, but, best-case scenario, he'll burn a lot of gas in afterburner doin' it and hopefully see the need to break it off and go home. But don't *ever* count on that, just because he has to light the cans to catch up with you. It could turn out to be worst *and* last mistake you'll ever make. He *could* turn out to be a determined son-of-a-bitch.

"Meanwhile, the E-dub is gonna be elbows and assholes, jammin' AI radars, droppin' flares, and dumpin' chaff to counter whatever infrared or radar-guided missiles the bad guys might be packin'. The trick is to keep the fighter in the gun cone as long as possible. That goes for stern attacks, too. Their geometry's a lot simpler. Keep those guns pointed at him. If a fighter sneaks up within about twelve-hundred yards and hasn't opened fire on you, your gunner oughta be tearin' him a new asshole. Your job is to help manage the battle. Let the defense team know what you're seein'.

"Unfortunately, we really don't talk about this stuff enough. SAC likes to brag about trainin' like we're gonna have to fight, but that ain't the truth.

"Anyway, most of the Russkie aircraft we're likely to encounter are likely to be interceptors, rather than 'fighters;' the Su-15 or the MiG-25. Flagons or Foxbats. But, neither is really capable of post-intercept maneuverin'.

"They'll be a substantial threat at high altitude, but they're almost totally dependent on their ground-intercept controllers. Their pilots aren't taught autonomy and they don't seem to be able to think for themselves if they lose contact with their GCI. As a matter of fact, the Foxbat A's flight controls can be linked to and flown by the ground controllers, leavin' the pilot to only fly the actual engagement. That's not conducive to a very overall effective fighter-interceptor pilot, but don't take that mean they aren't dangerous.

"The Foxbat is less effective against low-altitude targets. The later E- and R-Models have a little better look down radar, but just marginally. Don't take any of this the wrong way. Chances are that if we ever launch on a SIOP strike, we're not comin' back. But, I ain't willin' to concede the issue. That's how losers think.

"Bottom line: get intercepted by a Flagon or a Foxbat and you *might* just get away, particularly if it's a low altitude, stern attack and your gunner can get off some rounds at 'em. Notice, I said, 'might.'

"All that bein' said, you know we're gonna fly into an EWO environment with the flash curtains closed, which means you're not gonna see *squat* outside. Trust the E-dub and gunner to do their jobs."

Buffy was referring to the metalized curtains which could be drawn to protect the pilots from the blinding flash of nuclear detonations. Prior to descending to low level and penetrating Soviet airspace, SAC tactical doctrine required those curtains be closed and secured until exiting hostile airspace.

"Then, why worry about all this?" Outlaw asked.

"Well, the EWO situation speaks for itself, but you remember when Belenko defected with A-Model Foxbat into Japan in '76?"

Outlaw nodded.

"Well, that airplane was a brand-new A-Model. Well, *we* call 'em the A-model. Ivan calls 'em somethin' else. Our intel and engineerin' people gave it a good goin'-over. We learned a lot about it and were able to reverse-engineer most of it."

"So, there's an 'up' side here?" Outlaw asked.

"Yeah, sorta. Not too long after they got their jet back, those Foxbat-As began showin' up in the air forces of Soviet client states. They were dumpin' 'em on the arms market, as they brought the upgraded versions of the MiG-25 on line and the MiG-31 came on line. NATO calls it the "Foxhound" and it scares the shit outta me.

"Remember, we're one of only two bomb squadrons in SAC, right now, that are tasked with non-nuclear, iron bomb contingencies. Every other wing is strictly nuke strike. Bottom line: somebody steps out of line in the Third World and we gotta go give 'em a dose of 'act right,' you just may see the odd Foxbat or two bird-doggin' you. They *can* be defended against. If we go in with MiGCAP, they might not lay a glove on us, particularly if we got F-15s along for the ride."

"Thanks, Buffy. I 'preciate our little talks. God knows we don't hear any of this through official SAC channels," Outlaw replied.

As Buffy got up to leave the room, he bent over and put his right index finger in front of Outlaw's nose and continued, "You just remember, Outlaw, the BUFF ain't an airliner. It's a *warplane,* man, with a range and payload nobody else in the world can match. And you can bet your cracker ass, Ivan is shit-pants scared of ya. You're a *bomber pilot,* man. Don't ever give yourself credit for anything less."

"I've never heard it put quite like that," Outlaw replied.

Buffy concluded, "Keep in mind what General LeMay said, 'Flyin' fighters is *fun.* Flyin' bombers is *important.*' He was right on both counts."

5. "Phizzy"

423rd Bombardment Wing B-52G, Tail # 58-0385
Radio Call-sign "Pipe 12"
Somewhere over Maine

The day had dawned into a magnificent, almost cobalt-blue sky, which put both McQuagg and Outlaw in a good mood and delighted them to be back in the air. The crew launched from Spurlin and headed out west on a practice nuclear strike mission that duplicated the sequence of events they would perform on an actual SIOP sortie: air refueling with one of the Spurlin tankers, message decoding and simulated Emergency War Order communications procedures, as well as low level navigation and bombing. They were scheduled to fly a low-level route known as "Hastings," through parts of Nebraska, with a mission duration of approximately eleven hours.

Climbing through ten thousand feet on the departure, Outlaw directed the crew to perform their required oxygen system checks, which they all reported as normal. The crew cabin didn't appear to be pressurizing, however, and the cabin altimeter didn't stabilize at its normal reading of 8,000-feet. Some valve somewhere in the plumbing was malfunctioning and, as the aircraft climbed higher, so did the cabin altimeter. Outlaw and McQuagg discussed it briefly and then ordered everyone don their oxygen masks. Outlaw worked the problem from the Dash-1 while McQuagg continued to fly the airplane.

McQuagg leveled the aircraft at 25,000 feet, which was as high as they could fly, according to regulations, without cabin pressure, and Outlaw directed the crew to perform their respective level-off checklists, which included another oxygen check. McQuagg then tapped Outlaw on the shoulder and made a twisting motion with his hand; the signal to go to private.

Interphone, where he and Outlaw could not be heard by the rest of the crew.

When McQuagg came up on private interphone, he said, "Dillon, tell me everything you know about decompression sickness."

Outlaw asked, "Where are you hurtin'?"

McQuagg replied, "My right shoulder, elbow, and wrist have all had sharp pain since passin' through 13,000 feet."

Outlaw responded, "You can't fly like this. Let's get you on one hundred percent oxygen and immobilize that arm. Keep that arm absolutely still."

"Switching to one hundred percent oxygen," McQuagg replied, while reaching down for his oxygen-regulator panel with his left arm.

"Good. Let's tell the crew what's goin' on," Outlaw advised.

"Co, you're now in command of the aircraft."

Outlaw simply nodded, as he switched his interphone selector switch back to "normal," so he could address the rest of the crew.

"Crew, Copilot; Spaulding's got the bends. Cabin altimeter's still reading twenty-five thousand and it doesn't look like we'll get cabin pressurization at all. Gunner, get your scarf ready to bring up here, along with Henry's, to make a sling for Spaulding's arm, but stay put until we get below ten thousand feet and I give you the okay. I'm now 'king for a day' and we're gonna descend below ten grand to burn fuel down to landin' weight. We're gonna have to declare a 'phizzy' and get Spaulding on the ground."

"Co, Gunner; roger. Lemme know when you need me," Stokes answered.

Outlaw keyed his microphone switch and told the Boston Center air traffic controller, "Boston Center, pipe 12 Heavy is requestin' immediate descent out of two-five-thousand to any altitude block below one-zero thousand with a physiological incident."

The Boston Center controller responded immediately, "Roger, pipe 12 Heavy, you are cleared out of flight level two-five-zero for the block five-to-seven-thousand. State intentions, when able."

"Wilco, Boston, pipe 12 Heavy," Outlaw replied.

Before leaving twenty-five thousand feet, Outlaw quickly ran through his descent checklist.

He again keyed the microphone and told the controller, "Boston Center, Pipe 12 Heavy requestin' airspace to burn down fuel. Estimate three to four hours before we're light enough to land."

"Roger, Pipe 12 Heavy. When level, you can fly box patterns, figure-eights, or standard holding patterns, at your discretion. You have the whole northern half of Maine. Will advise transient traffic and keep them clear of you. Report level in the block."

"Pipe 12 Heavy, wilco, out of two-five-zero for the block, five-to-seven-thousand. Thanks," Outlaw responded.

He then told Henry Chinchilla, "E-dub, Co; take the #2 UHF and talk to command post. Let 'em know we have a physiological incident with the pilot and to recall the tanker. Our intentions are to burn fuel down to maximum landin' weight and put it on the deck, so the flight docs can have a look at Spaulding."

Henry Chinchilla's discussion with command post set things in motion Outlaw and the crew couldn't have known. The wing commander, deputy commander for operations, deputy commander for maintenance, two flight surgeons, the Old Man, and Major John "Mac" McClellan, the 609th Bombardment Squadron's operations officer, were all hastily summoned.

Had any other crew dog but the aircraft commander gotten the bends, the solution would've been simple and the discussion brief. The pilots would simply burn down fuel to an aircraft gross-weight of 325,000 pounds, which was the heaviest a B-52G could safely land, under normal, peacetime operations. However, a physiological emergency with the aircraft commander changed the scenario completely. Copilots weren't trusted to land the aircraft unassisted and indeed some were not fully competent at landing the big beast without a squadron IP in the left seat.

With a copilot at the controls, the "wing king" in crew dog parlance, and the deputy commander for operations, the DO, thought they needed to weigh risks-versus-rewards of having him attempt a landing. The lives of all six crew dogs were at risk, if the copilot couldn't pull it off.

The wing commander, Colonel Dalbert Rogers, floated the idea of having Outlaw fly out over the Atlantic and have the crew eject, under controlled conditions, into the ocean. That idea was met with a flurry of protest from the Old Man and Major Mac, who'd both flown with Outlaw enough to know that he was indeed a competent, smooth pilot. In the end, the wing king deferred to McClellan. Colonel Rogers was simply passing the buck and intended to walk away from this potential mess with his hands as clean as possible. They weren't going to be completely clean, given that this in-flight emergency was happening on his watch, but he would have no moral reservations whatsoever about skinning McClellan alive, should this whole situation go south.

Major Mac told Rogers, "Sir, Lieutenant Lawless is a totally different breed of cat. Best copilot I've seen in all my years in SAC. The kid can handle this. He'll put that airplane down on that runway as smooth as a fat baby's butt.

"Besides, if we order him to fly out over the ocean and bail that crew out, he's gonna tell us to pound sand up our asses because he's in control of that aircraft and it's not really our call, anyway. He also knows that ejecting into the North Atlantic, this time of year, isn't gonna let his crew survive more than a few minutes before the onset of hypothermia, subsequent to which will brew-up a tremendous shit storm, if we lose a crew that way. That'll be a Big Shit Sandwich none of us wants to eat. He's *that* savvy, Colonel."

"You think so, John?" Colonel Rogers asked.

"Sir, I *know* so. He's flown on a crew with an IP the whole time he's been here, aside from the few months he's flown with McQuagg. He can refuel the damned thing, and take it off or land it as well as any AC in this wing you can name, includin' *me.* The odds of him dingin' that bird are almost nil. The odds of that crew dyin' of hypothermia or gettin' lost at sea are almost one-hundred percent. He knows that and so do we."

McClellan was well-aware that he may have just crossed a line of insubordination with Rogers. He had just told the wing king to kiss his ass in the most diplomatic of ways, but he didn't care if the colonel liked his assessment or not. Six of his boys were out there twisting in the wind and he trusted the odds with Outlaw at the controls.

"Alright, then," the wing king continued, "somebody call Flight Records and let's get his training folder over here. We need to look at his check ride results, landing currency, and all the things CINCSAC is sure to ask us about before a copilot makes a heavyweight landing in one of his airplanes. Get the ACE detachment commander over here, as well, and let's see what he has to say about the kid's flying skills in the T-37."

As he said it, Colonel Rogers was already thinking of ways to burn McClellan, if this whole thing didn't work out. The Old Man knew where the colonel was going with it, but also knew that his ops officer was spot-on with his assessment of Outlaw's flying skills. McClellan had been around the block enough times to make an accurate appraisal of the situation. Some commanders of Rogers' particular stripe were cut from the same bolt of cloth and nothing was too small or petty for him to hammer a red-hot spike of misery up an ops officer's ass, if he so chose.

Outlaw flew around northern Maine for over three hours with the landing gear and flaps down to increase power settings and thus fuel consumption.

When the aircraft was down to the required landing weight, McQuagg read the checklist items to him as the crew prepared for final descent and landing. Outlaw requested radar vectors to final approach from Spurlin Approach Control. He then checked with the weather shop on the way down and, in addition to the weather being nice and clear, the wind was "down the runway at ten knots," which made for absolutely perfect landing conditions.

Up until that point, everything had been routine. Outlaw saw it all as just doing his job: flying the airplane to get his boys back down on the ground safely. A crew of medics and the flight surgeon were going to meet the aircraft with an ambulance, once it had taxied clear of the active runway. Henry Chinchilla was handling the #2 UHF radio with command post and fielding a lengthy list of questions about Outlaw's flying hours, currency, and proficiency. On the way down final approach, Outlaw took the #2 UHF radio away from Chinchilla and talked to them himself.

The command post controller indicated that CINCSAC, General Hatcher, was patched-in to their frequency. Given the demands of flying a large, heavy aircraft down a precision final approach, Outlaw talked to them as much as he could, but no more than absolutely necessary. Once he established the airplane on the ILS glideslope, he began to get annoyed with this prodding and probing. So, he told command post, "Everybody knock off the chatter on this frequency. I'm *not* wearin' 'copilot' wings. I'm wearin' 'pilot' wings and I'm wearin' 'em for a reason. Tell the CINC I'll have his goddamned airplane on the ground in about five minutes."

He then switched the #2 UHF off and checked in with the Spurlin control tower, who told him the wind was still down the runway at ten knots and that he was cleared to land.

The flight surgeon and medics took McQuagg to the hospital. After the crew got through the maintenance debriefing and back to the squadron, the Old Man called Outlaw down to his office.

He said, "That airplane was steady as a rock on final and the landing looked great. You did everything by the book, and I thought it was smooth the way you handled yourself when you told command post you'd have the airplane on the ground in five minutes. But, you shouldn't swear at the controller. He was just badgerin' you because the general told him to. Nice work, though."

6. "A Shot in the Dark"

423rd Bombardment Wing (Heavy)
Operational Readiness Inspection (ORI)

One month after the physiological incident, the 423rd Bomb Wing was subjected to an ORI, the periodic but necessary pain in the ass. Things had gone very well from the outset for McQuagg and the crew, until the Initial Point on the bomb run for the last low-level target. They were "IP inbound" and Banjo and Outlaw both had their stopwatches going, timing from the IP to the release point. They were right on track and right on time.

Forty seconds before the first bomb release, Stumpy shouted over the interphone, "Shit! My scope just died and I don't have time to fix it!"

Outlaw responded immediately, "I'm visual on the target, crew! The tank farm's a boomer!"

This particular target was a complex of large, white petroleum tanks.

Stumpy responded, "Roger, Co. We'll release on your mark!"

McQuagg pointed the nose of the aircraft directly at the center tank, on a heading Banjo gave him that compensated for wind drift. They continued on and, as the target disappeared under the nose of the aircraft at three hundred feet of altitude and three hundred and sixty knots indicated airspeed, Outlaw counted down and Stumpy released the electronic "bomb" on his verbal mark.

As was his quirky custom on these practice bomb releases, Stumpy announced, "Just think, that could have been real *Roo-shuns* down there," in imitation of Slim Pickens's Major Kong character from the cult-movie, *Dr. Strangelove.*

Subsequent to the bomb release, Henry Chinchilla had to amend the release type to the 1st Combat Evaluation Group bomb-scoring site radar operators as a "copilot visual release," to let them know that Outlaw had done the bombing and not Stumpy, Banjo, and the ASQ-38 Bomb-Nav System.

While climbing out of low level for the four-hour, high altitude cruise back home, the "bomb plot" relayed the encoded scores to Banjo.

Banjo read some very good scores to the crew and said, "Jesus, Outlaw, you threw a shack!"

Banjo meant the bomb landed within a one-hundred-foot "circular area probable" and was considered a "bullseye." Outlaw's "bomb" landed within eighty feet of the designated "ground zero," which, when slinging a 1.1 megaton nuclear warhead, would have put the target out of business for the next ten thousand years or so.

McQuagg's crew was the first bomber crew to land from the flying portion of the evaluation. Henry Chinchilla's ECM scores in the target area had been good, as had the first two bomb releases Stumpy and Banjo made before the system went haywire. The reports Stokes had been required to send out over the AFSATCOM system were on time and accurate. Overall, it had been a productive sortie, albeit a long one at nearly thirteen hours in duration. Crew R-13's bomb scores were the best in the squadron.

They landed shortly after midnight and, during the maintenance debriefing, McQuagg received a call from the squadron administrative office that the Old Man wanted to see the whole crew in his office immediately after they were done. They had no idea what their boss wanted, but being summoned like that in the middle of the night was ordinarily an unsettling experience with every possibility of being served a Big Shit Sandwich for reasons as yet undetermined. They were delightfully surprised when they found out they'd been completely wrong in their assumptions.

They rode the crew bus back and walked into a darkened squadron. In the entrance hallway, there was a sign illuminated by a spotlight. The sign was a large hand with a pointing finger that read, "THIS WAY FOR A SHOT IN THE DARK."

Down the dark hallway, they saw another illuminated sign pointing to the Old Man's door. McQuagg and the crew went in and found him standing there in the dark, behind his desk, which was set with a tablecloth, bottles of expensive liquor, and candles burning at each end of the desk. Stokes wondered aloud what sort of pagan ritual the Old Man might be conducting. The desk was set with the finest single-malt scotch, bourbon, vodka, gin, and tequila money could buy at the Spurlin Class VI Package Store. He even had Coke, Sprite, and ginger ale for the teetotalers.

The Old Man told them, "Gentlemen, this is my way of saying 'thanks' for all you do here in defense of our country. You've worked hard and now you can play hard, but always know that I am personally grateful for the things you guys do to make *me,* and all of us in command positions around here, look good."

The entire crew was very moved by this and saluted the Old Man there in the dark. He then asked them, one by one, what their poison would be. McQuagg looked over the whole setup and chose Sprite. Outlaw and the rest opted for the hooch as the Old Man poured them each a shot.

After every shot glass was filled, the Old Man lifted his and said, "This is for you, gentlemen of crew R-13," and they downed their shots.

He then offered seconds, which they all gladly accepted. The Old Man did this with all fifteen returning crews and had a snoot-full by sunrise, when he finally made it downstairs to the basement, where the all-night party was still in full swing. There, he offered toast after toast to his crew dogs, their wives, their kids, and their accomplishments. The squadron wives had all brought food of some sort and set up an impressive buffet. There were two kegs of beer and an ocean of booze, to the fuzzy, inebriated delight of most. To top it all off, the Old Man announced the IG team informed him that because of McQuagg's crew's bomb scores, they would be recipients of the 8th Air Force Blue Ribbon Crew Award.

7. "McQuagg"

423rd Bombardment Wing

Alert Facility Picnic and Family Recreation Area

July 4, 1982

Four-year-old Beasley McQuagg appeared before his mother, holding a half-eaten hotdog in a death grip with his left hand, a balsa wood glider airplane in his right one, a large dollop of green snot snaking its way out of his right nostril, and a mustard-and-ketchup grin on his face that stretched from ear to ear and into his unruly mop of blond hair.

"Oh, Beasley," Martha McQuagg said, reaching into her handbag for a Kleenex, "maybe it wasn't such a good idea to bring you out to the picnic with this cold."

It took three tissues to clear Beasley's runny nose and two more to remove the condiments from his face. Beasley then held out the hotdog, offering her a bite, which she declined, knowing that at some point, it would've come into direct contact with that river of snot.

"Out-naw cook Beezer hotdog," he said, still grinning hugely.

"Beezer?"

"Out-naw call me Beezer," he replied, "Out-naw give me pane, too!"

He gleefully handed her the glider for her to examine.

"Outlaw, huh?"

"Yes, mama. Out-naw pay Winnie Pooh song on git-tah."

Earlier, she had seen Outlaw and Bergen sitting on one of the benches, playing and singing for a group of the children. She had heard them playing "House at Pooh Corner" and had the children clapping along. "Beezer," as he now insisted he be called, was an enthusiastic fan of A.A. Milne's stories and cartoon characters, which decorated his room, and had squealed with delight when he realized Outlaw singing about his cartoon hero.

"Nook, Mama," Beezer said, putting his hot dog down on the ground, "Out-naw teached Beezer how fye pane, too."

He turned away from her, adjusted the wing in slot just the way Outlaw had shown him, and gently launched the little glider into a perfect loop, which quickly returned and skidded to a halt in the grass in front of him.

"See, Mama. Beezer grow up and be pie-not, just Nike, Daddy and Out-naw! Beezer nub Out-naw. He *coooo.*"

"He's cool, huh?"

"Yep, Beezer nub Out-naw," he repeated with a huge smile.

Martha McQuagg looked to find Outlaw cooking a new batch of burgers and hot dogs on the grill, assisted by Montel Stokes, who was grooving on the attention from the little kids. Outlaw caught her eye, smiled, and nodded in the direction of Beezer, who was having a grand time with his glider. She gave him the faintest of smiles and a quick wave of the hand. He smiled again in return.

While he had met McQuagg's family on several of their earlier trips to the alert shack, this had been the first time he had ever spent any time getting to know, or really noticing, any of them. He and Beasley had hit it off, immediately.

Martha had watched Outlaw and Bergen, from time to time, with conflicting emotions of awe and carnal jealousy. She was quite stricken with Outlaw's rakish good looks, that charming southern drawl, the ease with which he ingratiated himself to others, and the ways by which he showed himself to be gone-around-the-bend in love with Bergen Cyr, who was a strikingly beautiful women and equally as ingratiating, in her own way. Not only was she awed by Bergen's physical presence, but also with her unusual name, which gave her still more sparkle and shimmer.

She had once been similarly smitten with her now balding, sourpuss of a husband, before he became the litany of things that made him the man she now knew to be Spaulding McQuagg: sneering, self-absorbed, and unavailable, both emotionally and physically, and running to paunch around the middle. The big "however" in his story was the façade he put up for the Air Force to see and the other side him, which it didn't see. She wondered how long he could keep up the false-face act and suspected the truth might already seeping out for his perceptive peers and superiors to observe.

Once Beasley had gone on his meandering, curious-about-everything way, her thoughts strayed to the unlikely fantasy of taking Outlaw to bed and felt herself getting aroused. She quickly blushed at the thought. Without a doubt, other men would still find her attractive and a willing, enthusiastic lover. However, she couldn't pinpoint anything she had ever said, done, or become that would explain her husband's lack of interest in her. The fantasy of sex with Dillon Lawless completed itself and she felt herself getting more aroused at the thought, yet all she could do was stare blankly at him and daydream.

While the alert facility had family visitation rooms, they did not, in any way, compensate for parents' absences from home during the alert cycles. Periodically, the alert force crew wives would organize these Saturday afternoon picnics, weather permitting. The Old Man and the two tanker squadron commanders would normally dig into whatever recreational slush fund money they had to provide burgers, hotdogs, chili, chips, treats, and soft drinks for these affairs. Everything else was covered-dish, which to the average crew dog was the highlight of the event, aside from getting to spend time with their spouses and children.

Like Outlaw, those who took musical instruments on alert with them brought them out for the entertainment of both the children and adults. It was Outlaw and Bergen's performance of "House at Pooh Corner" that had captivated Beasley; that, and the fact that Outlaw had purchased the entire stock of balsawood gliders from the Base Exchange checkout counters for the kids. They were only twenty-nine cents apiece and, to his satisfaction, the kids loved them. Thus, for an investment for something less than ten dollars, the alert force rug rats were having a good time, courtesy of Outlaw, although one glider landed on the grill and immediately caught fire, to the shrieking dismay of one little fellow. Outlaw quickly replaced it and sent him happily on his way.

While Beasley McQuagg was quite the social butterfly, curious about and making friends with everyone, the other two McQuagg children, Brace and Amy, were wallflowers. From his briefest of interactions with him, Outlaw had found the ten-year-old Brace to be a reticent sourpuss, much like his dad, while the seven-year-old little girl never seemed to venture much beyond arm's reach of her mother. She too, was quiet and standoffish, though cordial to Outlaw, Bergen, and others with whom she came in contact. Outlaw had the sneaking suspicion that if he said "boo" to either of them, they would jump right out of their skins.

Although something had not seemed right, on other occasions, Outlaw became fully cognizant of it on this most pleasant of summer days in area where the temperature never ventured much above eighty-four degrees. Spaulding McQuagg seemed oblivious to his family's presence. While other families had spread blankets across the ground and other fathers were tossing balls or playing in dogpiles and laughing with their children, Spaulding was content to seek out those crew dogs who were willing to "talk shop" with him, while his wife sat alone and Amy and Brace sulked against a tree just out of earshot down the hill. Outlaw, by contrast, couldn't have cared less about talking shop on an outing such as this. He was too absorbed by the fun of it all.

Bergen noticed Martha sitting alone and prepared her a plate with a cheeseburger, a hot dog, potato salad, and a brownie. When she took it to her, Martha graciously accepted, made a bit of small talk, and then put it aside, untouched. Bergen then returned to sit beside Outlaw, who had once again picked up his guitar.

Two weeks later, on the subsequent alert tour, Beezer pointedly ignored Outlaw when the McQuagg family visited the alert shack. Martha was noticeably less cordial than normal and neither Brace nor Amy said a word, but instead just fumed with shades of heavy storm clouds in their facial expressions. He wondered again what in the world could be going on within the McQuagg household, but quickly decided it was none of his business.

While McQuagg had a good pair of hands and could fly the airplane well, he proved himself prone to disregard regulations, take chances with the airplane, and improvise, all for no apparent reason. All of the freestyling with the regulations endangered the lives of his crew, though he seemed completely at ease with the idea. Although the terrain avoidance system in the B-52 would technically keep the aircraft at a predetermined altitude, while flying over mountain ranges and the like in the weather, SAC Regulation 51-52 specifically stated that crews were not to fly the "terrain trace," a line across the little green TV screens in the cockpit generated by the bombing-navigation radar and computers, during peacetime training missions.

During wartime EWO missions, it would have been necessary, because the pilots would have been flying with the aluminized flash curtains closed to protect them from nuclear detonation-induced flash blindness. That protection was further bolstered by the PLZT flash-blindness goggle attachments the pilots and copilots wore over their regular helmet visors.

Not many of bomber crew dogs trusted the TA system, which required "hands on" flying. It seemed far too sloppy and crews seemed to induce errors into by performing the checklist procedures used to test it in flight before actually using it.

SAC Regulation 51-52 notwithstanding, one afternoon, McQuagg decided to spontaneously prove to his crew that the TA system was safe and flew them right up the side of a Maine mountain, in the weather, using the terrain trace. Outlaw sucked in his breath, moved his hand toward the ejection seat arming levers, certain they were seconds from flying into a mountain.

When McQuagg's demonstration was over, Outlaw let out a sigh of relief and told him over the interphone, where the whole crew could hear it, "Spaulding, don't you ever do that, again!"

Stumpy's terse voice was heard next on the interphone, "Pilot, Radar; the radar altimeter bottomed out at fifty feet when we cleared that peak. That's way too close and that shit better cease when you can't see outside the goddamned window!"

McQuagg merely looked at Outlaw and grinned.

8. "Big Shit Sandwich"

609ᵗʰ Bombardment Squadron (Heavy)

Spurlin AFB, Maine

October 15, 1982

Crew R-13 had become quietly, and sometimes openly, contemptuous of McQuagg, and Outlaw found himself almost continuously involved in the process of attempting to soothe their fraying nerves and ruffled feathers. It wasn't a matter of being disrespectful of or wanting to subvert authority for the sake of subversion alone. Stumpy, Banjo, Henry Chinchilla, and Stokes felt their lives were being needlessly endangered. To a lesser degree, so did Outlaw, who at least had his hands and feet near the flight controls, if he needed to override McQuagg during an impending disaster.

McQuagg had taken to violating standing policies and regulations, such as pulling power on two outboard engines and flying six-engine approaches when, in fact, all eight engines were operating perfectly. That sort of practice approach was forbidden by regulation without an instructor pilot occupying one of the pilots' seats. None of those prohibitions seemed to faze McQuagg in the least. To his way of thinking, these sorts of rules weren't really rules at all, but mere suggestions.

Word of Crew R-13's discontent filtered up to Major McClellan and subsequently to the Old Man. After the TA stunt over the mountain, the entire crew dreaded flying with McQuagg, though they trusted Outlaw as much as any crew was going to trust its copilot, and Outlaw was leaps and bounds better than most. Several weeks later, while the crew was enroute to one of the STRC low level routes out west, word came from the bomb scoring site that the route was closed due to extensive thunderstorm activity. Thus, they requested and were put in a holding pattern over Lake Superior until the weather system had worked its way east of the training route. McQuagg had the idea for yet another confidence-building lesson for his crew and figured this would be a good time to practice steep turns, which were forbidden by SAC regulations.

Without bothering to tell any of the rest of the crew what he was about to do, McQuagg reefed the aircraft into a couple of sixty-degree-bank turns. He even rolled the aircraft to ninety degrees of left bank, making sure to keep the aircraft "unloaded" to zero-g, before rolling wingslevel, again. Outlaw had seen that done by his IP as a training requirement in the CCTS training program, but McQuagg was not an IP and this was not a training demonstration. Outlaw was at a loss to understand McQuagg's dangerous inclinations.

When offered control of the aircraft, Outlaw declined, despite McQuagg's insistence, preferring instead to keep his hands fairly close to the ejection seat arming levers, should McQuagg inadvertently "over-g" the airplane and snap one or both of the wings off. He was cagey enough to not be an active participant, should disciplinary action cease to be an eventuality and progress to a certainty.

Stumpy began to howl on the interphone, wanting to know what was going on. The nav-team downstairs had no windows for outside reference, so Banjo, who was normally a taught bundle of nerves and had a nicotine and caffeine-stressed gut that couldn't abide such foolishness, threw up all over his radarscope, chart table, and himself. He even managed to spew a chunk onto Stumpy's right sleeve. Stumpy nonchalantly thumped the chunk right back at him. Then, without saying a word to Banjo, he doffed his headset and put on his helmet, clipped on his oxygen mask, and selected "100%" on his regulator to preclude himself from smelling the vomit.

As much as the crew began to dread flying with McQuagg, Outlaw told them, "Let's just keep a close eye on him and each other and hope he doesn't kill us or fuck somethin' up. It's all we can do, right now, but I do intend to have a talk with the flight commander about him."

All were in agreement, but several more conversations took place in these "top secret" enclaves involving Outlaw and the crew.

Outlaw's glowing moment in the wake of the ORI bomb scores proved to be to be a short one. One dreary Thursday morning, Major Mac showed up at Base Operations, as the crew was getting on the bus, to head out for another routine, nuclear strike training sortie. He didn't say a word the entire flight, except to acknowledge his oxygen-and-station checks. He simply sat in the IP jump seat, watched, and listened. Outlaw tried to engage him in conversation several times, but he never said a word and just sat there, pokerfaced. The next day, word came by way of one of the sergeants in the squadron administrative office that Major Mac wanted to see Crew R-13, individually, in his office, beginning at 1300 hours.

Outlaw made sure he was the first one there, unsure of what bad omens might be wafting on the wind. He went and stood outside McClellan's door for ten minutes before the major arrived, walked into his office, and closed the door without acknowledging Outlaw's presence. Through the door, Outlaw heard McClellan hang up his flight cap and jacket, make a quick telephone call, and shuffle some papers. He then knocked three times.

Outlaw was by now certain this couldn't be anything good and thus reported in a formal, military manner when he heard McClellan say, "Enter."

Outlaw closed the door behind him, stopped two paces in front of McClellan's desk, saluted, and said, "Sir, Lieutenant Lawless reporting, as ordered."

McClellan returned the salute, but did not say, "At ease," as was customary. So, Outlaw remained standing at attention, certain that the major was preparing to serve him a Big Shit Sandwich. McClellan then plowed into him for all he was worth.

The major insisted, "Lieutenant, you may think your shit doesn't stink, but right now, it does, *real bad.* You've got a great pair of hands, maybe the best hands on a copilot to ever float through here, but there may as well have been a brick wall between you and Captain McQuagg on that flight deck, yesterday. Your crew coordination was terrible and that's the kinda thing that's gonna get you and your crew killed."

Outlaw heard everything, in detail, about what needed improvement, everything the major didn't like, and every nuanced, potential bad habit he'd exhibited; some imagined, some real. The ass-chewing and analysis were extremely long on the negative and short on the positive. McClellan also told him that if he thought McQuagg was a bastard, he was going to reassign him to an even bigger bastard, if one could be found.

After McClellan was done and Outlaw was convinced that he had absolutely no ass left to chew, he asked, "So, do you have anything to say for yourself, Lieutenant?"

Outlaw straightened his posture a bit and said simply, "Major McClellan, you are absolutely right about everything you just said and I won't offer any excuses about anything that happened yesterday or throughout this entire, sorry mess. You won't have any more problems with me."

The major's tone and face softened. The kid had balls. And smarts.

He then leaned forward and asked, "Do I have your word as an officer and fellow pilot on that?"

Outlaw replied, "Yes, sir. You do."

McClellan responded, as the faintest ghost of a smile appeared at one corner of his mouth, "Get outta here, before I throw you and your circus act out on the street."

As Outlaw was about to open the door, McClellan stopped him and asked, in a hushed tone, knowing that McQuagg and the rest of the crew were standing in line outside his door, "Do I need to take action on this crew situation?"

Outlaw responded in a low tone, "Yes, sir. If I was sittin' in your chair, I'd have to."

"On second thought, siddown and tell me everything you've seen him do outside regulations. I'll make sure nothin' you say will blow back on you. Your flight commander and I have already talked about this several times, and Colonel Spraggins asked me to look into it, so I have some idea of what you're gonna say. But, I wanna hear it from *you.* This is some *serious* shit; life-and-death shit. So, let's hear it. "

When Outlaw at last walked out of the major's office, McQuagg was waiting to go in. Henry Chinchilla was in line behind him, patiently waiting with the others for their bite of the sandwich.

Henry Chinchilla told him later in the day, "Man, McClellan really let Spaulding have it. I heard the whole thing through the door."

As tempted as he was to smile, Outlaw couldn't. He was beginning to have some very bad "vibes" about McQuagg. According to Henry Chinchilla, McQuagg wanted to quibble and make excuses for everything McClellan threw at him. He played the blame-game like an impassioned shithouse lawyer, but McClellan didn't buy a word of it.

Henry Chinchilla overheard the major say, "Captain, excuses are for failures and *you* are a failure. I just had your copilot in here, a twenty-five-year-old lieutenant, who was man enough to suck it up and not make any excuses at all. He owned up to everything and I respect the hell out of him for it! He's *exactly* the kinda guy we need around here."

Chinchilla recounted the world-class reaming McQuagg received and stated that McClellan raised his voice significantly when McQuagg began his verbal tap dance. Major Mac even dressed him down for not reporting in a military manner, as Outlaw had done. A Big Shit Sandwich was served to all six crew members and what Burnt-the-Fuck-Up and Outlaw would, in later years, refer to as the "Great Crew R-13 Mutiny," was over. So they thought.

Late that afternoon, Outlaw went to the Officers' Club bar and ordered a beer, knowing that Bergen was working all night and wouldn't be able to meet him. After nursing half the beer, which didn't taste right to him, he asked for glass of Perrier, which coincided with Major Mac's arrival. McClellan plopped down on the barstool beside him, guffawed at the Perrier and ordered shots of Irish whiskey for both of them.

He then clapped Outlaw on the shoulder and said, "Don't take that ass-chewin' personal, Dillon. It's *bidness*! Hell, everybody needs one, once in a while. It puts things in perspective and keeps ya sharp! I just hadda to make a point. You stood your ground with me exactly the way you shoulda."

Outlaw nodded as he took a sip of Tullamoor Dew.

"As much as I woulda liked to," McClellan continued, "I woulda preferred to have some incense burnin' and some new age, sitar music playin' softly in the background, but that wasn't the situation for it. I had to do it that way, just so ya know."

"I know you did, Major," Outlaw replied as he raised his glass to meet Major Mac's.

McClellan carried through on the idea of making some crew changes and McQuagg was reassigned to work in the Vault; DOX, which meant the War Plans office. For several weeks, the crew flew with two of the IPs from Training Flight, as well as the Old Man himself, which Outlaw found to be a bit of a treat. The Old Man had done a tour as a T-38 IP at Garriott Air Force Base and still had an impressive skill set.

After a month passed, Major Mac appeared in the mission planning room one day as the pilot for the next day's mission. The day after the flight, as Outlaw was passing him in the hallway, McClellan grabbed him by the sleeve and pulled him into the A Flight commander's office, which was the office closest to them, and said, "One-million percent improvement, yesterday. That woulda gotten you a qualification level-one 'excellent' on a checkride or CEVG eval. Keep doin' it that way. Consider yourself off the Shit List, as of right now."

Outlaw gave the major a quizzical look, to which McClellan responded, "Look, Lawless, nobody ever stays on the Shit List for very long. Of course, there's the odd exception to that, but there's too much competition to get to the top of it in any SAC unit. Been on it a coupla times, myself, but I learned that there's always somebody waitin' in the wings to take your place. Everybody has to take a bite of the ol' Shit Burger, every now and then, but don't worry about it. Just do your job and keep your nose clean. Do you roger?"

"Affirmative, Major."

9. "Black Space"

113 High Street
Apartment C
Captown, Maine
October 24, 1982

Bergen sat on Outlaw's couch, smoking her first cigarette of the morning with her ankles crossed and her bare, immaculately pedicured feet propped up on the coffee table. Her gaze was fixed on the big, wet snowflakes falling soundlessly from a grey, dawning overcast as they danced in the pale, pink glare of the nearby streetlight before settling to the ground and onto the street. The view from his third-floor picture window was spectacular, even in the first, faint stabs of dawn. It was the highest vantage point in Captown, as far as she could tell, and commanded a view of virtually the whole town and the small valley below. Outlaw once told her that picture window was the primary reason he wanted this particular apartment. She understood its charm and appreciated his good taste.

That picture window also had the effect of radiating a bit of the cold into the room, but it was bearable. She'd grown up northern Maine and preferred things a little cool. This morning, the short, satin robe that Dillon thought so alluring was enough to keep her comfortable with the room temperature and her reverie, even though it didn't cover much leg and revealed just the right amount of cleavage she knew appealed to him.

Being from Georgia, Dillon would, of course, start grousing about how cold it was when he woke from his Sunday morning sleep-in and came out to join her for coffee, which reminded her that she hadn't started a pot, yet. It could wait, she decided. He wouldn't be up until 1000 hours or so and it was only 0800, with the daylight just stirring in the east; still a bit dark and quiet. Then, he could adjust the old, steam radiator to his liking.

There wasn't much traffic on the street below, beyond the local faithful making their way to Sunday school and morning worship at the nearby church. She couldn't remember it ever snowing in northern Maine this early.

It was barely the fourth week of October. She'd seen plenty of early November snows, but nothing like this. Traffic was just sparse enough for the snow to cover the tracks of passing cars before another one came along, etching more black scars into the snow, which were slowly turning the snow to a gray-brown mush. Quickly on the heels of the last car she saw pass, a snowplow followed, sending a dirty wall of snow and slush up over the curb and onto the sidewalk.

She reached for a cigarette, lit it, and shifted her thoughts to Dillon. There was nothing at all wrong with this man. He was considerate and devoted to her. He never complained about anything and was the most ingratiating individual she'd ever known.

Specifically, it was the small things he did, day in and day out, that made people like him. With dinner or party guests, or when a friend would stop by or call, he always made a point upon parting to tell them how delighted he was to see or hear from them. With cranky little children in the checkout lines in the Commissary or Base Exchange, he always had a kind word and the ability to turn a little frown into a big smile. He was scrupulously polite to everyone, particularly his elders.

Despite his youth, "debonair" was the word which perhaps described him best. Dillon Lawless was easy company and she'd never run across anyone who seemed not to enjoy spending time with him. People drawn into his world became caught up in his story, and most seemed grateful to be so. He was never contentious with friends. At social functions, he scrupulously avoided conversational topics that might've made others uncomfortable. Rarely did he engage in shop talk with other pilots or aircrew members and made it a point to take an interest in the endeavors of the wives and children of his commanders and squadron mates. He seemed to be able to move mountains with that affability.

In restaurants, should a server bring him a cup of coffee or a meal that wasn't exactly what he'd ordered his thanks were always profuse. If that server later came by asked if the coffee or meal was to his liking, he would always respond, "It's perfect; just right. Thanks a bunch."

If someone made the effort for him, he felt gratitude was always in order. He was the same way with her at home. While he enjoyed cooking, it had never been her strong suit. If she burned the toast and went to toss it in the trash, he would stop her and say, "No. It's perfect. Just right. Bring it here."

Then, he would scrape off the burnt layer with a butter knife, and eat it with a huge, Cheshire-cat grin. Sometimes, he didn't even bother scraping and insisted that enough butter and marmalade went a long way toward changing a small problem into no problem at all.

Then, there was the music. Outlaw wasn't just some hack, when it came to playing the guitar and singing. He was a bit of a prodigy and had no difficulty at all learning to play new stringed instruments since the age of ten. He played and sang every night he was home, often with her as his rapt audience. The music was a perk of the relationship few other women ever got to experience with their men, or *vice versa*.

Since shortly after the day at the firing range, they had essentially been living together, although she maintained her small suite in the Unaccompanied Officers' Quarters in the interests of propriety. She would occasionally stay overnight at her place, if work demanded she remain close by, and sometimes when he was sitting alert, rather than drive all the way back in to town.

Sex with him had always been earth-moving. He never seemed to make it about himself, but seeing to her satisfaction, which, he maintained, was *his* satisfaction and she couldn't ask for a more enthusiastic or passionate lover. When he awoke on the weekends, she knew that if she heard him in the bathroom, brushing his teeth and gargling with mouthwash, he would inevitably stroll into the den naked and put his best moves on her, hoping to stir up another round of lovemaking. This morning, she was in the mood for it, and even if she wasn't, he would be hard to resist, standing there with that Greek-god body and his impish grin. Though she tried to dismiss the image, she found herself getting aroused at the thought.

Yet, she was also frustrated by her arousal, knowing she had some serious thinking to do about this man and this relationship. For the better part of the last month, she'd felt it: the *black presence*. That's how she referred to it, but she never said anything to anyone else about it; certainly not to Dillon. She'd been a bit guarded, lately, and wondered if he'd noticed, but reasoned he hadn't, as he seemed his usual, glad-to-be-here self.

It was that old, familiar pain that made her want to run from men, as she'd done several times since the day her husband had walked out on her. When that darkness crept into her thoughts, it felt like a pair of hands with cold, prickly fingers gently gripping her neck. Then, as the doubts about the relationships became more pronounced, the grip would tighten, bringing with it the dread of rejection and humiliation. On and on the despair would creep, choking the joy out of everything until she would eventually be smothered by the emotional blackness. When she got to that point, it would be time for her to bolt and she always did.

As she mashed her cigarette out in the ashtray, she decided that Dillon Lawless might just well be worth battling the demons. This time, she would fight them. For now.

She decided a good cup of coffee would do to knock the chill off, after all, and walked into the kitchen to start a pot. As she loaded the Mr. Coffee with the French Roast blend she and Dillon preferred, he walked out of the bedroom and goosed her on his way to the bathroom.

"That ass should be cast in bronze and put on display in a museum or somethin'," he said, chuckling behind it.

"Think so?"

"Worth a try. We could get rich, if we charged admission," he said, causing her to grin at the praise because he knew she worked hard on it at the base gym.

She heard him start the shower. That was good, she thought. Last night's lovemaking had been a bit steamier and sweaty than normal. She could've joined him in the shower, but she'd already had one, so she went back into the den while the coffee brewed.

She heard him heard him singing, after his shower, as he shaved and brushed his teeth. When he was done, per her prediction, he presented himself naked in the den. Right now, seeing him like that, she wanted him. Her eyes met his, as she put her cigarette in the ashtray without mashing it out. With her gaze still firmly locked with his, she untied the robe sash and opened it, exposing herself to him. Moving between the couch and coffee table, he slowly stepped between her legs and nudged them apart with his hands. She reached for the cigarette and felt that familiar jolt of electricity as he went to his knees, leaned forward, and fluttered his tongue over her clitoris. She knew he thought it was a turn-on when she smoked while he went down on her.

"Oh, Dillon," she moaned, "you've got to be the sexiest motherfucker in the whole world."

10. "Cold Comfort"

Coley Residence
Officers' Family Housing Area
Spurlin AFB, Maine
November 2, 1982

"C-Square." One simple phrase that proved there was a God and he loved crew dogs. Most of them thought that way. Banjo and his wife, Katrina, were the hosts of this Saturday night's C-Square revelry. Almost all of the members of the four crews, who had just come off alert, were there, as well as other crew dogs from the bomb squadron and Katrina's tanker squadron. Spaulding and Martha McQuagg weren't there, of course, and Stumpy was last seen leaving the alert shack parking lot in his 60s-vintage, rust-bucket VW microbus, driving off to his netherworld existence, not to be seen nor heard from again until his next required appearance at the squadron.

Over the course of the previous months, Outlaw had worked an impressive stretch of very long weeks before the Old Man personally ordered him to "stand down" and get some rest. He had endured a full-blown ORI, four alert tours, double-digit bomber sorties, and numerous ACE sorties in the T-37 during his C-squared time and some weekends. While the Old Man appreciated his efforts, where his exponentially increasing flying proficiency was concerned, he knew Outlaw and a few others like him were burning the log at both ends and ordered them home. He needed the rest, which Bergen had been telling him for weeks, to no avail.

Earlier in the day, Bergen had told Outlaw she would meet him later in the evening at the Coleys' house. She needed some time off and the opportunity to "decompress," as she termed it, but couldn't get away earlier, due to a case that she felt was crushing her emotionally, not to mention the black space closing in around her. She'd been working 16-hour shifts, assisting local law enforcement and the local district attorney's office in the investigation of a staff sergeant from the Avionics Maintenance Squadron accused of murdering the mother of the young Captown man who drove while extremely drunk and killed the sergeant's wife and two-year-old son.

When she finally finished her report for the DA's Office, she headed out to her truck at 2310 hours for the drive to the Coley on-base residence. She didn't know if it was actually the weather or if she was just tired, but the cold seemed to grate on her in ways it normally wouldn't. It was only the first week in November, but cold and snowing. As she lumbered along at the posted speed limit of 15 miles per hour through the family housing area, she decided it was likely exhaustion. Not only was she cold, but cranky and tired, as well, given her case load, and hoped Dillon didn't plan on staying too late. That night, she would've preferred to go to her own quarters on base and flop into bed for ten or so hours.

The party chugged along as all of these C-Square parties did: some crew dogs got drunk, some fell asleep, some comported themselves as gentlemen and ladies, and some managed to howl at the moon until the wee hours. They'd all been working hard, prepping for the recent ORI and, as a result, the evening's festivities were a bit more subdued than usual, though not much.

Per standing "orders," from the rest of the A Flight crew dogs, Outlaw brought along his acoustic guitar and performed to always delighted audiences; wives and girlfriends, in particular. After performing ten or so songs, he put the guitar back in its case and took turns with Banjo playing video games against Henry Chinchilla on Banjo's Atari set. Being an obsessive competitor, Banjo refused to be pulled away from the Atari by his very drunk wife, who kept insisting he dance with her to the music blaring through the stereo speakers.

She tugged at Banjo's sleeve one time too many, pleading, "C'mon, baby, dance with me."

"Nope. I'm playin' 'Space Invaders' and I'm whippin' Henry Chinchilla's ass. That don't happen too often. I'm on a roll, here, so lemme alone. Okay?"

"Please, baby."

Banjo shot an annoyed glance at Outlaw and said, "Would *you* please go dance with her, before she starts workin' my last nerve?"

"You don't mind, man?" Outlaw asked, shrugging his shoulders.

"No," Banjo responded. "Hell, no. You're harmless, dude."

Looking up from to couch at his wife, he nodded in Outlaw's direction and asked, "Will *he* do, if you absolutely gotta dance?"

"Hell, yeah, Honey. He'll do just fine," Katrina cooed, beaming a sloppy, drunk smile at Outlaw.

"Okay, then," Outlaw said. "Let's go cut some rug."

"No fuckin'," Banjo called after them and Outlaw raised his hand in acknowledgement.

After draining the last of uncounted margaritas, she took him by the hand and led him into the living room, where two other couples were dancing. As they entered, the next song on the LP was a down-tempo tune, necessitating a slow dance. She moved up close to Outlaw, stepping on his right foot as she did so. After a quick apology and a drunken giggle, she snuggled close, reached around, and put her right hand on his left ass cheek, then fell asleep in his arms.

Bergen reached the top of the front steps, just in time to see it through the curtain flimsies. She grew livid. The black presence had finally worked its dark magic, overwhelming her, and she knew the breaking-point had been reached. Time to bolt.

"Goodbye, Dillon," she said, under her breath.

She turned, walked to her truck, and drove away. On the way to her quarters, Bergen gave brief thought to driving to Outlaw's apartment and confronting him with what she'd seen, but she wasn't even sure exactly what that was: an obviously drunk woman with her hand on his ass, and she knew Katrina Coley and Banjo well. Did Dillon and Katrina have a thing going behind her back? And Banjo's? He'd never given any indication at all of dissatisfaction with their relationship. Maybe it was innocent enough. After all, Jeff Coley was certainly somewhere in there, as the party was at his house. It didn't matter, she determined, and drove to her quarters. It was time to move on, and Dillon Lawless could have any woman he wanted. He wouldn't be lonely long, if he had time to get lonely at all. She knew that and was certain he did, as well. She found that to be cold comfort, but realized that was sometimes better than no comfort at all.

11. "Ivan's Dead"

423rd Bombardment Wing Alert Force Crew Bus
Spurlin AFB, Maine
November 12, 1982

After the "assumption of alert" briefing, the crews went outside into a cold, gray dawn that revealed an overcast and wisps of snow dancing across the pavement, and boarded the crew busses that would take them out to the alert birds. "Rumor Control" had it that the alert force might well assume a higher alert posture. Crew dogs usually took information from Rumor Control with a healthy dose of skepticism, but it certainly wasn't beyond the realm of possibility. Depending on how close the Soviet nuclear attack submarines, or "boomers," were to the east coast, it usually meant taxiing the aircraft out to the end of the active runway, shutting down engines, and sitting in the aircraft, once the fuel had been topped-off and the aircraft had been re-cocked.

Outlaw remarked, "It's those damned subs, again. Ivan's just fuckin' with us."

Other than that remark, he wasn't really in a conversational mindset. It had been nearly two weeks since he'd heard from or seen Bergen. She "wasn't available" at work and he dared not stop by the OSI office. He'd left a message for her at work that wasn't returned and apparently the answering machine in her quarters was disconnected from the phone line, as well. Thus, here he was on the outside looking in, for the second time.

Henry Chinchilla, who was reading a newspaper, lowered it and announced, "Hell, Ivan ain't fuckin' with us, Outlaw. Ivan's *dead!*"

He then held up the newspaper for the crew to see the headline, "BREZHNEV DEAD."

Aside from a brooding Outlaw, the crew all whooped and hollered with glee about the old bastard cashing-in his chips. Outlaw only managed a smile. Banjo wondered aloud, echoing a deeper, unspoken concern, as to exactly who was now minding the Soviet store. Would it be someone with a less hawkish bent, as far as relationships with the West went, or would it be some old, hardline, Bolshevik pain in the ass?

Apparently, Rumor Control had gotten some "good poop," because the alert force was briefed later during target study to prepare for an increased alert posture until things sorted themselves out in the Soviet Union. Two cycles of pissed off alert force crew dogs later, things settled down and an old KGB fossil named Yuri Andropov assumed power. Things seemed to have returned to normal and alert crew dogs no longer had to bear the chill of an oncoming Maine winter, by sitting in the alert aircraft and trying to keep warm by drinking enough coffee to kill a small country's worth of kidneys.

The Old Daigle House
Northern Vicinity, Captown, Maine
November 25, 1982

"Oz" took off the respirator, tossed it aside and admired the final, deep blue paint job he had just sprayed onto to the second of the two Dodge pickup trucks he had procured for the mission. He had rented a fairly remote house and used the detached garage as his paint shop. He would next begin the meticulous job of stenciling the required U.S. Air Force markings on each front door. His KGB point of contact had done a remarkable job of providing him with photos of the stenciling and other details, right down to the official stickers all such vehicles carried on their left front bumpers.

He had flown into Quebec aboard Aeroflot and received instructions from an envelope stashed at a designated airport drop-point, which directed him to a safe house. There, he was equipped and supplied with American currency, credit cards, a Maine driver's license, and then briefed by another KGB operative. Subsequently, he had worked his way into Maine through the wilderness along the Maine-Canada border without notice, or so he thought.

He was tasked with establishing, as inconspicuously as possible, a base of operations, preferably a remote house away from well-traveled roads or highways. Additional funds would be put in his account at two-week intervals by operatives at the Soviet Embassy in Washington. When he was ready to procure the two "pickup trucks," as the Americans called them, he was to call a specific phone number, which he had committed to memory, for yet additional funds.

Once established, he would purchase an old panel-van in which to conduct his "errands." These included the procurement of two Dodge pickup trucks. Another contact would help with driving them to the safe location, after which he would be killed. Instructions would come later as to when and where to meet the team. Oz made the decision, independent of command, to avoid face-to-face contact with the team at all costs. Inside American borders, it was far too dangerous, given the competent intelligence and law enforcement agencies that could be brought to bear.

Done with the painting of the two trucks, he again called the memorized telephone number and requested the funds he would need to secure two more vehicles. In this case, he had decided on a Ford Bronco and a Chevrolet Blazer; both four-wheel-drive vehicles in which the Spetsnaz team would ingress and egress the target area. The blue "U.S. Air Force" vehicle would get them to the target area and the Bronco and the Blazer would be placed at locations where the blue trucks would be discarded on the egress route. No one would question military vehicles enroute to a military base, but, once the news was out, they would be suspect.

Back in the Soviet Union, the men who had planned and briefed this operation to him told him this would be one of the easiest operations he would ever conduct. Within their own borders, the Americans were much laxer with their laws and security than they were abroad, especially where their military and naval bases were concerned. Getting on American air force bases, particularly the bomber bases of their Strategic Air Command, would pose more stringent challenges, but civilians were routinely given tours of the bomber bases and were invited *en masse* by the installation commanders for airshows and festivities called "open houses." If the American public could get on these bases so easily, a well-trained and experienced Naval Spetsnaz team would be able to infiltrate one.

Oz, however, had been a part of too many of these covert operations to be as overly optimistic as his briefers. He'd seen some of the simplest plans take unexpected, disastrous turns that got operatives killed and learned, long ago, never to take anything at face value. While the Americans might be considered freewheeling, nothing was guaranteed. Their law enforcement, particularly their Federal Bureau of Investigation, along with their Central Intelligence Agency, and their military intelligence agencies, were nothing less than outstanding. He knew, just when things seemed like they were falling into place exactly as planned, that was the time to expect surprises. Knowing that, there was always an alternate plan that he dared not divulge to his handlers, for fear of being seen as lacking confidence in the party *apparatchiks* who planned and ran things. This plan could and would be done, he knew, but something disastrous was certain to occur along the way that no one could have foreseen. What exactly that might be was anyone's guess.

12. "Crazy Suzy's"

Crazy Suzy's Bar and Resort
Mars Hill, Maine
November 27, 1982

Outlaw was enjoying himself and glad for the time away from work. He also needed to clear his head of Bergen, even if only for a few hours. A month before, he and some friends had made the trip down to Crazy Suzy's in Mars Hill on a C-Square Friday night. The bar food had been good and the entertainment great, so he and Mark Tolbert decided to go back. The drinks were flowing and the music from the band, Big Hippie Bush, which specialized in the country-rock, *Southern California* sound of the early '70s, was just what he needed. The entire club, which had, at one time, been a very large warehouse of some sort, was jumping. During the band's first break at 11:00 p.m., Outlaw struck up a conversation with the lead guitarist and bought him a drink. They talked guitars, equipment, and set lists.

"So, during our next break, you wanna get up there and play us a short, acoustic set?" the guitarist asked. "I brought along my Martin, for the songs where we need an acoustic. Got it rigged with a pickup, so it sounds off pretty good."

"I'd love to," Outlaw told him.

Big Hippie Bush took a break and Outlaw took the stage. The house light operator turned the spotlight on him as he was plugging the acoustic-electric guitar into an amplifier. The crowd gave him a quick, tenuous round of applause. In college, when he had performed with bands, he always stood on stage. When he performed solo, he always sat on a high stool. He thought it made for a more intimate rapport with the audience. He chose a barstool that had been stashed behind the stage that he found to be the perfect height.

When he started the intro to the famous Jim Croce, up-tempo blues number, *You Don't Mess Around with Jim,* the buzzing of the crowd died off noticeably. This guy was obviously quite the guitarist; so good that he really didn't even need a band. By the end of the first verse and chorus, he had their rapt attention. Aside from the occasional clink of a glass or shuffling of feet across the floor, the only sounds that could be heard were coming from his guitar and his mouth. The silent crowd erupted into applause when he struck the last, resonant E-chord of that first number.

"Thank you!" he shouted to the crowd into the microphone. "My name's Outlaw! Is everybody havin' a good time, tonight? I sure am!"

More applause and whistles.

"Here's a song by the guy who did *'American Pie.'* This one didn't get as much radio play as I thought it deserved, but it's a good 'un!"

He received still more applause, this time tempered by anticipation. He began the opening bars of *"Vincent."* Don McLean's tip of the hat to the Dutch post-impressionist painter, Vincent van Gogh. The crowd had heard it before and the next smattering of applause had a pleasant, appreciative feel to it. No one moved. Many sat at their tables, spellbound. Patrons sitting at the bar or standing in line for drinks all turned their attention to the stage.

As he strummed the last chord to "Vincent," the crowd again erupted into applause and he thanked them, then added, "Okay, I've got time for one more, before we get Big Hippie Bush back up here!"

He addressed the band, which was sitting at a table near the restrooms, "Thanks, guys, for lettin' me do this!"

They just waved at him, smiled, and raised their glasses in salute and acknowledgement or held up the flames of cigarette lighters to signal their approval of his performance.

Outlaw finished his abbreviated set with an impressive acoustic version of Jackson Browne's *Fountain of Sorrow*. Again, the crowd signaled its approval with more raucous applause, as he finished. Big Hippie Bush crowded around him on stage, patting him on the back and shaking his hand. The lead guitarist asked him if he wanted to join them for *Rocket in My Pocket* and he readily agreed. He hadn't played on a stage with a band since college. They even asked him to sing the lead.

"Okay, ladies and gentlemen," the guitarist said. "Outlaw has agreed to join us for one more tune, this evenin'!"

Applause.

When Outlaw was satisfied his guitar was tuned, he looked again at the lead-guitarist, who told him the tune was a standard blues riff in the key of E.

Outlaw counted it down, "A-one, two, a-one, two, three four," and off they went in front of a wildly cheering crowd.

Outlaw gave his best, spiciest blues voice, along with the perfunctory, rock-and-roll primal scream, and riffed two blistering solos on the Stratocaster, bringing the tune to a crashing halt some four minutes later. For anyone entering the bar late, they wouldn't have known that Outlaw hadn't been a part of the band, all along.

"Ladies and gentlemen, let's hear it again for the Outlaw," the guitarist shouted into the microphone as Outlaw left the stage.

"We need to see more of him here at Crazy Suzy's, don't ya think," he concluded.

The crowd roared an enthusiastic, "Hell, yeah!"

Outlaw returned to the table at which Mark Tolbert was sitting, sipping a glass of single-malt scotch.

"Damn, buddy," Tolbert said. "I knew you played, but I didn't know you had that in ya! You were great, man!"

"I'm a...whatchacallit...a *prodigy*, or so I've heard. Had to work at flyin' a little, but music comes to me real easy. Anyway, thanks man. You gonna buy me a drink or what?"

A cloud of concern spread across Tolbert's brow.

"A quick one, then we gotta split, man."

"Split? Why?"

"Did ya happen to notice the guy at the bar wearin' the New England Patriots jacket?"

Outlaw nodded and said, "Yeah. Why?"

"Well, he's still there, so don't turn around and look at him. I need you to go to the payphone outside, call Bergen, and tell her to meet us at her office as soon as we can get back to the base," Tolbert told him.

"But..." Outlaw started to protest.

"But nothin'," Tolbert countered, "Look, I know you and Bergen are on outs, right now, but this can't wait. I'll tell you what you obviously wanna know on the drive back. Now, go call Bergen and tell her you're with me. I'll grab us each a coffee for the road. It could be a long night."

Outlaw found the payphone, pushed a dime into the slot, and dialed Bergen's home number.

He knew he had awakened her by the sleep in her voice.

"Hello?"

"Hi, Berg. It's me. Sorry to wake..."

She cut him off with an icy hiss, "Dillon, what do you want? I was asleep."

"I know. Sorry. This isn't about me, you, or us. It's business," he said.

"What kind of business? Where are you?" she demanded.

"I'm down at Crazy Suzy's in Mars Hill. It's Air Force business. Can you meet us at your office in, say, an hour and a half?"

"I'm not in the mood for games, Dillon. Who is 'us?' What's this about?" she asked in a snippy tone.

"I'm with Mark Tolbert. It was his idea to call you, not mine."

"Tolbert? Oh, I see. That it's Tolbert gives me a better idea of what kind of 'business' you're talking about. We received a 'heads up' a few weeks ago. I'm sure Mark'll brief you on the way back. You guys stop and call me when you get back to Captown. I'll head to my office, then. Meanwhile, there's a call I need to make."

She hung-up without saying, "Goodbye."

Tolbert turned the key in the ignition and the Mercedes convertible purred to life. He then put it into gear and drove out of Crazy Suzy's parking lot, as lazy flakes of snow glittered in the headlight beams.

Outlaw said, "Okay, man, what's with the cloak-and-dagger, and why'd you have me drag Bergen into this? She was madder'n a gut-shot Indian when I woke her up."

"Don't get your bowels in an uproar, man," Tolbert said.

"I'm listenin'," Outlaw insisted, "The guy in the Patriots jacket; what's the deal?"

"He's Russian," Tolbert said simply.

"How can you possibly know that?" Outlaw asked.

"I know because my real name isn't 'Mark Tolbert,'" he said.

Outlaw's initial response was stunned silence.

"Go on," he said after a hushed ten or so seconds. "What's your real name?"

After clearing his throat, Tolbert continued, "Until I saw that guy in the bar, you didn't have the need to know any of what I'm about to tell you. Because you happened to be with me, you're inadvertently in on it, too. I still probably shouldn't tell you, but it's my judgment that you have a top-secret security clearance and the wherewithal to keep your mouth shut. This conversation doesn't leave this car. Got it?"

"Got it," Outlaw replied and nodded.

"Don't worry about my real name. I'm farmed out to other government agencies, from time to time, and it's not important which agencies. OSI knows about me; even Bergen. They just don't know who I really am or who I work for."

Outlaw responded hesitantly, "Okay. Makes sense. When I mentioned I was with you, she said she could guess what kind of 'business' we had with her."

"Relax, man." Tolbert chuckled. "I'm still your friend and still on your side."

"How did you know that guy was Russian?"

"My father was Russian. He was liberated from a Nazi slave labor camp at the end of World War II. He'd been an NKVD officer assigned to a Red Army infantry unit until he was captured by the Germans in 1944. He had the presence of mind to steal and wear the uniform of a Red Army sergeant, before the Nazis bagged him, which gave no hint of who and what he actually was. They would've shot him on the spot, had they known."

"Forerunner of the KGB?" Outlaw asked.

"Exactly," Tolbert replied.

"When the German SS guards hauled ass from the camps ahead of them bein' overrun by the Allies, Dad saw his chance at a new life. When he was being processed by our intelligence people, he identified himself by name and his actual position and said he wanted to defect and work for Western intelligence.

"They knew they could use a native Russian speaker, particularly an NKVD resource, so they got him out of the camp immediately and took him to Paris. They made sure his name never appeared on any captured German documents or any rolls of displaced persons or POWs. As far as the Soviet authorities knew, he'd been captured by the Germans, executed, and buried in a mass grave somewhere; just disappeared from the face of the earth.

"The OSS gave him a completely new identity, put him on the federal payroll, and taught him English. He worked in counterintelligence and married a French girl. He stayed on with the CIA, after it was formed in the late '40s.

"His time as a guest of the Third Reich wrecked his health and he never fully recovered. It didn't wreck his mind, though. He stayed with the CIA as an analyst until he died from lung cancer in '69."

"So, I'm guessin' you speak Russian," Outlaw surmised.

"Fluently," Tolbert answered, "but, until I came on active duty, I didn't know how to read or write it. My dad spoke it to me at home from the time I was learning how to talk. He wanted to keep that alive in me, as a hedge against an unforeseen future, I guess. The Air Force sent me to the language school at Monterrey to learn to read and write Russian. All this happened after I completed UNT and electronic warfare training."

"Amazing," was all Outlaw had to say.

"So, why do you hide in a B-52 squadron?" Outlaw asked.

"Not exactly hidin', man. I'm a mission certified E-dub, though I don't sit alert, like the rest of you guys. The people I work for don't want to risk me fallin' into the wrong hands, in the event of a shoot-down. That's why they keep me in Training Flight. I get to use those skills by teachin' and flyin' occasionally, but did you ever notice how I seem to disappear for a while, from time to time?"

"Yeah, I heard somebody mention it in the alert shack, a while back."

"Did anyone ever explain to you why we get the OPSEC/COMSEC warnings over the intercom at the squadron a couple of times a week?" Tolbert asked.

Tolbert was referring to those warning announcements over the squadron PA system, now and then, about Operational Security and Communications Security, OPSEC/COMSEC advisories, which basically meant "keep your mouth shut about classified information" and, above all, not to discuss it over the unsecured telephone lines.

"Yeah, we were told durin' mission certification that's because Aeroflot can't fly into the States, anymore, and they have to fly into Quebec City."

"That's right. They fly just close enough to the Maine-Canada border on their approach routing to be able to have a look and listen to us at Spurlin, based on whatever surveillance gear they have in the back of those airliners...and they *do*.

"Sometimes, when you guys get the OPSEC/COMSEC warnings, I happen to be aboard those Aeroflot birds."

"No shit?"

"No shit. My 'other job' is to fly to Moscow, whenever there's gonna be a change of diplomatic personnel at the Soviet Embassy in D.C. or any of their consulates. I'm their escort into the United States."

"So, that's why you disappear, every now and then?" Outlaw observed.

"Yep."

"Do you think the Russians know anything about who you really are?" Outlaw asked.

"The safe assumption is, *yes,* they do. Don't ever underestimate 'em. They may stand for arguably the worst cause in human history, but they're resourceful.

"Anyway, I don't advertise the fact that I'm fluent in Russian. They probably know, but I'm careful to always work through an interpreter, which really puts a burr in their shorts, and I always travel incognito. I like to make 'em work hard for whatever they get."

"You go in disguise?"

"Sure do," Tolbert answered. "That's why that Russian at the bar, if he'd been payin' attention to me, probably wouldn't have recognized me, anyway.

"I knew he was Russian, right away. I'd seen him on two separate flights into Quebec, over the course of the last eighteen months or so.

"I watched him interact with other people at the bar. He was standoffish, but he wasn't shy about chattin'-up the ladies. Based on his teeth, he likely didn't get very far with any of them, on account of his breath probably smelled like toxic waste.

"I must've seen my dad strike a million matches and wave 'em out. That guy did it exactly like he used to. He held and smoked that cigarette just like my dad and the way I've seen countless other Russians smoke 'em.

"Think about how many Americans you see light cigarettes with matches, these days; not very many, and it's usually only older men. We now live in the Land of the Disposal Lighter.

"Not only the business with the cigarettes, but I've also seen my dad and other Russians drink vodka, and that guy was slammin' it with every Russian nuance I've ever seen. Nobody else in that bar would've noticed, but I did."

"So, I'm guessin' all this is leadin' up to the idea that you think this guy hoverin' around Crazy Suzy's is up to no good?"

"Exactly. Why would a Soviet citizen be hangin' around a bar in northern Maine? Their diplomatic people are supposed to stay within a specified radius of D.C. or from cities where consulates are located, and there's no Soviet consulate in Maine. There's no way in hell that guy's a Soviet diplomat. He looks too rough to be embassy staff."

"So, why didn't we just wait until he left and follow the bastard wherever it was he was goin'?" Outlaw asked.

"Because I don't want to get us killed," Tolbert answered. "A guy like that can spot a tail within about ten seconds of pullin' out onto any city street or country road.

"You leave that kind of guy alone. You're a bomber pilot. You don't have the trainin' or skills to deal with guys like him."

"You think he's KGB?" Outlaw asked.

"Yeah, or worse. We might have a bigger problem on our hands: A SAC bomber base with nuclear weapons targeted on his country, remote area, and a Soviet infiltrator. That whole thing adds up to a long list of grim scenarios. I sure hope Bergen's called the right friends in on this one."

They drove north through a lazy, wispy snowfall until Tolbert asked, "So, bud, you got any questions?"

"Yeah, just one."

"What's that?"

"These other agencies you work for…do they make it worth your while?"

"Oh, hell yeah," Tolbert responded. "I'm drivin' a Mercedes."

He held up his right hand and said, "Just treated myself to this diamond ring."

"No further questions, Your Honor."

Tolbert stopped at a quick-mart so Outlaw could call Bergen, again. She told him the meeting couldn't happen until 0600, at the earliest, but the individual who needed to be there was already on a flight. To kill time, Tolbert pulled into an all-night diner where they could drink some more coffee and eat doughnuts or eggs and bacon, before heading to the OSI Office.

13. "So-Called Dave"

Tolbert drove straight to the OSI Office, when they arrived back at Spurlin. Both knew where it was, but Outlaw had ever been inside. All of the windows were shaded and the entrance was strictly controlled. Bergen had to vouch for them and sign them in on the visitors' log. Outlaw surmised OSI had plenty of secrets of its own to protect. She led them to a conference room in the back, where they found a burly, dark-complected character with a distinct Middle Eastern look waiting for them. There were several folders on the table in front of him.

Without bothering to tell them his name, Bergen introduced them. This was neither the time nor the place for familiarity, although Bergen's greeting to Outlaw had been a terse, "Lieutenant Lawless," with a nod of her head.

Outlaw simply responded in kind, "Agent Cyr."

Outlaw shook the stranger's hand and said simply, "Dillon Lawless."

Next, the stranger addressed Tolbert, "So, what do you gentlemen have that I need to know?"

Tolbert told him the story of the Russian in the bar and made note of the fact that he had seen the suspect on two previous Aeroflot flights into Quebec City. The stranger initially made no eye contact with either of them as Tolbert told his story. He simply smoked a cigarette and nodded, occasionally.

When Tolbert was done, the stranger looked at him and asked, "Do you think you'd recognize him in a photo?"

Tolbert replied in the affirmative, reiterating that he had seen him twice previously and got an adequate look at him in the bar.

While shuffling through the folders, the stranger asked Outlaw, "You?"

"Sure," Outlaw replied. "I was on stage, performin', but I had a pretty good look at him from about thirty feet away."

The stranger opened a dossier and pushed across the table in front of Tolbert.

"Is that the guy?" he asked.

"No, that's not him," Tolbert replied.

Outlaw concurred. The stranger retrieved the first folder and pushed another over to Tolbert.

"What about this one? Is this the guy?" he asked.

"Yep, that's him. I recognized the mole on his forehead and another one on the left side of his neck," Tolbert answered.

Outlaw leaned over and looked at the photo in the dossier.

"That's the guy, without question," he said.

"I was afraid you'd say that," the stranger said. "Before I say anything else, let me tell you gentlemen this: If you see this man, again, do not, under any circumstances, attempt to confront him. Don't even make eye contact or try to strike up a conversation with him. Leave him alone. This guy is a world-class motherfucker and he's up to no good. You can bet your last money on it."

"Call Agent Cyr, *immediately,* if you encounter this guy again. She knows how to contact me and I'll be in the local area. I'll say it again, gentlemen: do not attempt to confront this man. He *will* kill you, if he perceives you to be a threat, and he won't bat an eye about it. Then, he'll disappear and turn up on the other side of the world within twenty-four hours or so."

Tolbert shot a glance at Outlaw and raised his eyebrows in a look that said, "I told you so."

The stranger continued, "This guy is known to British intelligence, MI-6, Israeli Mossad, and probably every other one of our allied intelligence agencies, too. The Brits refer to him as 'Oz,' as in the 'Wizard of.' The name fits. We have an idea who he is and, until right now, no definitive idea of what he looks like, but he figuratively sits behind curtains, pulling levers and strings that make a whole lot of shady shit go down around the world. He can vanish into thin air, like a fart through an open window. I don't like the bastard, but I *do* admire his skills.

"He's a cold-blooded, murderin' sonofabitch. We're not even certain what his real name is, but he's been known to kill outside the realm of operational necessity."

"How do you know that?" Outlaw persisted.

"I've been close enough to see his work and close enough to see some of his victims. Those photos of him in Muslim clothes, they're from Afghanistan, but he was heavily bearded, then. I took those photos myself. He was a major shot-caller in the plot to overthrow the Afghan government in '79 and orchestrated the murder of President Amin and nearly everyone else in the presidential palace, just before the Soviets landed their Spetsnaz teams at Kabul Airport. They flew in aboard Aeroflot airliners. Almost everyone in the presidential palace was shot, execution-style, with silenced weapons. Like I said, this prick was a major player."

The stranger continued, "I appreciate your diligence and lettin' us know about this.

"We got word several weeks ago through our Canadian friends that this guy had been seen getting off an Aeroflot jet in Quebec. They lost track of him, but told us he was last thought to be headin' south. They just couldn't pin him down. He's too slippery and he's a hard target to track. He almost certainly crossed the border through a wilderness area or was somehow smuggled across, because U.S. Customs and other agencies were advised to keep an eye out for him at all border-crossing points. He's sharp enough to think through that scenario.

"My guess is that his presence in northern Maine may have something to do with this base. Now that we know his general location, we can refocus our search area. We want this guy and so do some other governments around the globe."

Tolbert added, "I think this guy might be gettin' a little complacent."

"Whaddaya mean?" the stranger asked.

"Well, for someone who wants to remain as inconspicuous as possible, he was wearin' a New England Patriots jacket. I guess he thought it made him look like any other American, but that thing was really bright red and my eye was drawn right to it. Could be that he's a bit more careless here than he would be someplace else. I guess he figured all Americans were ignorant of Russian mannerisms, but he was wrong."

The stranger nodded his head and thought a second before responding, "Well, he just made his first mistake on this caper. One slip like that might be the difference between us baggin' him and him doin' whatever it is he came here to do.

"I've seen him come close to slipping up, a couple of times in the past; namely, hanging around too long after he's done his mischief. He's still slippery as hell, though."

"Is that all you need from us?" Tolbert asked.

"Yeah, for now. Captain Tolbert, we may need you as an interpreter, if we uncover any written communications or radio transmissions from this bastard. So stay close. I have a working knowledge of Russian, but nowhere close to your fluency. Thanks, gentlemen."

As Outlaw shook hands with him before leaving, the stranger grinned and said, "By the way, my name's Dave."

Outlaw grinned while he shook his hand, but knew there was no way in the world this guy's name was really "Dave." So-Called Dave.

As Outlaw and Tolbert left, So-Called Dave asked Bergen to stay behind. He then left the room briefly and came back with a master sergeant, in uniform, who Bergen thought she recognized as being assigned to the 423rd Bomb Wing DOX shop; the "Vault," where the war plans were kept.

So-Called Dave told her, "Agent Cyr, the incident we just discussed coincides with another incident that my people recently became aware of and is being worked by another office in counterintelligence. After an investigation and a brief interrogation of an individual downstream of this, it leads us back here to compromised war-plans at this base."

Bergen was stunned. This was bad, if entities she couldn't even name were getting involved. This was espionage, plain and simple, and it foretold of "deep shit" for someone.

"No one else on base knows about this, right now," Dave told her, "not even the wing-commander, and he won't know, until we've made an arrest and interrogation of the individual in question. Master Sergeant Tucker here will brief you on what he has been privy to and what's been going on in your War Plans Office."

14. "Burglars in Our House"

Northern Vicinity, Captown, Maine
December 1, 1982

Soviet Naval Spetsnaz Captain Lieutenant Arkady Ivanovich Beloglazov led his team of nine men through the dark woods north of Easton, Maine, parallel to Highway 1, in the direction of the safe house. They were quiet enough, even though he'd seen them move in almost complete silence over snow that would've squeaked and crunched under the footfalls of less capable troops. It was a relatively short walk, just a bit over two kilometers, and they may easily have been mistaken for just a group of hunters, from the sound of things. Aside from that, they were wearing the fatigue uniforms and headgear of U.S. Air Force Security Police and he surmised they would simply be assumed to be on a training exercise of some sort, which he could easily explain away to any ordinary American citizen. Had they been in an Afghan combat zone, he would have ensured his team's almost complete silence. Thinking further on it, they would have seen to it themselves. They were "special operators," as the Americans referred to them, and totally reliable.

By the pace count and his compass heading, he figured he and his team would arrive at the safe house shortly. There, they would find four vehicles; two of them "pickup trucks," as the Americans called them, which would be identical to the type used by the U.S. Air Force. Their contact would have seen to all of those details. The other two would be civilian vehicles which could operate on or off prepared roads.

Because of the cramped confines of the small submarine in which they had made their way to the American shore, their advance operative had also been tasked with providing them with the black-arms market M-16 rifles, two American M-60 machine guns, one mortar tube, and the ammunition and mortar rounds they required. Beloglasov surmised that what would be provided had been captured from Afghan battlefields and reconditioned. He has no way to ascertain this, however, and perhaps the weapons would be procured on the lucrative American arms black market, but it was of little consequence. His team was thoroughly familiar with American weaponry and would break it all down, clean it, and ensure it was in working order, once they reached the safe house. They wouldn't need to be told; it was instinctive to them. The only weapons they had loaded aboard the insertion submarine had been "the Package" and a complement of 9K32 *Strela-2* shoulder-fired surface-to-air missiles and two launchers.

Members of Beloglazov's team were taking turns hauling the Package on their backs, though they refused to allow him to carry it. To a man, they knew what his six months of captivity with the Afghan mujahedeen had cost him and that he still experienced recurrent back problems, subsequent to cramped confinement and physical abuse. Although he never complained aloud, the team could tell by his occasional wince when he was hurting and they admired his stoicism.

The Package weighed approximately thirty kilos and was a ponderous load, even for highly conditioned troops. The ankle-deep snow and sloping ground only added to the difficulty, which became close to impossible after just a few minutes. Even in the cold, the operator carrying the load would begin puffing and sweating in short order, but it was a team effort and no one complained. They were Naval Spetsnaz, the most elite, toughest, and most disciplined of all Soviet combat forces.

Beloglazov's mind kept jumping back and forth between the march and his hunger. His last meal had been a light one, early in the morning aboard the submarine. As with submarine crews in other navies, Soviet submariners ate well aboard ship. Beloglasov and his team hadn't been aboard long enough for the good rations to be exhausted, which they undoubtedly would on the return voyage.

His team had been cramped in their quarters aboard the boat, but didn't venture out, except to the head or dining area, nor did they interact with the boat's crew. Aboard the submarine, Beloglasov's team had worn the uniforms of ordinary naval infantry, which aroused little curiosity among the submariners. Had they worn submariner uniforms, the real submariners would have been more eager to engage them in conversation. The team would likely not have been very cordial, if they responded at all, which would have caused further questions and concerns among the submarine's regular officers and men. Beloglazov and his team kept to themselves out of operational necessity. The boat's crew had no need of their mission specifications and the naval infantry uniforms served as an adequate buffer.

The only submarine officers who had even a remote inkling of the nature of the Spetsnaz team's mission were the captain and the executive officer, but even they had been kept in the dark about the Package. They were given sealed orders that were only to be opened after the boat had been at sea for twenty-four hours. The only information the order contained was a set of geographic coordinates as an insertion and pickup point, as well as the times of each. Once there at the assigned time, they were to release the midget submarine from the aft deck and surface again at the designated retrieval time at the same place. The midget vessel need not be re-mated with the mother boat, in the interests of time, the orders stated.

Isolated even from the Spetsnaz team was the technician known only to Beloglazov. A loner by nature, he was known by most back home only by his surname: Zimin. He was an engineer with expertise in the design of miniaturized nuclear weapons and responsible for the final assembly and electronic systems check of the Package. Zimin took up quarters in the rear of the boat, aft of the engine room. He took his meals alone and stayed in his cramped, partitioned area, rarely to be seen.

Zimin briefed him on the operation of the RA-155, which contained a six-kiloton, fissionable warhead. Beloglazov had orders that only he or his second-in-command, Warrant Officer Yermakov, were to fuse the Package, which meant if anything unfortunate happened to both of them, the mission would be aborted and the weapon abandoned.

This weapon's blast radius would be dwarfed by other tactical and strategic nuclear weapons of the day, but was ideally suited for the small area destruction Beloglasov knew would be sufficient to destroy the alert aircraft parking area and most of the flight line maintenance hangars at his target base. It would also likely shut down airfield operations indefinitely, which would impede the Americans' ability to stage operations destined for the fighting in Europe.

It was only in the hours prior to the team leaving the boat that the reclusive Zimin approached Beloglazov and said simply, "The Package is ready, Comrade Captain-Lieutenant. It will perform as intended. I had to make two minor repairs to slightly corroded wiring, but everything is now in perfect working order. If anyone attempts to neutralize the weapon, or if the container is punctured in any way, it will detonate with the nuclear yield.

"You have a battery life of approximately seventy-two hours. As the battery charge depletes itself, it will need to be connected to an outside power source to re-charge. Any American alternating current power outlet will do. I have two hundred feet of power cord for you to take along for that purpose. Be advised, Comrade Captain Lieutenant, if the battery depletes itself, the Package will not detonate."

Beloglazov nodded his understanding. Should the blast of the RA-155 elicit collateral nuclear detonations from the Americans' alert bombers, the results may well by cataclysmic for eastern Canada, the northeastern United

States, and perhaps the Soviet Union itself. The Americans might well launch a full-scale nuclear response and that possibility worried him.

Before boarding the midget submarine, they donned the fatigue uniforms and berets of U.S. Air Force Security Police troops; an act that directly violated the rules of warfare under the Geneva Conventions and would warrant them summary execution, should they be caught so clothed. As a hedge against that possibility, Captain Lieutenant Beloglazov had his men wear the shirts and tunics of Soviet Naval Spetsnaz under their American clothing. In the event of a firefight with American troops or law enforcement, they could quickly doff their U.S. Air Force jackets and shirts, thus enabling them to fight and likely die as what they actually were: Soviet troops.

15. "Safehouse"

The Old Daigle House
Vicinity Easton, Maine
Night of December 1-2, 1982

The KGB contact had chosen the vacant house well; off the road and nestled into some quiet woods which provided ample concealment behind stands of evergreens. In the summer, the deciduous trees would make for adequate shade and even better concealment. While the contact had not had the electricity restored to the house nor left any firewood for the team, Beloglazov understood it to be prudent, so as not to call any undue attention to the fact that the team would be resting there, even for a short time. He thought the petrol-powered generator in the garage would be able to charge the Package, but none of his team could get it to start, even though there was petrol in the tank and a full, five-gallon can beside it. Thus, the two hundred feet of power cord with which Zimin provided him would be useless. He would have to ensure the Package was placed and fused within the time-frame Zimin had specified.

The house, did, however, have running water in the kitchen faucets and bathroom, so at least he and his men could wash-off some of the stink from the submarine. While not luxurious by American capitalist standards, it would have been a veritable palace of sorts, back home in Russia. Their operative had done a very good job of indeed of securing this safe house and providing food, cigarettes, and the weaponry and ammunition they required.

As soon as they arrived, Beloglazov took two of the men and reconnoitered the route of escape, based on the instructions and map left for them. The team would be briefed on the egress-route to the rally point, where a 1973 Ford Bronco and the 1972 Chevrolet Blazer awaited them to facilitate a clean escape. Beloglazov rightly assumed it would not take the "dark forces" very long to come to the conclusion that the two blue, Dodge trucks were not authentic U.S. Air Force vehicles. The Ford and the Chevrolet might at least buy them a few hours.

Because of its weight, Beloglazov decided to leave the Package in the back of the Blazer, rather than keep it in the safe house. Anyone who would have to leave with it on his back, most likely under fire, would surely be slowed to the point of being killed or captured. Such an eventuality would, of course, mean they had failed in the mission altogether.

Beloglazov also decided not to leave the Package unguarded. One of the men promptly volunteered to stay with him for a four-hour shift and Beloglazov sent the others back to the safe house with orders to return at the appropriate time with two more men to continue the watch. Even though the latitudes of Maine were well south of those of Europe and the western Soviet Union, darkness still arrived early in Maine, this time of year. It was fully dark at 1700 hours. Beloglazov reckoned three four-hour shifts would suffice, before they headed north just after dawn in the direction of Spurlin Air Force Base. The others would bring breakfast to the two who sat the last shift with the vehicles. Outside the safe house itself, the team alternated watch-shifts as a hedge against any night-time approach by American troops or law enforcement.

Beloglazov knew that he could've left his two men with the vehicles and returned to the safe house. They would not have complained nor even begrudged him some rest in a "real" bed, as opposed to the wafer-thin mattresses aboard the submarine. Beloglazov was not the sort of combat leader who would leave anyone out there until he had first completed the type of watch shift he had demanded of them. While December was bringing cold and snow to Maine, it was not what his men would have called, "Russia cold." It was brisk enough for the clean air to stimulate the senses and necessitate the wear of winter clothing, but nothing his men couldn't tolerate. On many of their training exercises back home, and certainly in the mountains during an Afghan winter, they had become inured to far worse, particularly the two team members from Siberia.

At 0600 hours, the two men left to watch the Package were to drive both the Bronco and the Blazer and rendezvous with the blue Dodge trucks at the Big Wheel Truck Stop, just north of a "Visit Beautiful Canada" billboard two miles north of the town of Easton along the highway.

As weary as he was, he'd been happy to finally be able to sprawl across the double bed, but Beloglazov couldn't stop his mind from racing. There was simply too much in the form of unforeseen circumstances that could spell disaster for this mission. Regardless of how good his team was, he knew the odds were next to impossible of ever seeing home, again. Should things go wrong, there was no base of support here whatsoever. His months as a prisoner of the mujahedeen in Afghanistan had robbed him of whatever sense of optimism he may have had left. This time, they were deep inside the belly of the beast; deeper, in a philosophical sense, than they had ever been in Afghanistan. Beloglazov understood that time was fleeting and it wasn't going to be long before the Americans were onto them.

While the provisions left for the team were more than adequate, Beloglazov found himself craving good, Russian food. To deal with his insomnia, he employed a trick he had learned while a prisoner of the mujahedeen to stave off the hunger pangs and help himself sleep. He simply envisioned the things his mother and her friends would put on the table for birthdays and celebrations of national holidays, such as New Year's Eve, National Defenders' Day, and Women's Day.

Beloglazov and his men had made short work of the bananas, apples, and citrus fruits the contact had left for them, as well as something packaged as "Twinkies" and beef jerky for protein. Fresh fruits were often in short supply back home, save for brief periods in December and January when citrus would be available in the government-run markets. In America, they were apparently available year-round. He had heard tales of the large stores the American's called, "supermarkets," and the abundance they contained, but had yet to see one. He took a narcotic pill to ease his back pain and, with a full belly, drifted off to sleep and dreamt briefly of his mother's wonderful Russian cooking.

Once he was awake and shaving in the bathroom basin full of cold water, Beloglazov heard the radio operator, Topostokov, walk into the bathroom and saw in the mirror that he was wearing an expression of alarm and disbelief.

"Sir, I've just decoded and authenticated a message we received over the HF set. It says we are to proceed with our mission and destroy our assigned target. The message also stated that 'the Operation' had begun. I don't understand, Comrade Captain Lieutenant. What does it mean?"

It was now time to inform the men, Beloglazov decided, and he assembled them in the kitchen to brief them. Some, but not all, had been aware of the RA-155 weapon and knew what it was. What they didn't know, yet, were the events transpiring in Europe. He would brief the men guarding the Package once they were on the road toward the aerodrome the Americans called, "Spurlin Air Force Base."

Some were still eating at the kitchen table when he began his briefing.

"Tovarishi," he said in Russian, choosing against his almost perfect, American-accented English, "the time has now come for us to proceed with our appointed task and destroy the Spurlin aerodrome with the RA-155, which is currently in one of our newly procured vehicles and under guard by the remaining members of our team."

"Then, sir, can we assume the device to be a nuclear weapon?" asked Yermakov, his second-in-command.

"Da," Beloglasov answered, "Some of you have seen this type of weapon before and some of you have not. The device is powerful enough to destroy their entire force of nuclear armed bombers and their supporting tanker aircraft. It should also serve to disrupt airfield operations and impede their support of the war in Europe. This Spurlin base is their primary staging point for support of their forces in Europe. It's the aerodrome in the United States closest to Europe. We've known its importance, in that regard, for years."

Several of the men gasped.

"Sir, are you saying we are now at war with the Americans and NATO?" asked Yermakov.

"Our forces, accompanied by our Warsaw Pact allies, have already crossed the border into capitalist Germany and are engaging the NATO forces, as we speak," Beloglazov answered without a trace of emotion on his face or in his voice.

"It has begun, *tovarishi*, and we can only hope that the western forces are as disorganized, cowardly, and unmotivated as our Party leaders have insisted. But, I doubt that they are. I perceive them to be very well trained and organized. This will not be an easy victory for the Motherland, so let us steel ourselves to our task."

With that, he unfolded his map spread it across the table, before going into detail about the vehicles, where they would be positioned, and how exactly they would gain access to the Spurlin alert aircraft parking area. The tension in the room was palpable, but he assured his team he had every confidence that they would prevail.

16. "Ill Winds"

Highway 1
Northern Vicinity, Easton, Maine
December 2, 1982

Sheriff Jasper Hood was nearly forced off the side of the highway by his coughing fit. He was in the beginning stages of his annual November bout with nasal allergies, which inevitably dripped down his throat and ended with bronchitis or something akin to it. However, he'd taken action on it early and was medicated enough to feel relatively well when the coughing fit caught him off-guard. This morning, he had two deputies call in sick; both so bad that they told him they were, without question, going to see a doctor. As a result, Hood was having to work a double shift; 7:00 a.m. to 3:00 p.m., after working all night. While he would've preferred to go home and put his aching body to bed, he didn't mind. Others had worked doubles for him, in the past, and he was grateful to have a crew in the Sheriff's Department that worked so well together and covered for each other in times like this.

That was all part of working in a small law enforcement office. Besides, he'd seen a doctor before he came on duty, last night, and already had two doses of antibiotics in him. He'd taken the prednisone tablets to open up his lungs and sinuses, and had cough syrup with codeine, which he hadn't yet taken, to keep that in check. Realizing he was still going to have to drive for the better part of the next eight hours, he decided he would take less than the prescribed dose of the cough medicine, in hopes of minimizing the effects of the codeine while he was out on motor patrol. He didn't have a spoon with him in the cruiser, so he just took a very small sip straight from the bottle. There was no need to go back to the station because he wasn't going "end of watch." After a quick breakfast at the Big Wheel Truckstop, which was more of a café with a small, attached garage, he would just continue on the rounds Deputy Carter normally made.

When he rounded the last curve that would bring the truckstop into sight, he saw four vehicles fifty or so yards beyond it, all parked along the right shoulder. Pulling in behind them, he could see that the two pickup trucks nearest him were Air Force vehicles and the Blazer at the front of the column and the Bronco behind it were civilian trucks. The hood was up on the Blazer and he could see someone bent over the engine. He'd retired from the Air Force out of Spurlin Air Force Base and was always glad to assist his fellow "blue suiters," whenever and wherever he could.

"Hello, Officer," said Captain-Lieutenant Beloglazov in his American-accented English.

Sheriff Hood waved as he walked forward and asked, "Hello, Sergeant. You fellas need any help?"

"No, Sheriff," said Wally Davis, whose hulking, potbellied form emerged from under the hood of the Blazer. "These fellas just needed a new alternator belt for the Blazer here. Good thing the old one snapped right in front of the truckstop. Easy fix!"

"Oh, hey, Big Wally," the Sheriff answered. "I thought it mighta been you, since I didn't see a company truck out here. Just a short walk across the parkin' lot for ya, eh?"

Closing the hood with a loud clunk, Wally said, "Yep, and I'm all done here."

Wally then offered his hand to the senior master sergeant who appeared to be leading this group and said, "You fellas have a safe trip, ya hear?"

Beloglazov, disguised as a U.S. Air Force senior master sergeant, shook his hand, smiled, and asked, "Thanks, Wally. How much do we owe you for the repair?"

"You don't owe me anything, Sergeant. We'll just send an invoice to the Spurlin Accountin' Office. They'll take care of it. They had an airman get in trouble down this way, about six months ago. When the SPs came down to get him outta jail, the thermostat blew on their van and we fixed it for 'em and sent a bill. The Spurlin folks pay-up like Roscoe. Well, Sergeant, I gotta go. Got a call from a stranded trucker about eight miles south of here. Gonna need the tow rig for this 'un! It was good to meet you fellas."

Beloglasov grimaced internally at the thought he didn't know what "pay-up like a Roscoe" meant and that this might be the first thread of his mission to unravel. He could only hope that he and his team could complete its mission before the invoice arrived from the truckstop. If they were successful in detonating the device, flight operations at Spurlin would cease to exist and the base would be evacuated or destroyed, by that time. He and his team would be back at sea aboard the submarine and headed home, hopefully to a national victory celebration, once NATO had been subdued in Western Europe.

Big Wally shook hands with Sheriff Hood and asked, as he headed off, "Ever'thing good with you and ever'body at the Sheriff's Office, Jasper?"

"Not as good as they could be, Wally. Carter and Blythe are out sick today with this crud that's goin' around. Happens every damned year about this time. I'm fightin' it, too."

"Everybody's got it at my house, too, 'cept me," Big Wally laughed, as he waddled away.

Turning his attention to the senior master sergeant, Hood read his name tag and asked, "Sarn't Steinfeld, is there anything I can do for you fellas before you get goin'? Cupacoffe or somethin' to warm you up?"

"No, thank you, Sheriff," Beloglazov answered with a smile. "We've been on an exercise down at the Plattsburgh base and we just want to get home to our families."

Hood took note of the fact that none of the other Air Force SPs had said a word to him. Most of them just smiled, some rather sheepishly, smoked cigarettes, and kept their distance. All, except one, avoided eye contact.

Not intent on giving that instant, ill feeling away, he simply shook the senior master sergeant's hand and said, "Gentlemen, I'm gonna go back there to the truckstop and get some warm chow and coffee. I've got a long day ahead of me."

Beloglasov sensed the subtle, almost imperceptible difference in the Sheriff's demeanor, then merely nodded and said, "We understand, Sheriff. Get some rest when you can and thanks for your offer."

Sheriff Hood returned to his patrol cruiser, a big, white Ford Crown Victoria, noticing that four of the airmen stayed close to the rear of the two Air Force vehicles, almost as if guarding the contents of the truck beds, which were covered with olive-drab tarps. Two of them seemed almost defensive in their body movements, preventing the Sheriff from shaking this sudden, ominous feeling. Hood had been a part of law enforcement for thirty-five years, the first twenty in Air Force Security Police, then the last fifteen in the Wallace County Sheriff's Department; long enough to be suspicious of everyone and everything. Things were seldom what they seemed, where criminals and their behavior were concerned.

He coughed again as he climbed into the cruiser, certain that things were askew, but he couldn't narrow it all down beyond an extremely disconcerting "hunch." Thinking on it for ten or so seconds, he thought about what senior master sergeant had said about being TDY. He'd used the phrase, "The Plattsburgh base." A "wingnut" wouldn't have said that. It sounded stilted and unnatural. Any airman or officer would've simply said, "We've been TDY down at Plattsburg." The word "base" was superfluous, to the wingnut way of phrasing and understanding things. He didn't even allude to being on "temporary duty" or "TDY" down there.

As he pulled his cruiser into the parking spot the truck stop owner reserved for law enforcement, he didn't remember a single time he'd been sent TDY from Spurlin for an exercise or additional training where he and those with whom he was traveling didn't fly out of Spurlin aboard military transport or commercial aircraft. They didn't drive pickup trucks on TDYs to Plattsburgh or anywhere else. As critical as serviceable vehicles likely were at Spurlin, due to the harsh weather and pressing concerns of the bomber and tanker alert force, the Spurlin brass certainly wouldn't have sent two of those trucks away. Everything here was adding up to one big negative, but he had no clear indication, yet, as to which direction these ill winds would blow, but he strongly suspected in the direction of Spurlin Air Force Base.

Then, he remembered one small detail that convinced him that his suspicions were correct. The license plate on the rear vehicle spoke volumes. It carried a Maine plate and he assumed the Air Force pickup in front of did, as well. That plate was stolen. Every military vehicle in the entire U.S. military inventory carried federal plates; never state plates. To top everything else off, why the hell were these guys way over here on Highway 1? If they were in a hurry to get back to Spurlin, they would've made substantially better time by heading north on Interstate-95.

Something was very wrong, but he wasn't going to call it in, just yet. There were some things he first needed to investigate. He shifted the Crown Vic into reverse and backed out of his parking-space, regretting he would miss breakfast. It could wait, but maybe he'd get to the bottom of this by lunchtime, even though he calculated the odds of that being the case as "between zero and none."

On his way north, this morning, he'd noticed tire tracks several miles back in the partially melted snow on the northern access road that led to the old Daigle place. Nothing had caught his attention on the southern road in. Hood hadn't thought anything about it, at the time, even though the Daigle house had been vacant for several years. His instincts now told him to investigate those tire tracks. Whatever caper these "airmen" were involved in might've included a stay there. It wasn't much to go on, he knew, but it was as good a place as any to start. In this business, gut feelings were sometimes the crux of settling investigations...and survival.

Hood found the thought of these men disguised as airmen extremely disconcerting. What could they possibly be up to, here in Maine? Drug or gun-running? Or something far worse? In any event, he knew federal authorities would have to be notified, due to the Air Force angle alone.

As he turned east onto the northern access road to the Daigle house, Hood had momentary doubts about investigating by himself. If there were ten of them in the vehicles, he had no way of knowing if there was anyone else holed-up in the house. He approached it slowly, carefully scanning each side of the road ahead of him as he eased the Crown Vic down the unpaved driveway and into the thick evergreens surrounding the old house. The snow wasn't deep enough to preclude the big, rear-wheel-drive Crown Vic from plowing ahead, though he wished he'd taken the department's four-wheel-drive Blazer out on patrol, instead. The saving grace was that he had the snow tires on the Crown Vic and those would have to do, for now. Before switching-off the ignition, he decided it prudent to report in with his dispatcher, Lorraine, and let her know where he was.

Taking the radio microphone from its cradle, he keyed it and said, "Dispatch. Unit One. Over."

"Go ahead, Sheriff. Over," Lorraine replied cheerfully.

"Just wanted to give you my ten-twenty. Over," he said, using standard law enforcement code for his location.

"Go ahead, Sheriff. Over," she answered.

"I'm at the old Daigle place, off Highway One, on the northern access road. You know where I'm talkin' about? Over."

"Aay-firmative," Lorraine replied. "How long are you gonna be at that ten-twenty? Over."

"Don't know, an hour, maybe more," he speculated. "But, I'm gonna need you to patch a call through to the 423rd Security Police Squadron at Spurlin Air Force Base, when you hear from me, again. Then, I'm gonna need a patch to the FBI office in Augusta. Have that info ready to go for me. Over."

"Got it, Sheriff. Whatever you're doin', be careful. I'm not feelin' warm and fuzzy about this. I just heard news over the radio war has broken out in Europe. Fightin' in Germany, right now. Over."

"Ten-four. That might explain a lot. Unit One out," he concluded.

Before leaving the cruiser, he pulled his service revolver from his holster and gave it a quick look. Cleaned and loaded. Next, he thought about unracking the shotgun from the floorboard under his legs, but decided the revolver should be enough, if he got in trouble at close quarters. However, the scoped Remington 30.06 hunting rifle he carried in the trunk might be useful, if he needed to do some precision shooting, which he earnestly hoped wouldn't be the case.

The Daigle house was screened and shaded a bit by a stand of evergreens and the snow in the shaded portion of the drive and around the house itself had not melted to the degree that the sunlit snow had. Hood could see numerous footprints in it all around the house, which he examined thoroughly, before going inside. From the looks of things, the house had been recently occupied. He decided not to knock on the front door for fear of alerting any threat which might lurk inside, but turned the knob slowly and found it unlocked. Shifting his revolver to his right hand, he opened the door fully and entered, carefully checking each room and all closets as he went.

Whoever had been here had not bothered to clean up. In addition to muddy footprints all over the hardwood floors and what few rugs remained, food wrappers, soda cans, juice bottles, and cigarette butts, had been strewn on the floors and all over the kitchen counters and table. The smell of cigarette smoke and sour body odor hung heavily in the air. The group who had been here last had obviously left within the last hour or so. Even the banana and orange peels, in addition to the five apple cores he found, appeared relatively fresh and still moist. Despite the mess and waste in the house, he could find nothing that would lead to a determination of what these "airmen" might actually be up to.

It was in the detached garage where he found evidence that their intended mischief might, in some way, be directed at Spurlin Air Force Base. The garage had been used to paint the two "Air Force" trucks. There, he found a gasoline-powered AC generator, a kerosene space heater, a spray gun, respirator, masking tape, newspaper, leftover blue paint, and stencils for the U.S. Air Force markings on the doors, as well as the leftover yellow enamel paint for the stencils. Outside, he found tire tracks from four vehicles, which he surmised to be the two Dodge pickups, as well as the Blazer and Bronco he'd seen. No doubt, these were bad actors, but the individual responsible for the trucks had been careless enough to leave all this evidence behind. Hood guessed that they had no intention of returning to what was obviously their base of operations. Before investigating the numerous footprints out back, which had come from the south, he decided to call Lorraine, again.

"Go ahead, Sheriff," she said, answering his call.

"Are you ready to patch me through to the Spurlin Security Police squadron? Over," he asked.

"Ay-firmative. Hang on and I'll get 'em on the line. Over."

Twenty seconds later, a voice crackled through the radio speaker, "Four-twenty-third Security Police Squadron, Technical Sergeant Wilson speaking. This is not a secure line. How may I help you?"

Hood keyed his mic and responded, "Sarn't Wilson, this is Sheriff Hood. I'm just north of Easton, right now, just off State Highway 1, and I've got a situation that might involve your people. Over."

"How can we help, Sheriff? Over," the sergeant responded.

"Less than an hour ago, I encountered four vehicles near a truckstop along Highway 1. Two were Dodge pickups, painted Air Force-blue and marked accordingly. One of the civilian vehicles was a late model, red-over-white Chevy Blazer and the other was a dark green Ford Bronco, both mid-seventies models. I don't have license plates on the two civilian vehicles, but the two Air Force vehicles had Maine plates, repeat, Maine plates, instead of federal plates. They appear to be stolen plates. Over."

He felt like kicking himself for not getting the plates of all four vehicles, but his instincts and uneasiness told him to get away from that group of men as quickly as he could. Should a confrontation occur, he would have found himself at a certain, mortal disadvantage.

"Please check with your transportation people to see if you have two pickups signed out for a TDY to Plattsburgh, dates uncertain. A Senior Master Sergeant Steinfeld appeared to be in command of the nine airmen he had with him. He stated they had been TDY to Plattsburgh and were headed back your way.

"I've uncovered evidence down here that these people are *not* who they say they are. Over."

"Copy all, Sheriff. Wilco on the motor pool and I'll also run a computer check on our base personnel locator system for a Senior Master Sergeant Steinfeld. Do you have a first name on him? Over," Sergeant Wilson answered.

"Negative on the first name. That last name is 'Steinfeld.' Sierra-tango-echo-india-november-foxtrot-echo-lima-delta. Mind if I stay on the line while you check? Over," Hood wanted to know.

"Copy all, Sheriff. Wait one. Over."

106

Two minutes later, Sergeant Wilson's voice crackled through the speaker again, "Sheriff Hood. Are you still on the line? Over."

"Affirmative, Sarn't. Over."

"Sheriff, the transportation people say 'negative' on two vehicles signed out to any NCO named Steinfeld or anyone else for a TDY to Plattsburgh. We don't have any vehicles at all signed out off-base, right now. Also, be advised that the base personnel locator system doesn't show anyone by that last name assigned to this duty station. Over," Sergeant Wilson said.

"I was afraid you'd say that, Sarn't. I've got one more thing to investigate, in this regard, and will contact federal authorities. Meantime, your people need to BOLO for those four vehicles and a group of ten, repeat one-zero, individuals disguised as airmen, in your area. There may be more, but numbers unknown, at this time. Suggest you advise state and all local law enforcement. I don't know what these guys are up to, but I don't see it as anything good. Over."

"Copy all, Sheriff. We're about to get *really* busy around here, but we'll notify OSI and all the other appropriate agencies. Thanks for the 'heads up.' Good luck. Out."

17. "Justifiable Homicide"

The Old Daigle House
Vicinity Easton, Maine
December 2, 1982

Before following the footprints out back of the Daigle house, Hood decided now might be a good time to take another swig of his cough medicine to keep him from giving himself away on the trail. Before starting out, he cycled the bolt on the Remington to make sure he had a round in the breech. If he needed to shoot anyone, the big Remington would reach out over long distances and make sure they stayed down.

Just as he had frequently done on countless patrols outside the wire at Phu Cat and Phan Rang air bases in Vietnam, he walked in a half-crouch, careful of his foot placement. He scanned from side to side and up and down, mindful of the lessons he'd seen others learn the hard way from the Viet Cong and their wicked booby traps; the difference here being he couldn't rely on the smell sense of Bear, the German Shepherd who'd accompanied him, on those patrols.

Hood felt his chest settle down as the codeine warmly worked its way through his system. It took him nearly an hour to cover the mile because he was careful and wasn't in the same physical condition as in his military days. Still, he was very apprehensive about what he might be walking into.

By his own mental pace count, he had gone just a little over a mile when he saw it in the secluded cove. A large, camouflaged tarp covered something floating in the water, and that something was tethered to a large pine close to the bank. From where he was standing at the crest of a small rise along the trail of footprints, he was looking slightly downward at a range he estimated to be approximately one hundred yards.

He quickly found concealment behind a snowbank and uncapped both ends of the Remington's scope. Peering through it over the top of the drift, the tarp-covered shape he'd noticed was obviously some sort of water-going craft. To date, any military activity in his county was made known to civilian law enforcement and he was unaware of any exercises being conducted by any branch of the U.S. armed forces along this stretch of Maine coastline. Something very unusual indeed was afoot.

As alarming as the thought was, what he saw emerge from behind it was even more startling. He saw a young man, obviously a sailor, with an AK-47 slung over his shoulder, nonchalantly smoking a cigarette. This sailor wasn't from the U.S. Navy or Coast Guard, based on the appearance of his uniform. When viewed through the rifle scope, even at a distance of just over three hundred feet, the uniform had a foreign look to it. He could make out some sort of name strip on the uniform through the scope and the letters weren't English letters; Russian perhaps. This was a foreign boat. Where did it come from and what in God's name was it doing here?

"It doesn't matter," he said to himself. "We're at war, now."

The sailor remained unaware of Hood's presence, sat down cross-legged on the bank, and continued to enjoy his cigarette. Hood had never fired a shot at another human being during his entire tenure in civilian law enforcement, but had fired plenty, and even killed, on air base defense duty in South Vietnam. This would be the first shot he would fire as a peace officer. The question he needed to answer was did he want to kill or merely wound.

Given that this sailor was armed with an automatic weapon, "shoot to kill" seemed the prudent option; the choice tilted in favor of personal survival. Obviously, the sailor wasn't going to let him near that vessel without some sort of fight. Based on what he had seen near the truckstop and at the Daigle house, this was the safe bet for a "justifiable homicide." It, in fact, amounted to a military action against a foreign power that had landed troops on U.S. soil; a foreign power with which his country was now at war.

He sighted in on the sailor's head. There was only the faintest puff of a breeze. He'd killed deer and elk at greater ranges than this. A tremor rumbled through his torso. Did he need to cough or was this the old mix of fear and exhilaration he'd felt on perimeter defense Phu Cat? It didn't matter. This was a necessary shot. There was a better chance of a hit with a center-mass body shot, but also a better chance the sailor wouldn't die instantly and would be able to return fire. Just one look at the ammunition pouches on the sailor's web gear and the AK-47 he carried, told the sheriff the foreigner would have the advantage, should this devolve into a firefight.

He applied a steady pressure to the trigger and felt the recoil of the Remington. Though his scope, he saw the sailor's head explode in a pink mist and then watched as the corpse slid down the bank and into the water in front of the tethered vessel. He immediately turned and scoped the area behind him, but neither saw nor heard anything. Then, he again looked down-range through the scope to the vessel, the bank, and the rise and woods behind. This sailor had been left alone to guard this thing, whatever it was.

Confident that he hadn't alarmed anyone else who might be nearby, he slung and shouldered the rifle, drew his revolver, and started carefully toward the vessel. Before he attempted to remove the tarp, he looked at the sailor, who was floating on his back and staining the water red with blood. Definitely Russian. That was confirmed when he pulled back the tarp and saw the Cyrillic stenciling on what revealed itself to be a Russian miniature submarine.

Hood continued to stare at the dead Russian for another minute. He'd felt a certain sympathy for the first Viet Cong he had killed, but not this Russian. After all, he been an unwelcome presence in that strange, little Southeast Asian country. But, this Soviet sailor had ventured onto American soil, intent on creating some sort of trouble, even if it was simple espionage. In a very strange, small way, it bothered him that it didn't bother him.

He realized he was right on the edge of his hand-held radio's range, but decided to try and call this in from his present location, as opposed to making the trek back to his cruiser with its more powerful radio.

"Dispatch, Unit One, mobile," he radioed.

"Go ahead, Sheriff. Over," Lorraine answered.

"Before you patch me through to the FBI in Augusta, I'll need backup out here, and I mean State Patrol, ambulance, coroner; anybody who can shake loose from whatever they're doin'. Tell 'em to take the south road in here; not the northern road running to the Daigle house. Over."

"Ten-four, Sheriff. Do you need medical assistance, yourself? Over."

"Negative, Dispatch, but I do have an 'officer-involved' shootin' and one fatality. Looks like a foreign national in military uniform. Don't know what he was up to, but suffice it to say the cat's outta the bag. Over."

"Copy, Unit One. Please state your ten-twenty."

"I'm in a little cove, approximately one mile south-southeast of the old Daigle house. Probably be easiest to spot from a helicopter. Over," Hood answered.

"Roger, Unit One, I know right where you are. My husband and I camped there and fished that cove, the summer after we got married. His family was friends with the Daigles. I'm advising State Patrol and coroner's office, now. Stand by for your phone patch to FBI. Over."

Sheriff Hood noticed that Lorraine's tone wasn't so breezy, now.

110

18. "Tripwire"

3022nd Army Security Agency Battalion, Company D,
Detachment M

Mount Mesmer

Vicinity *Ostweg,* West Germany

December 2, 1982

Sergeant Major Claude Bolden eased his stiff, aching back into his chair inside the MP duty hut and glanced out over the antenna-field, but noticed nothing unusual. The day had been a light, gray overcast, but it hadn't started snowing, despite the forecast. However, he could smell it in the air. The day had been cold, but not a biting, windy cold; just the sort of weather in which he'd liked to run when he was younger. He really didn't like running at all, these days, but still made himself do it. Bolden had completed a three-mile run that afternoon before beginning his shift and realized just how quickly the years were beginning to catch up with him.

Nevertheless, Bolden was enjoying his second tour of duty at Detachment M. His presence had been specifically requested, this time, and he was glad to be away from the stress and strain of the hellhole that was United Nations Joint Security Area at Pan Mun Jom on the Korean Demilitarized Zone. Bolden regarded the DMZ the strangest and potentially the most dangerous place on the planet, courtesy of Kim Il-Sung and his goons. Yet, Bolden knew well from his previous tour of duty here on the mountain that his lifespan would be measured in mere minutes, if not seconds, should the Soviets send their armored units and other ground and air forces across the border through the Fulda Gap.

There was a lethal side to Mount Mesmer unknown in most other MP posts. The Detachment was an antenna farm and a signals intelligence unit, known in military jargon as SIGINT. The American antennae, which were plainly visible, were inside a fenced compound adjacent to the MP Duty Office, from which they had a view of most of the compound. Their West

German sister outfit, which also performed SIGINT duties, was located on the northern end of the compound.

From its position atop Mount Mesmer, Detachment M had an unimpeded view of the border, which lay in the valley below some 11 kilometers distant. On a clear day, the view was almost completely unobstructed and good enough for Detachment M personnel to plainly see Soviet activity in the valley near the border.

The mountaintop site was protected, or at least screened, in the valley below by a platoon of M-60A1 main battle tanks from an armored cavalry regiment. The tank platoon certainly wasn't going to stop any major Soviet armored incursion, but it just may give the Soviets enough of a face-slap to slow them down long enough for Detachment M personnel to get a message out that an invasion was underway, set their thermite charges on the safes to destroy the classified documents, and scramble rearward for whatever safety they could find.

A Soviet armored invasion at that point along the border might have been a stretch in defensive thinking. The more likely scenario, as Sergeant Major Bolden and the others had been briefed, was that the site would likely be the target of a tactical nuclear missile, or, at the very least, a sustained barrage from Soviet heavy artillery, possibly with chemical warheads. That way, they could be done with the site and its SIGINT-gathering capabilities in short order and bypass it altogether.

The incoming CO was an old-school infantryman who had found a home in the intelligence world when the Army tried to invalid him out of the service due to wounds he had received with the "Big Red One," the 1st Infantry Division, in Vietnam. The major was still more "grunt" than "spook," but the entire complexion of Detachment M took on a completely new look and feel under his leadership.

"Make 'em look like soldiers and they'll act like soldiers," the major was fond of saying.

His first appeal was to Bolden and the other MPs, who were literally the only armed troops on the mountain. Bolden bought into his way of thinking. The others followed suit, some reluctantly, but no one could argue with the major's results. Even the linguists and others who worked inside the operations center seemed to fall into line. The whole detachment had a distinctly more "GI" look and feel to it. Bolden felt like he was "in the Army," again.

Things were running well when the major received word he'd been promoted to the rank of lieutenant colonel and Bolden was glad of it. But, for all the things the CO had gotten right, Bolden couldn't figure out why the chemical defense suits were kept under lock and key, nor could he help but wonder why the gasmasks they were required to have on their persons were only fitted with teargas protective filters, instead of the war filters that would be needed to protect against real chemical weapons.

Late one night, as the new lieutenant colonel and the sergeant major were downing a bottle of Scotch to celebrate the CO's promotion, Bolden raised the issue, stating that a visit from the inspector general, the dreaded "IG," during which they found that, could potentially prove to be a career-ending disaster for them both.

"It wouldn't do us any good, Claude," the colonel told him. "If those Communist bastards come across the border, they're gonna make short work of us, most likely with a tactical nuke; either that, heavy artillery, or chemicals. If they attack in force, you know your job is set the thermite charges on the safes and the radio operators have their orders to get out message traffic to the effect that the war is *on.*

"Then, it's gonna be elbows and assholes to get the hell off the mountain. To get all that done, while tryin' to do the dick-dance of gettin' into MOPP gear at the same time, gettin' away clean likely won't happen. We *will* incur casualties."

As the CO spoke, he took note of the skeptical and disapproving expression on the sergeant major's face. He supposed it to be about the inaccessibility of the war filters.

"If the shit hits the fan, just get off the damned mountain and to the rally point you and your guys have selected. I know you have some emergency rations, commo gear, ammo, weapons, and other stuff there. Hell, come to think of it, that might be the ideal place to stash some additional MOPP gear. But, maybe you're right, Claude. Maybe we should take another look at the whole scenario.

"I suppose it's always been done as a cost savin' measure, as the damned things only last a couple of weeks, once they're unwrapped. Put 'em in the mask and start breathin' through 'em and they only last a couple of hours. I don't have any problem spendin' Uncle Sugar's money. Do you? Hell, we probably oughta get the suits out from under lock and key and put the damned war filters in the masks. Any IG people come around and see things as they are, in that regard, and they might not like it. Glad I have you around to keep me out of trouble, Claude."

Subsequent to that conversation with the CO, lockers were installed just inside the door of the main building for the chemical defense suits. All personnel were to have their gasmasks, *with* the war filters, on their persons at all times while on duty, which met the requirements of Mission Oriented

Protective Posture Level-Zero. "MOPP-Zero," as that posture was called, meant masks carried with gloves and suits immediately accessible.

Bolden kept his chemical ensemble in a footlocker underneath the desk in the MP duty office, hoping he would never need it. This so-called "cold war" could go on for another century or two, with both sides continually squabbling over the right ways to live. All this posturing along the "Iron Curtain" was just for show.

0200 hours. Five more to go. Then, he could head to the mess hall and eat breakfast, cooked by Rudi, the marvelous little German cook who had learned his trade while a POW in Oklahoma during World War II. Bolden was looking forward to his Colorado omelet, hash browns, and peppered bacon, prepared as only Rudi could. He thought about that breakfast through the process of stretching his stiff back once more and lighting another cigarette.

He didn't hear the SCUD missile coming. It detonated at an altitude of 500 feet, directly above the antennae field, but the blast wasn't overly destructive or even particularly stunning. At first, Bolden dove to the floor. He rose to his knees a few seconds later, wondering if there would be further detonations, then looked out the window to see Privates Pickard and Childs, both on the ground, twitching and gasping for breath. Apparently, they had inhaled some of what vapors were settling to the ground. It was then that he noticed the mist on the windows. The vaporized nerve-agent could and would blow away quickly, but the droplets wouldn't. The only "up" side was that it gave him a few more precious seconds to don the suit. Glancing toward the German buildings, he saw three of their troops in the same predicament as Pickard and Childs.

Grabbing the microphone to the public address system, he shouted, "All personnel! All personnel! Gas! Gas! Gas! This is not a drill!"

So far, he was feeling no ill effects. He was inside and that was buying him some time.

He ripped his gasmask and hood from the pouch on his web belt and donned it, being sure to clear the mask by placing his hands over the filters and inhaling, to ensure an intact seal on his face. He quickly retrieved his protective suit and wiggled into it as quickly as he could. He'd practiced this very thing numerous times on the Korean DMZ and was very efficient in his movements. Lastly, he tugged on his protective gloves and checked to make sure his atropine-sulfate syringe was readily at hand. Should he begin twitching and gasping for breath, the first sign of a nerve agent asphyxiating him, he knew to jab himself very hard in the thigh depress the plunger. Atropine sulfate was the antidote to the nerve agent and might very well keep him alive. Apparently, Pickard and Childs hadn't heeded that bit of doctrine and had, by now, stopped twitching, as had the three West Germans on their side of the compound.

Directly across from the MP duty office, one of the linguists had opened the door to the Operations Building. Both Bolden and the linguist could clearly see each other and the sergeant major gave him the hand-signal for "gas," touching the tops of his shoulders with his fingertips.

He then grabbed the microphone and shouted through the mask into it, "This is not a drill! Gas! Gas! Gas! Close that goddamned door!"

Garbled as it was through the gasmask, the linguist understood him and, with an expression on his face that bespoke absolute horror, closed the door, but not before Bolden could see personnel scurrying in the background, one an MP obviously setting a thermite charge atop a large safe. Good. The MPs were doing their jobs.

Glancing out of the duty hut to the east, he could hear the ragged "crump-crump" of artillery impacting nearby and see the horizon on the East German side of the border alight with the muzzle flashes of the big artillery pieces. This was most assuredly not a drill.

Bolden took stock of his surroundings in what was a pre-briefed, "every man for himself" scenario. He could plainly see the droplets of nerve agent on the north and east windows of the duty hut but saw none at all on the western window, which was also the door. If this was VX nerve agent, it was exponentially more deadly than sarin because of its "motor oil" consistency and much slower evaporation rate. Yet, this door was his only way out and the prevailing wind, light as it was, would blow the deadly mist in an eastward direction as it descended on the mountaintop. Bolden hoped some it had blown back on the Communist bastards, as well.

The MPs' escape and evasion plan had been briefed and reviewed weekly, per Bolden's standing orders. They had prepositioned additional MOPP gear, weapons, ammunition, and food in a cave some two miles distant, at the westernmost base of the mountain. Whoever survived the initial onslaught on the mountaintop, if anyone, would rally there, then begin moving westward in search of friendly forces. Bolden decided not to take his M-16, which would only prove cumbersome and would not do him much good in the face of what was coming. He could replace it at the rally point.

The light from the door of the main building got his attention, again. He turned to see a masked and hooded soldier peeping out the door, and giving him a thumbs-up sign with a hand wearing a chemical protective glove. It was Danoff, the big kid from Connecticut, judging from the size of him. He was signaling that the thermite charges had been set atop the safes the fuses were about to be pulled.

The phone rang. Out of habit, Bolden picked up the receiver, having temporarily forgotten about the mask and hood.

Sticking receiver up under the hood and next to his ear, he could barely discern the voice of Lieutenant Forrest, one the SIGNINT officers, who was literally shouting into his end of the phone through his own mask, "Sergeant Major, the charges are set and fused! We have some personnel leavin' out the opposite end of the building! Get outta here!"

Bolden dropped the receiver, sucked in a deep breath through the mask, opened the door, and bounded out the western-facing door across the parking lot and the road that ran parallel to the site. The Detachment sat atop a lip on the eastern side of the mountain and Bolden had a slight uphill stretch of two kilometers, nearly a mile, to go before he could reach the crest and descend the western face. He was glad of the bright moonlight that made the trail easier to see. He had made sure to run the course to the cave on the occasional off day, both in daylight and in the dark. He knew the way.

Breathing hard through the gasmask, he crested the hill and started down. A half-mile down, his leg began to go numb for the pounding of downhill running, forcing him into a labored, ambling gait. His breathing was hampered considerably by the gasmask and he felt like his lungs were going to burst, but he wasn't about to take it off. The thought crossed his mind that a coronary event might kill him, but he'd be damned if any communist, chemical attack would.

Bolden stopped and turned to have a look back at the mountaintop, where he discerned movement on the trail behind him and recognized the long gait of Peirson and the measured strides of Middleton, right behind him and both in full MOPP gear. He was glad to see that they'd had time to get into the suits and get off the mountaintop. He waived his arms over his head and they acknowledged, bounding down the slope toward him.

It was then he heard what appeared to be two more SCUDs detonate above the site. From this distance, the explosions were somewhat muted. Once the two others caught up with him, the three continued downward. Several minutes later, they heard sustained explosions from the site, indicating the Soviets were now bringing heavy artillery to bear, killing those who hadn't already been killed by the nerve agent and destroying the site completely. Hopefully, the radio operators had notified both Frankfurt and Augsburg that an attack was underway. But, if this was indeed a major Soviet invasion, chances were that Frankfurt and Augsburg had already found that out for themselves.

As he turned and continued his limping gait down the mountainside with Middleton and Pierson in tow, Sergeant Major Bolden realized he was going to sorely miss Rudi, those omelets, and those damned hash browns.

19. "We Interrupt This Program"

113 High Street

Apartment C

Captown, Maine

December 2, 1982

0702 Hours (Local)

Outlaw sat on the edge of his bed with a towel around his waist and his hair still wet. That would give him plenty of time to dress, eat breakfast, drive the twelve miles to the base, and make the 0800 assumption of alert briefing. His A-4 bag was already in the trunk of his car, loaded with all the gear he would need for his alert tour. His suitcase, in which he would carry his toiletries, underwear, socks, and four flight suits, was packed and sitting at the top of the kitchen stairs.

The telephone on the nightstand rang, startling him.

"Hello," he said, placing the receiver to his ear.

"It's Mark," Tolbert said, on the other end, "Turn on your T.V."

"What channel?"

"Any channel. Hurry, man. I'll stay on the line."

Outlaw had no idea at what Tolbert might be hinting, but stepped quickly through the kitchen into his den. His mouth dropped when the TV sound and picture came to life and he saw the headline graphic scrolling across the screen below the newscaster, "SOVIETS ATTACK U.S. AND NATO FORCES IN GERMANY."

The network was obviously playing the feed over and over.

"...at this juncture, we have been able to piece together information that U.S. and NATO forces are being pushed back in heavy fighting, both from the Fulda Gap in the south and across the North German Plain. In addition to U.S. forces, British, Dutch, West German, Danish, and other NATO forces have come under attack. Casualties are thought to be heavy, based on reports filtering in to our affiliated sources in West Germany and Brussels.

Again, Pentagon sources confirm that extensive fighting has erupted in Germany..."

Outlaw dashed back through the kitchen, ignoring the towel as it fell to the floor, and picked up the phone, again.

"You still there, man?" he asked.

"Yeah. Hard to believe," Tolbert said.

"Have they started a squadron recall, yet?" Outlaw asked, "Hell, never mind. I'm on my way in. I just got done packin' for alert, anyway."

"Sit tight, man," Tolbert admonished, "No need to go jumpin' into this all dick, balls, and foreskin. I know you're goin' on alert, but wait for the call, then call the next guy on your list, *then* get your ass to the squadron. If you haven't already, don't even take the time to shave or shower. You can do that in the alert shack. That's the way it works.

"Oh, yeah, and be careful on your way in. From my window, I can see that the on-base dependents have already started to bugout. Traffic might get bad. I gotta go, man. See ya at the squadron."

Outlaw hung up the phone and quickly got dressed in his flight suit. As he tugged on his flying boots, he thought about what Tolbert had said about military dependents fleeing the area and was glad of the fact he was still single. He'd heard a discussion about it once in in the alert shack. Some married crew dogs maintained that they kept "bugout bags" and cash set aside for their families to leave the local area in scenarios identical to this. Plans inevitably centered on them leaving and driving away to stay with relatives until the world situation sorted itself out or hostilities ended.

The call came three minutes later. As McQuagg had recently been reassigned to work in the Vault and a replacement had not been assigned to the crew, the A Flight Commander was initiating the recall for Crew R-13. Under established recall protocol, each copilot was to then call his radar navigator. Outlaw quickly dialed Stumpy's number and woke him from a sound sleep.

When Outlaw relayed the news, Stumpy sputtered fully awake and ended the call with, "Okay, gotta go. I'll call Banjo. See you at the squadron."

After the dial tone came back on, Outlaw quickly thought about calling Bergen to let her know. He realized she'd likely already gotten the word, as well, through her own unit recall. Besides, he hadn't heard from her in over three weeks and decided he was most likely *persona non grata* with her, for reasons he was still unable to determine. He could worry about Bergen Cyr when the war was over. Or not.

On the drive to the base, Outlaw passed the long line of dependents leaving Spurlin and wondered how many local civilians might be in the traffic mix, as well. Arriving and turning right into the front gate, he noticed that the bearded, old fisherman who sold fresh lobsters and seafood from his truck across the street was not there. Whenever he was there with a fresh truckload, he would sometimes pitch a tent and camp beside his truck until he had sold out. Yet, there was no sign of him, now. Outlaw surmised the old man might be somewhere in the bugout traffic, as well, because he likely wouldn't be selling many lobsters in the coming days.

20. "War Council"

The Joint Chiefs of Staff entered the room just ahead of the President Basil Harvey. The President's national security advisor and the directors of the CIA and DIA were already seated at the conference table, as was the Director of the FBI; so were most of the Cabinet members. Their respective assistants and aides sat around the periphery of the room. The President motioned for them all to be seated, as he entered with a sense of urgency evident on his face.

Addressing the Air Force General Hubbard, Chairman of the Joint Chiefs, he asked bluntly, "General, are we sure that this isn't just some cross-border misunderstanding?"

The Chairman removed his glasses and set them down on the table before he spoke, "That's affirmative, Mr. President. SITREPS we've gotten from our forces and NATO all indicate the same thing. This is a major Soviet attack into Germany, from the Fulda Gap all the way to the North German Plain."

"So, it's on," the President said to no one in particular.

A murmur swept through the room as the chairman responded, "I'm afraid so, Mr. President."

"Well, then, I'd prefer we dispense with the euphemistic phrase, 'National Security Council' and call this damned thing what it is. It's a *War* Council; our tribe against theirs."

The Joint Chiefs were each relieved to hear this from the new President. He was a former Air Force fighter pilot who'd seen service in World War II, Korea, and Vietnam and wasn't going to use any soft, euphemistic language to describe the situation. Basil Harvey had flown over 450 combat missions during his Air Force career and had been shot down over Europe in World War II and once over North Vietnam.

Harvey had also served one term in the House of Representatives, subsequent to his retirement from the Air Force. Disillusioned with the constant posturing, grandstanding, and pocket-lining that seemed endemic to Congress, the "Shit Show," as he called it, he decided against standing for re-election, opting instead to return to the Texas ranch on which he'd been raised. Persuaded by wealthy friends of his parents to run as an "independent" in the 1980 presidential election, he didn't seem to stand much of chance at being elected against a sitting president from Georgia or the actor-turned-Democrat-turned-Republican former governor of California. Gaining little traction, initially, Harvey's odds skyrocketed in the wake of the Republican candidate's debilitating stroke, two months before Election Day. Thus, Basil Harvey had progressed from "dark horse" to the Oval Office with a slim margin in the Electoral College, thanks largely to the incumbent's inept handling of the Iran hostage situation and its monumental misfire of a rescue mission.

"So, what're we hearing from NORAD?" the President asked, referring to the joint U.S.-Canadian North American Aerospace Defense Command and its system of Distant Early Warning radar-sites stretching from the Alaskan Aleutians across arctic Canada and all the way to Greenland and Iceland.

General Hubbard answered for the Joint Chiefs, "I just got off the horn with Cheyenne Mountain, Mr. President. They're telling us that none of the DEW sites are seeing anything in the way of Soviet bomber activity that would hit us from the Arctic, coming over the pole. Our PAVE PAWS and COBRA DANE radar systems are fully functional to warn us of any SLBM launches or ICBM launches from the eastern Soviet Union. If their missiles had been launched, we would've been incinerated, by now, anyway. We can't envision a scenario with their bomber force attacking without their ICBMs and SLBMs getting here first, Mr. President.

"NORAD has seen nothing, as of ten minutes ago, to indicate that bomber or missile strikes against the CONUS are imminent. This whole thing doesn't fit with our intelligence forecasts about a major attack by the Warsaw Pact on NATO. We've always strongly considered the possibility, or rather *probability,* of an attack in force against NATO that would coincide with ICBM strikes, with follow-up bomber activity a certainty.

"Other than that, Mr. President, our airborne interceptors have reported some maritime surveillance aircraft off both coasts. Three Bears have been sighted and are being shadowed by F-106s, as we speak, sir."

"Splash 'em," the President replied tersely. "I want any aircraft bearing the red star shot down before they get within 250 miles of *any* U.S. land mass; that includes Hawaii, Alaska, Puerto Rico, and Guam, too. Any Soviet or Soviet-built aircraft is fair game."

General Hubbard again spoke up, "Mr. President, are our interceptor pilots cleared to engage with Genie?"

The President nodded his head once, then asked, "Genie is a nuclear-tipped missile, correct?"

"Yes, Mr. President, a semi-guided rocket, actually, but the Douglas AIR-2A the Genie, is indeed nuclear-tipped and designed to destroy Soviet bomber formations."

The President continued, "I'm assuming there are different protocols relating to employment of these weapons, given the time-sensitive nature of enemy bombers approaching our coasts and the fact that we employ them from single-seat fighter-interceptors."

"That's correct, Mr. President," General Hubbard answered, "By an executive order signed by President Eisenhower in 1956, the 'Authorization for the Expenditure of Atomic Weapons in Air Defense,' protocols were indeed established for employment of nuclear air-defense weaponry against aircraft known to be committing hostile acts against over U.S. territory or those demonstrating manifestly hostile intent. Established protocol dictates that the first interceptor to engage enemy bombers do it with conventional, air to air missiles, with Genie's being loaded into aircraft still on the ground."

The President cut him off, "General, I'm waiving that requirement, right now. I want every F-106, F-101, or any other aircraft capable of and available for air defense duty armed with Genie immediately, to the maximum extent possible. I don't want to wait to lose a U.S. city or military installation while those ground crews wait for the call to arm. I want the interceptor force ready to engage formations of three or more enemy bombers with Genie, if need be, before anything like that happens."

"Yes, sir," General Hubbard said crisply. "We can make that happen."

"General, engage with Genie, if and when the situation calls for it," the President added.

"Anything else related to the air defense issue?"

The bespectacled National Security Advisor spoke next, "Yes, Mr. President."

"What do you have for us, Mr. Director?"

"Mr. President, *none* of NSA's listening posts along the Sino-Soviet border, which we have per some very high-level, sensitive agreements with the People's Republic of China, have picked up any unusual chatter among their strategic bomber bases or from their ICBM fields. This information is also ten minutes old. Both CIA and DIA also confirm no unusual movement. Our next satellite pass in about thirty minutes will tell us more."

"Thank you, Mr. Director. Okay, next question: Berlin," the President said.

The Chief of Staff of the Army answered, "Another puzzle, Mr. President. SITREPs we've gotten from inside the city indicate Warsaw Pact forces haven't entered it. Not at all what we would've suspected, based on the symbolic importance both sides have historically placed on it."

"Thank you, General," the President responded, "One might suspect they'll need it as a bargaining chip, should this devolve into some sort of negotiated settlement. If that situation changes, I need to know ASAP."

All heads in the room nodded in agreement.

The Chairman then asked, "Mr. President, have all contingencies associated with our continuity of government plans been implemented?"

"They have, General. Within the next few minutes, members of Congress and the Cabinet will begin movement to the Mount Weather facility. The vice president and his staff are being moved to the Pennsylvania site, and I'm standing by to move to the Maryland site, along with you gentlemen."

The president paused to take a sip of water from the glass in front of him and then asked, "What're we hearing from SAC out at Offutt?"

The Chairman answered, "They report 'ops normal' on LOOKING GLASS, Mr. President. As you know, they have EC-135 command and control aircraft airborne around the clock, flying twelve-hour sorties."

"Good. Let's hear what you have next," the president responded.

"Mr. President, our embassy in Moscow is currently incommunicado."

"What do you mean, General?"

"We can't contact them. They might be receiving, but they aren't responding. None of our military attaches have responded at all. We had urgent message traffic from them early on that sustained small arms and heavy automatic weapons fire and explosions could be heard in the vicinity of the Kremlin, followed shortly thereafter that mortar rounds were landing inside the embassy compound and armored vehicles were maneuvering to surround it. That last message concluded that the Marine garrison there had already engaged Soviet forces which were firing into the compound and preparing to breech the walls. That's the last we heard, Mr. President."

"So, they appear to have taken our embassy," the president stated.

"So it would seem, sir," the Chairman added.

"What about the hotline? Have we tried contacting Andropov or his staff in the Kremlin?" the president wanted to know.

The fabled "hotline," installed after the Cuban Missile Crisis in 1962, had been installed between Washington and Moscow to enable U.S. and Soviet leadership to expeditiously work through crisis situations. In reality, it wasn't a red telephone, as many believed. It was simply a teletype system.

"We're trying continuously, Mr. President, but the Kremlin hasn't responded; neither has anyone else in Moscow," the chairman said dourly.

"So, assuming our embassy has been overrun and Andropov's people aren't responding by the established channels, do you think it's safe to assume that the existing Soviet leadership has fallen victim to a *coup d'état?*"

"That's where the logic leads us, sir," the Chairman answered.

"Any idea on who's behind this *coup*?" the president asked.

"At the Politburo level, two names come immediately to mind. Several others are suspect. Succession has always been problematic within the Soviet system, dating all the way back to Lenin, and apparently there are those who think Andropov's advanced age and political inclinations aren't in line with the nuances and complexities of the modern world, Mr. President. Due to the attack on our embassy and what's going on in Europe, rogue admirals and generals are also undoubtedly in on this. Currently, our people at CIA, DIA, and the various armed forces' intelligence services are scouring dossiers and running down leads on exactly who these military leaders might be," the general explained.

"How did we not see this coming," the president pondered, addressing no one in particular.

"Mr. President, Brezhnev's death just happened to coincide with large-scale military exercises in Eastern Europe. If this coup had been long planned, this would've been the most opportune time for them to spring it. It could just as well've been a *coup* to overthrow Brezhnev as Andropov. As far as we know, Brezhnev could've been murdered, although we'd known for some time that he'd been drinking a great deal, was increasingly dependent upon sleeping medications, and generally in wretched health.

"We suspect the telecommunications aspect of the planning could've been toned down considerably to avoid arousing our curiosity. A great deal of this was likely done by courier, as opposed to telephone, teletype, or any other sort of electronic communications we have the ability to monitor," the Chairman concluded.

The President replied, "We can save all the 'whys' for later. Has Operation REFORGER been instituted?"

"Yes, sir. It was triggered when the first Soviet boot stepped across the border. As soon as we realized this thing was bigger than we wanted to believe, we sent the *Lariat Advance* notification out to our forces," the Chairman responded.

"*Lariat Advance?*"

"A general muster in Europe, Mr. President, mainly aimed at the defense of the Fulda Gap. When troops receive the call or a radio broadcast with the words, 'Lariat Advance,' they know to report immediately to their designated transport muster points for a ride to war," the General explained.

Mr. President, we've received a partial message from one of our SIGINT posts near Ostweg, West Germany, that indicated they were under chemical attack."

President Harvey leaned forward in his chair, "You did say that was a *partial* message. Is that correct, General?"

The Chairman nodded and replied, "Yes, Mr. President. Our crypto-centers in Frankfurt and Augsburg both received the same message, in the clear. In addition to the electronic signature indicating that it was the post at Mount Mesmer, all we got was '*Under che…this time. This is not a drill.*' It's not conclusive, sir, but we all agree that the intent of the message was urgent and to inform us that they were under chemical attack. Various headquarters units attempted contact with them via land line and radio, but they're not answering."

The President said simply, *"This is not a drill…*just like the telegram sent stateside from Pearl Harbor. I see. Does any other evidence corroborate this?"

"In all likelihood, Mr. President, that unit probably *was* attacked with chemical weapons. Mobile SCUD-C batteries were moved within a fifty-mile radius of that detachment several weeks ago, as part of this so-called military exercise they're conducting. Why the SCUD-Cs, we didn't know, at the time, but, now we do.

"Because the Mount Mesmer Detachment is, or *was* a SIGINT operation, with both a U.S. and West German presence, the Soviets would've wanted it neutralized at the outset of hostilities. If any of those troops are still alive, they're now *behind* enemy lines, Mr. President, and forced to operate in an impossibly toxic environment."

The Chairman continued, "The bottom line here, Mr. President, is that NATO tactical doctrine dictates that we respond to Warsaw Pact chemical attacks with in-theater tactical nuclear weapons."

The president interrupted, "And why is that, specifically, General?"

"Mr. President, over the last decade, we've essentially stopped our production of chemical weapons. The Soviets haven't. They're not prone to any humanitarian crises of conscience and tend not to wring their hands about

126

much. Currently, they possess enough of a chemical stockpile to completely eliminate every NATO troop in Western Europe several times over. Chemicals play a major role in both their strategic and tactical doctrine.

"As our chemical stocks age and remain stagnant, in terms of size, the Soviets' stockpiles continue to grow. They have something on the order of 45,000 troops in the Warsaw Pact countries specifically dedicated to the employment of chemical weapons. Thus, we can't match them on a warhead-for-warhead basis. So, our most realistic retaliatory option is to respond with our tactical nuclear weapons."

The president again sat back in his chair and said, "Makes sense."

"Mr. President, do you wish to give release authority for the use of tactical nukes in-theater, at least, the Victor Alert sorties we have left in the U.K.? As you recall, we stood down our Victor Alert force on the continent, in the wake of Secretary General Brezhnev's death and converted them to Zulu Air Defense alert," the Chairman explained.

"No. Not yet. I stood them down to telegraph to the incoming Soviet regime that we didn't, in any way, wish to take advantage of or inflame tensions after Brezhnev died. In hindsight, perhaps not the best decision I've ever made, but we at least have the F-111 Victor birds still on alert in the U.K. I've never been an ardent fan of one-way suicide missions, which is basically what the Victor packages are. As you gentlemen know, I sat that duty in the F-105 in Germany during the early 'sixties. I think throwing away aircraft and pilots like that is a waste of human and material resources," the president replied without hesitation, "We won't react with the Victor force until we have definitive confirmation that large-scale chemical attacks against NATO forces have occurred. I don't wanna run the risk of this devolving into theater-level commanders thinkin' they can start slingin' nukes at their own discretion. It'll turn into a shit fight, like chimps at the zoo; a nuclear shit fight. If we absolutely must employ theater or strategic nuclear weapons, I want the Soviets to understand, in no uncertain terms, that a message is bein' sent directly by the highest levels of this government.

"So, let's raise our stateside strategic forces posture to DEFCON-2, for the time bein'. Everyone here has a great deal on his plate, right now. We'll adjourn and meet back here in four hours, or sooner, if circumstances dictate. You're all dismissed, but don't hesitate to let me know pertinent developments, as they occur."

21. "Alphas, Charlies, and Foxtrots"

Spurlin Air Force Base

423rd Bombardment-Wing Alert-Facility Theater

December 2, 1982

The crews for the Alpha alert bomber sorties and the generating Charlie and Foxtrot sorties were assembled and in their theater seats by crew in the alert force briefing room; a total of fifteen bomber crews, in all. The bomber crews sat on the right side of the aisle in crew order; the tanker crews on the left. Two staff sergeants from the 423rd Weather Detachment briefed their projected departure weather for the next twenty-four hours. A master sergeant from command post briefed them from an overhead projector slide as to what the day's radio call-signs were to be. Following those two portions of the briefing, a no-nonsense, very businesslike, female lieutenant from the wing intelligence shop gave them a very quick overview of what was unfolding in Germany. She was followed by the Deputy Commander for Operations, Colonel Mike Lopez.

"Ladies and gentlemen," Lopez began, "the day has arrived that we never wanted to see. We may have to fly our SIOP bomber sorties. We may not. Let's *hope* not. Too early to tell, but I can guarantee you that some of you tanker crews are gonna earn your money.

"What the lieutenant just told you is about all we can piece together on the intelligence front, right now. As you might guess, we can't focus too much on what's goin' on in Europe. We gotta get ready to play our part *here*. As we learn more, we'll get it to you through the process of gettin' all of our generated force sorties, bombers and tankers, ready. In the meantime, do your jobs the way you've been trained to do 'em. God willin', we'll win this fight.

"Operation REFORGER is fully in motion. Notice I didn't say *'Exercise* REFORGER. 'It's the real deal, now. Everything and everybody will be balls to the wall to get people, equipment, and supplies to Europe.

"You're gonna see some strange things goin' on around here: Civil Reserve Airlift Fleet birds, the CRAF, all sorts of old Century Series stuff from the Reserves and Air National Guard, airline pilots comin' and goin' here in the alert shack; a whole bunch of stuff you've never seen here, before. Don't be surprised by any of it. It's a big job and we gotta take care of it, both with our own people and aircraft, as well as everybody involved in REFORGER.

"Alright, the tanker crews are dismissed. We'll follow in zero-two minutes with the bomber strike-routing intelligence and weather. After that, we'll get the Charlie and Foxtrot crews to target study and then out to their birds to get 'em generated. Smoke 'em if you got 'em.

"Colonel Lopez concluded his briefing to the Alpha, Charlie, and Foxtrot crews, whose aircraft were already being towed to their parking stubs, where the process of generating them to full alert status would be completed.

"Captain McQuagg, I need for you and your guys to sit tight when I let the rest of these guys go," he told them.

Although Outlaw's crew was scheduled to begin its normal rotation onto the Alpha Alert force, that Thursday, he had also been a part of three total force generations; twice as a Charlie and once as a Foxtrot. McQuagg had been called from Vault duty and reassigned to Crew R-13 for this force generation, due to a lack of qualified, healthy aircraft commanders within the squadron.

When the other crews had left the briefing room, Colonel Lopez addressed McQuagg and the crew, "When you get to target study, you guys'll need to study your Alpha routing, which you should already be thoroughly familiar with.

"You all know that that Alpha Sortie #3 is also the 'Pale Horse' CONALT Option sortie for this wing; the Contingency Alternative Option. The war plans people have that mission package ready for you, as well. Be sure to have a good look at it. My guess is that it may well be the sortie that gets launched from here first, assumin' this thing in Europe doesn't go ape-shit nuclear, before then. If we get the word from on high, we'll download your gravity weapons and adjust your fuel load accordingly. Our CONALT package is strictly a high-altitude PALM-launch sortie. If you gotta fly it, should be a piece of cake. On the last ORI, you guys showed the wing and SAC leadership what you can do. I have complete confidence in you guys. Any questions, gentlemen?"

McQuagg and the crew answered simultaneously, "No, sir!"

The Colonel smiled grimly and concluded, "Outstanding. Go do what we pay you the big money to do."

Spurlin Air Force Base, Maine
B-52 Alpha Alert Force Parking Stub #3
December 2, 1982

The driver kept the bus door closed against the cold and kept the engine running as McQuagg leafed through the AFTO 781 maintenance forms and noticed the glaring lack of jocularity in the crews he was ferrying, today. No jokes, bullshit, nor much banter at all. Even the lieutenant they called "Outlaw" appeared somber and he was usually the friendliest of this crew. They were likely to be flying combat missions to God-knows-where and some of them wouldn't be coming back, he supposed.

As McQuagg leafed through the forms, he apprised the crew of any maintenance write-ups from previous crews and whatever fixes had been made. The Air Force Technical Order 781 series was the most important paperwork associated with any individual aircraft in the Air Force inventory. It chronicled each aircraft's maintenance history and stayed with the aircraft all the time.

When McQuagg was done briefing the crew on all pertinent maintenance write-ups and discrepancies, they all stood to exit the crew bus, as the driver opened the door for them.

Outlaw motioned for McQuagg to stay seated and whispered to him across the seat in front of him, "Hold on a sec, Boss. Somethin' you need to know about this bird."

The driver closed the door, again, so as not to let the heat escape.

Once the other four had exited the bus and begun its "bag drag" to the aircraft, Outlaw told him, "Before you got here, this jet was a hangar queen."

"Great," McQuagg responded, "just the kind of airplane I wanna take to war."

"You don't know the half of it, Spaulding," Outlaw continued, "Things got so bad with this bird that it became the *can*-bird."

When an aircraft was in "can" status," it was the aircraft the maintenance troops went to for spare parts when other aircraft needed them posthaste. In short, it was "cannibalized."

McQuagg asked, "What sort of problems?"

"You name it," Outlaw answered, "Engine problems, all sorts of generator and electrical problems, and ASQ-38 problems *all* the damned time. Crews had to do a lot of copilot visual bombin', on account of that. ECM and fire control seemed to work fine, but that's about it.

"I'm tellin' ya, man, ol' two-five-seven there ain't nothin' but trouble. I'm hopin' against hope that they got it all sorted out enough for it to be a reliable alert bird, but I wouldn't bet the kids' college money on it," Outlaw added.

"Is that all the good news you got for me, Dillon?"

"Uh, no. This jet has been notorious for problems with the rudder-and-elevator hydraulic systems. Twice, when Ivanoff and I flew it, the two right side systems failed, both the Primary #1 Pump and the Aux Pump, and we had to air-abort sorties. A couple of other crews did, too. I know the Dash-1 says that the possibility of all four rudder-and-elevator systems failin' is next to impossible, but *nothin'* that happens with this bird surprises me."

"Okay, bearer of bad tidings," McQuagg said, "let's hope that if we have to aviate in this bucket of bolts, she'll hold together."

"Yeah, let's hope," Outlaw answered, in an attempt to calm the still-troubled waters running between McQuagg and the remainder of the crew, "We've done it before, Spaulding. We can do it, again."

22. "The Wizard Unmasked"

The Old Daigle House
Vicinity, Easton, Maine
December 3, 1982

As Oz cautiously approached the house through the darkness, he noticed no fresh tire tracks. He'd parked his vehicle on a secluded side road approximately one mile north of the house and approached on foot, remaining completely unaware of the southern access road that led to the cove where the midget submarine was moored and the crime scene that it now was. He intended to make a quick sweep through he the house to make sure he'd left nothing behind that could identify him to American intelligence, and that included fingerprints, although he was certain he wiped everything down in that regard, prior to the arrival of the Spetsnaz team.

His orders, as originally briefed, were to board the midget submarine with the remaining Spetsnaz force and return to the submarine awaiting them in deeper waters. He'd done a thorough mental calculation of the odds that the "Spets" force would be successful and survive its mission and determined that those odds were far from favorable. This wasn't some Third World hellhole like Afghanistan with its corrupt, inept, and spotty law enforcement and security forces. This was America, with a dedicated intelligence infrastructure and competent law enforcement.

Consequently, he determined that the Spetsnaz troops were expendable in the service of the Motherland. None of them were likely to survive unscathed or uncaptured and, if captured, were unlikely to last through what would doubtless be brutal interrogations at the hands of American intelligence operatives. He alone would board the midget submarine and, along with its pilot, would return to the mother submarine for the voyage home.

As he moved closer to the house, he noticed nothing unusual, save for the footprints left by him and the team. Glancing at his watch, he calculated that he had about ninety minutes left before sunrise; more than enough time for him to make it to the cove. The house was set far enough back from the highway that things here were likely to remain unnoticed by passing traffic and, to hear the man who had rented him the house tell it, no one paid much attention to the Daigle house these days, anyway.

Oz had a moment of doubt concerning the wisdom of having the water service restored to the house when he rented it, due to the paper trail it would leave behind. He put aside his concerns, reasoning that the risk of the house and garage lights being seen from the highway were minimal, he had only occupied the property for a week, and the Spetsnaz team had only occupied it for one night. It wasn't going to matter for long, if at all. Within hours, he would be aboard the midget submarine and headed out into deep water. The captain lieutenant and his team would likely be dead or in custody sooner than that.

As So-Called Dave waited inside the house, he fought the gnawing urge to light a cigarette. Perhaps the "nicotine fit" he was experiencing was just the nervous tension involved in his impending confrontation with the capable and crafty Oz, who he knew was going to be a tough customer.

Dave didn't even know the bastard's real name. Nobody in the Western intelligence services did. They knew him by the half-dozen or so aliases he used, and six was a conservative estimate. It could very well be that Oz himself didn't even know his real name anymore, given the myriad masks he was undoubtedly forced to show the world.

This Oz obviously needed to dispose of a great deal of evidence in the garage, from what Dave had seen, and certainly would need to remove fingerprint evidence, which he knew would match his known prints kept on file with both the CIA and FBI. Dave knew those files existed and had seen them himself, although no known birth name was attached to them. So-Called Dave was playing the odds that Oz would return to the house, even though it wasn't a site of his direct, bloody mischief. He'd seen him do it several times in far-off, Third World places like Kabul, Islamabad, and Beirut. Should his ego dictate, he would most likely do it here, as well, though he hadn't actually killed anyone in or near this house.

In the pre-dawn silence, he realized his hunch was paying off as he heard deliberate, almost imperceptible footsteps crunch through the snow outside. As still as things were, it would've been hard to miss them.

Who else would be here, this time of the morning? The local sheriff had concluded his business at the "crime scene" where he had found the midget submarine and killed the Soviet sailor. Naval Intelligence was now on scene, but this house remained largely out of sight and out of mind, per his specific request to the sheriff.

Jasper Hood, the astute sheriff and seasoned Air Force ground combat veteran, knew better than to question the clipped wording of an intelligence operative's "request." Hood had dealt with them, on occasion, in Vietnam and knew them to be an unsettlingly spooky and lethal breed of cat, even though they never seemed to let on exactly which federal agency cut their paychecks. But, Hood had seen enough to know that when their unsavory brand of shit went down, there was no telling who could get hurt.

Patience was his best asset in these situations and Dave waited remained absolutely still and silent as he heard the slow, creaking turn of the front doorknob. He knew Oz would be hyper-vigilant to any threat lurking in the house. Dave knew how to play that game, as well, taking only the slightest of breaths to avoid even the faintest rustling of his clothes.

So-Called Dave was peripherally aware of the moonlight streaming to his right from the door Oz opened. Separating them was a hearth and fireplace, which protruded from the front wall some twelve inches, concealing Dave's presence from line of sight, keeping him hidden in darkness and shadow. Peering around the edge of the fireplace, Dave saw the pistol moving slowly from side to side in a moonbeam, as Oz eased into the house. Sensing no immediate threat, Oz continued forward through the front parlor and angled right toward the hallway.

His own pistol drawn, So-Called Dave took aim at his lower back as Oz made for the hallway to the kitchen. A light squeeze of the trigger sent a silenced nine-millimeter round directly into his adversary's lower spine, which caused him to collapse immediately with paralysis, but the light round ricocheted off a disk and otherwise harmlessly exited his left side without any organ damage.

Oz crumpled to the floor, yet the pain was only a flash, lasting only fractions of a second. After that, he could feel nothing below his waist. For all of the human misery he'd caused and seen without the slightest twinge of fright or remorse, he now found himself terrified at the idea of life without legs, however long that may be. That was his last thought before So-Called Dave's pistol smashed into his left temple and the darkness engulfed him.

"Gotcha, motherfucker," Dave said, as he stood over him in the darkness.

23. "The Raw Exercise of Power"

National Security Council
Secure Site Alpha
December 3, 1982

"Ladies and gentlemen, please let me have your attention," the White House Chief of Staff announced, "The president is currently on a call with the Chinese Premier and will be with you, shortly. He said to tell you that this is 'a big fish he has to fry, right now.' His words, ladies and gentlemen, not mine."

A murmur swept through the room and weary smiles could be seen on faces where they had been noticeably lacking for the last few days. Everyone currently assembled in the off-site Situation Room had been in and out of this room and the Executive Office, as the president's office at this site was called, repeatedly for the past fifty hours. The Joint Chiefs of Staff, National Security Advisor, the Directors of the CIA and DIA, Secretary of State, Attorney General, Director of the Nuclear Regulatory Agency, and various briefers from the defense and intelligence communities, as well as the Director of the FBI. Everyone had been scrambling with his or her end of this latest war in Europe; the third in the twentieth century.

"Ladies and gentlemen, the President of the United States," the president's military aide, a Marine lieutenant-colonel, announced ten minutes later, as President Harvey entered.

The Joint Chiefs and the other military personnel in the room stood to rigid attention, while the civilians on the "War Council" merely stood. President Harvey gestured for them to be seated as he made his way to his chair at the head of the conference table.

"Ladies and gentlemen, I apologize for the delay. I was on the phone with Premier Deng, who has assured me that he and the good folks runnin' the People's Republic of China don't have and don't want any part of this current mischief their communist cousins have instigated.

135

"While their military has increased its overall force posture, they aren't mobilizing, nor have they detected any potentially hostile moves by the Soviets against them, as we and they have long feared. He also stated emphatically that the Chinese government, like us, has heard nothing from the Soviet government, whoever that might currently be.

"Premier Deng also gave me assurances that North Korea will be held in check, forcibly, if need be, and won't exploit the current situation by any hostile moves toward South Korea."

"So," he said, pounding a fist very lightly on the table, "that's our first real bit of good news."

Addressing the National Director of Intelligence, he asked, "Do the Premier's assurances match what your people at NSA and elsewhere are seeing and hearing?"

"Yes, Mr. President," the Director replied, "We've seen some shuffling of troops, vehicles, and aircraft on the last few satellite passes, but nothing that would telegraph hostilities toward us. They also confirm no hostile moves by the Soviets toward the PRC along their common border, like we saw in '69."

The Director continued, "Sir, our most recent satellite imagery confirms that the Soviets have indeed overrun our embassy. In addition to numerous Soviet troops seen moving in and around the compound, we have images of Russian gun and missile emplacements on the roof of the main building and elsewhere in the compound. HUMINT sources also confirm the presence of Soviet Army and KGB troops inside the compound.

"As to the major players involved in this *coup,* if that's indeed what it is, still no concrete information regarding names. Apparently, KGB and military troops loyal to the *coup* plotters haven't completely secured the Kremlin, yet, although they have apparently been able to shut down the electrical power from primary and emergency sources and effectively cut it off from the rest of the world."

The president observed, "All parts of the puzzle that don't seem to fit anywhere.

"I've had several telephone conversations and a sit-down with the Soviet Ambassador; the latest, a little over an hour ago. Ambassador Poydashev seems to be deaf, dumb, and blind concerning the status of his government, from which he has received no communication at all. He has even requested political asylum, which I'm inclined to grant."

He asked the Secretary of State, Marvin Parham, "Mr. Secretary, has Foggy Bottom heard or seen anything in the Soviet diplomatic channels?"

Parham replied, "No, Mr. President. Nothing. Very puzzling."

Just prior to the president's arrival, an Air Force lieutenant colonel had hurried into the room and handed a document to the Chairman of the Joint Chiefs, himself an Air Force general.

"Mr. President," said the Chairman, "before we continue, I was just handed a piece of actionable intelligence, right before you came in. It's something we've been watching since its earliest stages."

"What is it, General?" the president asked.

"Sir, just prior to the start of hostilities, two very astute B-52 crewmembers from the 423rd Bombardment Wing at Spurlin Air Force Base spotted a suspicious-looking individual at a bar in nearby Mars Hill, Maine. They reported it to Air Force OSI and OSI handed it off to CIA. The Agency confirms this individual's identity as a known Soviet intelligence operative and a *significant* source of trouble.

"He was thought to be one of the major players involved in the overthrow of the Afghan government and the murder of President Amin in '79. Our HUMINT assets took numerous photos of him there before the Soviets flew their Spetsnaz teams into Kabul. He's been apprehended in Maine and is being interrogated, but he's not talking."

"So, you *got* the bastard? Do you realistically expect him to talk?" the president asked.

The General shook his head a said, "No, Mr. President. One of our CIA operatives shot him in the spine and paralyzed him from the waist down, but he's now conscious and in stable condition at a safe CIA location where he can receive medical attention. He's still going to be a tough nut to crack, if he cracks at all. He's KGB or Spetsnaz, possibly GRU."

"Understood. Go on, General."

"Additionally, Mr. President, the sheriff in Wallace County, Maine encountered two Air Force vehicles near a diner along Maine State Highway 1, yesterday morning. Both vehicles were Dodge extended-cab pickups, identical to the type SAC purchased as their alert response and general-purpose vehicles. The two trucks the sheriff saw were painted the standard blue, with the correct stenciling on the doors and elsewhere, but both had Maine plates, instead of the federal plates all military vehicles carry."

The president raised his eyebrows in a mix of interest and alarm.

The General continued, "The sheriff's a retired Air Force Security Police troop, from Spurlin, incidentally, and thought that very suspicious. He returned to investigate when the vehicles left. He'd spoke to the men outside the diner as he was going in for coffee and thought it odd that only one of the "airmen," a senior master sergeant, actually, and they were all dressed in Air Force fatigues, did all of the talking.

"Long story short, Mr. President: the sheriff did some backtracking after the vehicles left him and headed north. Less than five miles down the road, he found tire tracks on an unpaved access road leading back into a wooded area near the coast. He found what appeared to be a safe house, a house he recognized, and then followed footprints in the snow for approximately a mile. He knows the coastline of his county quite well and found a midget submarine tethered in a small cove. He shot and killed the Soviet sailor guarding it, and then phoned it in to the Augusta FBI Office. Things were set in motion from there."

"Midget sub?" the president asked quizzically.

Addressing the Chief of Naval Operations, Admiral Jason Willard, President Harvey asked, "Admiral, do you or anyone on your staff have an explanation as to how a Soviet boat got close enough to the U.S. coast to drop off a midget submarine, which is currently moored along the coast of Maine?"

The admiral cleared his throat and said with a hint of hesitation in his voice, "The realities of the peacetime Navy, Mr. President."

The president cut him off abruptly, "I'm not interested in any bullshit excuses, Admiral. We are at *war,* here, not peace."

The CNO's eyes flashed angrily, as he leaned forward and clasped his hands on the table in front of him, "I wasn't offering excuses, Mr. President. They're not in my playbook, sir, and you know that. The reality of this situation is that India boat left port more than two weeks before hostilities began. The Soviets built their India-class subs in numbers so small we can readily account for them, as we need to. They were purpose-built to deliver special operations troops to foreign shores and the likelihood of them delivering them to our shores seemed like the remotest of peacetime scenarios."

The president shrugged and nodded, indicating regret at having castigated the admiral in front of the others and motioning for him to continue.

"The India's are newer, diesel-electric boats and fairly easy to track when they're operating on diesel power. When they're running on their batteries, they're very quiet and tracking them presents a much more complex problem; so much so that they're very difficult to track without our boats knowing they're nearby. The boat in question was noted leaving its moorings near Murmansk and, at the time, was believed to be on a routine training-mission.

"That India very likely ran our GIUK gap on battery power to be as stealthy as possible when passing over our underwater SONUS arrays.

"It's their main route out of the Murmansk-Monchegorsk area into the North Atlantic. We have a network of underwater sonar arrays to track them.

Every second day, the India-class boats have to snorkel to recharge their batteries. When they are on the surface like that, we can generally locate them via satellite and alert our attack-boats, if there are any nearby.

"When hostilities began, as you might expect, our attention turned to their boomers: their Victor, Charlie, and Akula-class missile boats. That lone India became a much lower priority for us. The three classes of boats I just mentioned, Mr. President, are very much the varsity team; the best the Soviets have, along with the best crews. The Indias...well, sir, we consider them strictly the second and third string, with crews to match. Apparently, the Soviets see it that way, too."

The Admiral paused to pour himself a glass of water from the carafe in front of him and took a quick sip. The president nodded for him to continue.

"However, Mr. President I'd the guess that the skipper of that India didn't come from the second string. It's likely he was handpicked and specifically placed in command of that boat by elements of the Soviet naval forces complicit in this *coup*. They would've wanted somebody reliable and loyal to their cause."

The president took a sip of coffee from the cup that had been placed in front of him and opined, "So, what you're sayin' is, we got played, Admiral?"

"Precisely, Mr. President. This operation was carefully planned to take advantage of what appeared to be a routine peacetime situation, which they surmised could be further exploited by our own prioritizations, once the shooting started," the admiral added.

President Harvey nodded his understanding and added, "We got sucker-punched all the way across the board.

"But, we're better than they are. I know it, Admiral, and so do you and so does everyone in this room. So, what else do you have for us?"

"Sir, what Naval Intelligence was quickly able to piece together for us is that this so-called midget sub appears to be a lengthened hybrid of the Soviets' 'Project 908;' the *Triton-2,* which is thought to normally have a crew of six. To date, we believe somewhere in the neighborhood of fifteen to twenty have been built, with twelve or so currently in service."

"You said 'hybrid,'" the president interjected, "How is this thing different?"

"Mr. President, the original version of the *Triton-2* was nine-point-five meters long and could accommodate at least six crew, as I said, which included an unknown number of combat-divers; Naval Spetsnaz, if you will. The sub we found on the Maine coast is at least three meters longer and our initial estimates are that it can hold up to ten divers or special operations troops. We're not sure what they can accommodate, as far as troops *and* weaponry. Whatever they're up to, they may have weapons prepositioned in the CONUS. They would be packed pretty tightly in there, but that squares with the ten so-called 'airmen' the Maine sheriff encountered."

"I'm waiting for the good news, here, gentlemen," the president said.

"There is none, Mr. President," said the Chairman of the Joint Chiefs.

"What are you telling, me, General?"

"Sir, the FBI called in Naval Intelligence and they confirm the midget sub to be of Soviet manufacture and nearly identical to the ones photographed in the Swedish incursions, last year, before your inauguration.

"You may not be familiar with the Swedish episode, Mr. President, but the divers, whose nationality could not be absolutely pinpointed, were spotted along their coast, even a few on the beaches. Neither NATO nor the Swedes were conducting any naval exercises in that area, so speculation was that Naval Spetsnaz teams were conducting penetration exercises into foreign countries. Their intent may well have been just to flex their muscles or to see exactly what they could get away with. We did manage to get a few satellite photos of the midget subs they used. That was our first visual confirmation of the existence of the *Triton-2* boats.

"The operative we bagged was likely sent into Maine as the point-man for a sapper team. As you know, sir, Spurlin is our main staging base for Operation REFORGER. We have every reason to suspect a Spetsnaz team has been inserted to neutralize Spurlin, and I say 'neutralize' in the strongest, most definitive sense."

"By 'neutralize,' you mean 'destroy?'"

"Precisely, Mr. President, and the means of destruction would most likely be a man-portable nuclear weapon. It's the only way a force of ten men could neutralize a base of that size. But, the whole base doesn't need to be destroyed. Just disrupting its flight line and POL facilities and destroying REFORGER aircraft is all they need to do. Any B-52 and KC-135 alert aircraft they happen to destroy with the blast would be a win for them, of course. Any secondary nuclear detonations they could get from that would be a huge bonus to them and a monumental disaster for us. That it hasn't happened yet tells us they may be waiting for Spurlin to become even more saturated with REFORGER aircraft and personnel before they light the fuse, so to speak. We have other options for REFORGER on the east coast, but Spurlin is the closest to Europe, geographically."

"Backpack nuke, huh?" the president asked.

"So, my understanding here is that all analysis, including the midget submarine, and the presence of that India so close to the Maine coastline, make a compelling case for just that scenario," the president stated.

"Yes, sir. We're all in agreement. The Soviets wouldn't insert a Spetsnaz team just to make a traffic count of aircraft in and out of Spurlin; not at this stage of hostilities.

"In any event, our operative who was tracking this guy caught him in a moment of carelessness when he returned to the safe house near the midget sub's berth for reasons unknown. We may get something out of him; we may not."

The president nodded his agreement and said, "Go ahead and make the sonofabitch talk, if you can. I don't care how. That he is a member of a hostile intelligence service or a hostile military force, with which this country is currently at war, we can call him a 'spy.' He won't be goin' home, not even in a box. He's a burglar in our house, as far as I'm concerned.

"*Sin loi,* Mike-Foxtrot," the president then added, lapsing into his Vietnam-era military slang.

"*Sin loi*" meant "I'm sorry" in a "tough shit" sense, in Vietnamese. "Mike Foxtrot" was phonetic U.S. military slang for "motherfucker." Tough shit, motherfucker.

Everyone present in the room nodded or acknowledged their understanding in some way. This president had the stomach to wage war and didn't flinch at the uglier aspects of it. They knew he'd seen too much throughout his Air Force combat experiences to feel otherwise.

President Harvey added, "I want as many assets devoted to baggin' these guys as we can spare: NEST, FBI, military, whatever. Everybody's a player."

Inclining his head in the direction of the Chief of Staff of the Army, he said, "What can you spare us, General? I know the Army has a full plate, right now."

"I can give you a Delta team and a Ranger company, Mr. President," the General replied.

"How fast can you get 'em saddled up and in the air, General?"

"Within the hour, Mr. President. They're already chomping at the bit to get into the war and they're gear's packed and ready. They can plot their landing zones on the way up in the C-141. It's best, in my opinion, to let 'em jump, rather than land 'em and truck 'em out. If that Spetsnaz team has the airfield under surveillance, they'll spot it, right away. That Ranger unit is fresh off an Arctic training exercise in Norway, so a little snow on the ground isn't going to slow them down."

"Good. Make it happen. I want those bastards dead, every one of 'em," answered the president. "If they've come here to wreak that kind of damage, I don't want 'em to have any sort of sense they might've accomplished anything.

"Anything else goin' on up in Maine I need to know about?" the president asked to no one in particular.

"Admiral," President Harvey then said to the CNO, "I want that India sunk."

"We have surface assets headed that way, Mr. President. Air assets are on-station and our P-3 aircraft are running their sonar nets, as we speak. USS *Sturgeon* is now at sea and close to being on-station, as well."

"Sink it, Admiral. I don't care if you have to do it yourself with a rowboat and a bag of hand grenades, and I apologize for my earlier sarcasm. Things're pilin' up on me."

"SUBLANTCOM is aware of it, Mr. President. The Navy and Coast Guard'll take care of it, and apology accepted, Mr. President. None of us are getting anything, lately, but what I call 'junk-sleep.' We're all on-edge and jumpy. It comes with the job."

Both Army Chief of Staff and the Chief of Naval Operations nodded to their aides, who both left the room to put the president's orders into motion.

Harvey looked around the room to see if anyone was present from the Nuclear Regulatory Agency. The Agency Chairman was there, at the far end of the conference table.

"Mr. Chairman, are NEST assets on scene in Maine, yet?" the president asked.

"Yes, Mr. President. We have four of the new OV-10Ns flying grids over the suspected areas, right now. Helicopters should be on-station in about two hours and all required ground personnel are enroute to Spurlin."

"New OV-10s?"

"Yes, Mr. President. We procured them from the boneyard at Davis-Monthan and reconditioned them. They're faster and can survey larger swaths of land more quickly than our helicopters. Their cargo compartments can hold the required radiation-sensing equipment. Plus, we can arm them with machine guns and rockets, if we suspect we'll have to engage enemy or terrorist targets on the ground. Our assets currently in the air *are* armed, Mr. President."

The president seemed genuinely surprised.

"OV-10s, huh? I learn somethin' new on this job, every single day," he said.

"Ladies and gentlemen, we have addressed the immediate threat within our shores and borders. Let's get to the brass tacks of what's goin' on in Europe," the president said after decanters of coffee, cups, and condiments had been placed around the conference table, "What do the intel people have for us?"

The National Security Advisor nodded to his aide, who went to the easel for his prepared presentation.

"Good morning, Mr. President, ladies and gentlemen," the aide began, "the U.S. Armed Forces, as well as those of the United Kingdom, West Germany, the Netherlands, Belgium, Denmark, and Luxembourg are currently still engaged in extensive combat operations against Soviet and East German forces. The Norwegian Air Force is presently flying constant Combat Air Patrols to protect against Soviet air threats from the north, but have encountered nothing, so far. The Italians, Greeks, and Turks stand at full readiness, but, as of yet, have had no moves made against them.

"Notice, Mr. President, ladies and gentlemen, I didn't say 'Warsaw Pact' forces, because that appears not to be the case. The Poles appear to be standing fast, as are the Czechs and the Hungarians. Romanian forces were involved in the initial onslaught, but turned back almost as soon as they met resistance; in some cases, even *before* they met resistance. We've heard nothing from or about the Bulgarians, but they're effectively in the Warsaw Pact rear area.

"Chatter the NSA is hearing is that those governments were as surprised as we were by the Soviet attack and appear to be willing and eager to stay on the sidelines. HUMINT and SIGINT sources, as well as satellite imagery, both tend to substantiate this. Our embassies in Eastern Europe are hearing the same thing through their diplomatic channels; that, according to the latest information from the State Department."

The president again made eye contact with the Secretary of State Willard, who merely nodded.

The briefer continued, "As previously discussed, things appear to be stable in regard to China and the Soviet Far East."

"What about the situation in Afghanistan?" the president asked.

"Everything we are seeing and hearing, Mr. President, all HUMINT, SIGINT, aerial, and satellite imagery indicate that the Soviets are staying within their garrisons. Not much activity, other than routine patrolling around their firebase perimeters. We're seeing little to no tactical air, fighter or helicopter, nor tactical airlift. As to the *why* of it all, we simply can't pin it down."

"As to the Middle East," the president interjected, "I spoke with the Israeli Prime Minister, late last night, and he said that Israel was, in fact, mobilizing and putting its armed forces on a wartime footing. They have no intention of ever being surprised, again, like they were during Yom Kippur, back in '73.

Any evidence of full-scale mobilization from the Syrians, Egyptians, or anyone else in the region hostile to Israel?"

"No, Mr. President," the Secretary of State answered. "The State Department received word from the Syrian government that it has no hostile designs on the 'Zionist aggressors,' at present.

"Egypt has stated its intention to fully abide by the terms and conditions of the Camp David Accords and its armed forces are staying put. The Jordanian government has made no statement at all, but King Hussein will likely never make another move against Israel, based on the pounding his forces took during the Six Day War."

"Hmm. Camp David. The high-point of my predecessor's administration. Anything goin' on down in Cuba," the president wanted to know.

"Other than Castro's obligatory statement of solidarity with his Marxist brethren, nothing unusual, Mr. President," the briefer answered.

"What about the Soviet government itself? Still no idea of who the hell is in charge of this *coup*?" the president then asked.

"Mr. President, our sources within the Warsaw Pact intelligence agencies are as stumped as we are, but, from what we're beginning to piece together, this whole thing has all the hallmarks of rogue elements within the Soviet military high command, the upper echelons of the KGB, and the Politburo, who were disgruntled with shifts in the power structure following Brezhnev's death. Even the State Department's contact with Warsaw Pact embassies and consulates are saying they don't have anything definitive about what's going on."

"So, the Soviet government, in its totality, might not stand behind this madness?" the president asked.

"Our best appraisal, Mr. President, is *no*. This is very likely a move by certain senior generals and admirals seeking to consolidate a greater share of power within their overall governmental structure, post-Brezhnev; a potentially catastrophic risk, to say the least."

"Well, that certainly clouds the issue. As long as the Kremlin remains incommunicado, we're basically flyin' blind. If there has been a *coup,* and all appearances indicate that there has been, the parties involved are taking an enormous risk," the Secretary concluded.

The National Security Advisor responded, "Those are the assumptions, Mr. President, and they, no doubt, are broad, sweeping ones. Without knowing exactly what's going on inside the Kremlin, our analysis is limited essentially to educated guesses based on past experience. Their takeover of our embassy in Moscow sends a very dark message, however. Across the spectrum of mischief the Soviets have caused throughout their history, they've never strayed that far outside accepted, diplomatic protocol, the way the Iranians did in '79."

"Is there anything else that would give us reason to believe that the Soviet government, in its entirety, is not behind this invasion?"

"Yes, Mr. President, there is," answered the Chairman of the Joint Chiefs, "U-2, SR-71, and satellite imagery suggests little movement in the Soviet rear areas."

"I'm all ears, General," said the president.

"Sir, it appears that their railroad yards aren't very active, at least not to the degree we'd expect with a full-scale invasion of Western Europe under way. We simply haven't seen a great deal of vehicle traffic, either troop transport or logistical, from their known garrisons and supply depots to their side of the lines. Not much heavy airlift, either. The only airlift activity we're seeing is tactical, in immediate support of their side of the FEBA."

The president sat noticeably more upright in his chair. The room went quiet and still.

"From what we're seeing, Mr. President, it appears this is not an all-inclusive effort by the Soviet military, nor the Soviet government. Somebody, somewhere, has pulled the plug on their logistical system. They don't seem to be getting much resupply by motor transport, rail, or air, at this point."

"So, what you're saying is…"

"Mr. President, their whole offensive could stall, if they don't receive the fuel, ammunition, and supplies they need. We've really only picked up traces of logistical activity in their rear areas, by all our means and sources."

"So, this entire thing could collapse and fall on its ass?" the president asked.

"That's one possibility, Mr. President, albeit an unlikely one. A major concern is that their aircraft and various other types of vehicles were engineered to utilize NATO electrical power, fuel, some spare parts, and facilities. So, as they overrun us, they can resupply what they need from our resources, food stocks and water included," the briefer responded.

"So, the down side, as I see it, is that the Soviets could be reluctant to tip their hand and, if things start to go south on 'em, they could, theoretically, release their reserves of manpower and equipment. Right, General?" he asked.

"Yes, Mr. President. That's the wild card they appear to be holding. It's the safest assumption, based on what we know and what we *don't* know."

The remaining members of the Joint Chiefs all nodded their assent.

The president then asked the Chairman, "General, how's it goin' with REFORGER? Is everything gettin' in that needs to be gettin' in?"

A dark frown spread across the General's face, as he responded, "Mr. President, Soviet forces have now advanced through the Fulda Gap and across the southern part of West Germany to a point where they can, to some degree, disrupt the approach and departure routes into and out of Rhein-Main Air Base, our main point of resupply for Germany.

"Currently, there's a backlog of traffic on the ground at Spurlin until we can contain the SAM threat around Rhein-Main; that, and just the sheer volume of personnel and equipment we need to move."

"How are the bad guys controllin' it," the president wanted to know.

The Chief of Staff of the Army nodded to his aide, who went to another easel, flipped to a map, and addressed the president, "Sir, they've formed a pocket of sorts around Frankfurt. We control the airfield between the two-eight-zero and one-seven-zero azimuths. They control everything else. We know they have brought in their mobile SA-6 and their newer SA-11 SAM systems, one of which shot down a C-141 about six hours ago, and they have ample SA-7s sprinkled throughout their infantry and armored units to make things very challenging for our airlift people. The bottleneck at Spurlin notwithstanding, we're still getting most of what we need into alternate airfields in France."

"What else are we doing about it," the president demanded.

The Air Force Chief of Staff answered, "Mechanized infantry and armored counterattacks and our A-10s and anything else we can hang a bomb, rocket, or missile on, are hitting those Soviet forces in what we call the 'Frankfurt Pocket' relentlessly. We've also dedicated a squadron of F-105G Wild Weasels from the Georgia Air National Guard to help nail down the SAM threat around Rhein-Main. We're very fortunate that GANG squadron was already deployed there for training. Our F-4G Wild Weasels at Spangdahlem, permanently assigned to USAFE, have already been dispersed and stretched to the breaking point. Fighter-drags to get the remaining GANG squadron and the one from George Air Force Base, as part of our Rapid Deployment Force, are currently underway, sir. As you know, Mr. President, our Air Force is the only one in the world with aircraft and crews dedicated to SAM suppression on a fulltime basis. Chances are, sir, those Weasel crews will arrive in theater and go into combat as soon as they can be refueled and armed, with no time for crew rest."

"Then, I guess they'll have to rely on Dexedrine, the 'go pills,' for a while. How are our air losses, General?"

"Heavier than we'd like, but not as bad as we expected, Mr. President. The most recent numbers for air and ground losses, as well as equipment losses, were still being crunched as I headed out the door for this meeting.

"We've gotten SITREPS from our armored forces that the A-10s are making a difference. With the losses they've been inflicting on the Soviet armored columns, they tend to even the score a bit and maybe even tip things in our favor. We've even had several reports of Soviet tank crews abandoning their vehicles under imminent attack by Warthogs. As intended, they're taking a huge load off our armored forces."

President Harvey observed, "You're right, General, hashin' out the numbers, right now, won't do us any good. There'll be time for that and all the hand wringin', later."

The General nodded.

"Yes, Mr. President. But, there is a bit of bad news which we got wind of in the early going, but confirmed conclusively, just before this meeting began."

"What's that, General?"

"Mr. President, in their opening barrage in and around the Fulda Gap, we incurred casualties from blister and nerve agent chemical munitions. As you recall, we thought as much in our first 'war council,' as you called it. Now, we can confirm the chemical attacks as widespread."

"Confirmed?"

"Confirmed, Mr. President. An NCO from the Mount Mesmer monitoring station was able to escape and evade after a chemical strike and made it back into friendly lines. It was an MP sergeant-major, I believe, who made it out with two of his soldiers. Once he made contact with friendly forces and they could get the three of them safely decontaminated, they all told the same story.

"They confirmed the use of what appeared to be a nerve agent, based on the casualties he saw on his way out. We're getting reports from our aid people in the field and there have been reports from civilian hospitals and clinics, as well. Wounds consistent with blister and nerve agents have been confirmed; Lewisite and VX, specifically. The Army Chemical Corps people back that up conclusively."

The president was now leaning forward, sitting on the edge of his chair. The tension in the room had been ratcheted up noticeably.

"Are they still usin' gas?" he asked.

"Mr. President, as far as we can tell, they appear to have stood down their chemical rocket and artillery units; either that, or we've destroyed them. We've encountered Soviet wounded and corpses that are no longer wearing chemical protective gear, like they were in the opening hours of the offensive."

The Chief of Staff of the Air Force spoke next, "Mr. President, as soon as we confirmed that this wasn't just another isolated border incident, we put tactical air assets on their known chemical supply dumps and the motorized transport routes in and out of those dumps. We hit 'em with conventional high-explosives, cluster bombs, and then napalm to burn off the residual. We also hit their known rocket launching sites and artillery positions we suspected were capable of firing chemical munitions. Those were preplanned mission packages and they appear to have worked. Our Blue Light teams and HUMINT sources in East Germany gave us very good intelligence, on that score."

"What about our casualties in the sectors where the gas was used?"

"Not as bad as we expected, Mr. President, with the re-emphasis on chemical defense training over these last few years. The MOPP gear and decontamination procedures seem to work fairly well, and most of the troops have taken the training to heart; that, plus employment of chemicals tends to be tricky, at best, given winds and weather. For the fatalities, however, it was a horrible way to go."

The president shook his head almost imperceptibly with a look on his face that bespoke both sorrow and disgust.

"What about the French?" the president asked.

"They're flying CAP for our airlift assets landing at their airfields and providing some SAM suppression, to the extent they are able, in the Rhein-Main area, Mr. President," General Hubbard, the Chief of Staff of the Air Force responded, "Our overhead imagery also indicated they are fully deploying their ground forces along the Franco-German border."

"I guess they don't intend to sit idly by and be overrun for a third time, this century."

The president stood suddenly from his chair and adjourned the meeting with an admonition to his Cabinet members to notify him of major changes pertinent to their respective departments, as they occurred. He asked the Joint

Chiefs and their aides, the intelligence people, and the Director of the FBI to stay.

President Harvey took stock of his latest war council, rocked back in his leather chair, then reached into his jacket pocket and withdrew a rather large cigar. Reaching into another pocket, he pulled out a clipper and lighter.

"Anyone mind if I smoke?" he asked, as he clipped and lit it, then thought about his question for a few moments.

"Ah, hell, I'm the President of the United States and I don't care whether you mind or not. Smoke 'em if you got 'em.

"Okay, gentlemen, let's examine the facts, as we know 'em, about our enemy's state of mind, the overall military situation, and our various courses of action."

All of the military heads in the room nodded, almost in unison.

"First," the president began, "we've been hit hard in West Germany. We've been pushed back, but we're holding on. The bastards haven't yet pushed us back to the Pyrenees or into the English Channel. No overt moves against Finland, Sweden, or Norway and nothing against NATO's southern flank. Neither the Italians, Greeks, nor Turks have reported any moves by hostile forces, though they stand ready to engage. Those are the *facts*.

"The Soviets have apparently not made any moves anywhere else on the planet, as far as we can tell. Our best intelligence leads us to the conclusion that none of their satellite countries nor their Communist friends around the world were aware of their intentions and apparently have no desire to get dragged into the current fracas."

Every ear in the room waited anxiously for what the president had to say regarding the present state of the Soviet government.

"We can't nail down who's runnin' the show in the Soviet Union, yet. One might assume they'll be fightin' amongst themselves, at some point, though it's too early to tell and a dangerous assumption, at best.

"Supplies and reinforcements don't appear to be reachin' their forces in West Germany in what we would consider sufficient quantity to sustain major combat operations across the NATO front. I think it safe to assume they're usin' whatever NATO supplies they can for their ground and air forces.

"Beyond that, Soviet forces have used chemical weapons on U.S. troops, perhaps other NATO forces, and undoubtedly, German civilians have fallen victim to them, as well.

"Our best evidence indicates they have at least one Spetsnaz team in the CONUS, intent on detonating a nuclear weapon at Spurlin Air Force Base. Is everyone in agreement that those are the facts, regarding the present situation and what we know and don't know about the intentions of our enemy?"

Everyone in the room nodded his assent.

"Okay, let's examine our options, gentlemen," the president said as he puffed his cigar and rocked back in his chair.

The president then exhaled a cloud of smoke and said, "Unless we act aggressively, our casualties could quickly soar into astronomical numbers. We're already pumpin' everything into Europe we can and the Soviets don't show any signs of lettin' up, their supply and rear area problems notwithstanding. If they push through into France, we've basically lost the war. We'll have lost Germany, Belgium, and the Netherlands, at that point; possibly Norway and Denmark, too. They won't leave their northern flank unprotected long enough to give us a chance to counterattack there. Neither Finnish nor Swedish neutrality will mean anything to the Soviets.

"With continued resistance by conventional forces alone, we'll lose air and possibly naval assets due to attrition, as well. We can't rule out Soviet moves in the Mediterranean and Southwest Asia, at some point. They won't leave their southern flank in the Mediterranean out in the wind for very much longer.

"Our forces have already been attacked with chemicals and, if our people in Maine aren't successful in baggin' that Spetsnaz team, northeastern Maine and the adjacent parts of Canada will be turned into a radioactive mess. That's a situation neither we nor our Canadian neighbors can accept.

"Gentlemen, we *must* respond to the use of chemical weapons on our forces and the presence of a Soviet nuclear weapon on U.S. soil. Whoever is runnin' the show in the Kremlin needs to be put on notice, in the harshest terms we can present, that we will meet force with force. As I see things, our only prudent option is to up the *ante* and escalate our response.

"Just so I know, gentlemen, what sort of casualty count could we expect in a full-scale nuclear exchange with the Soviets?"

Everyone in the room silently cringed at the question, but understood that it was one that now needed to be addressed.

The Chairman answered, "Approximately seventy to one hundred million immediate deaths in the U.S. and maybe twenty to forty percent less in the Soviet Union, due to varying demographics and population dispersion, Mr. President. No true estimate of the number of citizens who'll die of from any lingering effects of radiation exposure, in the short *or* long runs. Best case, a few million; worst case, tens of millions."

A deep frown crossed the president's face as he asked the Chairman, "General, short of launchin' our fleets of SAC bombers and missiles, what immediate options do we have that'll allow us to respond without telegraphing the intent of launching all-out nuclear war? Right now, we don't need fleets of ballistic missiles headed toward the Soviet Union, nor do we need large numbers of our bombers prowling their airspace."

General Hubbard leaned forward over the table on his forearms and answered, "Mr. President, each of our SAC bombardment wings has its requisite SIOP target packages, as you know. Additionally, each wing has one of its Alpha alert sorties tasked with an on-shelf mission designed to address just this sort of contingency. The Alpha sorties are those that are always kept on alert. Within that force structure, we have what we call 'CONALT Options;' Contingency Alternative. Spurlin has one that just might fill the bill."

The president exhaled cigar smoke and said, "Go on."

The Chairman continued, "Mr. President, the Spurlin people call this their 'Pale Horse' package. Their number-three Alpha alert sortie will have its gravity bombs downloaded and its fuel load adjusted to compensate.

"This CONALT sortie is designed to launch out of Spurlin at H+48 hours on a peacetime flight plan currently, but the plan is flexible and the launch time can be adjusted, as needed, without difficulty.

"The strike bird will proceed across the North Atlantic and cancel the peacetime portion of the flight plan at a predetermined point, somewhere northwest of the British Isles. It will then proceed under radio silence to its launch point, and then launch seven Precision-Guided Air-Launched Missiles, which we call 'PALMs,' at designated Soviet-controlled targets in East Germany. It'll resume the peacetime flight plan again at a predetermined point west of the UK on its return routing."

"Lone penetrator, huh? Do we have any CAP available to ride shotgun on it into contested airspace?"

"Yes, Mr. President, RAF and perhaps Royal Navy over UK airspace, then F-15s out of Camp New Amsterdam, exigent circumstances notwithstanding and the availability of tanker resources to re-fuel them. We have a contingency plan with the British Royal Air Force and Navy. The strike aircraft, in this case, will fly a high-altitude profile only."

Fifteen seconds passed before the president responded.

"I'm guessin' we have a way to recall this bomber, should the Soviets come to their senses while it's enroute?" the president asked with a raised eyebrow.

"Yes, Mr. President. We always have a way to recall our bombers, under SAC's concept of positive control," the General Hubbard responded.

The president nodded as he blew another cloud of cigar smoke.

151

"Gentleman, what I am about to say will most assuredly relegate me to the status of a one-term president, but I don't care. I'm making this decision with a great deal more clarity than the one John Kennedy faced with Cuba in 1962. He was dancin' around the idea of a first strike against a nation that had not attacked us nor any of our allies. In my case...*our* case...we're already fightin' a war *we* didn't start. We *were* attacked, this time. My focus is on bringing it to a quick end, if I can. I'll leave my political legacy to be sorted out by the politicians and bullshit artists in the media and college history classrooms.

"I'm about to tip my hat to Julius Caesar and cross both a personal and national 'Rubicon,' if you will, and the way I see this is I'm damned if I do and damned if I don't. So, I prefer to be damned if I *do,* given the chemical attacks on our forces in Germany and what might very well happen in Maine."

"Do you want us to order the Pale Horse strike out of Spurlin, Mr. President? My best advice is to keep put our entire force structure at DEFCON 2 and elevate the 8th Air Force to DEFCON 1, as that's our numbered Air Force responsible for the strike," the Chairman asked and added.

"Put it in motion, General. Gentlemen, the gloves come off, right now.

"I agree with DEFCON adjustments, but keep your bombers on the ground, for the time being. Tow 'em out to the end of your runways, as you see fit, but a flush launch of any sort, at this stage, unless absolutely necessary, would likely send the wrong message to whomever the hell is currently holding the orb and scepter in the Kremlin."

Again addressing the Chief of Staff of the Air Force, he asked, "General, is the crew sittin' alert for this strike capable of pullin' this off?"

"Yes, Mr. President, I can safely speak for CINCSAC in saying that all mission certified B-52 crews are capable of handling this. Their training is almost exclusively in the nuclear strike realm. Those crews up at Spurlin are damned good, based on what we've seen on their past five ORIs," the General replied.

"Good. That's all I need to hear," the president assured the group.

"At the conclusion of this mission, I don't want the names of this crew released. Period. Beyond the scrutiny they would undoubtedly garner from the left-leaners and their cohorts in the media, they would very likely be subject to some sort of reprisals from our enemies. The KGB has some very long arms. Their identities will, over time, leak out, but we need to keep a lid on that information as long as possible."

Addressing the Air Force Chief of Staff, the president continued, "General, if your people spot any potential problems with this crew, let me know, ASAP."

"Yes, sir. I don't foresee any problems, sir."

"Thank you, gentlemen," the president said, as he stood up, effectively dismissing them.

24. "Pegasus Eye"

Nuclear Emergency Search Team OV-10N

Final Approach to Spurlin AFB, Maine

Runway 01

December 4, 1982

Major Butch Conyers retarded the Bronco's throttles to idle over the large, white numbers and settled the little aircraft smoothly onto the runway. Although he was regular Air Force, he and the three other OV-10N pilots were on loan to the U.S. Nuclear Regulatory Agency Project Pegasus Eye, in reference to the radiation detection equipment, referred to as "sniffers," installed in the rear cargo bay the aircraft. They were an augmentation force for the Nuclear Emergency Search Teams and the Broncos' back seaters were civilian radiological specialists who worked full time in the NEST program, although all of them were ex-military.

Conyers and his "GIB," the "guy in back," John Tuck, were both frustrated from their lack of results, thus far. Both knew that, if there was indeed a nuclear sapper team out there, those guys were good. Or lucky.

As he taxied to the area where the other three Broncos were parked, Conyers asked, "You couldn't pick up anything?"

Tuck answered, "No, nothin', man. This whole area's hot as hell. Always is, around SAC bases.

"I counted fifteen BUFFs on alert out here, as we were comin' down final approach. Assume, and I *am* assumin', each one of 'em is armed with four nukes. That's at least sixty weapons and that guess is probably on the low end.

"No tellin' how many of those warheads leak radiation. We know that some of the PALM warheads leak, and I don't think the Air Force as bothered to tell the bomber crews, but I'd be willin' to bet good money the munitions maintenance people know about it."

"Then, there's the bomb dump, over there to the east," Tuck continued, referring to the weapons-storage area. "No tellin' how many they've got in those bunkers. Plus, they've had nukes here since, what, the early fifties, draggin' 'em all over the airfield and whatnot?

"The bunkers are definitely hot, but so are a lot of the trolleys they haul the weapons on, as well as vans and trucks full of hot tools; all residual radiation. It's a mess."

"My sniffers back here are pretty good at differentiating' natural from man-made radiation, but here, it's *all* man-made. Not necessarily dangerous levels, but a whole lot more than most every other place I've scanned.

"If the Russians have a team out there, and they're close, any satchel or backpack nuke they have is likely just gonna get lost in all the clutter. I could be wrong, but I ain't seein' anything out of what I'd consider ordinary, given that this is a SAC bomber base."

Conyers followed the hand signals of the marshaller and taxied the Bronco into its parking spot.

He cut the throttles and, as the props were rotating to a stop, he said, "I don't know who's up next, but maybe, just maybe, they can get the bastards to stick their heads up long enough to zap 'em with the rockets or the guns.

"If we can pinpoint their location, maybe we can light 'em up," said Tuck.

"Let's see if we can scare up a cuppacoffee and a sandwich, while they refuel this bird and give 'er the once-over. I'm game to go back up. Maybe this overcast'll lift a little and we can put our eyeballs on the ground a little more than we've been able to, so far. You up for it?"

"Best idea I've heard, all day," Conyers replied.

25. "Behold a Pale Horse"

Spurlin Air Force Base, Maine
Alpha Alert Parking Stub #3
December 4, 1982
1200 Hours Zulu (0700 Local)

All eight engines started smoothly, which wasn't always the case in the frigid temperatures of wintertime northern Maine.

When the "before taxi" checklist was complete, McQuagg simply nodded to Outlaw, who transmitted on the #1 UHF radio, "Spurlin Ground, Pale Horse Three, Alpha stub three, taxi with information Tango."

Ground Control responded, "Roger, Pale Horse Three. Information Uniform is now current. Altimeter is two-niner-eight-six. You are cleared to taxi to runway zero-one."

"Copy Two-niner-eight-six. Taxi runway zero-one, Pale Horse Three."

Outlaw and McQuagg both turned the small knobs on their respective altimeters until 29.86 showed in each window to correct for the outside barometric pressure.

"Two-niner-eight-six set. Pilot," McQuagg said over the interphone.

Outlaw and Banjo responded likewise with the correct altimeter setting and their crew positions. In front of the aircraft, the crew chief began waving his arms, giving them the signal to taxi forward. McQuagg advanced the throttles and the bomber rolled forward out of the parking space. Outlaw glanced to his right and looked for any obstructions and other aircraft on the taxiway, but saw nothing.

"Clear right," he told McQuagg over the interphone.

McQuagg glanced to his left to ensure that nothing was approaching Pale Horse 3 from his direction.

"Clear left," he said, as he applied right rudder to start the right turn onto the taxiway.

Outlaw noticed the crew chief, Staff Sergeant Alberson, snap to attention and render a textbook-perfect salute, which he returned. As Pale Horse 3 taxied past Alert Sortie #1, Outlaw wondered just how long it would be before the other alert birds launched on their SIOP sorties, which would involve deep penetrations into Soviet airspace. There was an unsettling, "lambs to the slaughter" feel to it all; a *gladiatorial* feel.

From the vantage point of her pickup truck in the parking lot just across the street from the alert facility, Bergen Cyr watched the bomber roll forward and turn right as the windshield wipers rhythmically wiped the fat, wet snowflakes away. She guessed a sortie was launching for Europe, but she didn't know who the crew was. Mark Tolbert tapped on the driver's side window, startling her.

She cranked the window down as he leaned down to make eye contact and said, "Hi, Berg. Watchin' the show?"

She responded, "Hi, Mark. What's going on? Why is there only one bomber taxiing?"

"Nuke strike," he replied, "They're sendin' Ivan a message. God knows what happens, after that."

Tolbert was cognizant of the fact that he had just violated OPSEC by telling Bergen that. However, he figured that she, being an OSI agent, had the security clearance and certainly wasn't going to tell anyone. Besides, the whole world was going to know in several hours, anyway. The whole industrialized world might well be flames and ashes, by then.

"Who is it?" she asked, but she could see from the look on his face exactly who it was.

"McQuagg and Dillon," was all he could get out of his mouth.

"I was afraid you'd say that," she said, breaking eye contact with him.

Determined not to show her alarm, she asked, "Why are you in civvies, instead of your flight suit? You're not on alert with the rest of the squadron?"

"No," he said. "My services have been requested by another of our fine federal agencies. You can guess which one. They bagged the guy they call 'Oz' and need a Russian linguist to help with the interrogation. Apparently, he's forgotten how to speak English. He also seems to have forgotten how to speak Russian."

"Glad they caught him," she nodded, having momentarily forgotten that NEST teams were combing northern Maine, searching for what they thought would be a team of Soviet special operators that just might be attempting to shut down Spurlin AFB with a nuclear device.

"Why's McQuagg back in the cockpit?" she asked. "I heard he was working in war plans."

Tolbert answered, "Their new AC, Satterfield, fell and broke a leg while movin' a bed up the stairs in his quarters. McQuagg was the only extra AC available who happened to be current in the aircraft and up to speed on all his recurring-training requirements. They were forced into it by the wing commander, basically. The squadron brass still has command responsibilities associated with the rest of the alert force.

"Hey, I gotta go, Berg," Tolbert said, "Don't worry, Outlaw and that crew are solid. McQuagg might be a bit of a wild card, but the rest of 'em are good. They'll be fine."

After Tolbert walked away, Special Agent Cyr's first instinct was to scream, but she fought against it. Instead, she sat in stunned, disbelieving silence. She was horrified by the thought that she may very well never see him, again; her sweet, gloriously talented Dillon, the man whose only mistake had been to fall in love with her. Though he'd never said so, she knew he loved her. It was evident in the way he talked to her, the way he looked at her, and the small, thoughtful things he did for her. Underneath all that, she knew she loved him, too, and it made her ashamed for treating him so callously.

26. "Package Delivery"

Spurlin AFB, Maine
Wooded Area, Southeast of the Runway
December 4, 1982

Captain-Lieutenant Beloglazov glimpsed the taxiing bomber through his night vision viewer as he scanned the runway and the tree line to the east. The low, heavy overcast and the resultant lack of moonlight made it much darker than normal. As far as he could discern, none of the Americans' security police patrols seemed aware of their presence, as evidenced by their activity, given that they were undoubtedly in an increased readiness posture. His team was holed-up in an abandoned shed near the old alert aircraft parking area and, for reasons unknown, no one seemed to think to investigate those few abandoned structures on that side of the aerodrome. The fencing on this forsaken end of the aerodrome and long since fallen into a state of disrepair and had proven quite easy to penetrate.

Beloglazov had determined that getting his mortar team into position farther north along the runway may present problems, though nothing his men couldn't surmount. The team would have to travel between the runway and the storage area where the Americans kept their nuclear weapons. He'd studied aerial photographs of other U.S. bomber bases and saw that this Spurlin base was somewhat different. It appeared that much of the natural vegetation surrounding the base had been left in place during its construction in the early 1950s. He agreed with the soundness of the decision in affording the base some natural camouflage, but for a different reason; namely, the concealment it presented would, in fact, serve the same purpose for his teams as they moved into position.

Additionally, logging trails and other roads in the area had been left intact, rather than the predictable, grid-like layout of many military air bases around the world, even those in the Soviet Union. He was confident his mortar team could make it into position in time to start the ruse he needed to get the Package positioned and fused.

As he drew in another deep breath of clean, Maine air, he was enough of a realist to know that by now the Americans must certainly be aware that something was afoot, in light of the fact that their contact had not rendezvoused with them at the appointed time and place the day before. Perhaps he'd been compromised or even captured.

The team had been careful in its movements, sweeping footprints in the snow with small tree branches and burrowing in to avoid as much movement as possible. They were only moving as perimeter security dictated, and then only very slowly and carefully. His men were experts at concealment and, while he had concerns, he knew detection of them would be difficult at best for the Americans. Most of their movements had been conducted in darkness, which afforded them a much greater degree of security.

Since the encounter with the sheriff, Beloglasov had kept a keen ear and eye to the skies overhead. Based on the sheriff's body language, the questions he asked, and the ones he had *not* asked, Beloglazov knew the constable was suspicious, perhaps much more than the typical American citizen would have been. The prospect of encountering a law enforcement officer in such a manner hadn't even entered his thought processes before this mission began. Try as he might, he couldn't put the ominous thought out of his mind.

He'd heard enough helicopter and fixed-wing traffic overhead to be gravely concerned. Beloglazov was a worrier by nature and worrying about the safety of his team was just part of his job. Thus far, his team had not been directly overflown, but he reasoned that it was only a matter of time before they were. Helicopters overhead would have been impossible to spot by the heavy overcast. This close to the enemy aerodrome, they would have been difficult to hear, given the amount of air traffic in and out and the almost constant taxiing of aircraft and engine test-runs being performed on the aerodrome by maintenance crews.

He was conflicted about the overcast. On one hand, he would be able to get a better feel what was going on with the air traffic overhead. On the other, they would become much more visible targets once the sun came up, in the absence of cloud cover. For now, he was content to have the overcast for benefit of the added concealment.

Warrant Officer Misha Yermakov, Beloglazov's second-in-command, plopped onto his belly in the snow beside him and asked, "Should we bring up the *Strelas* and take down their bomber, once it is airborne, sir?"

"No, not a good idea," Beloglazov insisted.

"We have two tubes and a compliment of ten *Strelas*," Yermakov maintained.

"A very bad idea, Misha. One of our missiles very likely will not knock a B-52 from the skies, unless we are extremely lucky. It's an enormous aircraft and it has eight engines. We would have to shoot two, maybe three missiles to take it down. Doing so would give away our position to whatever base defense forces they have looking for us, and make no mistake, they know we are here. Somehow, they *know*. I have a very bad feeling about the constable we encountered along the highway.

"Further, our orders are to detonate the Package as close to the center of their airfield as possible; the closer to their alert aircraft, the better. That will diminish their striking capability against our forces in Europe and the Motherland itself. This airfield is their main channeling base for their operations in Europe. Destroying it takes away that advantage. Let's hope we're fortunate enough to be able to get the Package into position, set the timer, and get away, before it detonates.

"We have the *Strelas* to defend ourselves from air attack, in the event we are discovered prior to delivering our Package. We cannot display that advantage until we absolutely need it to enable us to carry out our orders or to escape back to our boat. So far, the Americans here seem oblivious to our presence. Besides, that bomber is not a direct threat to us and one bomber is not likely to make a difference in this war."

"You are right, of course, sir."

He handed the night vision scope to his Yermakov and pointed to the three small, dark grey, twin-engine, propeller-driven aircraft parked north of the alert force parking area.

"Do you see those grey aircraft, Misha?" he asked.

"Yes, sir," his second answered. "What are they?"

"They are American observation and light-attack aircraft. The Americans call them, 'Broncos.' Nasty little things," Beloglazov answered, "I saw them in Vietnam in late 1972. They may well be the reason we have to conserve our missiles, but being in the woods so close to our objective and with these low clouds, let's hope that will not be the case."

"Misha, have the men check their weapons, ammunition, and gear.

"How did your reconnaissance of the weapons storage area go?"

"Very well, sir. Not as much lighting as I would expect, but they undoubtedly are keeping it somewhat dark as an additional security measure. Moving between there and the runway should pose no problems, as long as we move through the woods between the runway and the compound. The weapons storage facility is disguised to look like an office complex, but to my trained eye it looks exactly like what it is: a munitions storage depot.

"If we move before dawn, we should be able to manage without difficulty. Besides, if our teams are seen, they will look just like the American security forces on a routine patrol, Comrade Captain-Lieutenant," Yermakov offered.

"What has your reconnaissance of the aerodrome itself revealed?" Beloglaszov asked.

"Sir, everything seems to match what we have known for some time, based on the intelligence reports given to us before we departed. Their security forces appear to indeed be in a state of increased preparedness from the north end of aerodrome to the south, as well as the area where their nuclear munitions are stored. Why they haven't come to inspect this shed, I don't know," Yermakov answered.

"Tell me more?"

"There is a rise in the terrain, near the northern end of the runway in the woods, but outside the fence. From the tree line and that rise, we can deploy our machine gun and mortar to fire over the fence onto the aerodrome. There will be no need to penetrate the fence on the far end."

Pointing toward the parked alert aircraft, Yermakov continued, "As you can see, sir, there is a white tower behind the second and third bombers, where their primary alert aircraft are parked. The personnel in that tower have a commanding view of the parking area and most of the aerodrome. They also appear to have a heavy-caliber machine gun in that tower, which concerns me. I think it is safe to assume there is some sort of alarm system in the tower, should a threat present itself. They have an armed sentry posted in front of each bomber and mobile teams in *groozoveeks* which seem to each protect two bombers. From what we have seen, all foot sentries within that area and those patrolling inside and outside the fences carry small arms. Fortunately for us, they have not penetrated the woods east of the aerodrome deeply enough to encounter any of us. We've also noticed that they wear gear indicative of flare pistols, so it may be safe to assume those on foot patrol do not carry radios. We have no way to determine what their alarm system entails, where their security command center is located, or what their response protocols entail.

"But, sir, we have noticed maintenance vehicles moving freely around the aerodrome, both the *groozoveek* type and the paneled vans. To get from our position to where we need to deliver our Package should present little difficulty. We will readily blend in with all the other vehicles moving about on the field. The Americans are rather busy over there, as you have certainly noticed."

"You do excellent work, Misha. We move in ten minutes and need to be in position before daybreak. Let's hope it continues to snow, even if lightly. It makes us more difficult to see, even though it slows us a bit. We'll send Dubrov and Zavarzhny with their tube and five mortar rounds to the northern end. They will have to move quickly to get into position. Once they begin their diversion, I will drive the Package into position. I've selected a mound of plowed snow behind which to leave it. If should provide just enough concealment in the midst of the ruse our mortar team will provide.

"Should covering fire become necessary, Dubrov and Zavarzhny will have their machine gun and we will have ours in place near their old alert aircraft parking apron, south and east of the runway. My hope is that I will not be noticed, as their security forces rush to defend the perceived attack at the north end. Those two will need to move quickly, once the Americans realize what's happening to their parked aircraft on that end of the apron."

"Sir, I would recommend you send one more man with them, as one will need to carry the tube and the other the base plate. They will also need to carry the five mortar rounds, the machine gun, and ammunition," Yermakov admonished.

"You're right, of course, Misha. Send Yagovkin with them. He's the strongest of us all; a bull. He will be able to carry the machine gun, ammunition, and the mortar rounds," Beloglasov agreed.

Yermakov added, "Sir, I was just informed of a bit bad news; an unforeseen development."

"What is it, Misha?" Beloglazov asked.

While repositioning one of the blue *groozoveeks* for better concealment, Krazalkovich slid off the road and drove it into a snowbank, which concealed a ditch. It fell in and broke an axle. The front left wheel broken completely off and we have no way of repairing it. I'm sorry to have to report that, Comrade Captain Lieutenant."

"Not good," Beloglazov responded, "Now, we are down to one vehicle, in which to get the Package into position and escape from this area. If our other blue vehicle is lost, we will be forced to make it back to our civilian vehicles on foot, but our remaining blue *groozoveek* is the one I will use to drive the Package into position. I've noticed several vehicles of different types parked close to their alert aircraft; maintenance vehicles, no doubt. I might need to procure one, should the *groozoveek* I drive become unserviceable, at some point. We'll be fine, Misha," Beloglazov assured him, smiling through his own doubts.

He well knew this would complicate things enormously, relegating the whole task to what amounted to a suicide mission. But he'd known to a greater degree than any of his men that the odds of them escaping the area and making it all the way back home were extremely long. Yet, he surmised they were perceptive enough to assess the overall situation for themselves.

The one detail Beloglazov hadn't briefed to his team was the possibility of secondary nuclear detonations once the Package itself detonated. Based on his extremely limited knowledge of the B-52 and what his own intelligence people had told him, there were in excess of one-hundred nuclear weapons, both gravity bombs and missiles, at the Spurlin base. Assuming each bomber carried four bombs internally, that totaled a minimum of sixteen nuclear weapons in the four primary alert aircraft alone. He'd not been briefed on how many of their air-to-ground missiles were carried aboard each aircraft, not to mention how many other nuclear weapons the Americans might have in storage. Should secondary detonations be a reality, the conflagration wouldn't be survivable, even at considerable distances. The radiation left behind would leave the entire region uninhabitable for the human race's foreseeable future. His men didn't need to know that, either.

Beloglazov was going to need the remaining vehicle to get the Package into position. If he encountered resistance, which was likely, the survivors of his team were going to have to extricate themselves on foot and make their way south to the Bronco and the Blazer. On foot, it would take them at least an hour, perhaps more, moving through the snow.

Yermakov seemed to want to say something, but seemed reluctant.

"What is it, Misha?" Beloglazov asked.

"Sir, I don't know how to say it."

"Say what is on your mind, Misha," Beloglazov answered. "You've always known you can speak freely with me when the rest of the men aren't nearby."

"Well, sir, you have taken the lead on everything since we boarded the submarine and I can see you're struggling with your back."

"*Da.* I had a spasm at the safe house and I fear it's more serious than that. I still cannot manage to stretch it out. It's beginning to affect my freedom of movement. The twisting and contorting I must do in order to walk normally has apparently caused one or more of the bone-chips in my lower spine to shift. I was advised by our regimental surgeon to have the chips removed, last year, but I refused, citing operational priorities with the team in Afghanistan. He was adamant, but so was I. Eventually, my will overcame his, but I fear I made a serious mistake."

"Exactly, sir, and the men all appreciate the example you set for them, as do I, but they dare not mention it to you," Yermakov explained.

"So, what exactly are you thinking, Misha Petrovich?" Beloglazov asked, smiling at his warrant officer.

"Sir, I am asking you to let me place and fuse the Package. You yourself stated that our orders are for only either of us to do it. I don't see that we can risk you hurting your back worse and not being able to remove it from the *groozoveek.*"

Beloglazov appreciated the gesture, but told him, "Misha, I cannot, in good conscience, ask that of you. It's far too dangerous. I prefer to do it myself."

Yermakov protested, "Sir, I must insist. With your back in its present condition, you must allow me to do this. That way, you can egress the area with the remainder of the men. They can assist or carry you, if you find you cannot walk. If I lag behind, I can catch up. I may have to hot-wire a *groozoveek* or some other type of vehicle to escape. You've seen me do it, before.

"As I say that, sir, the men and I have already surmised that surviving this mission is an impossibility. Very likely, the Americans are aware of our presence and our intent. I would guess that, by now, our means of escape moored in the cove has been discovered and perhaps the submarine in which we crossed the Atlantic now rests in pieces on the seabed. The best we may be able to accomplish is to place the Package, fuse it, and get away from it, as best we are able.

"Once we start our diversion, it should be easy enough to blend with their security vehicles responding to the attack, as well as their maintenance vehicles attempting to find cover. That should afford me ample time to drive the *groozoveek* into position behind their parked tanker aircraft, set it on the ground, fuse it, and drive away. I'll meet you here and the others at the designated rendezvous point.

"We just might make good on our escape from the airfield, but I fear we may be here in America for quite a while, and that is speaking optimistically. We are here on a suicide mission and the men have come to accept that. It isn't the first time we have been placed in such extreme, unfortunate circumstances. We are here to follow orders and destroy this aerodrome, which we will."

"I'm afraid you don't know the worst of it, Misha Petrovich," Beloglazov said.

"What do you mean, sir?"

"A short time ago, I was scanning the sky south of us with my field glasses. Through a break in the clouds and against the moonlight, I saw a cargo aircraft that appeared to be dropping paratroops."

"That's not a good thing, sir."

"No, it isn't, Misha Petrovich. That was not a training drop; not now and not here. Those were likely special troops of some sort and I'm sure they will seek us out, once they are on the ground and assembled. Further, I would imagine the Americans are tactically sound enough to make another drop north of the field, in hopes of trapping us in a pincer. I have seen or heard nothing, since, and thus have no way of knowing how far away from us they are," the captain lieutenant explained.

"Nevertheless, sir, I must insist on being allowed to place and fuse the Package," Yermakov answered.

"Very well, Misha. You have used your considerable reasoning skills to think this through. Your judgements and observations have always been sound, as long as we have served together," Beloglazov observed, "Come, let me brief you once more on the switching sequence for the Package. It's quite simple, really."

Spurlin Air Force Base
December 4, 1982
0705 Local (1205 Zulu)

At the runway hold line, McQuagg and Outlaw watched the dark grey OV-10 float past in its landing flare and taxi clear of the runway, once it had slowed sufficiently.

"What's that all about?" Outlaw asked over the interphone.

"No idea," McQuagg replied, although they both knew it was an OV-10.

The voice of the Spurlin tower controller jerked their attention back to the task at hand, "Pale Horse Three, wind is three-six-zero at five. Contact Departure Control when airborne. Cleared for takeoff, runway zero-one."

"Roger, Tower. Pale Horse Three, switching to Departure, cleared for takeoff, runway zero-one," Outlaw responded as he reached with his right hand to ensure his sliding window was closed and locked.

He then reached up with his left hand and switched the preset channel on the #1 UHF radio to Spurlin Departure Control's frequency. With that, McQuagg advanced all eight throttles and the bomber lurched forward and rolled smoothly onto the active runway through a moderate snowfall. The wet snow was sticking to the windows just heavily enough for McQuagg to activate the windshield-wipers until they were airborne.

Dawn would soon be stirring, but the sky was heavy with a dark overcast. There was a low-pressure area just off the Maine coast, kicking up moisture which would fall back to earth as big, wet flakes. At present, it would prove to be of little concern, as the runway RCR was still considered "dry" and the weather shop had told them they would break out on top of the clouds at three-thousand feet. Reports from F-106 interceptor pilots who had let down through the weather to land after returning from their designated air defense patrol sectors bore that out.

As Pale Horse 3 crossed the runway hold line precisely at the scheduled takeoff time of 0730 hours local, Banjo started the mission timing clock. As McQuagg swung the aircraft in line with the runway centerline, he reached forward with his right hand and moved the steering-ratio select lever forward to the "TAKEOFF AND LAND" position and keyed the interphone, stating such, per the checklist, as he advanced the throttles and Outlaw fine-tuned them to his computed engine pressure ratio settings. McQuagg kept his right hand on the throttles, in the event he needed to retard them and abort the takeoff for any reason. The engines spooled up evenly and roared with an increased pitch in the cold air. As Outlaw made several more fine-tuning EPR adjustments to three of the throttles, he kept his eyes on the airspeed indicator, which rapidly approached the "seventy-knot hack," which was entail the beginning of a process which would determine if the aircraft was accelerating adequately to get off the ground in the remaining runway.

"Seventy knots...now," he said, as the airspeed indicator needle reached the mark.

Banjo started his stopwatch on Outlaw's seventy-knot call. Outlaw had computed the time it would take to accelerate to one hundred and twenty-one knots, based on a combination of pressure altitude, temperature, wind, and runway slope.

Outlaw glanced quickly at the rows of engine instruments in front of him. No caution or warning lights and all needles "in the green" as the bomber's eight engines thundered in the darkness.

As the airspeed indicator rapidly wound toward the mark, Banjo announced, "Coming up on sixteen-point-one seconds...now."

McQuagg quickly checked his airspeed indicator, and, seeing the correct computed S-1 speed of one-hundred and twenty-one knots, keyed his interphone switch and told Outlaw, "Committed. Your throttles."

"Roger," replied Outlaw, as he reached around the throttles and advanced the throttle-friction lever to a point of tension where they wouldn't creep back and slow the aircraft.

Pale Horse 3 was now committed to the takeoff and had enough momentum to do so, picking up speed through the darkness. Now that Outlaw had control of the throttles without his assistance, he kept both hands on the control yoke.

Well before the aircraft became "unstuck," McQuagg had literally begun "flying" the wings with lateral movements on the control yoke. As the B-52's speed increased, the drooping wingtips would rise off the runway, as the wings began generating enough lift to support themselves, though not the entire aircraft.

McQuagg kept the wings level until Outlaw announced, "Coming up on unstick...now," and the bomber lifted off the runway at precisely 160 knots indicated airspeed, as McQuagg applied back pressure to the yoke. Outlaw checked to ensure that the airspeed indicators, vertical velocity indicator, and altimeters confirmed that the aircraft was both accelerating and climbing, as he waited for McQuagg's "gear up" call.

Once Outlaw informed McQuagg that all gear was "up and locked," which McQuagg quickly confirmed by a glance at the landing gear position indicator panel located on his side of the instrument panel, followed by a quick glance at the hydraulic panel beside his left thigh. All four gauges were "in the green" and normal.

McQuagg maintained wings-level as he accelerated to the flap retraction airspeed, at which time Outlaw announced, "Flaps comin' up."

McQuagg flew the aircraft smoothly through the flap retraction speed schedule and allowed the aircraft to accelerate to two-hundred and eighty knots for the climb to cruise altitude.

Outlaw keyed the radio microphone switch on the right horn of his control yoke and said, "Spurlin Departure, Pale Horse Three, passin' three thousand."

The departure controller replied, "Roger, Pale Horse Three. I-dent."

Without Outlaw having to say anything, McQuagg reached down to his left and nudged the "Identification" switch on his IFF, Identification Friend or Foe, on the transponder panel, which sent an electronic signal to the controller's radar, identifying the aircraft, its altitude, and direction of flight. It was also coded to identify the aircraft as "friendly" to air traffic controllers.

"Pale Horse Three," the departure controller responded, "radar contact, seven miles north of the field. You are cleared on course, as filed. Climb and maintain flight level three-one-zero. Contact Boston Center on three-six-two-point-seven. Good day and good luck."

Outlaw contacted Boston Center on UHF frequency 362.7, who acknowledged radar contact, as Pale Horse 3 climbed steadily on course and had broken out of the weather at three-thousand feet, per the prediction of the Staff Sergeant Phillips in the weather shop. Passing through a wispy cloud layer at ten-thousand feet, they were greeted with a deep, blue sky and a brilliant sun rising far in the east.

27. "Covered Wagon"

Spurlin AFB, Maine
December 4, 1982
0845 Local (1345 Zulu)

Major Butch Conyers reached for the landing gear handle and moved it to the "UP" position just after the OV-10 broke ground and began climbing away. The wheels snapped to the "UP AND LOCKED" position even before he could begin retracting the flaps. The three green lights were all extinguished, indicating all three wheels were safely retracted as the small aircraft accelerated past one-hundred and twenty-five knots.

A flash of light in his right rearview mirror caught his attention, as the moved the flap lever to the "RETRACT" position. He saw it, again: tracer rounds emanating from the ramp toward the woods, east of the runway. An assault on the airfield was underway. The Soviet bastards had gotten past everyone and he hoped to Christ they wouldn't get away with what they came here to do, assuming all the intelligence and speculation had been correct.

In an instant, his options raced through his mind. He could continue straight ahead and hope to outrun the nuclear blast that was sure to come, or, he could level off and increase his airspeed, then trade that excess airspeed into a climbing, 180^0 turn. From that perch, he could attack the attackers on the descending portion of the turn. He pushed the nose over to level flight and left the throttles at full power, determined to get in the fight as soon as airspeed permitted.

"What the hell are you doing', Butch," John Tuck wanted to know from the backseat.

"I see automatic weapons fire at about the seven-thousand-foot marker, across the runway. Tracers," Conyers replied stiffly.

With the wide range of visibility afforded by the Bronco's bulged, bug-eyed canopy, Tuck twisted his upper torso and craned his neck to see for himself. As he did so, Conyers kept an eye on his airspeed indicator as he instinctively reached for the "MASTER ARM" switch, which would electrically charge the machine guns and rocket pods.

"I don't fuckin' believe what I'm seein'," Tuck said with a grunt, as he remained twisted around to get a view of what was unfolding on the airfield below and behind them, "I never thought…"

"Welcome to the war, pal," Conyers interrupted.

The word "pal" was punctuated with a grunt, as Conyers pulled back on the stick and raised the nose of the Bronco to initiate the wingover. Tuck had the presence of mind to turn around, face forward, and begin his anti-*g* straining maneuver, a second before Conyers started the climbing turn.

Before applying lateral pressure on the control stick to move the ailerons and spoilers, Conyers quickly decided to go to the left, which would enable him to swing the little Bronco around and better position it for an attack that would hit the sapper team from their right-front. He would follow the tracer fire coming from the security troops along the flight line and other points on the airfield. If he went right, he would pull out and be lined up over the woods east of the field and spotting the sappers would be more difficult.

At the apex of his turn, he looked over his left shoulder at what was unfolding below. He saw the right wing of a C-130 explode in a huge fireball followed in quick succession by the radome on the nose of a B-52 exploding in a shower of sparks and debris. The Herk was quickly consumed by flames, as ground crew scurried for firefighting equipment or to take cover. He saw several individuals run down the back ramp of the C-130; two on fire. He had no way of knowing if anyone else was trapped inside.

The B-52 didn't light off, as had the Herk, but ground crewmen were running away from it and seeking cover, as well. Apparently, the sappers had a mortar tube, in addition to their automatic weapons. To the south, near the approach-end of the runway, he could see more red tracers arcing toward targets unseen. One of the two sources of the hostile fire was likely a diversion, but a diversion that could kill military and civilian personnel alike, in addition to destroying some very expensive aircraft, vehicles, and equipment. Nevertheless, he was glad to see the security police fire teams responding so quickly.

Conyers continued his turn part 180^0, allowed the Bronco's nose to fall through the horizon on the back side of the wingover, and aligned his gunsight with the point he saw the red tracers flying into the woods. He shot a quick glance as his MASTER ARM panel and saw all green lights. Then, he squeezed the trigger on the front of the control stick grip, felt the little aircraft shudder, and watched as his own tracers first struck the snowy ground in front of the tree line, churning up black chunks of earth, as they walked their way toward where he thought the sapper team would likely be. He spotted movement just inside the tree line and realized the Bronco had now become a target. He heard sounds like hammers hitting metal and that of shattering Plexiglas, as the ground fire impacted the aircraft.

"Aw, Christ, I'm hit," Tuck shouted over the interphone.

Conyers intended to swing the Bronco around in a wide, left turn to line up for another strafing pass, during which he intended to hit the sappers with at least one salvo of rockets. Due to the concealment the trees provided the sapper team, he didn't see his results and had no way of knowing that he had indeed destroyed the machine gun team and the mortar tube. He also didn't see the Russian sergeant step quickly out of the tree line and bring the SA-7 missile tube to bear on his aircraft. Tuck, now attempting to determine if he would live or die, didn't the see the near-instantaneous trail of white smoke in his rearview mirrors as the small missile streaked toward the aircraft.

Although the OV-10's turboprop engines didn't emit the same intense heat signature of a jet, the exhaust was broadcasting a signature which should have been sufficient for the missile's infrared seeker head to lock on, but the missile flew harmlessly past. Conyers then applied right stick and put the aircraft into a right turn, as he quickly formulated a plan to extricate himself and his GIB from this extreme and unforeseen predicament.

"How bad you hit?" he asked Tuck as the nose of the Bronco swung right toward the Spurlin control tower.

Tuck's voice was awash in pain, but he was still lucid.

"Took one through my left wrist and one in the left side. I don't think its bleeding' *too* bad," he answered, though Conyers could hear the strain in his voice.

"Hang on, man. I'm gonna put this thing on the ground as near the base hospital as I can."

"Hurry, man!"

Conyers keyed the OV-10's microphone button on his right throttle and transmitted, "Spurlin Tower, Nest One has a 'mayday' with a casualty. Headin' for the main-gate road, near the hospital. Let 'em know, if able."

The Spurlin tower controller peeped up over his console at what could only be a described as murderous firefight taking place at both ends of the runway, but dared not stand straight up, lest he get hit by a stray round or become a target himself. He glanced at the old B-36 hanger long enough to see hundreds of soldiers boiling out, weapons at the ready. Infantry squads were fanning out, north and south, to engage the sappers.

The tower controller was able to locate his handheld microphone and reply, "Roger, Nest 1. Understand you have a casualty aboard. Will notify the

172

hospital. You're cleared to land, either runway, if you think you can make it in."

Conyers knew no one could get emergency medical help to Tuck on the airfield. As Nest 1 climbed for enough altitude to establish a "base leg," for his landing on the main gate road, Conyers responded, "Nest One will fly a right base leg for the road. Negative on landing either runway, Tower. Too hot down there."

Conyers noticed his number-two engine running a bit rough, but saw no fire warning lights and no other indications of impending catastrophic engine failure. The overcast was clearing a bit and, climbing past two-thousand feet, he could easily see the road and discern there were only two vehicles traveling on it and they were headed toward the main gate. By reversing pitch on the propellers after touchdown, the OV-10 had a remarkable short-field landing capability and Conyers had done it numerous times in Vietnam. It could also be safely landed on unprepared surfaces. If the tower controller could indeed get the base hospital on the horn, he could get his bird down on the deck, get it stopped, and maybe keep Tuck from bleeding out. From what he'd already seen, he might even be able to taxi right up to the emergency room entrance.

"Talk to me, John. How're you doing, man," Conyers said over the interphone.

He was minimally relieved to hear that Tucker's tone was noticeably more subdued, but less lucid.

"I'm holdin' pressure on the wrist, Butch. The through-and-through is toward the outside of the wrist, so I don't think it got an artery. Don't...know...about...side. Hurts."

"Hang on, partner! I'm gonna set this thing down on the main-gate road, as close to the hospital as I can. If I gotta land alongside the road, it'll be bumpy, but we'll be alright."

Tuck knew what Conyers had in mind, but felt himself fading and getting very cold.

"I ain't goin' anywhere, man," was the last thing Conyers heard him say.

Warrant Officer Yermakov cranked the truck thirty seconds prior to the diversionary attack at the northern end of the runway. The Package was already in the truck bed, placed there by Yermakov himself. He'd had to struggle a bit with its bulk and sixty-kilogram weight, but managed it sufficiently that he was satisfied that he could remove it without too much difficulty. It was of robust construction and he could simply roll it off the tailgate and into the grass or snow, if need be.

"Good luck, Misha Petrovich," said Beloglasov, as he reached through the driver's side window and clapped him on the shoulder, after Yermakov had removed his U.S. Air Force field-jacket, revealing his uniform and now wearing the distinctive, black beret of Naval Spetsnaz.

"One more thing, sir. All of the others have discarded their American disguises. They are all now fighting as what they are: soldiers of the Motherland."

Yermakov then nodded, put his foot on the brake pedal, put it in gear, and drove off in the direction of the alert aircraft. He was satisfied he could get the Package into position without arousing any undue suspicion. He could see the security forces' vehicles responding to the firefight to the north and emergency vehicles responding to both the cargo aircraft and the bomber that had been struck by the mortar rounds. Beloglasov knew this would be the response the American security forces would call a "Covered Wagon" and that their defense of both the aerodrome and their alert aircraft would be immediate and forceful. He also felt a momentary surge of pride at his mortar team's marksmanship: two direct hits on American aircraft with the first two rounds fired. To his dismay, however, it looked as though the tiny Bronco had made quick work of at least some of his team on the northern end.

Beloglazov became alarmed as he peered through his field glasses and saw hundreds of what appeared to be U.S. Army infantry rushing out of the large hangar uphill from the alert aircraft. They were deploying quickly and responding with small arms and automatic weapons, firing down the hill and across the aerodrome into the woods. He could clearly hear the deep, steady bark of the American .50-caliber machine guns, which had greater range and much more formidable hitting power than anything else being used against his team.

As the security and maintenance vehicles scurried about the aerodrome, some responding to the threat and others heading for cover, Beloglazov watched as Yermakov drove directly to his intended spot. Beloglazov was forced to take cover in a small depression when automatic weapons fire buzzed past his head. Perhaps he'd been spotted and recognized for what he was.

Peering through the glasses once more, he saw the *groozoveek* come to a halt between the runway and the alert aircraft parking area. Yermakov opened the door and dashed around to the back, apparently handling the

174

Package with relative ease. Beloglasov wasn't surprised in the least, given the effects of adrenaline on the human body.

Misha knelt beside the Package, obviously attempting to initiate the arming sequence. As he stood to return to the vehicle, Beloglasov saw his head literally explode in a pink spray as Yermakov's corpse toppled to the ground. Again, the heard the distinctive bark of a .50-caliber machine gun; this one closer than the ones firing from the hillside hear the hangar. The gun from the white tower had apparently seen Yermakov and realized he was not one of their own. The gunner then directed his fire onto the *groozoveek,* setting it afire in a shower of sparks and flame. He then saw rounds impacting the Package, toppling it.

Something was terribly wrong. Aboard the submarine, the technician, Zimin, had told him that should the container be breached or punctured, the Package would detonate with its nuclear yield. His instinct was to run toward Yermakov and the Package, but, even if he was in the best of health, he would undoubtedly be cut to pieces by the heavy machine gun before he got close to either.

Beloglazov thus knew it was time to move and assumed the surviving members of his team knew it, as well. As he stood, two security policemen appeared from his blind spot around to the left of the abandoned shed. He raised his sidearm and killed the first one before the second one raised his M-16 and shot him through the left shoulder. Staring in apparent disbelief, the security policeman didn't fire a second round, giving Beloglazov the blink of an eye in which to return fire, killing him.

He was hit high on the left shoulder and immediately knew it would not be mortal, only painful. Wincing against it and the pain in his lower back, he stooped to retrieve the *Strela* and began heading south to the team's designated rally point. The trek would have to be made on foot and he hoped the two civilian vehicles hadn't been discovered. If they had, neither he nor any of his men were leaving this state of Maine alive. Beyond that realization, he had no idea of how many of them besides Yermakov had yet been killed or captured. He had no idea how long they would be able to hold out, given their limited ammunition. Would they be able to escape and evade the forces heading their way, if not the infantry and security forces currently engaging them?

Beloglazov struggled southward for what he reckoned to be one-thousand meters, by his pace count. From the outset, he was experiencing numbness in his legs and extreme pain in his lower back. Deciding to rest, he sat down in a stand of trees. Examining his shoulder wound as best he could, he saw that the bleeding had apparently stopped, due, in part, to the cold. While it did indeed hurt, it wasn't serious. The problem came when he again attempted to stand, he found he couldn't. His legs simply wouldn't respond.

The timer in the fusing sequence should have detonated the Package, by now. He wondered aloud whether this was due only to unforeseen circumstances or whether this Zimin had intentionally sabotaged it. He had no way of knowing and never would.

Hobbled as Beloglazov was, he would just have to wait, on the improbable chance that members of his team would manage to escape the pincer and make their way south to the vehicles. In the interim, he would have to make himself as inconspicuous as possible, which he set about doing while dragging himself around by his arms.

28. "Positive Control"

Pale Horse 3
Overhead GIUK Gap, East of Iceland
North Atlantic
December 4, 1982
1800 Hours (Zulu)

Henry Chinchilla had been monitoring the radio communications on the #2 UHF radio between "Sideshow," the Boeing E-3 Sentry aircraft known as "AWACS," and Edsel Flight, two F-15 Eagles which had just shot down two Soviet Blinder bombers apparently on the prowl for U.S. and NATO naval targets. He'd yet seen nothing on his ECM screen to indicate the presence of hostile enemy fighter-interceptors. Both Outlaw and McQuagg had seen two flashes and black smears against the sky well off in the distance, but had no way of knowing for sure what they were. Their suspicions were aroused, however, by the two long streaks of black smoke leading to and extinguished by the cold Atlantic, miles below.

After a brief conversation with Sideshow, Henry Chinchilla announced, "Crew, AWACS says we have some clear, open-field runnin' ahead of us, as far as their radar coverage goes. A pair of F-15s out of Iceland just splashed two hostile heavies. I picked up their search radars. Looked like Blinders."

Outlaw silently agreed with Henry Chinchilla's assessment and asked, "You pickin' up any threat radars, either airborne or on the surface, E-Dub?"

"Negative, Co," Chinchilla responded, "All I'm seein' is friendly, for the time being. Those F-15s are looking at us, but they know we're friendly. I'm seeing a lot of naval stuff, but it's all ours. Expect all this friendly stuff to change in the near future."

"Roger," was all Outlaw could think of, by way of reply.

Then, he added, "Just keep workin' your weirdo-voodoo-magic, E-Dub. The fur's gonna fly, at some point."

Shortly thereafter, Spaulding McQuagg lost his nerve and attempted to abort the mission for reasons that would remain forever known only to him.

177

Once the tension over McQuagg's attempted abort and shooting had subsided a bit, Stumpy announced over the interphone, "Crew, we'll arrive at our PCTAP in one-zero minutes."

Ten minutes until the Positive Control Turn-Around Point.

"Roger, Radar," Outlawed replied, "we're under positive control and we're goin'."

"Affirmative, Co," Stumpy answered, "Tickets match and strike order's legit. We won't orbit at the PCTAP. We're gonna kill some *Roo-shuns*, instead.*"*

Then, he added, "Crew, stand by for the MPL checklist. Get ready up front, Co."

"Roger, Radar, standing by for the Missile Prep for Launch checklist."

No one responded to Stumpy's quip about killing Russians. Stumpy even sounded a little uneasy, when he said it, yet Outlaw was grateful for something coming along that would take his mind off McQuagg, even if for a moment. Everything that was happening now had been rehearsed countless times during stateside training sorties. This was no rehearsal. PALMs were going to be launched, nuclear warheads were going to be detonated, and untold thousands were going to die.

29. "Lair of the Foxbat"

Pale Horse 3

Overhead North Sea

December 4, 1982

Outlaw quashed the doubts lingering in his mind about the viability of this mission, now that McQuagg was out of the picture, and remembered his admonition to the command post controller the day McQuagg got the bends, "I'm not wearin' *copilot* wings; I'm wearin' *pilot* wings and I'm wearin' 'em for a reason."

His course of action was now crystal-clear in his mind: continue with the assigned strike mission and get the job done. None of the others had addressed the issue of aborting, and he considered that a vote of confidence in his abilities both as a pilot and a leader.

"Nav, Copilot," Outlaw said the offense and defense reported in on the checks, "I've got solid undercast, up here. By my dead reckonin', we should be passing the UK, now."

"That's affirmative, co. We're abeam Aberdeen, Scotland, right now," Banjo answered.

Outlaw then remembered the thing he hadn't done: don the PLZT goggles, which both he and McQuagg should've done as soon as possible after takeoff. He needed to get them on before things got too busy.

"Crew, Copilot," he told them, "I'm puttin' on the goggles, now. I'll be off interphone for just a sec."

The PLZT goggles were connected to the aircraft's electrical system by special connections on the pilot's and copilot's oxygen hoses and snapped into on receptacles in their respective visor covers to protect against the effects of nuclear flash blindness. Outlaw ensured the connection was secure, then snapped his PLZT onto his visor cover, which gave him a more bug-like, "science fiction" appearance than even his helmet and visor normally did. He knew they were working by virtue of the fact he could see through them. Had they not, he wouldn't have been able to see.

While he was donning the PLZTs, Outlaw gave himself a quick mental review of the questions and answers on his SAR Card, which was kept by the combat intelligence people in the 423rd Bomb Wing war plans office. This "search and rescue" card contained information unique to each crew dog and would be data-linked to SAR forces, in the event of a shoot-down over hostile territory. Outlaw well knew that any shoot-down on this mission would likely be over open water, *deadly* cold water, but he mentally reviewed his information just the same. SAR forces would query him by radio about it, before making the decision to swoop in and pick him up and each crew dog was responsible for formulating both the questions and answers to be entered on his or her individual SAR card.

Next, he gave himself a quick mental review of his post-bailout procedures, once he was safely in the parachute. He also reminded himself that as soon as he was "in the drink" or safely down on dry land, he would need to kill the emergency locator beacon on his survival radio, which was housed in the left side of his parachute harness. The thing emitted a high, pulsating tone to alert other aircraft and any nearby rescue forces to the fact that someone had to resort to the "silk letdown" and would be either walking or swimming home, if they weren't picked up.

Outlaw drew a deep breath and felt he was ready. He knew his crew was ready, as well, but that didn't at all tamp down the queasy sensation in his gut. The crew was shorthanded. McQuagg was dead and that toothpaste couldn't be put back in the tube. The remaining five would have to be enough to complete this strike.

"Crew, Copilot," Outlaw said, "I'm gonna leave the flash curtains open. I don't want anybody away from his station, in case we get jumped. Radar, confirm that our last missile'll be an 'over the shoulder' shot and we'll be headed away from the target area before the first detonation."

An over the shoulder shot was a maneuver the PALM could perform. It simply involved a turn, either in the vertical or horizontal plane, whereby the missile could strike a target behind the aircraft.

"Affirmative on the over the shoulder, Co. We'll be headin' home before the first detonation."

"Roger, Radar. So, is everybody good with the decision to leave the flash curtains open?"

The four others all responded that they were.

Henry Chinchilla broke an interphone silence of some seven minutes, "Crew, our first RAF CAP just broke escort. They're 'bingo' fuel. Expect to see our second CAP as soon as they're off the tanker, as we approach the coast of Denmark."

The Royal Air Force Lightnings had been protecting them since they entered British airspace, but had to return to base, being low on fuel. Outlaw had an uncomfortable feeling realizing they were now without fighter protection, but decided he could bear the thought, as long as they were still in British airspace.

Outlaw knew that the problems encountered by ejecting over the North Sea were going to be identical to those of ejecting over the North Atlantic. At the high latitudes in which they were flying, the North Atlantic and the North Sea were dangerously cold, all year long. Even in a one-man life raft, which was a part of each B-52 crewmember's ejection system, the odds were always tilted precipitously in favor of a quick, hypothermic death.

"Thanks, E-Dub. Crew, let's get another oxygen-and-station check before we start our turn to the southeast," Outlaw ordered.

All crew positions checked good with oxygen-and-station.

"ASQ-38 and the PALM computer okay, Radar?" Outlaw asked Stumpy.

"Affirmative. Piece of cake, down here, Co. PALM computer's good," Stumpy replied with his usual, unconcerned air.

"Guns, is defense still Code One?" Outlaw asked Stokes.

Henry Chinchilla looked to his right at Burnt-the-Fuck-Up and gave him the thumbs up.

"Affirmative, Co. All smooth, back here. ASG-15 looks good and I got the .50s cocked and ready to rock. Henry's got his witchdoctor show up and runnin'."

"Roger that. Get ready," Outlaw replied.

Thirty minutes later, the routine and boredom came to a grinding halt.

"Crew, accordin' to my chart, we're gettin' within range of their GCI coverage. That might mean bandits. Heads up," Outlaw told them.

"Roger that, Co," said Henry Chinchilla, "I'm pickin' up some hostile early-warning signals. Faint, but they're still lookin'."

"Copy, E-Dub," Outlaw responded, "Nothin' to see from the window seats, yet."

"Co," Henry Chinchilla reminded, "it's time to contact AWACs about the *Jade Thief* advisory."

"Roger that, E-Dub. I'll handle it. What's the AWACS call sign?"

"It's 'Flatfoot.' They should be up on the #2 UHF, now. Two-six-three-point-seven. Have 'em authenticate Sierra Hotel. Authentication is Juliet."

"Roger, E-Dub. Sierra Hotel and Juliet."

Outlaw reached up to the radio panel with his left hand and dialed 236.7 into the #2 UHF radio.

"Flatfoot. Flatfoot. Pale Horse Three," he transmitted.

"Pale Horse Three, Flatfoot. Go ahead," the AWACS controller replied immediately.

"Flatfoot, you are 'go' on *Jade Thief* advisory. Say again, you are 'go' on *Jade Thief*. Authenticate Sierra Hotel."

There was a pause as the senior AWACS controller checked his date-time grouping in the code books for the "Sierra Hotel" authentication.

Then, he responded, "Roger, Pale Horse Three, we authenticate 'Juliet' and copy a 'go' on *Jade Thief*. Flatfoot out."

"Affirmative on Juliet," Outlaw replied, "Pale Horse Three, out."

All pilots and aircrews in Europe were briefed within the last eight hours that, if they heard the term *"Jade Thief"* broadcast, they were to immediately break off whatever operations they had going, defensive maneuvering notwithstanding, head east, and get down on friendly concrete as soon as possible. They weren't briefed on the specific reason for the advisory, but they could speculate. Most would be far enough away not to incur any physical damage, but the pilots may well be subjected to nuclear flash blindness, which would effectively cripple them. Further, the electromagnetic pulse, EMP, from a nuclear detonation would likely "fry" their aircraft's avionics, and render the aircraft unflyable, from that point on.

"All players! All players! *Jade Thief! Jade Thief!* Say again, *Jade Thief! Jade Thief!* This is Flatfoot on Guard. Flatfoot out," Outlaw heard the AWACS controller broadcast.

"Guard" was the internationally recognized UHF frequency of 243.0 megahertz, which, for safety reasons, overrode every other UHF frequency being broadcast. Pilots never disregarded a Guard broadcast, whether they instinctively knew it was for them or not.

Without his being able to see them, all NATO aircraft within radio range of Flatfoot were disengaging and returning to base; some hauling ass in full afterburner, if the aircraft were so equipped and they had the fuel for it. A massive "skedaddle" was underway all across Western Europe.

Subsequent to the *Jade Thief* advisory, Outlaw heard other transmissions on Flatfoot's frequency. In the first transmission, a very calm voice alerted NATO aircrews to a SAM launch in the vicinity of Bremen. The second one, which sounded like it came from a very excited, SAM-hunting, Wild Weasel crew, advised, "Multiple SAM launches, vicinity Essen-Dortmund! Let's take it down!"

Stumpy transmitted over the interphone, "Sounds like they're pressin' northern Germany pretty hard; probably Holland and Belgium, too. If we don't stop it, Ivan's got this one in the bag!"

Stumpy was usually cool, almost serene, under pressure. This was the most excited tone Outlaw had ever heard him use. Then, again, this was actual combat. Perhaps he wasn't so eccentric and different from other crew dogs, after all.

Ninety seconds after the second *Jade Thief* advisory, Outlaw glimpsed movement just over a hazy, indistinct horizon. If it was an aircraft, it was still much too far away for him to identify it, or them, visually. Not noticing any contrails, he surmised the troops in the weather-shop had gotten it right, in regard to contrail altitude. The "bogeys" appeared to be at the same altitude as the bomber. Thus, if these bogeys weren't leaving any contrails behind, neither was Pale Horse 3.

His momentary respite was disturbed when Henry Chinchilla announced, "Crew, AI signals, twelve o'clock! High Lark, India band! Foxtbat! Jammin'!"

Outlaw heard the timbre of Henry Chinchilla's voice rise, knowing that his threat warning receivers were lighting up and realizing that they were under imminent attack. "AI" referred to a hostile air intercept radar. He again felt his pulse quicken. He didn't need to know in which frequency band the AI radar was operating, as there was absolutely no meaning in it for the pilots. Henry Chinchilla was simply talking to himself, in anticipation of what was about to happen.

"Roger, E-Dub! I see movement at twelve o'clock! Wait…looks like two, repeat *two* bandits, turnin' to port, comin' straight at us from twelve o'clock! Get ready, crew!"

Chinchilla's information on his directional threat warning display confirmed Outlaw's sighting.

"Roger, Co, I confirm *bandits*, twelve o'clock! Jammin'!"

Outlaw squinted into the distance, hoping that doing so might give him a visual edge. At the speeds the Foxbats were traveling, he wouldn't need to squint for very long. Though, to his knowledge, the MiG-25 didn't have a reputation of being a "smoker," like the F-4 Phantom, Outlaw could make out the faintest trace of jet exhaust behind the four huge Tumansky turbojet engines that were speeding the two interceptors his way.

"I still have AI-lock," Chinchilla said excitedly, "I keep jammin' and they keep burnin' right through! Same with the GCI! Shit! Dispensin' chaff!"

Outlaw's attention was caught by two white contrails rapidly lengthening away from the direction of Pale Horse 3 toward the MiGs. Air-to-air missiles. But, who fired them? He'd forgotten Henry Chinchilla's advisory about the second British CAP.

Realizing he'd switched back to the #1 UHF radio, Outlaw reached down with his right hand to his COMM panel and selected the #2 UHF, which Henry Chinchilla had been monitoring. He did it without even looking down. There wasn't much happening on UHF #1, at the moment. All the excitement was on the #2 UHF radio.

Outlaw's earphones exploded to life with the sound of an excited British pilot telling the area AWACS controller that he and his wingman were "fox one," meaning they had just launched radar-guided missiles. Outlaw looked up again to see the two trails of missile exhaust extending quite rapidly toward the MiGs. The bandits broke in opposite directions, in hopes of foiling the radar guidance of the missiles, but to no avail. The missiles were tracking.

The Foxbat was not a jet built to "turn and burn," in the style of true fighter aircraft. It was built to fly relatively straight and fast, "bat out of hell" fast, to keep U.S. and British bombers from reaching their targets inside the Soviet Union. Outlaw and the others had been briefed that the Foxbat could haul some serious ass, even though tangling with other fighters wasn't its *forte,* and it certainly wasn't going to maneuver violently enough to fool an air-to-air missile.

Outlaw faintly discerned objects falling from the Foxbat turning to port. The pilot had pulled too much *g* and ripped the missiles off their pylons. The first of the RAF missiles impacted the starboard turning Foxbat between its retracted landing gear. It was a solid impact and the Foxbat exploded in a brilliant flash of red and orange, which turned almost instantly to oily, black smoke. The second Foxbat didn't seem to turn as violently to port as his leader did to starboard. Nevertheless, the second missile struck its belly, just aft of the cockpit. It, too, exploded spectacularly. The distance between the Foxbats and the bomber was rapidly closing, but Outlaw saw no parachutes. These two MiG drivers were having a very bad day and neither one managed to get off a missile shot.

Outlaw watched as the explosions grew to look like huge, black spiders as the smoke trailed from aircraft pieces now falling to earth and the distance between them and the bombers diminished. Adrenalin was pumping through his body with the exhilaration of dodging the proverbial bullet with the MiGs.

"Splash two," he nearly shouted over the interphone, "Haven't seen the guys who shot 'em!"

Henry Chinchilla responded, "Roger, Co. Early-warning radar's down. No signals, right now, but stand by. This ain't over, yet, *muchachos.*"

Outlaw glanced out over the right wing and saw two Royal Navy F-4 Phantoms in loose, route formation, the nearest twenty or so feet from his wingtip.

The Royal Navy flight leader gave him a thumbs-up and stated, "Ripper Flight is 'bingo' fuel. Breaking escort. Gotta get back to the ship! Good luck, Yanks!"

Outlaw responded, "Thanks, friend."

He heard two clicks on the radio in response.

With that, the two F-4s reduced power slightly, turned west, and headed for the boat. They'd heard the *Jade Thief* advisory, as well, and needed to get on the ground.

Outlaw's brief interlude of good feeling came to a halt when he glanced over his left shoulder at McQuagg's corpse. The sight of it brought of it all storming back into focus; a vicious uppercut from the Fist of Reality.

"Crew, Copilot," Outlaw told them, "we're not outta the woods, yet. Chances are those weren't the only two Foxbats they have on hand for us. It's like the bastards knew we were coming; *us,* specifically, all along. Everybody ready?"

"Defense still Code One and ready," Burnt-the-Fuck-Up answered.

"Offense good," Stumpy responded.

"Co, Nav; I need a course correction four degrees south," Banjo told Outlaw.

"Roger, turning four degrees south," Outlaw responded, "Radar, everything lookin' okay with the PALM computer?"

"Affirmative, Co," Stumpy responded as he and Banjo continued to work through the various checklists they needed to complete before the launch-point.

The crew was quiet for the next three minutes. Henry Chinchilla broke the silence.

"Crew, early-warning radars are back up and they're lookin' at us," he said in a flat monotone.

Outlaw squinted into the distance ahead, looking for more Foxbats and fleetingly entertained a thought in the back of his mind that there might just be a rat working in the Vault and giving away some of the war plans to the Russians. The sudden appearance of MiG-25s in the skies over Western Europe seemed too much to be mere coincidence.

30. "Krasnaya Luna (Red Moon)"

Wolfhorn Aerodrome

German Democratic Republic

December 4, 1982

Major Boris Ivanovich Mikhalev acknowledged the control tower's instructions as he taxied his MiG-25 to the parking apron with his wingman, Lieutenant Ilya Petrovich Potopov, right behind him. He was instructed to stay inside his aircraft while he and Potopov were re-fueled and re-armed and to expect further orders personally from his commanding officer. The orders were "time critical," he was told.

Mikhalev knew that "time critical" would involve yet another sortie today and he was in no humor for it. He was tired, cranky, and his lower back ached from sitting on his ejection seat through two earlier missions. His back was growing stiffer by the minute and he could feel the stiffness settling into his hips. Even the exhilaration of shooting down a West German F-4 Phantom on the day's first sortie had worn off. All he wanted was a bite to eat, a glass or two of good vodka, and some sleep. If not vodka, some good, German beer would suffice. But, all that would have to wait.

Major Mikhalev was an experienced fighter-interceptor pilot and a good officer who knew how to give and how to follow orders. But, whatever order his commander was about to hand him was going to be a difficult one. He knew he was quickly approaching his limits with the stress of recent combat and was unsure how much more of it he would be able to stomach. This was very much a meat grinder of a war; to a much greater degree than the Party *apparatchiks* back in Moscow could ever have imagined.

His aircraft was overdue for a thorough inspection, as well as complete overhauls on both of its Tumansky engines, one of which had been running a touch rough on today's second sortie. Nothing he could definitively identify, but it just didn't feel right. He had flown this particular MiG-25 for the last eighteen months as his personal mount and he felt something was amiss. The oil pressure gauge needle on his left engine had waivered briefly, but the pressure readings were completely within the normal range. The contingencies of combat would take priority over an engine overhaul, just now, but the huge Tumansky power plants were notoriously temperamental and prone to failure, particularly after sustained supersonic flight at speeds in excess of Mach-2 and they had taken a quite a beating in the previous few days of combat, chasing enemy fighters and two American SR-71s, though pursuit of the black, American reconnaissance aircraft proved fruitless. They traveled so high and so fast that they could simply run away from threats.

Major Mikhalev would just have to trust in the hasty maintenance his crew chief, Senior Sergeant of Aviation Gennadi Andreivich Samokhin, had done over the past few days. Samokhin was as good as they came and Mikhalev's confidence in him was absolute. Sergeants as ground crew chiefs, in lieu of officers, in Soviet flying units were the exception, rather than the rule. But, Senior Sergeant Samokhin was a cut above the rest, in terms of his talents and detailed knowledge of aircraft systems, and thus assigned, per the major's request, as his personal crew chief.

"Comrade Major," Samokhin had told him before today's first combat sortie, "this aircraft is as sound as the day it rolled off the factory floor. I know every rivet, every nut, every wire, every weld, every vacuum tube, and every bolt in it. Just be sure you don't break anything and bring it back to me intact."

Samokhin laughed at his own joke, although it wasn't said totally in jest, as he clapped the major on the shoulder and climbed down the ladder after helping him strap in. Mikhalev knew his crew chief was as good as his word, but he also knew there were things over which the senior sergeant would have no control. That brief fluctuation of the oil pressure needle began to stick in his mind and bother him like a hangnail.

No sooner had he and Lieutenant Potopov parked and completed their engine shutdown checklists, Mikhalev saw his regimental commander, Colonel Churkin, scrambling up the crew ladder that had just been rolled into place.

"Comrade Major," the Colonel shouted into his ear over the ambient airfield noise, "you are to stay in your aircraft while it is being fueled. But, I suppose if you need to piss or have a smoke, dismount and do it quickly. We have an emergency situation, so you may not have time to be completely refueled and armed."

He then handed Mikhalev a written order that stated simply:

American B-52 inbound over North Sea, northwest of Denmark.
Intercept and destroy by any means necessary.
Launch immediately.
Contact controlling agency "Red Moon" as soon as airborne.

Colonel Churkin climbed down the ladder and jogged to his staff car, where Mikhalev saw him begin a conversation on the vehicle's radiophone. By the time Mikhalev had climbed down and pissed into the grass behind his aircraft, the colonel had finished his conversation and stood waiting for him at the foot of the ladder. With a sense of alarm, he noticed the fueling crews were rolling up their hoses and preparing to leave, as he zipped the lower zipper on his flying coveralls and rearranged his g-suit. Lieutenant Potopov's aircraft had flown the previous sortie with only one air-to-air missile, which he had fired, leaving only Mikhalev with one missile still hung under the port wing of his aircraft.

"Major," the Colonel said, "you are to launch immediately and intercept the American bomber. It must be destroyed. We are not sure of the nature of its mission, but our best intelligence reports tell us it is the only B-52 airborne, at this point. Let's hope that's the case. It may only be here to probe our air defenses, with the purpose of sending more of them to attack our frontline positions with conventional bombs, but maybe not. I think it safe that we assume the worst, based on the nature of what the B-52 was originally designed to do."

"But, Comrade Colonel," Mikhalev countered, "I haven't received a full fuel load and neither as Lieutenant Potopov."

"I am well aware of that, Major," the Colonel replied, "but, unfortunately, you will have to fly this sortie with what fuel and munitions you have. Both your tanks and those of Lieutenant Potopov are almost full. The order to send the bowsers away was *mine.* You have enough fuel, by my hasty calculations, to get you across the Schleswig-Holstein peninsula and out over the North Sea to intercept the bomber.

"Yours is the last air-to-air missile we have on this aerodrome, right now. We are not getting supplied from our rear areas and no one has been able to tell us why. I'll file the appropriate reports and send the required letters of inquiry when we've won this war. For now, go with what you have.

"We just received word that the two aircraft dispatched a short while ago to intercept the bomber have disappeared off the ground controllers' radar screens and aren't responding to attempted radio contact from Red Moon. They may very well have been shot down or run out of fuel. The American bomber is closer to us, now."

"Understood, Comrade Colonel," Mikhalev answered, "but, we have a faulty lot of seeker heads on these missiles. We don't seem to have any more heat-seekers and only two of my radar-guided missiles found their mark on my earlier mission. One didn't ignite all and simply fell off the aircraft. Lieutenant Potopov is, no doubt, in a similar situation. He shot at an American Phantom and the damned proximity fuse didn't detonate. A wasted shot, Comrade Colonel, and the American got away. He will return to fight us. Someone will doubtless answer for it all, once this is over."

The Colonel didn't respond to that last remark and Mikhalev was tempted to lean toward insubordination and tell the colonel to take Lieutenant Potopov's place and fly along, if he was so cocksure this sortie was worth the potential loss of two very expensive aircraft and two highly trained pilots. He quickly thought better of it. Whatever the Motherland needed, he would deliver. He was a good enough Russian for that.

"*Est,* Comrade Colonel. We will launch immediately," he said simply, giving the engine-start hand signal to Potopov as he climbed back into his cockpit.

The two MiG-25s roared down the runway, each with both Tumansky engines howling in afterburner and consuming fuel at floodgate rates. As soon as they were airborne and retracted the landing gear and flaps, Major Mikhalev eased his throttles back out of afterburner and directed a radio frequency change to contact Red Moon, which would guide the intercept of the American bomber. After Potopov checked in on the new frequency, Mikhalev was already keeping a close eye on his fuel, fretting about the partial fuel loads. That nagging oil pressure problem crept back into his thought process as he scanned his engine instruments during the climb to intercept altitude. Did he see the needle waiver? Was he imagining it? He wasn't certain, at this point. This entire mission was a gamble.

That aside, he was glad Lieutenant Potopov was flying as his Number Two. The lad looked like a schoolboy, but he had good "air sense" and was a more competent pilot than many older and higher-ranking ones with whom he'd previously flown. Potopov had put his time in the Young Pioneer youth organization to good use, developing his leadership skills and his understanding that good leaders must first be good followers. "Always ready" was the organization's motto and that was the essence of Potopov's character. There would be no need for the controller to fly this intercept remotely. Lieutenant Potopov was good for the task and Mikhalev was, too. His one remaining radar-guided missile should do the trick against a solitary B-52. Things could be worse, Mikhalev surmised. They always could.

The major was glad Red Moon was keeping them over land, or as close to it as possible. A blown engine or flameout due to fuel starvation would necessitate an effort to glide to the Danish coast, to avoid ejection into the North Sea and certain, icy death. The MiG-25 had an unpowered glide profile almost identical to that of an anvil, so proximity to land was paramount, just now. He was initially puzzled by a lack of response by the Royal Danish Air Force, but surmised it may be too busy with commitments east of the peninsula and in northern Germany. Undoubtedly, the Norwegians would be up and prowling about in their Starfighters, but likely too far north to intercept.

Without any air-to-air missiles on board, Potopov was essentially along as a spectator. The lieutenant's only option was to ram the American bomber and Major Mikhalev couldn't bear the thought of that, though he in no way doubted the lad's resolve. He just hoped the seeker-head on his missile would lock-on and track to the B-52. If it didn't, a failed intercept could mean disaster for his countrymen on the ground.

Pale Horse 3

Outlaw had called for another oxygen-and-station check, which the crew completed before Stumpy and Banjo began their final few items on the PALM-launch checklist. From Stumpy's reassurances, all of the bomb-nav systems and the PALM computer were working "as advertised."

Keeping it to himself for fear of putting a jinx on things, Outlaw thought, "That's pretty damned good, for *this* gremlin-infested contraption."

Had a problem manifested itself, Stumpy probably wouldn't tell him, anyway. There was nothing he would have been able to do about it from the flight deck. Stumpy and Banjo would handle it and Outlaw's trust in their abilities was total. The same held true for Henry Chinchilla and Stokes. The defense team upstairs was just as good at its respective jobs as the nav team downstairs. Too bad both of the pilots couldn't be counted on to do their jobs. McQuagg's corpse lay in mute testament to that. Conversely, the other four had complete trust in Outlaw's flying skills and judgment. If they were skittish about having only one pilot flying the aircraft, and the copilot, at that, none of them would have let on as such. They knew Outlaw, at least, wouldn't *try* to kill them.

After Outlaw heard Stumpy and Banjo read and acknowledge the last few steps on their PALM-launch checklist, Stumpy said over the intercom, "Thirty TG, crew. Bomb doors comin' open. Copilot, center the FCI and keep it centered."

Thirty seconds "to go" to the first PALM launch and the bomb-nav system was opening the bomb bay doors, which on the B-52 were enormous and would create a much larger signature on enemy radars, be they GCI or air intercept. Outlaw was forced to lean over, as he looked over the left side of the instrument panel and saw the yellow "BOMB DOORS" light illuminated, indicating they were open. He next checked the flight command indicator and made sure the needle was centered, per Stumpy's instructions.

Henry Chinchilla's voice crackled across the intercom, "Crew, GCI's active! We're bein' painted by Hi-Lark, again! More Foxbats. Jammin' and dispensin' chaff!"

Outlaw had not yet seen the two small dots on the Danish horizon when Stumpy said, "Missile away," in the most relaxed tone he had ever heard him speak.

Outside the windows, Outlaw fully expected to see a long, white trail of missile exhaust streak out ahead of the aircraft, exactly as he'd seen in the training films. Yet, there was no white trail at all.

"I don't see anything, Radar," Outlaw said over the interphone, "Bad missile."

"Damned propellant," Stumpy responded, "Standby, crew…launch in five, four three, two, one…missile away."

Outlaw saw the "Bomb Release" light flicker once, quickly followed by a bang and jolt to the aircraft so strong it disconnected the autopilot. Outlaw put his hands and feet on the controlyoke and rudder pedals, assuming manual control of the aircraft.

"Okay, crew, I'm hand-flyin' this thing, right now. Bad missile, radar."

At that moment, he had no way of knowing that a piece of shrapnel from the exploding missile had punctured the aircraft's skin in the aft fuselage and, in its path through the aircraft, had punched an almost microscopic hole in one of the #1 rudder-and-elevator hydraulic lines. Initially, it didn't cause enough of a fluid leak to activate either the main system pressure sensors or illuminate any warning lights.

Outlaw didn't even think to look over at the hydraulic systems panel. He was focused instead on the prospect of more MiGs on the way and getting the PALMs launched. He hadn't yet processed the thought that a missile propellant explosion under the aircraft might have caused structural or systems damage more severe than just disconnecting the autopilot.

As Outlaw held the bomber wings-level, craning his neck to the left to ensure the FCI, which was on the pilot's side of the instrument panel, was centered. Stumpy again announced, "Missile away."

This time, Outlaw saw the white contrail spread quickly from the nose of the aircraft as the missile streaked toward its target."

"Good missile," he said over the interphone.

"Missile away," Stumpy repeated and Outlaw saw the contrail of the second successful missile.

"Good missile," Outlaw reported, again.

It was then that Outlaw spotted the two Foxbats, still just small, almost imperceptible dots on the horizon, crossing from one o'clock to the twelve o'clock position and obviously in a turn to port and being vectored toward Pale Horse 3.

"Crew, two bandits, one o'clock, comin' across to twelve," he told them, trying to remain calm and not at all sure how that was coming across.

Four missiles had been launched, leaving three more, two of which were launched in rapid succession by the PALM computer as it turned the rotary launcher in the aft portion of the bomb bay. All that now remained was the turn and the "over the shoulder" launch.

The Red Moon controller called traffic to Major Mikhalev about the same time the suspect oil pressure gauge ran to "zero." His left engine seized and slung itself apart from oil starvation. The centrifugal forces within the engine caused turbine fan blades to fly off their shafts, turning them into shrapnel, chunks of which penetrated the right engine, hydraulic lines, and all sorts of wiring and plumbing. The right engine then slung itself apart, as well.

The major's heartrate soared as his entire cockpit lit up with every warning and caution light there was; red and yellow lights from the right side of his cockpit to the left. Realizing he would quickly lose the electrical power necessary to launch his missile, he squeezed the "trigger" on the control stick and launched it blind, unguided. He could only hope the seeker head functioned properly and picked up the bomber.

With his left engine seized and the right winding down rapidly to zero percent RPM, he attempted an emergency restart while steering his aircraft through a starboard, descending turn toward the Danish coast. At his altitude of 34,000 feet, he just might have the glide range to eject over land, assuming the catastrophe in his engine nacelles didn't get any worse. It did.

The restart drill didn't work. Mikhalev then repeated it, still to no effect, while making sure his oxygen regulator was supplying 100% oxygen to his mask as the cockpit filled with thick, black smoke. What the smoke prevented him from seeing in his rearview mirror was the long plume of flame and smoke emanating from the rear of his aircraft. Without either engine turning a hydraulic pump, he no longer had any control input and was simply a passenger.

Lieutenant Potopov saw the black smoke erupt from the rear of his leader's aircraft just before he saw the major's lone missile drop from its pylon, ignite, and begin streaking toward the American bomber. He also saw his leader begin a descending, right turn with smoke, and now flames, trailing his aircraft. The odds of this ending well for the major were now nonexistent.

"Glide to the coast, if you are able, Major," he transmitted, "I'll finish the Americans!"

Mikhalev heard the boy's transmission, but had his hands too full of aircraft at the moment to reply. He knew Ilya Petrovich would attempt to ram the bomber and the thought horrified him. Potopov was too good a wingman to lose in such a manner.

"Okay, Co, gimme me a right turn to heading two-six-zero. Expedite," Banjo said in a terse tone.

"Roger, heading two-six-zero," Outlaw repeated as he applied right-yoke to put the bomber into forty-five degrees of right bank, applying just a touch of right rudder as he did so to swing the nose across the horizon quicker.

Outlaw didn't see the missile coming. He was too busy, at the moment. Before the bomber actually responded to the control input, one of the missile's fins clipped the intake cowling on the #7 engine, but didn't detonate. It jolted the aircraft and everyone on the crew, but Outlaw had the presence of mind to keep his hands on the yoke and throttles and not reach for the ejection seat arming levers.

Once stabilized in the turn, Outlaw reached up with his left hand moved the heading set marker on his horizontal situation indicator to 260^0, giving himself visual confirmation of his rollout heading. The bomber turned quickly, as nearly two-hundred feet of wing span and the right spoiler's bit into the air. He began applying left yoke as the nose of the aircraft passed the 245^0 heading and rolled out exactly on 260^0.

Although Outlaw and the crew had heard the bang and felt the jolt, it was only then that Outlaw looked out over his right shoulder and realized what had happened when he saw that the lower left engine access-panel of the #7 engine was missing and noticed the large, jagged gash in the nose cowling where the missile's fin had torn through it. He could see all sorts of exposed plumbing and wiring, though nothing visually to indicate a fire or impending engine failure.

The next voice on the interphone was Stumpy's, "Bomb doors comin' open."

Outlaw glanced to his right and saw the yellow "BOMB DOORS" light illuminate on the pilot's side of the flight deck.

"Missile away."

Outlaw saw the missile streak away in a more aggressive turn than he thought the stubby fins on the thing could produce.

"Good missile," he replied.

"Let's get the hell outta here. Co, gimme all the airspeed you can," Banjo urged.

"Roger, nav, pushin' it up to point-eight-four," Outlaw responded, indicating he was increasing airspeed to .84 Mach, which wasn't going to outrun any fighter, but it was the maximum the B-52G could do to distance itself from harm.

31. "Stinger"

Lieutenant Potopov saw his leader's missile race toward the bomber and swore aloud when it didn't detonate, though he did see a piece of what he thought to be an engine-access panel fly off the B-52. The bomber seemed to turn up on a wing and pivot in the air, amazing him that an aircraft so big could have so tight a turn radius. When the bomber rolled out of its turn, Potopov could instantly see that he was in perfect position for a stern ramming attack. He gulped at the idea his life was rapidly coming to an end and pushed the throttles all the way forward into full afterburner, feeling the MiG lurch forward as his airspeed indicator needle began to rapidly rotate toward Mach-1 and the realm of supersonic flight. His fuel state was precarious and he hoped he would have enough to reach and destroy the bomber. Mother Russia demanded the sacrifice.

Behind him, Major Mikhalev's aircraft was arcing toward the ground like a blazing meteor, almost completely aflame from its engine intakes to its tail surfaces. His cockpit was now so full of choking, black smoke so thick that he could no longer see out through his canopy. Mikhalev reached for the two red handles just forward of his crotch, put his head against the headrest, straightened his back, and pulled the handles.

Mikhalev was instantly blasted into a horribly cold sky and found himself falling toward the waves below, desperately hoping the automatic-opening feature of his ejection system would open his parachute at 14,000 feet, which would provide for a far less violent opening shock than would occur at higher opening altitudes. As he continued his freefall, his thoughts danced briefly to the idea than any vessel that might be within sight of his water landing would rescue him quickly. It didn't matter whether that vessel was friendly or not.

Mikhalev knew his cold-soak in the North Sea needed to be as brief as possible, in order to survive.

Pale Horse 3

Burnt-the-Fuck-Up's search radar picked up the MiG even before Outlaw rolled the bomber wings-level. Very quickly, the track radar picked it up and Stokes realized just how fast the bandit was traveling: faster than any fighter he'd ever seen on a training intercept.

Once wings-level on heading, he announced, "Crew, I'm trackin' a lone bandit, inbound, six-o'clock level, movin' fast!"

Henry Chinchilla responded, "Roger. Not pickin' up any AI, yet. Dispensin' flares and jammin', anyway!"

The MiG was rapidly closing the gap and had not yet fired a missile. The MiG-25 was not equipped with any sort of machine-gun or cannon and Chinchilla was the first to realize this was a ramming attack.

"Crew, he's gonna ram us! Get ready," he said, with the timbre of his voice rising, "Still jammin' and dispensin' flares!"

"Gunner, standin' by to maneuver on your call," Outlaw told Burnt-the-Fuck-Up.

"Hold steady, Co. I got him in the cone and this sonofabitch is flyin' right down the middle," Stokes answered.

He knew his fire control system would compensate for closure, lead, and bullet-drop, but this was going to be an easy target, as long as the Russian stayed straight and level like this.

Stokes let the MiG close to twelve-hundred yards and couldn't stand it, any longer.

"Bandit, six o'clock, twelve-hundred yards, inbound! Firin'!"

Burnt-the-Fuck-Up grabbed the handles in front of him and pressed the buttons atop the levers that served as the "triggers" for the four .50-caliber Browning machine guns in the tail turret; the "stinger." Outlaw and the others felt the entire aircraft shake and shudder as Burnt-the-Fuck-Up unleashed a torrent of .50-caliber rounds at the bandit. He released the buttons after a three-second burst. Nothing. The bandit was still closing and he didn't notice any additional returns on his radar screen to indicate the bandit had been hit and was breaking apart.

Burnt-the-Fuck-Up did notice, right away, that the MiG's rate of closure had slowed. Nevertheless, the bandit was still on its deadly collision course.

"Bandit, *still* inbound, six o'clock," he told the others, "Firin'!"

The huge bomber shuddered once more as the tail guns roared to life. This time, Burnt-the-Fuck-Up knew he had hit the bandit, seeing the radar return balloon on the screen and blossom into a return three times its normal size and then turn into multiple returns, indicating the bandit had broken apart under the hail of heavy machine gun fire. The bandit's closure rate slowed drastically and then stopped altogether, as the multiple returns began to drop off Burnt-the-Fuck-Up's radarscope.

"I got the bastard," Stokes announced, not really believing what he was saying or seeing. He had practiced it dozens of times in the simulators, both at Castle and at Spurlin, but never thought he'd actually get a MiG.

Henry Chinchilla diverted his attention from his ECM screens, leaned to his right, and craned his neck to see the fire control radar screen. He saw the same thing Stokes was seeing.

"That's a confirmed kill, crew," he said simply.

Lieutenant Potopov glanced at his airspeed indicator and had not noticed the bomber's winking muzzle flashes when the first burst had been fired at him. His first noticed that he was under fire by way of a hammering sound as the .50-caliber rounds began impacting his radome and the horrible grinding sound his left engine made when they flew into the intake and sheared off compressor blades. One round had penetrated completely through the radome and instrument panel, amputating three fingers on his left hand, which was still on the throttles, knocking them out of full afterburner and all the way back to idle. He could feel the immediate deceleration and the strain against his shoulder harness as the interceptor slowed and a horribly cold wind howled and pounded him through his bullet-holed windscreen.

While trying to take stock of his shattered instrument panel and associated systems with their myriad attendant warning and caution lights, the second burst from the bomber again hit what was left of his radome, this time with two rounds flying low into the cockpit and striking his right rudder pedal, the shards of which mangled his right foot. Access panels were blasted free of the nose of the aircraft as shards of the radome detached themselves into the slipstream, banging into and breaking pieces off his vertical stabilizers as they did so.

Howling in pain, his survival instincts overwhelmed any remaining thought of ramming the bomber, causing him to sit erect with his head against the rest, and pull the right red lever at his crotch with his right hand. He wanted to live and knew he wouldn't, if the bomber fired a third burst into him. In an instant, he too was descending in a high-altitude freefall toward the frigid North Sea below.

32. "Peace Is Our Profession"

Final Approach to Runway 26
Mayerstettin Aerodrome
Vicinity *Mayerstettin,* German Democratic Republic
December 4, 1982

As he rolled his MiG-27M wings-level out of a left turn onto his final approach, Captain Artyom Vladimirovich Ivchenko of Soviet Frontal Aviation noticed that his pulse was no longer pounding in his temples. He seemed to have stopped the profuse sweating and his heartrate was back to normal. The top of his flying suit was drenched, from the armpits all the way down to the small of his back. He had been forced to raise his helmet visor and wipe away a stinging droplet of sweat from his left eye with his gloved hand and was relieved, almost to the point of pissing himself.

This afternoon's mission had involved him flying as Number Two for Major Zhykov in a formation of four aircraft to attack Dutch and West German ground targets. All four aircraft launched good order, and things even looked good as they approached the target area; this, despite the fact that none of the aircraft were carrying a full bomb load, thanks to the increasingly sparse re-supply efforts of the munitions depots in the rear areas.

The Dutch ground forces had responded to the presence of the MiG-27s with shoulder-fired surface-to-air missiles, apparently British-built "Blowpipes," which to date had proven largely ineffective against the fast, low-flying MiG-27s. However, NATO anti-aircraft automatic weapons were accurate and plentiful, and the Dutch certainly weren't shy about using them. The sky had come alive with tracer rounds as the flight of four entered their target area.

Despite their reputation for spotty effectiveness, a Blowpipe missileer was lucky enough to knock down Lieutenant Vlasenko, the Estonian, who was forced to eject from his stricken aircraft near NATO lines. He knew Vlasenko was a tough lad, but perhaps not tough enough to survive the windblast of an ejection at near-supersonic speed.

Of the remaining two, Captain Bok and Major Zhykov both fell prey to two F-15s, which seemingly appeared out of nowhere. From the outset of hostilities, Ivchenko and the others had been warned against F-15s sneaking in from the west out of their base near Amsterdam. The Americans and their technology were impressive and deadly. Bok and Zhykov were apparently victims of heat-seeking air-to-air missiles, the ones the Americans called, "Sidewinder," after the venomous rattlesnakes of the American desert southwest.

Ivchenko's regimental commander, who had flown with the North Vietnamese against the Americans, had this admonition for his pilots, "Never make the mistake of underestimating the Americans. I have seen them fly in combat and fought against them. The bastards are vicious and they're relentless. They are superbly trained and they do not scare easily, if at all. Their equipment is first-rate. Make no mistake, *tovarishi*, they are the best-trained air force in the world, and their NATO goons are almost as good."

His thoughts jumped back to the predicament from which he had just extricated himself. With Bok and Zhykov down, that left him as the sole remaining prey for the two Americans. At first, Ivchenko attempted to throw the F-15s off by maneuvering violently from left to right. As he slammed the control stick against his left thigh, he tensed his legs and abdominal muscles and strained against the g-forces to keep from losing consciousness. The aircraft shuddered under the g-loads of such violent maneuvering. Looking to his right and visually clearing the airspace in that direction, he slammed the stick against his right thigh and stayed on his anti-g straining. His vision went to grey, but he didn't black-out completely. He also knew he couldn't keep it up, indefinitely. No pilot could. Breathing was difficult under the strain and sounded more like a series of grunts.

He was limited in his ability to maneuver vertically by his close proximity to the ground. The F-15 pilots, obviously skilled and very experienced, weren't fooled by any of his hard, horizontal turns. They effortlessly matched him, turn for turn.

Ivchenko realized that he wasn't going to have the opportunity to strike any targets with his bombs and jettisoned them along with his external fuel tanks. He felt his sleek fighter lurch upward slightly and forward as the bombs fell away. He double-checked the variable geometry wings to ensure they were swept fully back, in order to make a high-speed dash for the safety of his aerodrome. His MiG-27M, codenamed "Flogger-J" by the capitalist forces, was meant to operate at blistering speeds. With no external stores hanging from the wings creating an enormous amount of parasitic drag, the MiG-27 could go like a scalded dog with the wings swept fully aft.

As Ivchenko zipped along over the treetops, oblivious to the world blurring by, he kept his focus well out ahead of his aircraft, looking for the now-familiar landmarks that would lead him home. Yet, he was horrified by the realization that the F-15s were having no difficulty at all keeping pace with him, even at his speed of 1,500 kilometers per hour, roughly 700 miles per hour, to the Americans' way of measuring.

While his MiG-27 was a single-engine aircraft, albeit with an enormous, very powerful engine, the F-15s were each powered by two of the magnificent Pratt & Whitney F-100 engines. Ivchenko knew he wasn't going to outrun them and had no idea what his salvation would be, if there was to be any salvation at all. The capitalist jackals were obviously stalking their prey, and perhaps having a radio discussion about who would shoot and be credited with the kill.

With a fleeting sense of awe, he watched over his shoulder and in his rearview mirror as they responded to his maneuvering. Whatever hard turn he tried didn't work. He wasn't going to throw them off or cause them to overshoot because they were too well rehearsed for that. The F-15s would maneuver side to side, over and under each other with each of his moves, bobbing and weaving like some great boxer and with the ease and grace of a pair of Bolshoi Ballet dancers. This American element leader and his wingman had flown together for too long to be fooled by any of his tricks.

Ivchencko didn't relish the thought of being a statistic or a trophy in some American fighter squadron's ready-room. The bastards should just shoot and be done with it, instead of toying with him in such a manner, which seemed pointless and even a bit cruel. Maybe they were following him home to what would undoubtedly be a target-rich environment for them. Realizing he had about five minutes of fuel left at this speed and that he had about the same time to reach home, Ivchenko felt his chances growing slimmer by the kilometer.

Then, it happened. The F-15s simply broke contact and headed west. As he glanced at them in his rearview mirrors and returned his gaze forward, he saw it: the aerodrome.

He'd made it home, once again. The F-15s were gone, suddenly and unexpectedly. Without a doubt and to a dead certainty, they'd had him boxed in, ready to pounce for the kill. Of that, Ivchenko was quite certain. The F-15s were now headed west in what appeared to be full afterburner, from the brief glimpse of them he got in his mirrors. Their exhaust nozzles glowed an angry orange as they sped away.

As to why they broke off the engagement, Ivchenko dared not hazard a guess, but was glad to be rid of the bastards. Their reasons for breaking contact didn't matter. He'd lived to fight another day, and there *would* be another day. NATO forces were far from beaten and they certainly weren't going to surrender, regardless of the talk and rumors being circulated by his unit's political officer. That talk was bravado and nothing more. He knew his fighter regiment and scores of others were going to be bled white, if not out of existence completely, by the time this was over.

Ivchenko pulled his throttle back and fanned his speed brakes to slow his aircraft. Turning onto a wide left downwind leg, swept the wings fully forward to sixteen degrees, lowered the wheels, retracted the ventral fin, and configured the wing flaps and leading-edge slats for slow-speed flight and landing. He felt like a man with a new lease on life.

"Happy birthday, Artyom Vladimirovich," he said joyously aloud to himself.

Although it was indeed his chronological birthday, he also meant it in the abstract sense that he didn't die and that he would live at least a little while longer. Tomorrow, or perhaps even later today, he would doubtless face the NATO pilots, again, but nevertheless thought it would be a shame to die on his birthday.

As he rolled wings-level on his final approach, he noticed nothing unusual on the aerodrome, aside from the sparse number of aircraft caused by combat attrition. He could see the anti-aircraft automatic weapons positions at the approach-end of the runway, as well as at the departure-end and several other spots on the field. Several aircraft were taxiing out for takeoff, while others were undoubtedly taxiing in after landing from other ground-attack missions. Maintenance crews were busy refueling, repairing, and preparing aircraft for new sorties at various points around the field.

Ivchenko slowed and flared his aircraft, causing it to settle smoothly onto the runway. He'd always enjoyed flying the MiG-27. It was easy to handle in the hands of an experienced, competent pilot, and he was both. By the time he reached midfield on the runway, he had slowed to a suitable taxi speed and applied right rudder to turn onto the midfield taxiway. He knew the December air would be brisk, but for all the sweating he had just done, he felt the cool-down would be refreshing. He would need it, before debriefing his commander on how Major Zhykov, Bok, and Vlasenko had met their respective ends. He was already dreading that most unpleasant of duties.

After the marshaller had directed him to his parking spot, he shut down the engine, completed the last of his checklist items, disconnected his oxygen, communication, and g-suit connections, then exited the aircraft and climbed down the ladder the crew chief had attached to the aircraft. Ivchenko hurriedly debriefed the maintenance crew on the status of his aircraft, which needed nothing other than to be rearmed and refueled. Once he had unzipped his flying coveralls and relieved himself in the grass, he then sat down on an empty bomb trolley and lit a cigarette to steady his nerves, before going to debrief his commander.

He hurriedly smoked his first cigarette and quickly lit another. As he smoked, he pondered which pilots he would join for the next combat sortie of the day. The numbers and faces in the squadron were dwindling. The losses of Zhykov, Bok, and Vlasenko left nine, assuming no one else had failed to return in the interim. In a day or so, unless replacement pilots and aircraft arrived, his squadron would effectively cease to exist.

He took the last drag off his cigarette and thumped it off into the dirt behind the parking apron. He gave thought to going for a shit, but thought it might be a bit of a struggle, given the scant breakfast he had eaten. It was then he noticed it: a ripple in the air, which he didn't have time to comprehend. The sonic boom had not yet arrived. Not that it would have made any difference at all. Fate had on just given him a loan on his life. Now, it had already come to collect on the debt. Yet, in the immediate post-mission euphoria of having survived another combat with the Dark Forces, Ivchenko remained mercifully unaware of what was happening.

At one-thousand feet of altitude, directly above the midpoint of the runway, a white flash eradicated everything on the aerodrome. In time that could be measured in billionths of a second, Captain Artyom Ivchenko and his aircraft were atomized, as was everything else on the field. Everything within the weapon's burn radius was incinerated or atomized and the blast radius, even bigger, destroyed much of what existed within a four-kilometer radius of the *Mayerstettin* aerodrome.

Witzok, German Democratic Republic

The Old Cemetery

December 4, 1982

Udo Lehmann lit a cigarette, stood before a copse of trees, and watched the thin stream of refugees move along the highway that ran through the narrow, shallow valley below him. Where did these people think they were going? The fighting was away to the West and the only vestige of it he'd seen was the previous day when a pair of what he took to be two British aircraft roaring low across the aerodrome at very high speed. The split-second violence of the war suddenly manifested itself as the British jets released what looked to be flares and he saw white smoke trails of what were evidently missiles streaking from the aerodrome on the far side of the trees. The decoys seemed to have fooled the missiles and the automatic weapons had been brought to bear a second too late. Because the British jets dropped no bombs and fired no missiles, he surmised they were merely performing a reconnaissance.

He and his ten-year-old granddaughter, Heike, had just strolled back from town through the old cemetery, where she enjoyed reading the names and dates on the headstones. In her early school years, when she was learning her numbers, they made a game of selecting a section of cemetery on each of their weekly treks, and had her determine which grave was the oldest. Sometimes, she was tasked with determining the newest. On several occasions, he made her write down the dates of death, or birth, and then take them home, add them together, and determine the average year of death or birth. She also learned how to determine how old a person was when they died, based on dates of birth and death.

When these mathematical games ceased to be a challenge for her, she decided to simply pay Herr Schmidt a visit as part of their weekly trips to town. Herr Schmidt's was the oldest grave in the cemetery. He old gentleman had died in 1732 at the age of eighty-six. In the spring and summer, she would pick flowers for him, as she did for her *Oma*, her grandmother, who was also interred there. *Oma* had passed away due to breast cancer, five years previously.

In the fall, she would collect brightly colored fallen leaves for Herr Schmidt. She knew that her *Opa,* her grandfather, loved the fall foliage and surmised that Herr Schmidt must have in his day, as well. But, winter was here and the brilliant oranges, reds, yellows, and browns of *Herbst* had all been swept away on the wind, leaving Uschi with nothing now for Herr Schmidt but a pleasant, verbal greeting and an occasional sweet song.

They had crossed the old, stone bridge over the creek, which ran perpendicular to the road out across the downward-sloping field, and crested the knoll, where they paused for Udo to light his cigarette. Overlooking the field and the highway, the knoll offered him a chance to look over his fields in the afternoon light. They lay along the far side of the highway, and offered a glimpse of the Soviet aerodrome on the far side of the trees, not quite three kilometers distant. Normally, he and Heike didn't go town in the afternoons; mornings, usually. Today, however, she insisted on an afternoon stroll and he was all too happy to oblige.

Udo lived in the small, wooded area across the way, as had his family for over a century and a half. The family had owned enough land for a fair-sized vegetable and wheat farm and, although the government officially took possession of it after the Communists established their government in the Soviet zone of occupation, they allowed him to continue living there, contingent upon the agreement that he provide vegetables to the Soviet troops operating from the aerodrome, for which they paid him surprisingly well.

Weather permitting, he and Heike would take time out of their week and walk to the south side of *Witzok,* where they would window-shop and he would buy her a treat from the confectioner, which was still privately owned. She loved the hard, lemon candies.

Though Udo shared the old family home with his son, Horst, and his daughter-in-law, Jutta, it was the time he spent with Heike that he enjoyed and cherished the most. When she beamed that pretty smile and looked up at him with those beautiful, blue eyes, he felt only waves of delight. She was active, precocious, and seemed to ask a million questions a day, eager to learn about everything that caught her eye, ear, or spurred her imagination.

Conversely, both Horst and Jutta were true products of German-Stalinist Communism: hard-working, stoic, unquestioning, and unimaginative. They played their cards very close to the vest, as far as political opinions went, and Udo thought that prudent. It was best just to lower one's head, lean into it, and get on about the business of life. He was the same way, though he still seemed to see the joys in everyday life they couldn't. He remembered what life was like before the Communists, even back to those heady days of the rise of the Nazis and the brief return of prosperity to Germany. His earnestly hoped Heike wouldn't lose those better parts of herself as she grew older and more aware of life in this "workers' paradise."

Udo also hoped that this war would bring about the end of the *Deutsche Demokratische Republik* as he knew it. It was a frightening proposition in many ways, but one he knew to be morally correct. Perhaps then, he could either escape with this family to the West, or the West would come to them. The DDR certainly didn't seem like much of a country, as it was run by dour, humorless bureaucrats, who were guided by the tiresome Marxist dogma heaped on them by their Soviet overlords. Much of the time, they squabbled amongst themselves and behaved like a pack of petulant ten-year-olds. Germans in the West didn't seem to consider it a proper country. They simply called it *Die Ostzone,* the East Zone, which was nothing more than a sock-puppet government totally under the heel of the Soviet jackboot.

Glimpsing his fields and the Soviet aerodrome, he surmised *why* these people might be leaving, even if their destinations, collectively or individually, remained a mystery. If the NATO forces were able to turn the tables in this contest, their aircraft and maybe even their ground-forces would arrive, and they were likely to be very angry, though he hoped civilians wouldn't bear the brunt of that wrath. From what he'd seen of Americans during the last war, he was confident that wouldn't be the case. Perhaps those two jets he'd seen twenty-four hours ago were a harbinger of things to come. Of course, he had heard the noise of the comings and goings of the Soviet jets to and from the front, but had yet to see any enemy activity over the airfield, until yesterday.

He supposed these people along the highway just wanted to put as much distance between the fighting and themselves as possible. There weren't many of them; a few lorries and even fewer cars. Most of these people were on foot, carrying what extra clothing and provisions they could on their backs or pushing them along in barrows.

Udo always took the small, worn footpath through the cemetery and across the fields to his house at the edge of the woods on this way home from his part-time job at the garage. He enjoyed the exercise and always paused atop this little knoll to have a smoke, look over his fields, and watch whatever activity was happening in the valley below. He liked this place, particularly in the fall, because of the glorious leaves and the refreshing, brisk air. It was simply beautiful and the air here still smelled clean.

Behind him, Udo heard Heike carrying on a one-way conversation with Herr Schmitt's gravestone and turned around to face her. As he did so, a bright, white flash, brighter than anything he had ever witnessed, lit the sky behind him. So bright, he could see the bones in his right hand as he raised his cigarette to his mouth.

"Opa! Was war das," Heike exclaimed, the alarm in her voice quite evident, as shielded her eyes with her hands.

Next, he heard the "thunder." When he turned back around, he could see it off to the southwest: a massive mushroom cloud boiling up over the horizon from the direction of *Mayerstettin,* the old, Prussian city twenty kilometers distant. The rate at which the mushroom grew in height was astounding. The cap of the enormous mushroom had a pinkish tint, at first, which roiled and churned with marbled colors of red, orange, yellow, and then turned to black, as it grew. It was a monstrous, obscene thing that Udo knew instinctively had just spelled the complete destruction of the aerodrome and a good portion of *Mayerstettin,* as well. He'd been there often enough to sell what surplus vegetables he could to the Soviet cooks at the aerodrome and to enjoy a picnic lunch of sausage, bread, and wine with his wife on the shores of the picturesque lake there. So, things had come to the unimaginable, after all.

Udo became instantly alarmed by the thought that if the NATO forces had just struck the aerodrome at *Mayerstettin,* they would very likely strike the one adjacent to his farm, as well. The *Witzok* aerodrome was sure to be on the NATO target list. He held out his hand and screamed for Heike, who was now shrieking with terror, to come to him. He intended to take shelter under the stone bridge, which, being on the near side of a small ridge, might provide them some protection from was about to come. He had no other options.

Udo scurried under the bridge and shouted again for Heike to come to him and she took three uncertain steps in the direction of his voice. The flash that followed was exponentially brighter than the one at *Mayerstettin.* The overpressure from the blast knocked Udo face-down in the creek under the bridge. Physical things in nature seek equilibrium, and the creek water was no exception, which turned instantly to steam; not steam from the spout of a teapot rumbling atop a stove, but steam from a heat source equal to the core temperature of the sun.

Udo was burned horribly from his face to his feet. He tried to scream, but only managed a garbled shriek from the burned tissue of his tongue and throat, as the heat wave rushed over and past the bridge, igniting everything, as it went. He was knocked back into the now empty creek bed when the air came roaring back into the vacuum that had been caused by the overpressure of the horrific blast.

He lay on his back for several minutes, stunned and unable to muster a coherent thought. Realizing he must check on Heike, he managed to lift himself onto his hands and knees, grunting against the worst pain imaginable, as he did so. Standing up, he thought his sleeves and pants had been torn and had fallen past his fingertips and down around his ankles. Udo didn't realize he was completely naked and that the "cloth" dangling past his fingertips and bunched around his ankles was actually the burnt skin of his arms and legs. He was in pain to the point of oblivion and the cold, December air now nipping at his naked muscles didn't even register in his brain.

He tried calling for Heike, but found he couldn't form the words. Turning around in a complete circle, could see flames everywhere. His fields were burning, as was the wooded area where he lived, only the trees were gone and no trace was left his house or barn. Horst and Gisela were gone forever, as well. They had stayed home to have some time to themselves.

Even his beloved copse of trees near the stone bridge was gone, as if it had never existed at all. Most of the gravestones were gone; others overturned, shattered, and scorched. The rubble on the entire south side of *Witzok* was ablaze.

A minute or so passed and he began to regain his senses, though only marginally. He again attempted to call Heike's name and again found himself unable. Heike was gone, he realized, with no traces to be found. Though he was still alive, he sat down and wondered, through his moments of fleeting lucidity, when the radiation poisoning from the fallout would take him. He didn't have to wait very long. The swollen, horribly burned flesh in his mouth, esophagus, and sinuses killed him in a matter of minutes.

33. "For Everybody Who Missed Sunrise..."

Pale Horse 3

Overhead North Sea

Return Leg

If the adrenaline was still coursing through Stumpy's veins, it wasn't evident as he said over the interphone, "Crew, standby for first detonation in five...four...three...two...one..."

Outlaw noticed nothing at all, and he was the only one on the crew with a window. The PLZT goggles functioned precisely as they were supposed to and he saw no bright flash. The flash was evident to the remainder of the crew, even with Stumpy and Banjo occupying the dark, lower deck. Four more flashes illuminated the crew compartment in rapid succession, without benefit of Stumpy counting them down.

True to form, Stumpy said dryly, "The kick is *up* and it's *good!*"

No one responded and the quiet of interphone sounded cavernous. They knew he was correct, in the sense that five of the seven Soviet targets they had come to destroy were no longer in existence, but they each knew untold thousands had also been consumed by the infernos.

Outlaw knew that, at some point, the moral purgatory aspect of it all would begin to wear on Banjo; being part and parcel to a homicide, only to enable him to take part in what he would inevitably view as murder on an industrial scale. He took everything too seriously; even that black-and-gold Z-28 Camaro he constantly babied. Outlaw just hoped the fretting wouldn't begin until he had them back on the ground and Banjo got to see his wife, again. She always seemed to have the ability to quell his morose spells.

Pale Horse 3 flew on for another minute in complete crew silence, only to have it broken by Burnt-the-Fuck-Up, who, now somewhat more composed, announced over the interphone, "For everybody who missed sunrise, stand by for a time-hack."

Outlawed laughed inside his oxygen mask at the gallows humor and rationalized that if there was ever a place and time for it, it was here and now. After all, stokes was at the apex of an extreme adrenaline rush and not dwelling on the five nuclear detonations that had just destroyed parts of East Germany. He had just destroyed a MiG-25 and that was the stuff of tail gunner dreams.

Outlaw keyed his interphone switch and said, "Crew, oxygen-and-station checks. Verify that we do or don't have any EMP damage. The good news is that the engines are still runnin' and we haven't fallen out of the sky, so maybe this so-called 'hardening' against EMP stuff worked."

A quick look around the flight deck told Outlaw that the engines were all good. He took a long look down to his right at the AC-generator panel and ensured that the generators on engines 1, 3, 5, and 7 were still on-line and had not failed or otherwise become isolated from the main AC power bus. Everything looked normal with the electrical system.

He was optimistic that all systems were normal until Stokes reported in, "Co, Gunner; the AFSATCOM's down. I'm resettin' some circuit breakers and tryin' to get it back. I got a post-strike report I gotta format and send."

"Roger, guns. Do whatcha can," Outlaw responded.

Outlaw asked Banjo, "Nav, what true airspeed do you need?"

"Gimme all you can, right now, Co. Mach-mach. I'll update you when we get away from this shitty situation," Banjo responded.

"Mach-mach" was an inside joke between the two that simply meant, "As fast as this thing'll go."

Outlaw reached to advance the throttles, but reminded himself they were already at .84-mach.

Outlaw's easy feeling ended abruptly when a red light in his left field of vision grabbed his attention. He also noticed the "Master Caution" light to the left of the throttle quadrant, which he reached for and pushed, which extinguished it, until the systems detected another malfunction of some sort, in which case it would illuminate, again, alerting him to another problem.

Fire-warning light. #7 Engine.

He hadn't noticed any problems with it, until now, other than the gash in the intake cowling and the lower access panel missing, but it made sense that some piece of metal, however small, had been ingested with the glancing missile blow. His emergency procedures training, going back to the T-37 and T-38, and extended to the B-52, told him to take stock of the situation before grabbing and snatching at things in the cockpit during a potential emergency situation.

"Maintain aircraft control" was the first thing to do in such a circumstance. With that in mind, he made sure the bomber was wings-level, on heading, on the airspeed Banjo had ordered, with an appropriate throttle setting, and on altitude.

The second step with an aircraft emergency was to *"analyze the situation."* Now, he could deal with the fire warning light. He confirmed fluctuating fuel flow on the #7 fuel flow gauge. The #7 exhaust gas temperature gauge was out of limits on the high end. He could also feel engine vibrations and surges, causing him to glance at the RPM gauge to see the needle bouncing up and down, along with a fuel flow indicator doing the same. All of these conditions confirmed an engine fire and necessitated a shutdown.

Once the situation was analyzed, the third step was to *"take the appropriate action."* The section of the Dash-1 that dealt with this type of emergency procedure, specifically "Engine Fire or Overheat," had the main steps in the drill set in boldface type:

THROTTLE(S) – CLOSED
FIRE SHUTOFF SWITCH(ES) – PULL (IF REQUIRED)

Before actually performing the "boldface" drill, as it was known, Outlaw told the others, "Crew, I have a fire indication on number-seven engine, confirmed, and I'm shuttin' it down. If you need to, get in your manuals and which of your systems, if any, will be degraded when the number-seven generator drops off."

"Defense copies," Stokes responded and Stumpy did likewise for the nav team.

The throttles, with their lozenge-shaped, grey knobs, were each clearly labeled with the engine number. Outlaw carefully placed his left hand on the "7" throttle and once again confirmed the errant #7 engine indications. He then smoothly retarded the throttle to "idle" and pulled the knob up and over the detent, closing it, and watched as the needles on all #7's instruments ran to "zero." Next, he reached up with his left hand and pulled the #7 fire shutoff switch. As the engine RPM dwindled, the fire warning light went out. Outlaw then pressed the bulb to test that the electrical circuit was still intact, in case there were any further problems. The bulb lit up, indicating that the fire detection circuit and the bulb itself were still intact.

"Crew, number-seven is shut down and the fire circuit tests good. I'm gonna try to reconnect George before I get into the Dash-1 for the cleanup items on the engine fire," Outlaw informed them.

With his left hand, he reached down to the center console and re-engaged the autopilot switch. George engaged for three or four seconds, then disengaged with a mild thump. He initially thought better of it, but decided to try it one more time, due to no other reason they were going to have to cross a great deal of open ocean to get back home. George disconnected, again. He would have to wait until all of the Dash-1 items related to the engine fire had been addressed before checking circuit breakers and other items related to the autopilot. He knew he was going to need to trim the aircraft perfectly for the brief periods of hands-off flying he would need to do, before doing his cleanup items in the Dash-1.

"Crew, Copilot; George ain't respondin'. Looks like I'm gonna have to hand-fly this big bitch all the way home…well, for a while, anyway. Last time I checked, we're still a little skinny on the fuel curve, but we can get the extra we need from the tanker.

"We still have seven good engines, battle damage on the number-four engine pod, an in-op AFSATCOM, and some sort of damage to the aft fuselage. We can put this thing down somewhere in England or go back home. I wanna hear from each of you what you think we should do; England or home," Outlaw told them.

Stokes spoke first, "Gunner's Code-One, Co. I got enough ammo left for a couple more bursts, if the boogeyman comes back. System's good, except for the AFSATCOM. I can help you with position reports on the HF radio, if you got your hands full and need me to. I can keep workin' the problem with the AFSATCOM. If I can get it back, I'll just get the position info from Banjo and make those position reports on AFSATCOM. That'll take some of the load off ya. I say we go home."

"Roger, guns."

Henry Chinchilla spoke next, "E-dub's still good. The magic-show's still workin'. Let's go home."

Stumpy added simply, "Home."

"Home it is," Outlaw responded.

Then, harkening back to his T-37 instructor pilot, he set about the most basic set of tasks pilots needed to perform, emergency situations or not: *aviate, navigate,* and *communicate.* For now, he could nail down the 'aviate' aspect of it all.

34. "Murphy's a Prick"

Pale Horse 3
Overhead the North Atlantic
Return Leg

After nearly three-and-a-half hours of hand flying, Outlaw felt his shoulders beginning to knot and the strain of it all was beginning to wear on him. For the entire crew, sleep had been a fleeting and precious commodity since the start of hostilities and the squadron recall. Although there had indeed been time to rest, crew dogs, for the most part, had not been able to shut down their minds from the stress and worry of it all.

Pale Horse 3 was approaching the twelve-hour point on the mission clock and Outlaw was carrying the whole load on the flight deck by himself. He'd trimmed both the spoilers and stabilizers to the point that the aircraft would remain stable, if he had to momentarily divert his attention to flight engineer duties, making slight changes to the trim as the gross weight changed from the fuel burn. The rudder hadn't required anything more than minimal trim to compensate for the asymmetric thrust condition created by the loss of the #7 engine and #8 running at idle power.

In keeping with the old military axiom, "hope for the best and plan for the absolute worst," his biggest, unspoken concern was any unpredicted increase in the jet stream velocity which might put the aircraft in a disadvantageous headwind situation, necessitating an over-water bailout, assuming the tanker didn't make the rendezvous. That, he reasoned, was the worst case scenario.

Beyond that, returning to Spurlin and finding it below weather minimums for a safe precision, instrument approach and landing may very well result in an overland bailout. He was an astute enough copilot to do the "head math" and realize they wouldn't have fuel enough to divert, either to the nearest base in Canada or other SAC bases farther east or south in the CONUS, should the tanker not show. As unappealing as the idea of arriving over the "home 'drome" with dry tanks might be, it was infinitely preferable to an overwater bailout. All one could do was say some "Hail Marys" and hope

213

Fortune smiled; and, of course, hope the troops in the weather shop were "on the money" with their forecasts. He'd taken the time to get out the performance manual section of his Dash-1 and compute the maximum range airspeed he should be flying for the aircraft's current gross weight; that is, the airspeed which would prove the most fuel-efficient and take them the farthest. Pale Horse 3 could make it, but with only by a precarious margin.

The crew had been relatively quiet for the last two hours, save for the oxygen-and-station checks and the occasional checklist items and responses required of the nav team, downstairs. Outlaw assumed they were all consumed, as was he, about the magnitude of what they'd just done and the stark terror of the encounters with the MiG-25s. They all knew they were extremely lucky to be alive, at this point, given that the Soviets seemed to know they were coming.

Stokes at last broke the long period of relative silence with a bit of good news.

"Crew, Gunner;" he told them, "looks like I got the AFSATCOM back. I guess the gremlin in charge of fuckin' with it went to lunch or somethin'. Co, I can help with those position reports, now. Banjo can just write down the lat-longs and I'll send 'em out for ya."

"Roger, Guns," Banjo responded. "I'll hand 'em up to you every ten degrees of longitude. I'm sure Mother SAC is dyin' to hear from us, but I assume they've gotten the news from Europe, already."

"Gunner, Copilot," Outlaw said. "When the SATCOM came back up, did you have any messages about what's goin' on, like maybe we hit our targets and this whole thing's over or World War III's in full-swing?"

"Nothin', yet, Co. I'll let you know if I get message traffic."

"Roger, Guns. I'm monitorin' HF, which don't seem to be workin' worth a damn, as usual, as well as UHF, and I've heard nothin'," Outlaw added.

Shortly after Stokes made the announcement that he'd sent the first of his position reports, Outlaw's attention was drawn to a yellow glow to his left: The Master Caution light, again. He leaned to his left and stretched to push and reset it and it only took a second for him to spot the problem on the hydraulic systems panel. The light was on for the #1 rudder and elevator hydraulic system and the auxiliary pump light was glowing, as well. The unseen microscopic hole in the hydraulic line from the missile propellant explosion could no longer contain the pressure in the plumbing and the hole had enlarged, causing a leak.

He told the crew, "Ladies and gentlemen, this is your captain speakin'. I just wanted to let y'all know that we consider it a pleasure to have Colonel Murphy flyin' with us, today."

Downstairs, Stumpy and Banjo simply looked at each other and shrugged, as if to say, "What now?"

Upstairs, Henry Chinchilla and Stokes both looked over their shoulders to the flight deck, attempting to determine what Outlaw meant by his sardonic remark. He was referring to the axiom of "Murphy's Law," which states, "If anything can go wrong, it will."

He was also sarcastically referring to the idea that some mission-ready crew dogs, who flew on a regular basis, didn't particularly care to fly with some colonels, who usually only got enough "stick time" to remain dangerous. In the case of their current wing king, Colonel Rogers, he required what they called a "seeing-eye major" IP in the right seat to keep him out of trouble.

"Colonel Murphy, huh? That guy's a prick. What did he fuck-up, this time?" Stokes asked.

"Looks like the #1 rudder and elevator hydraulic system has gone on the fritz," Outlaw said, as he alternately applied right and left foot pressure to the rudder pedals, before initiating a series of gentle climbs and descents to confirm he still had control-authority with pitch and yaw.

"Crew," he added, "looks like the systems we have left are workin' okay. I still have rudder and elevator authority and everything feels right. We should be okay, assumin' Colonel Murphy don't turn into a complete asshole. In a second, here, I'm gettin' into the Dash-1 and reviewin' the section on rudder and elevator hydraulic systems failure."

He was familiar with it almost to the point he could almost quote it, but wisely and properly thought to read through it, anyway. He knew he would be in the vicinity of a gross weight of 230,000 pounds by the time they were overhead Spurlin. Should things take a turn for the worse and the #2 system failed, he knew to a certainty he wasn't going to be able to put the aircraft safely on the ground by himself. In their required, periodic emergency procedures simulators, he and McQuagg hadn't been able to get one down safely. Ivanoff had gotten one on the ground, with Outlaw operating the throttles, but the simulator technology wasn't advanced enough for them to know whether anyone would've walked away from it. Thus, doing it himself wasn't a realistic possibility, given the fact that one engine was shut down, another on the same pod operating at idle power, and unknown damage to the rear fuselage. If the remaining system failed, he felt that he could maintain level flight long enough to get the crew over land for a bailout, however. So he hoped.

Soviet Krivac-Class Missile Frigate, *"Istomin"*
700 Miles East of Nova Scotia, North Atlantic
December 4, 1982

Captain Second Rank Vitaly Petrovich Gorshkov was not breathing any sighs of relief, even though the American ships appeared to have ceased hostile activity and broken contact. He would only stand easy when he read a message from the Monchegorsk Naval Command Center ordering the *Istomin* to stand down and return to port. Thusfar, nothing of the sort had been forthcoming.

Given that the American navy had broken contact, was it safe to assume the threat from U.S. air assets would now be minimalized or nonexistent, as well? Because of the battle damage to his communications center, there was no way of knowing. Nevertheless, he thought it prudent, given the perceived odds now against him, to set a course and limp directly for home, employing evasive maneuvers only as necessary.

The *Istomin* had, of course, come under fire and taken a beating from U.S. aircraft and surface vessels, and, in addition to casualties and damage in the communications center, had sustained casualties and somewhat less damage to its fire control center, which directed the 4K33 OSA-M surface-to-air missile batteries; all at a cost of four sailors killed and another twelve wounded. None of the other vessels in his small task force had been so fortunate. All were now resting on the bottom of the Atlantic, with their few survivors dead or dying of hypothermia while clinging to what bits of wreckage remained afloat.

He had only realized *coup* plotters had been the ones responsible for the outbreak of hostilities when he set his course for home and Lieutenant Zaporozhets, the political officer, informed him of that fact. With the aid of the naval exchange officer from the Democratic People's Republic of Korea, the militantly communist Lieutenant Commander Shin Chung-ho, Zaporozhets directed the captain to sustain combat operations in their assigned patrol sector of the Atlantic, rather than return to Murmansk.

Gorshkov had refused the order from Zaporozhets and the mutiny was short-lived. None of the crew had sided with the political officer and both Zaporozhets and Shin were quickly subdued at gunpoint. Gorshkov forthwith shot the haughty North Korean in the forehead with his sidearm, but Zaporozhets had wriggled free from the sailors' grasp, bolted from the bridge, and jumped overboard. Gorshkov immediately decided against a "man overboard" drill and gladly resigned him to his frigid fate. Shin's body was tossed overboard, as well. He wasn't going to regret being rid of his obnoxious guest from the Korean People's Navy one bit.

In the combat action report he was duty-bound to compose, the political officer and his liaison would simply be mentioned as "killed by hostile action, buried at sea." Before composing his report, however, he must first see to the soundness of his ship and the status of his sailors.

Gorshkov found himself relieved to be rid of Zaporozhets and his unending blather of political dogma, often parroted *ad nauseum* by the haughty North Korean. Gorshkov considered himself a loyal Russian and a dependable, capable naval officer, but decidedly not a Communist Party hack. There would be time to put that story together, later, back in port.

Picking up the handset on his wall, he contacted the communications center for a status report. The news he received was disheartening: the *Istomin* still did not have any sort of radio communications ability, given the damage, though his remaining, unwounded specialists were actively working the problem and responded they might well restore radio capability within the next two or three hours.

Gorshkov next requested a status report from his fire control center. The news here was better, though only marginally.

"Comrade Captain," his fire control officer reported, "our main missile fire control computer is operational, but persists in locking itself into 'automatic' mode, each time we attempt to reset it to 'manual' mode. While we may be able to defend ourselves against air attacks, our surface radar has been damaged beyond repair. We are completely blind to surface threats, sir. Our sonar arrays are still operational and we can still defend ourselves against submarine threats."

"Understood. If there is some sort of ceasefire in place, do you think you will be able to prevent the system from launching on any NATO aircraft transiting overhead? We do not wish to advertise our presence or make any unnecessary trouble for ourselves," Gorshkov admonished.

"Est, Comrade Captain," the fire control officer responded, "but we still should maintain the ability to defend ourselves. Perhaps not all of the Americans or their friends will be inclined to give us safe passage back to port. Our problem, as we see it, is that the system may well launch on NATO aircraft on its own, if we have no means of reverting to manual control."

"Understood," Gorshkov replied, "Just take all measures necessary to ensure it operates normally."

He then hung the handset back in its cradle and went to his basin to wash his face and clean his teeth. This war had been brief, but had seemed like it lasted for months and he was weary.

Pale Horse 3

Approaching Neptune Anchor Refueling Track

Overhead North Atlantic

December 4, 1982

"Crew, Radar," Stumpy told them, "I have naval surface contacts south of our air refueling track between thirty and forty miles, headed north-northeast. The contacts appear to be a Navy surface battle group."

"Roger, Radar," Outlaw answered, "You see anything else out there?"

"Affirmative, Co. One surface contact right in the middle of our AR track. It seems to be heading east-northeast."

Henry Chinchilla added, "That checks, crew. That's one of our battle groups to the south, but a hostile contact at our twelve o'clock along the AR track. Their SAM radar comes up for ten or so seconds, then breaks lock and goes down. It's very intermittent. I'm showing no other hostile signals at all."

"I still have chaff and flares. There's also a Navy P-3 in the area. Just heard 'em talking to the battle group on #2 UHF, and they're aware of the single surface contact. If we have a problem, those guys might be able to solve it for us."

Burnt-the-Fuck-Up added, "I still got enough ammo for a coupla squirts. We pass close enough, I can hose 'em off at the boat. I've heard tales of other gunners shootin' at whales on live-fire exercises. Might be easy enough to hit a ship."

"Roger, Gunner," Outlaw responded, "Everybody, stay on your toes. All we gotta do is sneak in there, get our gas, and then haul ass home."

35. "Break Away!"

Pale Horse 3

Neptune Anchor Refueling Track

December 4, 1982

The air refueling checklist was complete. The slipway doors on the dorsal side of the aircraft, aft of the cockpit, were open, the lights on the air refueling control panel were good, and Outlaw had his fuel panel set to receive the gas. The flight plan called for a 30,000-pound on-load, roughly 4,600 gallons, which would give Pale Horse 3 an extra measure of fuel to get home safely and enough for diversion to another nearby base, though only marginally, if needed. As soon as he could clean up the post air-refueling checklist items, he was going to put Henry Chinchilla to work on obtaining current and forecast weather conditions at Spurlin, if Spurlin still existed.

The join-up with the KC-10 "Extender" tanker had been accomplished in complete radio-silence, even though they could use the UHF radio, if need be. A quick check of the #1 UHF overhead on the radio panel confirmed he had proper frequency set. Stumpy, Banjo, and the inertial navigation system, the INS, of the KC-10, which had no human navigator, had the point-parallel rendezvous timed perfectly, enabling the "flying gas station" to roll out of its 180^0 turn exactly one-half mile in front of and one-thousand feet above Pale Horse 3. Outlaw could just see the outline of the KC-10 in the darkness, running with minimal lights on.

He remembered something Ivanoff told him, the first time he'd been behind the Air Force version of the enormous version of the McDonnell-Douglas DC-10 airliner, "Taking gas from a KC-10 presents a much different picture in the windows than the KC-135. He's so big, you're gonna feel like you're standin' on your tail, only you're not. It's just a matter of payin' attention to the director lights and then seeing what your window picture looks like when you're in the center of the refuelin' envelope."

As he approached the "contact" position behind the tanker, he felt his pulse quicken. He'd done enough AR with Ivanoff to feel comfortable behind the KC-135, but he and Ivanoff had only been behind KC-10s twice; once in daylight and once in twilight, but never at night. Nevertheless, he felt up to the task. Subsequent to shooting McQuagg, he'd gotten them in and out of the target area and almost all the way back across the Atlantic. So far, so good.

Still adhering to radio-silent procedure he stabilized the bomber below and behind the KC-10 in what he estimated the "pre-contact" position behind the tanker to be, then added power to close into the "contact" position. As soon as he sensed forward motion, relative to the tanker, he pulled off half the power he'd added and slid easily into the contact position. With a slight "thunk," he heard the refueling boom mate with receptacle, just aft of the flight deck. A quick glance out of the corner of his eye at the refueling light on the eyebrow panel showed green, meaning he was in fully mated with the tanker and ready to receive fuel.

Before the boom operator could began pumping gas, Henry Chinchilla's voice lit up the interphone, "I have uplink! SAM-launch! Dispensin' flares and chaff!"

Outlaw immediately pushed the air-refueling disconnect button on his control yoke and pulled the throttles to idle. He saw the "boomer" retract the probe and "fly" it up toward the stowed position under the tanker's empennage.

Pushing the yoke forward, the bomber immediately began to fall away from the tanker, as he keyed his radio microphone switch and transmitted, "Break away! Break away! Break away! SAM launch! SAM launch!"

Satisfied he was safely below the tanker and still in a descent, he initiated a steep left turn with the yoke and rudder pedals.

Henry Chinchilla's voice came back over the interphone, "Still jammin'! Brace for impact!"

Burnt-the-Fuck-Up instantly decided he wasn't bracing for anything. As the bomber descended, he was able to acquire a radar return on the surface contact and opened fire with the stinger. He intended to go down swinging, if he was going down, and knew the hitting power of the .50s would, at the very least, make life unpleasant aboard the ship for a brief second or two. Ideally, he would catch some Soviet sailors out on deck.

As the tanker grew smaller in Outlaw's right-side windows, he rolled wings-level as he continued to the descent at idle power. Henry Chinchilla was still employing his countermeasures, when the thought ran through his mind that the missile might indeed miss Pale Horse 3 and guide on the tanker, which had no electronic countermeasures capability at all. It was literally just a flying gas station and completely vulnerable to whatever threats were deployed against it.

As soon as he began applying back-pressure and adding power to level-off, the KC-10 exploded in a bright orange ball of flame a sparks. He knew no one aboard had survived.

Henry Chinchilla announced, "I've lost uplink, crew."

Outlaw responded, "Roger that, E-Dub. Missile hit the tanker. Nav, mark this position so we can forward it to whatever air-sea rescue forces we can get out here, but it ain't lookin' good."

Soviet Missile-Frigate, *"Istomin"*

From vantage point on the damaged bridge of the frigate, Captain Gorshkov was both fascinated with and horrified by the huge explosion he'd just witnessed overhead. He had no way of knowing what type of aircraft had been hit, or even if it was hostile, which he assumed to be the case.

Picking up the handset at his station, he queried the fire-control center, "What just happened? Why did you fire?"

The sailor replied, "The system launched on its own, Captain. We have no idea what we just shot down. We still are unable to manually command the fire control system."

"Well, kill electrical power to it, before we meet our end," were the last words he said as the first AGM-84 "Harpoon" fired from the U.S. Navy P-3 patrol aircraft hit the bridge, right below his feet.

The second and third Harpoons, RGM-84s fired from the U.S. carrier battle group, sank the *Istomin* in less than two minutes.

36. "A Wing and a Prayer"

609th Bombardment Squadron

Operations Office

December 4, 1982

Major McClellan mashed the butt of yet another cigarette in his ashtray. The last fifteen minutes had been quiet and he was glad for the brief respite. Command post had already received reports from SAC and USAFE that five nuclear detonations had been observed in the Pale Horse 3 target area. However, there had been no strike report forthcoming from the Pale Horse crew.

Shortly after the fifth detonation, Soviet units inside West Germany began disengaging and heading back east. Some battered and nearly nonexistent units even surrendered in-place to whatever NATO forces were in front of them, but the Pale Horse crew, if they were still alive and airborne, might well not know that.

Five detonations; not seven. That bothered McClellan, for it meant two missiles were either duds or had fallen victim to propellant cracks and never made it to their targets. Perhaps those two had been shot down by Soviet SAMs. That possibility still existed. The more ominous thought remained that the crew and aircraft had been destroyed by naval or land-based SAMs or taken out by fighter-interceptors before they had a chance to launch all seven missiles. At this point, all possibilities were still up in the air, figuratively and literally. Surely, word would have filtered back from the British air traffic control system, or perhaps the AWACS net, that Pale Horse 3 was on its return leg. There were also no reports from any NATO maritime assets indicating a B-52 had been seen going down in the North Sea or anywhere else.

With one crew out on a nuke strike, McClellan had begun his day thinking that it couldn't get any worse. The Soviet sappers, operating on the eastern side of the airfield, proved that it could. He was still fielding sporadic reports from the Spurlin security forces that a sapper had gotten within two hundred feet of the Alpha alert birds before being engaged with small arms and heavy automatic weapons fire. The SPs had taken casualties, along with some maintenance troops, but none of his crew dogs.

Mark Tolbert came into Major Mac's office for no other reason than to finish his cup of coffee and cigarette. As McClellan slid his ashtray across his desk to Tolbert, his telephone rang, startling them both from their thoughts.

"Six-oh-ninth Bomb Squadron, Major McClellan speaking. This is a secure line," he said tersely, after putting the receiver to his ear.

"Major, this is Sergeant Albritton at command post."

"Whaddaya have for me, Sergeant?"

"Sir, we just had a SKYBIRD contact from Pale Horse Three over the AFSATCOM. They're gonna make it back, sir. They're about two hours out and they confirm they are 'Winchester' status. They launched all their missiles, sir. However, they have one fatality aboard: Captain McQuagg. The copilot says they have some battle damage and one engine inoperative. The two left rudder-and-elevator hydraulic systems are out, but the other two, they say, are running fine.

"Major, they report their tanker was shot down by a SAM before they had the chance to take on any gas, so they're gonna be flyin' on fumes when they get back. They need somebody to come up and give 'em the once-over on the battle damage, sir. We should hear from 'em again, as soon as they get within UHF range. Alpha and Charlie are here at the command post and they need you and Lieutenant Colonel Spraggins over here, right away."

"We're on our way," McClellan blurted as hung-up the phone and sprang from his chair.

"The kid's flyin' 'em back in. They're two hours out. McQuagg's dead, battle damage, and they're low on gas. A wing and prayer. I gotta go," he told Tolbert, as he grabbed his parka and fur cap off the coat rack behind his chair.

He then bolted out the door and turned left for the Old Man's office.

He leaned into the office and said, "We gotta get to the CP, boss. The Pale Horse bird is headed back. I'll brief you on the way over."

Spraggins, who himself had not slept in the last forty-eight hours and had nodded off at his desk, was startled at McClellan's entrance.

"Okay," he said, blinking himself awake, "let's go. Good news, for a change!"

As they walked out to the staff car, the Old Man asked, "How're you holdin' up, Mac? It's been a while since you slept."

"I'm good, so long as there's coffee to be had. You had much of a chance to close your eyes?"

"I nodded off mid-cigarette. If you hadn't come in when you did, I would've burnt some fingers."

The Wing-King, DO, the Old Man, and Major Mac stood in a tight circle inside the command post and assessed the situation.

"They have some battle damage and they need us to have a look," Colonel Lopez said, "We can't send a BUFF up to do it. Could we send up a one-oh-six?"

The colonel was referring to the Maine Air National Guard F-106 Delta Dart fighter-interceptor squadron, which was also based at Spurlin.

"I'd rather not, sir," the Old Man said. "Those Six-drivers don't know much about our airplanes and wouldn't even know what to look for."

"How 'bout we send up a Tweet from the ACE Detachment?" Major Mac asked.

"How," the Old Man wanted to know, "All of our bomber copilots are on alert, right now, and all the ACE-qualified tanker copilots are either on alert or deployed for REFORGER."

"Sure, boss," Major Mac answered, "but the T-37 IPs *aren't*. Neither are we."

"Are those IPs even at work, right now?" the wing-king asked.

"Yes, sir. They're pretty much been in all along, doin' what they can, helpin' transient crews flight plan, that sort of stuff," Major Mac answered.

"If we can get one of their birds up quick enough, who wants to go with 'em?" the wing-commander, Colonel Rogers, asked.

"I'll go," Major McClellan said emphatically.

"Okay, Mac," Colonel Lopez, interjected, "I'll have Life Support send over your helmet, mask, some water wings, and a survival-vest. The ACE Life Support guys'll get you fitted for a 'chute. See which one of the Tweet IPs is up for it. You still remember how to bail out of a Tweet, right Mac?"

"I'm not plannin' on bailin' out, Colonel. My boys are up there, and I intend to get 'em down on the ground safe and me and the Tweet driver along with 'em."

Lieutenant Colonel Spraggins added, "I thought, they were *my* boys."

"You can have 'em back, when we get 'em back on the ground, Boss.

"Based on the fuel state Lieutenant Lawless called in, they should have enough to stay in the holding pattern for ten or fifteen minutes, before they really need to put it on the deck. We'll meet 'em at five thousand feet, over the VORTAC, just to keep 'em above any remaining mischief the bad guys out there in the woods might have left up their sleeves. By the time they're overhead, we won't have enough daylight to look 'em over. I can grab a flashlight from the OMS guys; one of those big ones. I'll figure out a way to use it without blinding the pilot. At least, we know from the physiological incident a while back that the kid can land the thing. He was heavyweight, then, but he's running on fumes, now," Mac told him.

"Mac, you'll run the risk of blinding the Tweet driver with that flashlight," Colonel Rogers added.

"You're right, Colonel. Say, is that T-38 from Garriott still here; the one their Wing Commander and another IP flew up here to visit the ACE Detachment?"

The DO, Colonel Lopez, answered, "Yeah. They got stuck here, when the trouble started and SCATANA was implemented. They were at Base Ops just a few minutes ago. The captain that came with him can take you up in the backseat of the '38. That solves the night vision problem with the flashlight. I'll contact Transient Alert and make sure they're gassed and ready to fly."

"Fine by me, Colonel," McClellan said, "Let's get airborne."

Office of Special Investigations
Spurlin Air Force Base
December 4, 1982

Since her conversation with Mark Tolbert nearly fifteen hours earlier, Bergen Cyr had been a bundle of nerves and wasn't handling Outlaw's potential death well. She'd sat at her desk, fidgeting and chain-smoking, for the last two hours. She'd tried to nap on one of the cots in the back room, but couldn't sleep. Twice, her boss had told her to go to quarters and get some rest, but, she refused.

Special Agent Simpson was in the back asleep on one of the four cots kept there. Even though the office was quiet, the phone ringing didn't startle her. Somehow, she expected it and picked up the receiver.

"Office of Special Investigations, Special Agent Cyr speaking. This is a secure line. How can I help you?" she asked in a disinterested tone.

"Bergen, Mark."

"Yes," she replied, unsure of what bad news, if any, was to follow.

"Listen," he said, "The strike bird just made contact with the command post. They're on their way back in with one fatality aboard."

Before she or Tolbert could say anything further, she dropped the receiver on her desk, reached down for her wastebasket, held it up to her face, and retched into it. The sound of it made Tolbert feel queasy, even on the other end of the line. After she was done, she picked up the receiver, again.

"Jeez, Bergen, are you alright?" Tolbert asked.

Tolbert could hear her choking back a sob, which, to her credit, she managed to do.

"Bergen, listen," he implored, "It's not Dillon. He's flyin' the jet. McQuagg is the fatality. Nobody else is even hurt. The word is they have some battle damage, but nothin' he can't get back down on the ground. Outlaw's a damned good pilot."

"Are you bullshitting me, Tolbert?" she asked. "Because I swear by all that's holy I'll feed your balls to the first bear I see, if you are."

"I was sitting in Major Mac's office when he got the call, Berg; just a few minutes ago."

"Oh, good," she said, composing herself somewhat. "I think I can relax and get a little rest now."

"You do that. I'll call you if I hear anything else. If you need me, call. I'm at the bomb squadron, okay?"

"Thanks, Mark."

She hung-up and really didn't feel like sleeping, when she gave the idea a second thought.

37. "The Once-Over"

Pale Horse 3

Overhead the Spurlin AFB VORTAC

5,000' Altitude

December 4, 1982

Join-up with the T-38, Garry 11, had been simple. Rather than the Boston Center controller, they had used one of the Spurlin Approach Control UHF frequencies and the controller had vectored the little trainer right to the lumbering B-52 at five thousand feet and 250 knots. The T-38 could handle that safely at five-thousand feet with partial flaps. The T-38 was a bit mushy at that speed in a clean configuration, but still flyable. It was an aircraft built for speed and typically maneuvered at 300-450 KIAS. Airspeeds below 250 KIAS were more of a sporting proposition. Nevertheless, Major Mac was enjoying the ride. It felt good to be in the "White Rocket," again, even if it was a backseat ride. Most UPT students fell in love with the T-38 the first time they flew it. McClellan had been no different.

Outlaw looked out his right windows and saw the formation lights of the little, white trainer at what he guessed to be about a hundred feet off his right wingtip.

"Pale Horse Three, GarryOne-One," McClellan transmitted, "what's your situation?"

"GarryOne-One, number-seven engine is shut-down. Missile glanced off the cowling, but I don't think it detonated. I had fire indications. Number-eight runs a little rough when I add power, but no fire light. It's runnin' fine at idle. I'll keep it runnin', just in case.

"Other than that, number-one rudder and elevator hydraulic pump is down. So is AUX pump number-one and both lights are on. Number-two main pump and AUX pump are good. No yellow lights. Pitch and yaw response is normal. Minimum sweat."

"Minimum sweat," McClellan thought to himself, "This kid's smooth."

Both Outlaw and McClellan knew that, while the situation wasn't optimal, it was certainly manageable and Outlaw possessed the piloting skills to pull this off. But, "minimum sweat" indicated there was still *some* sweat.

"What's your fuel status, Pale Horse Three?" McClellan asked.

"Borderline critical," Outlaw answered, "I'm gonna need you to gimme a quick look, then I gotta put this bird on the ground, Major."

"Roger, Pale Horse Three," McClellan responded, "are we cleared in?"

"Borderline critical," the Major thought, "This kid ain't gonna let any of us see him squirm."

Not "critical;" just "borderline." No admission from Outlaw that he might just have his hands full.

"Affirmative, Garry One-One. You're cleared in to my right wing."

The T-38 IP applied slight left and forward pressure to his control stick, careful to add just a touch of throttle he did so, to keep from falling behind the bomber. He was careful to dip well under the bomber's right wingtip to avoid the strong vortex it was generating. It was a vortex large and strong enough to flip a small aircraft like the T-38 and send it tumbling completely out of control.

Once established and stable under the bomber's number-four engine pod, McClellan looked up at the number-seven engine, which was almost completely exposed. The access panel, which normally dropped down and to the left for maintenance, was gone. He could see some wiring and plumbing that appeared sooty. Also visible was the disfigured cowling on the front. Lucky bastards. Had that missile been a solid hit or had the warhead detonated that close, it would have destroyed both engines and likely caused the separation of the left wing at the point of the engine pylon. Pale Horse 3 would now be just so much wreckage on the bottom of the North Sea.

"Bill Boeing built himself a hell of an airplane," McClellan said to the T-38 IP, who agreed with the notion.

"Pale Horse Three, I don't see any damage to your number-eight engine. Number-seven has no access panel and your fire indications were correct. No other damage to your wing. It's your call, but I'd recommend you fly it in no-flap, just to be on the safe side."

Outlaw and every other student learned early on in pilot training that structural damage was truly a wild card in the deck of manned flight. Aircraft are designed to exacting aerodynamic standards and any change to the manufactured profiles and geometry of airfoils and airframes could produce alarming and often uncontrollable situations. Wing flaps were a special case in point. They learned that if there was damage to a wing, particularly where a flap was concerned, to leave the damned things alone and make a no-flap approach and landing.

Outlaw was apprehensive at about the idea flying a no-flap approach. It was a maneuver he had practiced some, though not to a level of comfort, with Ivanoff as an IP, and one at which most other co-pilots had no experience at all and weren't even required to show proficiency, as far as training-requirements went.

Major McClellan's voice interrupted Outlaw's thought process, "Okay, Pale Horse Three, we're gonna slip back, have a look at your aft fuselage and tail, then your left wing."

Fortunately, the IP in the front seat had voiced no complaints at all about the big flashlight Major Mac was using in the backseat. The decision to use the T-38, instead of the side-by-side seat T-37, had been the correct one.

"Roger, GarryOne-One. You're cleared aft," Outlaw acknowledged.

As the T-38 driver reduced power and the little trainer moved aft, in relation to the bomber, McClellan could see no damage to the aft portion of the right side of the fuselage in the glare of his flashlight. Once established under the tail, he discerned a wide streak of what he thought to be pinkish fluid smeared along the underside of the fuselage and tail, aft of a panel. Hydraulic fluid, as attested to by the #1 rudder-and-elevator hydraulic system being bled dry.

As the T-38 pilot backed out and then moved forward, Major McClellan became alarmed. He was looking at the aft portion of the fuselage. The vertical fin and the left horizontal stabilizer appeared to have been peppered with shrapnel.

Disregarding proper radio procedure, McClellan said, "Outlaw, you're streaming hydraulic fluid and it looks like you mighta bled that number-one system dry. Sheet metal damage to your fin and left stabilizer, but your elevators both look good. Left wing looks good, too. No damage there. Did you guys get hit by a missile back here?"

"Uncertain, Major."

"Roger," McClellan added, "if you're not havin' any control issues, it's *your* call on how you wanna get down. How's your stabilizer trim?"

"Trim's good. We're light on gas. I'm gonna pull number-one and two back to idle and fly a four-engine approach, no-flap, with airbrakes position two, since we're unsure of what, if any, damage exists to the wings or flaps. I don't wanna run this thing outta gas, flying' with those barn doors down, if I don't need to."

"Roger, Pale Horse Three. Just remember, she's aerodynamically clean and light, so power increases need to be slight and you're gonna be flyin' down final approach in the landing attitude. So, no big end-swap to flare and touch down. Light as you are, you shouldn't have any trouble stopping. When we launched, the runway was dry; no ice."

McClellan knew the kid was obviously in control of his situation. Besides, he'd managed to get the damned thing all the way across the Atlantic and back, battle damage and all. The aircraft flew just fine when lightweight and on four engines. Any BUFF instructor pilot knew that. So did Outlaw, who'd practiced it both in the simulator and in the airplane with Ivanoff. He knew how the aircraft would handle, absent any major structural damage issues.

"Garry One-One is clearin' off. Good luck and we'll see you on the ground."

"Roger, GarryOne-One. Perrier's on me. See ya at the bar."

Major McClellan smiled at the Perrier remark. The kid had a breezy, smartass quality to him that he genuinely liked.

38. "Hurtin' Status"

Pale Horse 3
ILS Final Approach, Runway 01
Spurlin Air Force Base, Maine
December 4, 1982

With a sense of relief and satisfaction, Outlaw heard the "clunk" of the landing gear as the four main "trucks" locked into position. Glancing over at the landing gear position indicator panel, he confirmed that the four main trucks and the two-wing tip gear were indeed "down and locked." He then peered over to the hydraulic panel and confirmed that pumps 1, 2, and 3 were "in the green" and putting out normal pressure. The remaining rudder-and-elevator hydraulic pump was still operating normally, as evidenced by the lack of illuminated warning lights.

After being given the once-over by Major Mac, he'd taken radar vectors from Spurlin Approach Control on the descent onto a fifteen-mile final approach, which would give him time to configure the aircraft and ensure it was "flyin' right," as his father had often said. He'd already tuned in the proper frequency and intercepted the localizer radio beam, which would give him course guidance all the way to landing. The aircraft was wings-level, on airspeed, and at the appropriate altitude for glideslope intercept.

He had already declared an emergency with Spurlin Approach Control, advising them he had battle damage and a fatality aboard, which would give the firetrucks and other emergency response vehicles time to position themselves on various cross-taxiways along the runway. After the touched down, he knew some of those vehicles would follow him until he stopped straight ahead or cleared the active runway.

Outlaw wasn't running any checklist *per se,* but was glancing periodically at the instrument approach diagram strapped to his left thigh. He and Ivanoff had practiced this very scenario nearly every time they were planned for "transition;" that is, to practice instrument approaches and repeated touch-and-go landings.

Ivanoff once told him emphatically, "In a combat situation, you may very well have to fly home by yourself. It happened during Linebacker II over Hanoi and it happened almost daily during World War II. Things may get to the point that controlling the airplane and reading the 'before landing' checklist in a jet this big and complex may be too much to handle. Know what you need to do to get the bird on the ground."

And Outlaw knew instinctively: landing gear, flaps, airbrakes, and a "best flare" speed, computed from the plastic ring around the fuel totalizer gauge, which combined the total of all fuel remaining in each of the tanks. Only this time, there would be no flaps and airbrakes in Position 2. From that best flare speed, he knew to add indicated airspeed to that and fly that computed airspeed down final approach, once he intercepted the ILS glideslope. In weather, or even when it was clear, he would have both course and glideslope information, displayed by steering bars, right in front of his face on the attitude director-indicator, the ADI, all the way to touchdown.

Spurlin Approach Control had already directed him to contact Spurlin Tower and, realizing he was seconds from glideslope intercept, he checked his airspeed, moved the airbrake lever to position two and adjusted his throttle settings.

At ILS glideslope intercept, he lowered the nose of the aircraft slightly, reduced power to maintain his computed final approach airspeed. He was flying this one on four engines and things appeared just fine. Position 2 was smoother and easier, he decided, even given the extremely light gross weight caused by the low fuel state.

Despite his "borderline critical" remark to Major Mac regarding his fuel state, the needles were now dropping low enough on the individual main tank gauges to make him uneasy. The fuel totalizer needle was creeping down toward dangerous levels, as well. He expected to see a "MAIN TANK" light illuminate yellow at any second, indicating he was dangerously low on fuel. Outlaw knew he had to get his bird on the ground quickly, because there wasn't enough fuel for a missed approach and a trip around the pattern for another attempt.

The ACE detachment commander, a captain, former KC-135 pilot, and Oklahoma good-ol' boy Outlaw had first met during his UPT days at Garriott, had once made the remark, "Any time you see any sort of fuel low-level light come on, that qualifies as 'hurtin' status.'"

As the thought crossed his mind, Outlaw certainly didn't disagree with the notion, but knew that if a MAIN TANK light illuminated, things might rapidly escalate to "hurtin' for certain," should he be forced to abort this landing for any reason.

As the steering bar floating down from the top of his attitude director-indicator, indicating he was rapidly approaching the precision instrument glideslope, Outlaw adjusted his throttle settings for the descent and transmitted over the #1 UHF radio, "Spurlin Tower, Pale Horse Three is on the glideslope, gear down, with an emergency."

"Pale Horse Three Heavy, wind is three-six-zero at five. Emergency vehicles are rolling. You're cleared to land, runway zero-one" the tower controller said.

"Roger. Pale Horse Three Heavy, cleared to land, runway zero-one," Outlaw confirmed, as pilots always did.

Although Outlaw was now through a ragged deck of broken clouds and on instruments, he felt good about it and did his wiggle in the parachute harness, just as he always did, when things looked right for a landing. He was on course and glideslope, on airspeed, and the aircraft was properly trimmed and configured for landing. He had broken out on the bottom of the broken cloud layer at 2,000 feet and had the runway in sight. Given what his crew had endured for the last fourteen hours, things couldn't get much better, even though he knew they could always get worse.

Captain Lieutenant Beloglasov heard the bomber approaching. Straining through the pain in his left shoulder from the bullet wound and not being able to stand, he nonetheless willed himself to sit upright and see it approach. He'd gone as far as he could on foot and was completely surprised that two American Rangers walked right by him, less than twenty feet away. Then again, he was Spetsnaz, and fully capable of concealing himself, even from other elite troops.

Having heard automatic weapons to the north, earlier, he surmised that the forces sweeping down from north of the aerodrome and from the south had caught his remaining men in a pincer from which they likely wouldn't emerge. Nevertheless, he knew his men would put up a stiff fight, but he also knew they were in America, now, and would certainly be outnumbered and at an extreme firepower disadvantage.

The automatic weapons fire to the north was slackening, now, telling him that most of his team had likely been killed. He knew his fate was sealed, just not the moment at which he would meet it. Beloglazov shouldered the *Strela* launcher and tracked the huge bomber through the sights. As it passed overhead, the he thumbed the safety to "Off" and squeezed the trigger, unleashing the SAM in a shower of sparks, flame, and smoke, though he knew only a stroke of luck would guide the missile to its target, given its proximity, altitude, and the treetops which might impede its flight. Almost simultaneously, a 5.56-millimeter round from a Ranger's M-16 tore through his neck, severing his spinal cord and killing him instantly.

Though Beloglasov didn't see it, the Ranger sergeant did and was able to see the missile streak away through the treetops and, its infrared seeker head unable to lock onto the engines' heat signature, strike the tail of the B-52, which kept flying. The sergeant cursed himself aloud for not having spotted the Russian a minute and a half earlier, which he'd passed that position.

39. "The Only Real Emergency"

ILS Final Approach to Runway 01

Spurlin Air Force Base, Maine

December 4, 1982

Through all his hours of emergency procedures training and simulated emergencies, both in the flight simulators and aircraft through his pilot training days, CCTS at Castle Air Force Base, and even at Spurlin, Outlaw had always kept in mind one thing his first T-38 IP, an F-4E Phantom pilot, had told him, "No matter what's wrong with your aircraft, when it comes time to get out and walk home, there's only one *real* emergency, and that's if the seat don't eject."

That thought had flashed through Outlaw's mind, at some point, during every subsequent aircraft sortie and simulator session. At the end of the day, he realized, it was sound advice.

The bang was surprisingly loud and jarring when the missile struck the empennage right where the right horizontal stabilizer met the fuselage. The impact was severe enough to momentarily knock Outlaw's hand from the right horn of his control yoke. Regaining control, he immediately advanced the throttles and pulled back on the yoke. An instant of panic ensued when he realized the elevators were jammed in a downward position, causing the nose of the aircraft to lower.

He added more power and moved the airbrake lever to Position 4. The nose began to rise and he noticed the radar altimeter winding up past the 400-foot mark, which would give Stumpy and Banjo the altitude they needed for their downward-ejecting seats. *"Thank God"*, he thought, for the "pendulum effect" of those engines, mounted as they were on pylons below and slightly forward of the wing leading edges. With no elevator authority, the throttles and airbrakes were the only pitch control he had left.

The runway lay straight ahead, but there was no longer any prospect of a safe landing on it. He steered the big bomber to the right and was instantly relieved to see he still had lateral control. The spoilers on the wings still worked and the aircraft was now on a trajectory to pass between the runway and "bomb dump" east of the field.

As the radar altimeter needle passed the 600-foot mark, he reached down with his left hand to the center console, lifted the red safety cover, and flipped the switch for the "bail out" light. Instantly, he heard a bang as Banjo's hatch blew away from the belly of the aircraft, then a very loud whoosh as his seat fired. Then, nothing, for what seemed like an eternity. He was almost surprised when he heard another bang and whoosh. Henry Chinchilla. Another. Burnt-the-Fuck-Up. And then, one more. Stumpy. They'd all done it in order, in accordance with Dash-1 procedures.

It was now Outlaw's turn. He made sure the aircraft was tracking between the runway and the bomb dump and then, for reasons he could never fully explain, pulled the throttles to idle. He then assumed the correct posture, sitting erect with his head against the headrest, heels against the base of the seat, rotated the yellow arming levers on the front of his armrests, which exposed the triggers, and then squeezed with both hands.

There was no warping of time, as he'd heard some pilots describe after an ejection. Within a few seconds, the automatic opening feature of his system had him swinging beneath a fully-deployed parachute canopy. Outlaw knew there were trees, and plenty of them, between the runway and the bomb dump, but the darkness precluded him from having a good look at his landing area. So he prepared for a "tree landing," making sure his feet and knees were together, to help prevent the possibility of a tree limb puncturing a femoral artery on the way down. He also remembered to discard his oxygen mask, left his clear helmet visor down, and placed his hands over the lower part of his face to protect it from the trees. Operating now on instinct and adrenaline, the only thing he could clearly remember before the back of his head struck a limb and knocked him unconscious was gunfire on the ground, which he fervently hoped wasn't being aimed at him.

His next memory, a blurry one, was that of being nudged very lightly on the chest.

A voice from the darkness asked, "You okay, buddy?"

Completely disoriented by the blow to the head, Outlaw was unsure of his surroundings, but still cognizant of the gunfire he'd heard on the way down and answered, "Lawless, Dillon J., First Lieutenant, United States Air Force, zero-five-three-one-seven-nine-nine. Date of birth 1 March 1957."

Per his resistance training during Aircrew Survival School, he'd answered with the Big Four: name, rank, service number, and date of birth, all he was required to give under the Code of Conduct. The "Big Four and Nothing More."

The voice answered, "No need for any of that, Lieutenant. You're home, sir. Sergeant Newman, Echo Company, 2nd Battalion, 75th Rangers."

"Who was shootin'?" Outlaw asked.

"Lots of us, sir. Russians were attackin' the airfield. Took us most of the day, but we think we killed 'em all, by now. Hell of a fight, there for a while. We came up from the south. A Delta team came down from the north."

Through his mental fog, Outlaw remembered something about a Russian in a bar, but couldn't grasp the totality of the thought.

"You hurt, Lieutenant?"

"Dunno. Haven't tried to move anything yet."

"Well, don't try…"

"Ahhh! Jeez, that hurts!"

"Don't move, sir. I'll get you a medic."

"Okay."

"Mediiiic! Hey, Doc, we need ya over here," the sergeant called through the darkness.

"How bad you hurtin', sir?"

"I just tried to sit up. Think I dislocated both shoulders. Right elbow hurts like hell, too. Right knee. Hurts to breathe. Think I mighta cracked a rib or two on the way down," Outlaw told him.

"Lemme check, sir. Just be still."

With what little light he had, the sergeant felt along Outlaw's arms and legs. He had a flashlight, but dared not to illuminate it on the chance that all of the Russians hadn't been eliminated. He unzipped Outlaw's flying parka and felt his chest and abdomen for any warm, wet spots that would've indicated blood.

"Yeah, you might've dislocated those shoulders, sir, but it doesn't feel like you broke any bones. Your knee feels like it's dislocated, but I can't feel any breaks in your legs. Can't tell about those ribs, though. It doesn't seem like you're bleedin' anywhere, either. But, best you stay still until the doc comes and we can get you outta here. He'll give you somethin' for the pain."

"I hope he's got something stronger than aspirin," Outlaw told him.

"Yes, sir. *Lots* stronger."

40. "A Darker Power"

Oval Office

The White House

December 7, 1982

"So, that's it, huh?" asked president Harvey as he examined the shiny, silver sphere on his desk, which was no bigger than a ping-pong ball. He was surrounded by the Joint Chiefs, the Directors of both the CIA and DIA, and others. They were examining the core of the small, Soviet "backpack" nuclear weapon.

"Yes, sir. That's it," replied the Director of the CIA, nodding to the Chairman of the Joint Chiefs of Staff.

"And it's not radioactive?" the president asked for reassurance.

"No, sir," replied the Secretary of the Department of Energy, "It has a lead inner core and a stainless-steel outer core, to resemble uranium in terms of weight."

He spun the sphere for the president, and pointed to a very small Cyrillic inscription. President Harvey, who did not speak, read, or write Russian, was puzzled.

"What's that?" he asked.

"Zimin."

"Zimin?" he asked, "What does it mean?"

"It's the name of the man who assembled the weapon aboard that Soviet sub, Mr. President," the CIA Director interjected, "*Sturgeon* caught the damned thing at periscope-depth, presumably at their designated rendezvous point to retrieve the Spetsnaz team in the midget sub. Hard to say, but that's the most plausible explanation, given the location *Sturgeon* encountered it."

"Good," the president said, "my understanding is that were survivors."

"Yes, sir. Fifteen sailors and two officers. All are currently being interrogated and some are still being treated for various medical issues. When we're done with them, they'll either be repatriated or granted asylum, at your discretion. We managed to kill all ten of the Spetsnaz operators."

The president scratched his nose, nodded, and said, "Good. Any takers on the asylum offer?"

"So far, our guess is one of the officers and about eight of the sailors. They seem to think they'll be executed when they get back home, once their higher-ups find out they've been captured and interrogated. They're probably correct in that assumption, Mr. President; no reasons or excuses in their system," the CIA Director offered.

"I see. So much for the fabled dictatorship of the proletariat, huh," the president said.

"What's been done with the Spetsnaz bodies?" the president then asked.

"They were all cremated and disposed of at an undisclosed location, per your orders, Mr. President. No evidence of their presence on U.S. soil exists," the Chairman told him.

"The CNO tells me there's a good chance we'll be able to salvage the wreck of that India, Mr. President. It sank in fairly shallow water. Apparently, the Navy's taken on much more complicated and deeper salvage operations. If we can get a look at some of their code books, cryptology equipment, sonar, and the like, it could be a bit of an intelligence windfall for us," the Director added.

"So, who is this Zimin character?" the president asked, breaking the brief silence.

The CIA Director cracked a smile and responded, "One of theirs that we turned, Mr. President. Valery Ivanovich Zimin was or is a Soviet nuclear weapons engineer who specializes in the design and assembly of these things; specifically, the design of the RA-155. That's the weapon that the Spetsnaz team carried to Spurlin. His father disappeared during one of Stalin's purges, just before the Germans invaded the Soviet Union in 1941. He was never seen again, nor was his family ever informed of his fate. Zimin apparently had a personal axe to grind with the Soviet government.

"We first received word about him a little over three years ago from sources in the Finnish Embassy," the CIA Director explained, "We had one of our operatives in the Murmansk area make contact with him. He worked at the nearby Monchegorsk Naval Command Center, systems-checking these and other Soviet nuclear weapons.

"Monchegorsk is close to Finland and the Finns go to great pains to monitor what goes on there. They surmised Zimin might want to defect to the West and we set that process in motion, but lost contact with him for an extended period. Before we lost contact, we received word, again through the Finns, that he would help us wherever and whenever he could. We thought, initially, he had been exposed and either imprisoned or executed. We can look to this dummy warhead as proof that he wasn't compromised and that he did indeed help us.

"Our guess is that we'll find his body in the wreckage of the sub. But, one thing remains almost a certainty: if someone else had been responsible for the final assembly of that weapon, much of Spurlin Air Force Base would no longer exist and what remained would be unserviceable and uninhabitable. They were *that* close, Mr. President."

President Harvey responded, "That leaves us with the question, gentlemen: Where is the *real* core for that particular weapon?"

"Best case scenario, Mr. President, is that it's on the bottom of the Atlantic with that sub," the CIA Director answered, "or, it may not even have made it aboard that sub at all."

"What if it didn't?"

"Well, let's hope that Zimin was true to his desire to help us and not attempting to sell his know-how and hardware on the international arms black market. After the business with our hostages in Iran, the handwriting on the wall is clear enough to some of us in the intelligence community that there are hostile governments and groups out there with the desire to use just that sort of weapon against a U.S. city. We've received intelligence, not actionable at this point, that some of those weapons have gone missing within the Soviet Union. Until we can pinpoint them, let's hope they don't end up in the hands of extremist kooks, like the group currently running Iran.

"From the behavior we've seen with Islamic terrorists, in the form of hijacked airliners, suicide bombings in Israel, and the slaughter of the Israeli athletes during the '72 Olympics in Munich, we may very well be dealing with a much darker power than the Soviets. It won't be a threat etched across the world stage as clearly or as large as the Soviet threat, Mr. President, but it will come at us unseen, in places and circumstances we may least expect."

"Understood," the President said, "Put the highest priority you can on preventing that, Don, and let's hope we find that core with the sub. Just one less of the damned things to worry about. And while we're at it, maybe we need to take a close look at making sure we have a *proactive,* as opposed to a *reactive* policy toward terrorism.

The president continued, "I'll announce at tomorrow's called Cabinet meeting that I want a top to bottom review of all our existing national response protocols, where terrorism is concerned. I would surmise, even now, that this problem will continue to revisit itself indefinitely upon us and we need to be as thoroughly prepared as we can, gentlemen."

"Mr. President," the CIA Director added, "our HUMINT sources within the Soviet Union tell us that we may not be out of the woods, as far as weapons like the RA-155 are concerned."

"How so?" the president asked.

"Well, Mr. President," the Director continued, "there are two versions of this weapon that we know about: the RA-155 for land use by Soviet ground forces, and the RA-115, which is meant to be detonated under water. The weapon we found was the RA-155.

"We've had reports, vague ones, that some of the RA-155s have been placed inside the CONUS and some of our allied nations. At this juncture, we have no way of knowing how many or where."

"So, what are you telling me, Mr. Director?" the president asked, "Is this a continuing threat to us? Are there other Spetsnaz teams hiding inside our borders, just waiting for orders from the Kremlin to detonate more of these things?"

"The safe and sensible answer, Mr. President, is 'yes;' safe to assume that Spetsnaz, KGB, or GRU operatives put them here, but we haven't uncovered any evidence or specific intelligence that they're actively babysitting the things. From what we've been able to reverse-engineer on the one we found at Spurlin and another one an Army Blue Light team was able to literally steal from East Germany, these things are rendered useless if they sit too long without some sort of external electrical power source."

"So, if Soviet operatives aren't here actively monitoring them, they may just die on their own and we'll never know about them, unless we stumble across them," the president demanded to know.

"Not an assumption we'd want to stake anybody's life on," the Director added, "We do have Agency and NEST assets actively searching for them, based on the intelligence we have. NEST radiation-sensors are being steadily improved. Rest assured, Mr. President, we're not complacent, regarding these types of threats."

"I understand, Mr. Director. Do we have capabilities similar to these two versions of the Soviet weapons?"

"Indeed, we do, Mr. President. We can have a briefing team, comprised of members from the Agency and DoD, at your daily intelligence briefing, tomorrow morning. They will, of course, need to brief you in private. But, I can give you the big-picture view, right now, if you like."

"I'll find it enlightening, no doubt," the president concluded, "We may be entering a period in which the Soviets might pull back their claws and behave themselves for a while, but they can't be trusted; at least, not by *me*. So, you were saying?"

"Yes, Mr. President, we do have our own version of a 'backpack nuke.' We refer to them as SADMs: Special Atomic Demolition Munitions. Ours are smaller and lighter than the Soviet versions, although they're still noticeably heavy. They're the primary responsibility of the Army's 5th Special Forces Group in Europe. The SEALs have them, too, Mr. President.

"Had the war gone on much longer, we may have seen fit to ask you for the authority to use several of them. Our doctrine dictates that once these weapons are in place, they'll be watched until detonation,"

"So, basically," the president interrupted, "the special operators in question would be on a suicide mission. Am I hearing you right?"

The Chairman nearly stumbled over his own words, attempting to answer the president, "Ah…Mr. President, you're correct. We do have volunteers for just such a mission. They know that desperate circumstances would be at play, should such a mission be ordered, but they're willing."

The president cut him off by shaking his head, not wishing to hear more.

Nodding to the Chairman, the president said, "General, I want that briefing, as soon as you can set it up. Like I've said, many times before, I learn somethin' new on this job, every single day."

41. "False Flags and Kangaroo Courts"

Spurlin Air Force Base Hospital

Orthopedic Ward

December 7, 1982

Outlaw awoke in his hospital bed to a tap on his left shoulder. Lieutenant Colonel Spraggins was standing at his bedside. He managed a weak smile through lips that felt cracked. The pain medications dried him out to the point he felt like he had a mouth full of dust.

"I didn't know whether or not to bring flowers," the Old Man said with a wry grin.

"I woulda questioned your manhood, if you did, sir," Outlaw answered.

"Atta boy," Spraggins said, still grinning, "Still fulla piss and vinegar."

"What brings you by, Colonel? I feel like I broke every bone in my body. Even my *hair* hurts."

"Well, since you say you feel like shit, I'll add that you *look* like shit, too. The flight doc said you've got an impressive list of dislocated and sprained stuff and you're scratched all to hell, but he can get you patched up to fly, again."

"That's good news, sir."

"Listen, Dillon, I'm not really supposed to be here, but I'm not gonna leave one of my boys twistin' on the flagpole. You follow me?"

"Yes, sir. How much trouble am I in, Colonel?" Outlaw asked, having only an inkling of where the Old Man might be going with this.

"They don't have SPs posted outside your door, right now, but they're on the floor. How much do you remember about punchin' out of the aircraft?" Spraggins asked.

"I remember comin' down ILS-final and feelin' a jolt and a hearin' bang in the rear of the aircraft. Everything was fine, up until that point. I had the jet all trimmed up and it was flyin' right. Then, all the rudder-and-elevator

243

warnin' lights came on. I lost my two remainin' systems and immediately lost all elevator authority. Felt like they'd jammed and the yoke was stuck.

"I was passin' through 400 feet on the radar altimeter and added power and ran the elevator trim to give Stumpy and Banjo a little more altitude before I hit the bailout light. When I did, I heard four good ejections. After Banjo went out, there was a delay of a few seconds, but I'm not sure how long. Then, all the others punched. I tried to steer the jet east of the field.

"Did everybody make it, Colonel?"

The Old Man winced and shook his head.

"Stokes got on the ground with some bumps, bruises, and scratches. Henry Chinchilla busted his ass pretty good and dislocated his hip. Stumpy wrenched his back and cracked an ankle bone when he landed. They landed right behind a Delta Force team that was sweepin' down on the Russians from the north. Jeff Coley was KIA, Dillon."

The Old Man saw the alarm in Outlaw's eyes.

"How?" he asked, "I heard 'em all punch out when I turned on the bailout light."

"No, no, no, that's not on *you,* Dillon. Banjo got a good 'chute and made a good landin'. The problem was, he landed between the bad guys and a Ranger platoon movin' up from the south.

"You guys got hit by an SA-7 on final-approach. A Spetsnaz team was hightailin' it outta here to the south, tryin' to get away from their bomb, which they didn't know was a dud. I guess one of 'em decided to get in one last lick for Mother Russia, when he heard you comin' down final approach.

"Coley got sandwiched in a firefight between four of those Spetsnaz goons and the Rangers.

"A Ranger lieutenant told us, after the fact, that they heard somebody hollerin' in Russian. Banjo obviously heard it, too, and started firin' his pistol in that direction. He got off all six rounds and apparently zapped one of the bastards in the noggin. Russkies killed him with a grenade while he was reloadin'. Banjo just dropped into a situation he couldn't have foreseen."

Outlaw felt bile rising in throat, but managed to choke it back. In that moment, he fully realized the importance of Mark Tolbert recognizing the Russian in Moggy's Bar.

"Did the jet clear the active runway, sir?"

"Sure did. Crashed in the swamp, northeast of the field. It missed the bomb dump by about a quarter of a mile. We were able to sustain SAC and REFORGER operations on the airfield. We had to clean up all the FOD and trash after the big firefight, which you missed. We had to do another FOD sweep after your bird overflew part of the runway, but we were able to keep goin'. You did good, Outlaw."

"Sir, what's the damage assessment on our targets?"

"You destroyed five out of seven."

"That checks with what I saw, sir. The first PALM never made it past the aircraft. I thought, at the time, that it just didn't light off. I think the second one exploded right under us. It knocked the autopilot off."

"I'd say you're spot-on with that observation. The munitions people are takin' another look at the PALMs to see how pervasive those propellant cracks actually are. My guess is they're a lot worse than SAC thought," the Old Man added.

"Did we get results, sir? Did we win, or is it still goin' on?" Outlaw asked.

"To the extent anybody wins in a war like that? Yeah. Our ground units and USAFE fought like hell. So did NATO; enough to get the point across to Ivan and his gang of criminals that we're in Western Europe to stay, whether the assholes like it or not," Spraggins answered.

"Ivan stood down and began disengagin', just about the time they saw the mushroom clouds go up. You destroyed a good portion of Soviet air and rail assets supportin' their ground forces. Some of their commanders, who didn't think this invasion of Western Europe was such a shit-hot idea from the get-go, decided enough was enough. We even had some satellite evidence that they started fighting' amongst themselves, at that point. Radio traffic we intercepted indicated that some of the higher rankin' officers involved with the invasion were executed by their own troops.

"Washington was finally able to sort out the mess. The Soviets had a *coup*, but it was unsuccessful. It looks like they might well pull out of East Germany. Reports we've been hearing are that they don't want to clean up the mess. The Poles may very well use this as an opportunity to tell Ivan to take a hike, as well. But, who knows? They're restive as hell and this may have given their Solidarity movement some added juice. We'll see.

"Andropov and President Harvey have already issued a statement of mutual agreement to look for ways to avoid this, in the future. Let's hope so, anyway. The Warsaw Pact may well dissolve itself, unless the Soviets can do some mighty fancy talkin'."

"Good. Then, maybe losin' Banjo was worth it. But, I'm not sure that really makes me feel any better," Outlawed said.

"Me, neither," Spraggins added.

Outlaw felt uncomfortable with that line of conversation and changed the subject, "Colonel, somethin's been botherin' me about the whole mission scenario."

"Whaddaya mean?"

"Well, sir, it seemed like they knew we were comin'; a B-52 strike. You know, the MiG-25s bein' stationed so far outside Soviet territory and all."

Colonel Spraggins responded, as he walked to the door and ensured it was closed, "Well, apparently, they *did* know you were comin'. Special Agent Cyr was in on an operation with another government agency, we weren't told which one, but you can guess. Air Force Intel and some counterintelligence people were also in on it. Apparently, a senior NCO in the Vault had good reason to believe that another NCO was making unauthorized copies of documents and sneakin' 'em out. His suspicions were correct. Agent Cyr was brought in to be in on the actual bust. They pinched three people involved in it.

The sergeant in question admitted to giving them the essentials of the Pale Horse plan. Air Force Intel seemed to think that would be the only reason the Soviets would station a MiG-25 unit that close to West Germany and Denmark; a hedge against us launchin' that type of strike. The NCO in question was using that old man who sells fresh lobsters and seafood across from the main gate as his drop. Pretty ballsy move, when you think about it: right under our noses and in plain sight. I'll bet I bought lobsters from that old man a coupla dozen times."

The expression on the Old Man's face then became frosty.

"Look, Outlaw, I just got out of a wing staff meetin'. Apparently, Colonel Rogers is suspicious of McQuagg's death, seein' as how the autopsy showed he died of a bullet wound to the head. Your aircraft hit the ground at a shallow angle, which broke the crew compartment clean off, while the rest of it bounced off a small hill, then tumbled. As low as you were on gas, it didn't make for much of a fire. Anyway, McQuagg's body was recovered intact. That's how they know about the bullet wound.

"I have my suspicions about what you mighta had to do, but I don't know for sure and I don't wanna know; at least, not right now. There'll be plenty of time to debrief it all, later.

"The next thing that's gonna happen is that the wing exec and Colonel Rogers' secretary are gonna come by here and have you dictate your after-action report to 'em. That's his angle. You're all busted up, with one arm wrapped up, the other in a sling, a busted knee, and a million scratches. He says both Headquarters SAC and the Chief of Staff are hollerin' for that report, but I think that's just a ruse. It can wait and everyone knows it, except *you*. He's countin' on your youth and inexperience to get what he wants.

"What he's really aimin' to do, without actually tellin' us as much, is to use that after-action report as your 'statement' at an Article-32 hearing."

Outlaw sat upright and asked, "Article-32?"

"Yeah, Article-32, as in he plans to file some sort of charges against you and maybe your whole crew in McQuagg's death. He's gonna start with you and try to feed you a Big Shit Sandwich. So, when they get here, don't you tell 'em anything. Fake a headache. Fake like you're under some heavy medication and can't remember. Hell, play dead, if you need to. Hang on a sec."

He felt his pulse jump as Spraggins stepped outside the room and returned fifteen seconds later with a major Outlaw did not know and had never seen before.

"Lieutenant Lawless, this is Major Rick Ball, our Area Defense Counsel. He used to be one of us, until he got hurt in a car accident and got himself permanently grounded and went to law school."

Outlaw immediately noticed the senior pilot wings on the chest of the major's service dress tunic.

Major Ball said simply, "Nice to meet you, Lieutenant Lawless."

"I'd shake your hand, Major, but, as you can see, I got nothin' to shake with."

"So I see," said the lawyer, "Okay, Lieutenant, if you want me as your defense counsel in whatever shit storm heads your way, say so, now. I've got a few tricks up my sleeve that I'm pretty sure'll work to your advantage."

"You got the job, Major."

"Good. When they come for your after-action report, you are deaf, dumb, and blind. You are *Sergeant Schultz*. Understand? Your Fifth Amendment right against self-incrimination is fully in play. Do not, under any circumstance, cave to any bullying along the lines 'failure to obey a lawful order' by not telling them anything in regard to this *supposed* after-action report. You just tell them you're invoking your Fifth Amendment right to remain silent.

"They may also try the tactic that because the wing commander isn't part of any law enforcement arm of the Air Force, like OSI, Security Police, or the Judge Advocate General's office, you can go ahead and dictate your report without any fear of criminal liability. That's bullshit and it's exactly what they want to happen. It's basically a 'false flag' maneuver that only a world-class, sneaky sonofabitch would try.

"However, in this case, Colonel Rogers is fully within his authority as the wing commander to act as the convening authority for the Article-32 investigation. I can defend the kind of trick he's pullin' in court, all day long, but, once you start talkin', you're more than likely gonna shoot yourself in the foot. You'll be overwhelmed by the temptation to tell your story and, if you say anything, you may very well lock yourself into a set of facts that I may not be able to walk you out of, at trial. You don't need to tell your story. Let me tell it, as things unfold. That way, we control the narrative and you stay as far away as possible from self-incrimination.

"If they Mirandize you, when they say, 'Anything you say can and will be used against you in a court of law,' they're not kidding. They *mean* it. Don't answer any questions, unless I'm present, and then only when I tell you to and how to phrase your answer. I'll most likely advise you not to answer anything at all. The last thing we'd ever want to do is open a door for the other side to cross-examine at trial. The longer you invoke your Fifth Amendment privilege, the less chance you have of inadvertently talking yourself into the Grey Bar Hotel.

"Invoking the Fifth doesn't mean you're guilty of anything. Every lawyer and judge in the country knows that, too. It's that simple.

"In the meantime, I know every fiber of your being is screamin' to get out of the hospital, but we need to keep you here. We're also keeping Captain Stumpfegger, Captain Chinchilla, and Airman Stokes away from each other, as well. I'll be talking to each of them, later today. What do you think are the chances that their stories will jibe with yours and with each other?"

"One hundred percent, Major. We got nothin' to hide. That's all I'll say in front of Colonel Spraggins, until this is settled and we can debrief it from an operational standpoint," Outlaw answered.

Spraggins nodded and winked at him.

"Keep thinkin' that way, Lieutenant," Major Ball added, "and avoid contact with your fellow crew members. We'll get it sorted out.

"Basically, what you've got with an Article-32 hearing is a commander who is usually trying to get the 'Good Housekeeping Seal of Approval' to bump the whole thing up to felony courts martial and out of his hair. I've seen enough of these things to understand which ones are kangaroo courts commanders use to cover their asses and which ones actually deserve to go to trial. I feel pretty good about this one."

"Roger that, sir," Outlaw replied

"Meanwhile, you get some rest," Spraggins said.

"Thanks for the help, Colonel," Outlaw told him.

"Just keepin' the faith, Outlaw. You crossed an ocean and back to carry out a mission no one else has had to do since 1945. You're the only Air Force pilot on active duty who has flown a live nuke strike; same with the rest of your crew. Suffice it to say that the Air Force considers you a pretty important guy, right now, all this other business with Colonel Rogers aside. *I* certainly consider you important."

42. "Get Out of Jail Free Card"

Spurlin Air Force Base Hospital
Orthopedic Ward
December 7, 1982

The Old Man and Major Ball had been gone only fifteen minutes before Outlaw was again awakened from a light sleep by the faint creaking of door hinges. Peering through the haze of his pain medication, he was surprised to see So-Called Dave standing at his bedside. Outlaw was even more surprised when Dave produced a box of Cuban cigars from the bag he was carrying and placed it on the chair beside the bed.

"Dave," he asked. "To what do I owe the honor?"

"Nothin' to worry about, Lieutenant."

"How'd you know what my favorite brand of cigar was?" Outlaw asked.

"I'm Dave and resourceful in ways you can't begin to imagine."

He then grinned and added, "Actually, I just took the path of least resistance and asked Captain Stumpfegger."

Outlaw nodded and said, "You're quite the guy, Dave, bringin' me a box of contraband stogies here in the hospital. So, whaddaya want?"

"I did a little askin' around and got the go-ahead from various Powers That Be to see if you might be interested in a job opportunity," So-Called Dave told him.

"What kinda job," Outlaw responded.

"Flyin', of course," So-Called Dave answered nonchalantly.

"I already have a flyin' job, Dave."

"Not doin' the kinda flyin' you'd be doin' with my organization," So-Called Dave said.

"And what's the name of *your* organization," Outlaw countered.

"I'm not at liberty to say, right now."

Outlaw pursed his lips and thought before he answered, "If you can't tell me the name of your organization, can you at least tell me what sorta flyin' the job entails?"

250

So-Called Dave didn't even blink before he answered, "The less said here, Lieutenant, the better. But, I'll say that it'll involve an interesting variety of aircraft. We recruit solely from within the ranks of the military; all branches. You don't have to leave the Air Force, in any official sense, but we can arrange that, if you'd want to. I asked Mark Tolbert about you."

"What did he have to say," Outlaw wondered.

So-Called Dave told him, "It turns out that Tolbert and I work for some of the same people and it's his considered opinion that you're one of the finest young pilots he's ever seen. He says you're level-headed, deliberate in most things you say and do, and can keep your mouth shut when you need to. He also says you're not short on the kinda balls we need. Tolbert thinks you're just the kinda guy we could use."

Outlaw wondered if So-Called Dave knew about the Article-32 investigation. In light of the fact that Dave seemed to know everything else that was happening in his world, he was certainly privy to that, as well. What he found interesting was the notion that Dave didn't seem to give a damn about it. If whatever spook show for which So-Called Dave worked wanted him badly enough, he was certain they had a work-around for it.

"I'll tell you what, Dave, I'm gonna have to think this over. You got a number where I can reach you?"

So-Called Dave reached into his jacket pocket and handed Outlaw a business card. It contained no name, no organization's name, and not even a logo. All it contained was a telephone number.

Extending his hand, So-Called Dave said, "I understand, Lieutenant. If you decide to use that number, just ask for 'Dave.' For now, please accept my thanks for what you've already done in the service of our country. We work for different people, but you're a brother in arms, man. Get some rest, heal, and get back in the air, my friend."

Should things go south on him during the Article-32 hearing, Outlaw decided So-Called Dave might just be a good friend to have. The phone number he'd been given sure seemed like his "get out of jail free" card, although Dave had never directly stated such.

Office of Special Investigations

Spurlin Air Force Base, Maine

December 7, 1982

Special Agent Bergen Cyr entered her supervisor's office without knocking and took a sip from her coffee mug before saying anything.

"What's on your mind, Bergen? I've seen that look, before," he said.

"You owe me and I'm calling in the marker," she responded.

He blinked with surprise, peered over his reading glasses, and said, "Well, that's about as blunt a statement as I've ever heard. What marker?"

"The marker for almost getting me killed by sending me under cover in that drug ring operating through Captown and out at the Physical Plant," she countered.

"Oh, yeah, *that.* Fair enough," he said, taking off his reading glasses and rubbing his eyes, "What do I need to do to square accounts?"

"You remember that report the Captown PD forwarded to us from the hospital downtown about five months ago?" she asked.

"Which one?"

"The one Colonel Rogers put the kibosh on," she answered.

"Bergen, I wouldn't go near that one, if I were you," he warned.

"I don't have a choice, Ralph. It's important and we'd both be remiss if we let this one lie. If we don't act, an innocent officer could get burned. Besides, the line Colonel Rogers spouted to us was that the complaint had been dropped and, to his knowledge, was being worked by local authorities. The JAG people saw it as a waste of time, if we weren't gonna get cooperation from the source. Well, that folder hasn't been touched since. If an outside source were indeed working it, I think we would have seen at least one inquiry, by now. Don't you," she said.

"Okay," he replied, "You've always had good instincts, as far as investigations go. What do you need, specifically?"

"I need the case file and I need to know who *you* know, upstream from us on the food chain; as high as you can get."

"My Academy roommate works in the Office of the Chief of Staff. Is that high enough?"

"Actually, that's perfect," she said with a grim smile.

"Is the officer who stands to get burned a friend of yours?"

"You could say that."

"Okay. I'll be right back. Let me go get the file."

When Agent Simpson returned from OSI "vault" with the file in question, he handed it to her and said, "Take it into your office and look it over. Let's meet at 1300 hours and we'll determine a course of action, then. I sure hope this doesn't blow up in our faces."

"I'm willing to take the chance," she answered flatly.

43. "Top of the Food Chain"

Office of the Chief of Staff of the Air Force

The Pentagon

Washington, D.C.

December 8, 1982

"Office of the Chief of Staff, Lieutenant Colonel Holloway speaking, this is a secure line," said the very businesslike voice on the other end.

"Steve, this is Dale," Special Agent Simpson said.

"Hey, buddy," the colonel responded, "I'm guessin' this is business. You've never called me on a secure line, before. Are you still running your OSI spook show up at Spurlin?"

"Sure am."

"What can I do for ya, bud?" Holloway asked.

"I have some priority info for your boss."

"Okay, I'll bite. What's it concerning?"

"Does the phrase 'Pale Horse' mean anything, around there?" Simpson asked.

"Oh, you better believe it does! The general'll be back in the office inside of ten minutes. He's in a meeting just down the hall. I'll have him call you back, as soon as he gets here. Anything with that name on it is a top priority, right now."

"Great. I thought he might like to know this. The point of contact for this particular matter at Spurlin is Special Agent Bergen Cyr. That's spelled charlie-yankee-romeo. She'll brief the general on everything he needs to know."

"He'll be in touch. You can count on that."

"Hey, buddy, I gotta run. There're million things around here that need doing and I'm sure you can guess why. I'll be in D.C., next month. Maybe we can get together and get caught up, then."

Oval Office

The White House

Washington, D.C.

December 8, 1982

The president heard the telephone buzz, left the window from which he was watching the snowfall, walked to his desk, and picked up the receiver.

His secretary told him, "General Hubbard is on the secure line, Mr. President."

"Thank you, Mrs. Peed," the president told her and pushed the button for the secure, encrypted line.

"Sorry to bother you, Mr. President. I hope you're not in the middle of anything you can't put down, right now."

"Not at all, General. It's actually been quiet for the last five minutes or so, which hasn't happened much, lately. What can I do for you?"

"Well, sir. Your orders were to let you know, in the event we found a problem with any of the Pale Horse strike crew. I just received some information from OSI up at Spurlin and we have, in fact, encountered a bit of a speed bump, in that regard."

"Is it a big one?" the president asked.

"Definitely one you want to know about, Mr. President," the general answered.

44. "Witch Hunt"

Conference Room
Wing Headquarters Building
423rd Bombardment Wing (Heavy)
Spurlin Air Force Base, Maine
December 10, 1982

Outlaw and his Defense Counsel, Major Ball, were already seated at the conference table by the time the court recorder had set up her equipment. The representative of the Judge Advocate General, Major Keith Mickley, the military equivalent of a district attorney, and his assistant entered the room and seated themselves. Lieutenant Colonel Spraggins and Major Mac followed and seated themselves along the back wall. Everyone present stood to the position of attention as a colonel Outlaw didn't know entered the room and stood at the far end of the table.

"Seats," the colonel said simply.

When everyone was seated, the colonel addressed the hearing, "These Article-32 proceedings are now open in the matter of *United States versus Lawless*. Ladies and gentlemen, I am Colonel David Elsberry and I am presiding over this Article-32 investigation at the behest of Colonel Dalbert Rogers, Commanding Officer of the 423rd Bombardment Wing. He is the convening authority, in this matter.

"Lieutenant Lawless, we're convened here, today, to determine if there is enough evidence to proceed to felony courts martial in your alleged complicity in the death of Captain Spaulding J. McQuagg. I see you appear to have retained counsel. Is that correct, Lieutenant?'

Outlaw simply nodded, thinking the best course of action would be to say as little as possible.

"Very well, Lieutenant. Is the JAG ready to proceed?" he asked.

"Ready, sir," said Major Mickley.

"Is the defense ready?" Colonel Elsberry asked Major Ball.

"Ready, sir."

As Major Ball again took his seat, Colonel Rogers entered the conference room and took a seat away from the table in one corner. While he was the impetus for this investigation, he couldn't preside over it, as much as he might've wished.

Major Mickley had no idea of the thumb in the eye he was about to receive. Major Ball had not, however, had the time to apprise Outlaw of what was about to transpire. He'd received the call just before stepping out of his office to drive to the wing headquarters building.

The stenographer got up and took a note to Colonel Elsberry, who read it quickly and frowned.

"We'll stand in recess while our stenographer, Mrs. Broome, sets up an alternate machine, due to a malfunction with the existing one."

Before anyone could react to that, an NCO, wearing the dark blue beret of the Air Force Security Police and chevrons on his service dress sleeves that bespoke his position as the Chief Master Sergeant of the Air Force, entered the room and said sternly, "Ladies and gentlemen, the President of the United States."

All present in the room stood to rigid attention, with the exception of Mrs. Broome, who glanced up to see the president, but otherwise continued plugging wires into her new Dictaphone.

President Harvey entered and told everyone to have a seat. He then seated himself at the conference table and the White House Chief of Staff sat beside him. Two men, who were obviously Secret Service agents, entered behind them and stood on either side of the door. Their faces betrayed no emotion or acknowledgement of their surroundings in any way.

The Chief of Staff of the Air Force, General Theodore Hubbard, followed the president and into the conference room. Behind him came the scowling Commander in Chief of the Strategic Air Command, General Thomas Hatcher, and the Commanding General of the 8th Air Force, the dour-looking Lieutenant General Horace Lupold.

Bergen Cyr entered the room with Special Agent Simpson. Outlaw noticed that Bergen, at her business-suited finest, was carrying a box containing documents of some sort. She made only the briefest eye contact with him, as she set the box on the floor, stooped, and retrieved a folder, which she then held at her side.

The wing commander, Colonel Rogers, was flabbergasted by the whole spectacle and stammered, "Uh, Mr. President, what brings you here, sir?"

"I have an interest in these proceedings, Colonel," the president answered without a trace of emotion, approval, or disapproval on his face.

"I see, Mr. President. Begging your pardon, sir, but how did you get on base, without me knowing in advance?"

"I'm the President of the United States, Colonel. I have the aid and services of the entire U.S. Air Force at my disposal. With the assistance of the Secret Service and my White House staff, I can sometimes work what amounts to magic."

"Yes, sir. I understand," the colonel replied sheepishly.

"Colonel, the reason I am here and in the company of these general officers is to inform you that this Article-32 investigation is closed. This whole thing is a sham and you're trying to take down a very competent company grade officer who is, from what I have heard and seen in his training records and check ride results, one very fine pilot. His OERs cast him in the light of an outstanding young officer, as well. His most recent efficiency report was written by none other than Captain Spaulding McQuagg."

"Closed, Mr. President? May I ask why?"

"Yes, you may, Colonel. But, first, let me preface my answer with a bit of background information."

Turning to address the court stenographer, the president said, "Ma'am, your services are not needed for the forthcoming discussion and you are excused, but please don't go too far. We may need you again, shortly."

Addressing Colonel Elsberry, he continued, "Colonel, I'll ask you to stay, as a witness to what is about to transpire, as we'll be addressing *due process* issues."

The judge nodded his assent.

As the stenographer left the room, Outlaw was puzzled by these developments, but Major Ball nudged him and whispered, "Wait for it."

The president poured himself a glass of water from the carafe on the table in front of him, took a sip, and began, "Colonel, Lieutenant Lawless has committed no crime. He hasn't told you anything, I'm sure, on advice of counsel, and rightly so. However, I personally conducted telephone interviews with his surviving, fellow crewmembers, Captains Stumpfegger and Chinchilla, as well as Senior Airman Stokes, from the Oval Office, last evening. The Joint Chiefs were present on those conference calls and will attest to everything that was said.

"In their recorded, verbal statements, given under promise of immunity by me, each of them told the same story, and I mean the *same* story, in detail. My Chief of Staff has brought along the transcripts of those recorded conversations, should you wish to read them. I'm sure you would find them both surprising and fascinating."

The wing commander's face drained of color, as the president continued, "Colonel, the Pale Horse strike was an on-shelf plan here in the 423rd Bomb Wing, which you approved by your signature, when you assumed command of this wing. Implicit in that approval was that aircrews under your command would be able to follow orders and execute the mission.

"Captain McQuagg was the designated aircraft commander for that mission, when it was ordered, and I understand he was reassigned to that crew due to manning contingencies within the wing. There was no question whatsoever about the legality of the order that came down, based on the peril our nation faced that day.

"As I said, the surviving members of the Pale Horse strike crew all told the same story. Captain McQuagg took it upon himself to turn the aircraft around and attempt to return here to Spurlin, before any of the assigned targets had been struck. All three were quite clear and precise on that point. I've no doubt Lieutenant Lawless will echo that thought, as well.

"In effect, Colonel, Captain McQuagg was refusing to obey a lawful order from the NCA. Period."

"But, Mr. President..." Rogers attempted to interject.

The president cut him off with a raised palm and continued, "Captain McQuagg had neither the legal nor moral command authority to make that decision, Colonel. At the time of Captain McQuagg's decision, none of his crew reported any aircraft systems malfunctions whatsoever. There was no reason at all for Captain McQuagg to abort the mission. While it could be argued that he was having a 'crisis of conscience,' the actions his crew described to me smack of cowardice and resultant willful disobedience of a legal order. At best, his was a strategy of despair.

"The remaining crew members discussed the situation and came to the same conclusion. They then agreed to take the course of action that would enable them to proceed and strike their assigned targets. In order to make that happen, Lieutenant Lawless had to eliminate Captain McQuagg, unfortunately. Otherwise, a struggle between the two pilots on the flight deck may well have resulted in the aircraft departing controlled flight and crashing into the sea without having struck any targets at all and the consequent loss of the entire crew and seven nuclear missiles, along with a very expensive airplane.

"Colonel, this was in no way a 'mutiny,' as you stated in your original, written complaint, nor was it, 'murder.' The remaining crew members clearly understood their orders and did exactly what they promised this nation they'd do. They followed orders, which were fully within the guidelines of current national defense obligations, and took all steps necessary to accomplish their mission.

"Had this crew returned to this base without having struck their targets, we might well still be at war or perhaps would've lost it altogether. God alone knows how many more American troops would be dead, wounded, or missing, by now; not to mention civilians who would've been unfortunate enough to get caught in the way. We might have even had a full-scale nuclear exchange with the Soviets, by now, and none of us would be here. The fact that Captain McQuagg refused an order of that magnitude falls squarely on *your* shoulders, Colonel. Although he is no longer here to account for himself, I still intend to take action, in that regard."

Colonel Rogers' shoulders slumped and his face took on a horrified expression.

"With all due respect, Mr. President, how was I responsible for that?"

President Harvey raised an eyebrow to Bergen, who had taken the remaining seat, which happened to be to the left of Outlaw.

"Before Special Agent Cyr enlightens us, Colonel, let me say that we looked at the fitness reports, both OERs and APRs, of everyone involved, including yours and even Captain McQuagg's father. We know that, as a young lieutenant, you were his father's copilot for a while in the B-47. There was a personal connection there and, the way I see things, this whole Article-32 procedure was a vendetta against Lieutenant Lawless for killing your friend's son."

The president then nodded to Special Agent Cyr, who began, "Gentlemen, five months ago, the OSI office here at Spurlin received word through the Captown Police Department of a report given them by the Emergency Room staff at Captown Regional Medical Center. All dates and times have been verified as accurate and are contained in the briefing notes I've prepared for you, should you wish to examine them.

"Two ER physicians treated the McQuagg family, who went there the Thursday morning in question, after Captain McQuagg left home to report for a week-long alert cycle. Mrs. Martha McQuagg told one of the treating physicians that she waited until then to prevent her husband from further harming the children or her.

"Both physicians wrote in their treatment reports that both boys showed evidence of physical abuse, as evidenced by numerous bruises and contusions. The older boy, in fact, had a broken nose, which he stated was the result of his father punching him in a drunken rage. The younger boy, Beasley McQuagg, had a contusion around his left eye and bruising on both buttocks consistent with being punched and a severe beating with a belt, as well as evidence of a belt *buckle*. The attending physician further stated that x-rays revealed the child had a crushed eye socket, which would require surgery to repair.

"Gentlemen, this isn't the sort of information that's normally given to law enforcement, unless state statutes dictate such, due to it falling under doctor-patient privilege. We obtained permission from Mrs. McQuagg only yesterday to have it released to us."

The thought of little Beezer, of whom Outlaw had grown quite fond, on the receiving end of such a beating, brought a sick feeling to his gut. He also found the thought of "drunken rage" puzzling, because at work and in the alert shack, McQuagg had purported himself to be a teetotaler. Surprise at that revelation was evident on the faces of Lieutenant Colonel Spraggins and Major Mac, as well.

Bergen continued, "While Mrs. McQuagg's treatment report showed evidence of being slapped repeatedly, in addition to a broken rib resulting from a punch, the daughter's report proved to be the most disturbing of all. The treating physician and nurse who examined her, genital area, on the basis of the complaints she made, found evidence of possible sexual abuse. She reluctantly attributed that activity to her father being drunk, then suddenly stopped talking to the medical staff.

"Mrs. McQuagg further stated to the doctors that her husband did indeed drink copiously at home, particularly when returning home after alert cycles. She also stated this was an issue he carefully guarded and kept from his work environment.

"Finally, she stated that, although the McQuaggs reside in the family-housing area, here on base, she sought treatment at a civilian hospital to keep this issue away from neighbors and Captain McQuagg's superiors."

All eyes in the conference room were now squarely on the Colonel Rogers, whose hands were shaking noticeably.

Bergen continued, "We conducted interviews with several of the McQuaggs' on-base neighbors, who attested to hearing shouting coming from those quarters on numerous occasions and periods of time, as long as two weeks, when none of the McQuagg children could be seen playing outside with other children in the family housing area. Our suspicions were confirmed, to a degree, by Mrs. McQuagg, who indicated that those periods followed abusive episodes by her husband. These interviews lend credence to the reports we received from the civilian hospital, by way of the Captown Police Department."

Bergen concluded her briefing by placing her notes in a neat stack in front of her and asking, "Do any of you gentlemen have any questions for either Special Agent Simpson or me?"

Lieutenant General Lupold, Commander of the 8th Air Force, asked, "Yes, Agent Cyr. Why didn't your office investigate this matter further?"

Special Agent Simpson interjected and answered in Bergen's stead, "General, literally before our office could begin an investigation, we received word from the Captown Police Department that no further complaint or cooperation would be forthcoming from Mrs. McQuagg. She refused to cooperate, beyond the initial information given to the medical staff that treated the family."

The general persisted in his questioning, "Special Agent Simpson, OSI operates independently of the chain of command. You weren't bound by anything Colonel Rogers ordered, in that regard."

"That's true, General," Simpson answered, "but, I was forced to make a command decision, based on our manning at the time, which consisted then and still consists of only Agent Cyr and me. At the time, we were engaged in two major, ongoing investigations, not the least of which involved a fairly substantial drug ring operating locally, which found its way onto our base. The other involved espionage in our war plans division. We were very fortunate, in light of the fact only two of us were involved, to affect the arrests of four civilians working at the Physical Plant, six Air Force personnel, in addition to some twenty-two arrests made by federal and local law enforcement off base. That's all, in addition to the NCO who confessed to selling secrets to Soviet agents outside the front gate."

"Okay. Point well stated. I'll defer to your judgement."

Simpson continued, "General, Agent Cyr and I interviewed Mrs. McQuagg at her home, yesterday. The overwhelming impression I took away from our meeting was that she was relieved, to a degree, that Captain McQuagg was dead, as strange as that may sound. Agent Cyr echoed my impressions. That being said, Mrs. McQuagg also stated she was horrified by the thought, but that her husband, at times, had been 'a monster.' *Her* words, gentlemen."

Simpson then nodded to Bergen, who added, "Gentlemen, Mrs. McQuagg told me that Colonel Rogers called her at home and urged her not to say anything further, after her initial report to the medical staff at the hospital. To do so would have adverse results on her husband's career; ending it, so to speak. While she acknowledged the fact that there was an old family connection between Colonel Rogers and the McQuagg family, she indicated to me that the colonel was more threatening in his tone than anything else. She was emphatic on that point.

"Therefore, she told the Captown Police she would have nothing further to say and that no further cooperation from her or her children would be forthcoming. We pulled the pertinent telephone records and the McQuagg family quarters did indeed receive a call from Colonel Rogers' office that matched the date she gave us. We could find no evidence in those records of a phone call originating *from* the McQuagg household to the wing commander's office."

"Did you question Colonel Rogers about it, at the time?" the general asked.

"He told us he was aware of the issues in question and to shelve it," Agent Simpson answered.

"Did he say why, Agent Simpson?"

"Yes, sir. He said he was made aware of the situation, that he had spoken with Mrs. McQuagg, and that she told him the medical staff had either falsified or misinterpreted a great deal of the information gleaned from the physical examinations of the McQuagg family. Those were *his* allegations, General, not hers. She stated she had no reason to believe the medical staff had falsified or misunderstood anything at all. Colonel Rogers also told me that the local authorities would be handling it, if anything else were to come of it, but that they were closing their investigation. He specifically used the words, 'stand down,' General.

"Gentlemen, we followed up with the JAG office on this and briefed them thoroughly. It was JAG's opinion that a successful prosecution of Captain McQuagg could not be accomplished without the complete cooperation of Mrs. McQuagg and her children. The JAG staff further stated that prosecutions of that type are almost impossible without the cooperation of the victims. I had my reservations, based on the medical reports, but, as I said, we had other irons in the fire at the time which I considered potentially more detrimental to national security."

"Very well. Thank you, Agents Simpson and Cyr. You are both dismissed."

General Hatcher, Commander in Chief of the Strategic Air Command, spoke next and directed his remarks to a very visibly shaken Colonel Rogers.

He began, "Colonel Rogers, as you know, we hold all of our SAC personnel to the highest standards of legal and moral behavior. That's the basis of our Personnel Reliability Program, our PRP: to prevent situations exactly like the one that transpired with Captain McQuagg during the Pale Horse mission during a time of great national peril. Discipline and adherence to regulations and established policies and procedures are the lynchpin of our strategic deterrence mission. You failed us, every American, in that regard.

"Regardless of the status of the OSI's investigation, you had more than ample reason to pull Captain McQuagg's PRP certification and ground him. That's exactly what you should've done, according to the letter and spirit of the regulations. There were other pilots in your wing fully certified and capable of flying the Pale Horse mission in a pinch, yet you specifically directed Lieutenant Colonel Spraggins to reassign him to crew duty, knowing well he might have to fly the mission in question, given the situation at the time.

"Had you taken the appropriate action, we likely wouldn't be here, right now, and Captain McQuagg wouldn't be dead. He might well be in shackles and handcuffs over in correctional custody, but he wouldn't be dead."

Both Spraggins and McClellan nodded in agreement and CINCSAC addressed them by asking, "Were either of you two gentlemen aware of the McQuagg situation?"

Spraggins spoke for both of them, "No, sir. Nothing related to this ever made its way down to the squadron level. None of us had any idea that Captain McQuagg had alcohol-related issues. He'd never been in trouble of any sort and none of us had ever seen him take a drink. He put on a good act, apparently. That, and given the fact that he obviously passed his security background investigation for his 'Top Secret' security clearance, we certainly had no reason for concern, sir."

Major McClellan nodded his agreement, knowing that McQuagg had been a chickenshit excuse maker, but he, too, had been hoodwinked on the alcohol issue. He'd seen McQuagg and his wife at the O'Club having dinner, on occasion, but had never seen so much as a beer or glass of wine on his table or in his hand.

The general continued, "Thank you, Colonel Spraggins. I suppose Fate knows where and what every man hides."

General Hatcher then turned and again addressed Colonel Rogers, "To underscore the president's point, Colonel, your interference in this matter jeopardized the most important combat sortie flown by a U.S. Air Force bomber crew since 1945. Tens of thousands of American lives depended on it, potentially millions, as well as perhaps the continued existence of the free world."

President Harvey then spoke, "With all that taken into consideration, Colonel, we will give you time to find counsel, preparatory to convening yet another Article-32 investigation around the issue of your dereliction of duty and obstruction of justice, in the matter of alleged crimes perpetrated by

Captain McQuagg upon his family. Our court recorder, as you know, is standing by."

Rogers appeared broken and could only meekly respond, "Mr. President..."

The president again silenced him with an upheld palm, "I'll make this easy for you, Colonel. In lieu of the Article-32 proceedings, you'll submit your written request for retirement, which I will personally approve, within the hour. You'll retire at your present rank, with the annuity and all attendant benefits in place. However, you will receive an efficiency report that otherwise would be guaranteed to end to your career and one you certainly wouldn't want any prospective civilian employer to read. It's *your* choice, Colonel. You're being given your Fifth Amendment right to *due process,* here, within the strictures of the UCMJ. Which course of action would you prefer?"

"I...I'll take the retirement, Mr. President. I guess I have no options," Rogers stammered, barely audible.

"Wise choice," said President Harvey, "So, by my verbal order, you are hereby relieved of command of the 423rd Bombardment Wing. Your Deputy Commander for Operations, Colonel Lopez, will assume command, immediately. Outside the door, the Chief Master Sergeant of the Air Force and two security policemen will escort you back to your office, in order for you to prepare your letter for my endorsement and to remove from your desk and office what personal items you don't wish to leave behind. Consider yourself under arrest and in their custody, until your paperwork is completed and approved by me. You're dismissed, Colonel."

Rogers stood slowly and walked stiffly across the room and out the door. Outlaw found himself trembling, having just witnessed the takedown of a full, bird-colonel by some extremely heavy firepower. He could only guess at what was coming next. Based on the president's poker-faced handling of the situation, he was deathly afraid his neck would be next in the noose.

Once the colonel was gone, the president turned to Outlaw and asked, "Lieutenant, has counsel advised you not to answer any questions, according to your Fifth Amendment right?"

"Yes, Mr. President," Outlaw answered warily, straightening up a bit in chair.

The president nodded to his chief of staff, who removed a sheet of paper from his briefcase and handed it to him. The president reached inside his coat pocket, removed a pen, and signed the document. Once he had capped the pen and returned it to his pocket, he returned the paper. The chief of staff stood, walked around the table, and handed it to Outlaw.

"Lieutenant Lawless, in accordance the powers entrusted to me by Article II of the U.S. Constitution, I'm granting you a full, free, and complete pardon for any federal crimes you may have committed during the execution of the recent nuclear strike mission you flew against targets in Europe. That pardon also extends to any federal crimes, either felony or misdemeanor, you may have committed as an officer of the United States Air Force, from the date of your commissioning up to and including today's date. I am also granting the same to Captains Stumpfegger and Chinchilla, as well as Senior Airman Stokes. None of this will crop up to haunt any of you, in the future. Do you understand what I'm telling you, son?"

"Yes, Mr. President," was all Outlaw could get out of a dry mouth.

"Good. That blot on your training records from Garriott Air Force Base has also been expunged from your personnel records. You may now speak freely about the events of the Pale Horse mission, without fear of any sort of criminal consequence.

"Let's get the rest of your crew in here, before we continue, Lieutenant," the president added.

Stumpy, Henry Chinchilla, and Stokes entered the room and all three nodded grimly at Outlaw, unaware of what had just transpired. Once they had been seated and the president had informed them of their previously agreed-upon immunity and the pardons, they relaxed noticeably. Stumpy even gave the president one of his Mona Lisa smiles.

Addressing the other three crewmembers, the president said, "Gentlemen, we have transcripts of our telephone conversations from last night. You were aware transcripts would be made. Is that correct?"

The three answered simultaneously, "Yes, sir."

As the White House Chief of Staff took the folders from his briefcase, the president continued, "Gentlemen, for your individual safety and that of your immediate and extended families, your names have not and will not, in any way, be released to the press or the American public. The phrase, 'Pale Horse' is already being scrubbed from all air traffic control logs and any other documentation into which it may have been entered, to include the emergency war orders tasked to this wing.

"This was a decision I considered very carefully, given the reckless manner in which the American media is sometimes prone to act. The reach of our enemies is long, in our modern world. The safe assumption is that each of you has a dossier on file somewhere deep within bowels of the KGB, as no doubt do I.

"The Director of the FBI and I have already discussed this particular issue and, if at any point in the future, you or anyone else becomes aware of a threat to you or your families, the FBI stands fully ready to place you in what amounts to their witness protection program. Do you gentlemen understand?"

Outlaw and the others acknowledged that they indeed did.

The president then took a sip of water from his glass, smiled and said, "Okay, gentlemen, before we debrief this airplane ride, you need to know that the Air Force Chief of Staff, CINCSAC, and the 8th Air Force Commander, along with the Chief Master Sergeant of the Air Force, accompanied me on this trip for very specific reasons, which you will see, shortly.

"As we've already had the blow by blow from Captains Stumpfegger and Chinchilla, as well as Airman Stokes, let's hear your recap of the Pale Horse strike, Lieutenant Lawless."

Outlaw spoke to the president and the generals for nearly half an hour, recounting McQuagg's attempt at aborting the mission, the encounters with the four MiG-25s, the malfunctions with the two errant PALMs, the damage done to the #7 engine by the Soviet air-to-air missile, the subsequent issue with the #8 engine, the naval SAM launch and shoot-down of the KC-10 tanker, and the loss of two of the rudder-and-elevator hydraulic systems. He also recounted the ejections from aircraft on final approach.

When he concluded, the president responded, "Son, Colonel Spraggins and Major McClellan both tell me that your abilities as a copilot far exceed most of those of similar experience and training, particularly in regard to your ability to air refuel, take off, land, and defend against fighters. Why do you think that is, son?"

"Well, Mr. President, I was fortunate to be assigned to a crew with an IP, Major Ivanoff, when I got here, which meant I got a fair amount of experience in the left seat, as well as a pretty good amount of time air refueling; lots of opportunities to take off and land, as well. Most copilots don't fall into a situation that favorable. Ordinary line pilots can't perform touch-and-go landings without an IP in one of the seats and, obviously, can't allow copilots to perform touch-and-goes, nor can they allow them to attempt air refuelin'. Plus, I've been flyin' the T-37, every chance I get. But, I *do* have somethin' to add, Mr. president."

President Harvey nodded and said, "Go on, Lieutenant."

"The other thing is, we don't really train like we're gonna fight."

267

General Hatcher fixed his gaze on Outlaw and asked, "How so, Lieutenant?"

"A little book, General, a little book that's in all of the mission packages we have on file in the Vault. One day, durin' target study, I saw this little book in the folder called *Fighter-Interceptor Tactics*. I was curious, so I pulled it out and started readin'. I could tell from the spine that it had never even been opened, which goes hand-in-hand with the fact we never talk about that stuff. We talk a lot about SAC tactical doctrine durin' low level operations and for things like minimum interval takeoffs, the MITOs, but every time we run a fighter intercept exercise, we just have to bore along through the sky, mostly straight and level, and serve mainly as targets for the fighters. We don't ever talk about or practice how to defend ourselves at altitude, which is where the gunner would be most likely to engage targets. As things stand, the gunners may as well sit on their hands back there.

"To be blunt, gentlemen, we always have to play to our weaknesses and to the fighters' strengths, as far as fighter-interceptor exercises go; never the other way around."

The president snorted at the kid's remark, but the generals merely looked surprised.

"Well, Mr. President, I started askin' some questions to the one pilot in our squadron who's flown the F-4 with TAC in the SAC-TAC exchange program. He had some good insights and he and I talk a good bit, every time we're on alert. He agrees that we don't train like we're gonna fight, regardless of what's said to the contrary. My opinion, Mr. President, is there isn't enough information shared between us and the TAC guys, like maybe we need one of those F-5 aggressor squadrons to brush up on Soviet interceptor tactics and come work with us, every now and then."

Harvey looked to his generals and said, "Are you gentlemen takin' notes? I'm a fighter pilot myself and this guy's makin' a ton of sense."

The president then asked, "Lieutenant Lawless, your training records indicate you were a top graduate in your pilot training class. Guys who graduate at the top usually end up in either fighters or being plowed back into Air Training Command as instructor pilots. What's your story?"

"A vindictive student squadron commander, Mr. President."

"We're all ears, Lieutenant," said the president as he sat back in his chair and relaxed a bit.

"Mr. President, my original assignment out of flight school was an F-16 to Luke. I failed a quarter's inspection, subsequent to that assignment drop, because I didn't clean my oven to the satisfaction of the inspectin' officer. I also got what amounted to that DWI for squealin' my tires on base at

Garriott. I didn't blow enough on the breathalyzer to be legally drunk, but after that, the STURON commander decided I wasn't worthy of assignment to the F-16 and had me reassigned to the B-52 here at Spurlin."

The president interrupted, "So, you're sayin' that assignment was punitive?"

"Yes, sir. He was clear about that. Why he had a beef with me, I don't know. I'd never had any interaction with him at all, before that, even though he'd briefed our class on various things at the start of the program; that, and I'd see him around the T-38 squadron and at the officers' club, every now and then," Outlaw answered.

The president looked in the direction of the Chief of Staff of the Air Force and asked, "So, General, you're using B-52s, in some instances, as punitive assignments?"

The general feigned ignorance, but knew it was entirely true.

"Mr. President," Outlaw added, "I know of two FAIPs, First Assignment Instructor Pilots, at Garriott who'd received fighter assignments, then got reassigned to BUFFs for punitive reasons, both resultin' from alcohol-related incidents. I also knew two more FAIPs who were assigned to KC-135s for similar reasons."

The president rocked back in his chair and said, "Well, this is certainly somethin' that needs fixin', don't you think, General? After all, we've had a 'universally assignable pilot' training program in place since the Vietnam years. I understand that not everyone who graduates from pilot training is ready to handle the demands of a high-performance fighter, right off the bat, but, in light of what this crew has just accomplished, I find it an insult to pilots and officers like Lieutenant Colonel Spraggins, Major McClellan, and Lieutenant Lawless here to use assignment to the B-52 or KC-135 as a punitive tool.

"When I was flyin' the F-105 out of Thailand, I flew with some heavy drivers; C-141s, and the like, who volunteered for the F-105 program, just so they could get in a fighter cockpit and get in the war. Oddly, I saw very few B-52 pilots assigned to the PACAF fighter wings, during those years. Now, I see why. For the most part, the heavy drivers were good sticks in the Thud, and even in the F-100, and the F-4, from what I heard; a little inexperienced, and maybe a bit out of their element in the beginning, but, once they settled down, they did okay and pressed home those bomb runs. Sure, we did a little beefin' about heavy drivers pollutin' our pristine, fighter pilot universe, but those guys had the moxie to show up and do what was asked of 'em. You're CINCSAC, General Hatcher. How do you feel about that?"

"Not very good, Mr. President," the general answered, glowering at the Air Force Chief of Staff.

"I wouldn't think so. As far as I'm concerned, that whole idea is an insult to one of the Air Force's original, major commands. To top it all off, MPC is assigning discipline problems, alcohol-related problems, to this nation's main nuclear war-fighting entity. That rubs against my comfort level in a big way," President Harvey said.

Again addressing General Hubbard, he added, "General, I want a review of all B-52 and KC-135 pilot assignments, both FAIP and initial assignments out of pilot training, going back four years. I want to know which ones were punitive, in the manner Lieutenant Lawless just described. I also want to know the names of the wing and squadron commanders involved in those assignments and the circumstances that led to them. If any improprieties are found on the part of the commanders involved, I want to know that, too, and I want that report on my desk one week from today, as well as a briefing from you and the Secretary of the Air Force on what remedies you think are appropriate."

The president winked at Outlaw and said, "Now, *there's* a witch hunt, for ya."

The president next looked to Spraggins and McClellan, then asked, "Colonel Spraggins, I saw in your personnel folder that you'd flown the T-38 at Garriott. What are your thoughts on this matter?"

Lieutenant Colonel Spraggins leaned forward in his chair and began, "Mr. President, Lieutenant Lawless is right. I was assigned to Garriott as a T-38 IP after six years of operational flyin'. I'd done a tour in Vietnam as an O-1 FAC, right out of UPT, and two tours as a B-52 aircraft commander; one stateside and an Arc Light tour. In total, I'd flown three-hundred combat missions.

"I was the first B-52 pilot assigned to Garriott Air Force Base as an instructor pilot in the T-38. The Garriott command structure sure didn't make me feel welcome, either. Instead of treatin' me like a combat experienced captain with six years of operational flyin', they treated me more like a second lieutenant right out of flight school. The first eighteen months were very unpleasant.

"Finally, I was chosen to be a flight commander. The next day, right after I conducted my first morning briefing in that capacity, I was called to the squadron commander's office, where he told me he'd changed his mind."

The president's raised his eyebrows in surprise and asked, "Really?"

"Yes, sir. However, ATC Stan Eval showed up about a month and a half later, for what amounts to an ORI in the pilot training world, and, of the twenty no-notice check rides given, I was only one of three who passed. I bagged a Q1-Outstanding on an IP formation check. The following week, I was back in that flight commander slot and finished at Garriott as the only captain they'd ever had as a section commander. I proved to 'em I wasn't some second-stringer.

"In all, I'd say the fighter pilots running ATC and the FAIPs, many of whom *think* they're fighter pilots, don't seem to think too highly of the bomber world," Spraggins concluded.

President Harvey took it all in and asked McClellan, "Major, what are your thoughts on the matter?"

Major Mac cleared his throat before speaking and said, "They square with those of Lieutenant Lawless and Colonel Spraggins, Mr. President. Almost half my pilot training class went to Southeast Asia, right off the bat. I did a year as a B-52 copilot at Wurtsmith, when Colonel Spraggins was there on his stateside SAC tour. The carrot and stick dangled in front of our noses to get bodies in cockpits and into the war was that if we volunteered to go to Southeast Asia, we could go in the aircraft of our choice.

"I volunteered and wanted to go in the F-4, RF-4, or RF-101, but when the guys handlin' those assignments at MPC saw I was a SAC B-52 resource, I got shunted off to Vietnam in the C-123, instead. The same thing happened to all the B-52 copilots I knew who volunteered: C-123s, C-7s, and the occasional C-130. If there were any assigned to fighter cockpits within my narrow frame of experience, I remained unaware of 'em. MAC guys in the C-130s and C-141s, however, seemed to get the aircraft of their choice, as you previously alluded. I guess the C-141 crowd in the 'Airline Lead-in Program' had the market cornered on the plumb assignments, as well."

The president took a sip of water before responding, "I hear you guys, loud and clear, and yes, gentlemen, I've heard all the hogwash along the way about 'there are no bad assignments.' Some may indeed be preferable, however."

Outlaw spoke next, "Mr. President, I have a few thoughts to add, if I may."

"By all means, Lieutenant. This is the forum for you to say whatever's on your mind. You've earned the right, especially in light of what's about to happen."

Outlaw looked puzzled by the president's remarked, but continued, "Well, sir, I've come to see things in a very different light from what I perceived in pilot training. I'm gonna beg your pardon, in advance, as I know both you and the Chief of Staff are career fighter pilots.

"I think the Air Force, without intendin' to, has created a caste system within itself. By that, I mean if you aren't a fighter pilot, you're seen as a second-class citizen, at least in Air Training Command. Fighter pilots there seem to think that's 'gospel.' What Colonel Spraggins and Major McClellan both just said squares that.

"The fact is, gentlemen, bomber pilots and other bomber crew dogs are warriors, as much as anyone else in the Air Force. We get a bum rap and, to be honest, SAC isn't gettin' much in the way of top-drawer graduates out of the pilot training pipeline. They're mostly guys who graduate at or near the bottom of their classes.

"As we discussed, those assignments are sometimes punitive, where FAIPs are concerned and, in cases like mine, student pilots, too. As a result, BUFFs are talked down during pilot training, as if anyone could do it, but no one really wants to, and to be frank, nobody really gives a shit. I heard IPs crow and laugh about the idea that we don't have any 'tactics,' *per se.*

"Well, Mr. President, the fighter guys think they can do our jobs, but they can't. They fly itty-bitty jets that don't have the endurance for deep-penetration missions into the Asian landmass and require constant air refuelin' to get to their own targets and usually back home. Their payloads are miniscule, compared to what we carry, and that includes the fighters sittin' Victor-alert in Europe. Their ability to operate strategically is almost nonexistent. In tactical environments, they're fine and they do their jobs. But, when it comes to long-range, strategic bombin', we're the guys you call to do the heavy hittin'.

"Gentlemen, as to these nonexistent tactics, bomber tactics are what we have to do stay alive when the fighter guys protectin' us from other fighters and SAMs are out of gas, out of bullets, out of range, and we're shit-outta-luck. By the time we reach our targets, they're back at the bar, thumpin' their chests, showin' their asses to the world, tellin' war stories, and lookin' down their noses at the rest of the Air Force aviation world. Simply put, I think we need to take steps to ensure the bomber force, and the strategic force, as a whole, gets its share of credit, given how successful it was in Vietnam."

"Son, did you just say *itty-bitty jets, shit,* and *asses* to the President of the United States, all in the space of about fifteen seconds, and in the context of bad-mouthing fighter pilots?" CINCSAC asked with a laugh.

Everyone in the room directed their attention to the president, who was sitting with his chin on his chest and his shoulders bobbing up and down with silent laughter. He'd heard language of that sort, and far worse, in every ready room and officers' club bar from East Anglia to Thailand and every place in between, though not in the context of a lieutenant saying it to an audience of the President of the United States and a host of three and four-star generals. The Chief of Staff and CINCSAC were laughing, too. The Old Man was grinning from ear to ear, and McClellan thought he was only a few seconds away from rupturing internal organs to keep from guffawing.

"Excuse me, Mr. President. I mighta got a little carried away, there. I've been through a rough stretch, lately, and I guess I'm a little edgy, right now. Matter of fact, I'm shakin' like a leaf," a flustered Outlaw answered.

CINCSAC replied, "No, Lieutenant, no need to apologize. It was insightful and it was brilliant. You haven't said anything in here today that I haven't known and stewed about for years. And, after all, you're the guy who told me you'd have my goddamned airplane back on the ground in a few minutes. Son, you're the kind of guy who goes out there for us and gets results. The same applies to the rest of your crew."

President Harvey looked at the general with raised eyebrows and asked, "He said that? He said he'd have your goddamned airplane back on the ground in a few minutes?"

The general nodded and smiled, and then the president added, "No need to fret, Lieutenant. In light of what you've accomplished, you've earned the right to tell us we're full of shit, right here, in this room.

"By the way, Lieutenant Lawless, I looked at your 'dream sheet' in your personnel folder. It showed a B-52 to Spurlin as your number-one choice out of pilot training. I found that a little odd, for a top grad. I also happened to notice that your signature on that document did not match any other of your signatures in your personnel folder. Any idea why that is?" the president asked.

"I would say the STURON commander at Garriott either forged it himself or had it done, Mr. President. From what I understand, he retired right after my UPT class graduated."

"I see. General Hubbard, let's recall him to active duty and see what he has to say about falsifyin' government documents. If he's indeed still on active duty, he'll be easy enough to find. Get that process started immediately. Light him up with an Article-32, if he doesn't come clean, right away."

A sense of deep satisfaction swept over Outlaw, realizing that Marble Man was now going to be called on the carpet by the Chief of Staff of the Air Force and held to accounts. He would love to be a fly on that particular wall.

45. "Speed Record"

Conference Room
Wing Headquarters Building
423rd Bombardment Wing
Spurlin Air Force Base, Maine
December 10, 1982

Addressing the remaining Pale Horse crew members, President Harvey said, "Gentlemen, while the details of your recent mission will remain highly classified, each of you is nonetheless deserving of recognition by your president, your Air Force, and a grateful nation. "Therefore, First Lieutenant Coley will be awarded the Air Force Cross, posthumously. That's most unfortunate, but sometimes it's the price that has to be paid; a possibility each of us acknowledged when we raised our right hands and swore the blood oath. His wife was notified and invited to be here, today, but begged off, citing concerns around her husband's funeral arrangements and all that goes with that.

"Captains Stumpfegger and Chinchilla, you will each be awarded the Air Force Cross, as well. Your Commander in Chief and your nation are both in your debt and impressed with the manner in which you carried out your orders, under some extremely difficult circumstances.

"Senior Airman Stokes, you are being awarded the Distinguished Flying Cross for downing the MiG-25, which was confirmed by not only Captain Chinchilla, but by a Royal Navy frigate operating in the North Sea, which saw the aircraft hit the water less than half a mile away. Shortly thereafter, they fished out the badly wounded pilot. He confirmed what happened, so you're the first B-52 gunner to down an enemy fighter since the Linebacker II raids over Hanoi in '72. You may very well be the last gunner to do so, as technology and tactics evolve. Who knows? Also, I'm meritoriously promoting you to the rank of staff sergeant. Congratulations, *Sergeant.*"

President Harvey continued, "As all of you were injured, to some degree, as the result of enemy action, you'll each be awarded the Purple Heart, as will Lieutenant Coley, for the wounds resulting in his death.

"Gentlemen, I know I speak for the generals here and your squadron commander when I say I couldn't be more proud of you. You conducted yourselves according to the highest standards and traditions of all of us who've ever worn the blue uniform. But, before we get to Lieutenant Lawless, let me underscore one very important point: the citations accompanying these awards will be highly redacted and therefore devoid of details. That's for your own safety, as I stated previously. Your squadron mates know what you did, I know what you did, and so do the generals here.

"Now, Lieutenant Lawless, your entire chain of command is assembled here for one reason that hasn't yet been brought to light; namely, Captains Stumpfegger and Chinchilla, as well as Senior Airman...er, *Sergeant* Stokes, indicated to me last night that they thought your actions and performance during the Pale Horse strike were deserving of our nation's highest honor. They told a tale that indicated you had your hands full of airplane from the moment of Captain McQuagg's death and, given an inoperative autopilot on the return leg, you labored under quite a burden, given your myriad duties on the flight deck. Despite your tanker being shot down on the return leg, and given the fact you were hit by a surface-to-air missile on final approach, you managed to put your crew into a position from which they could eject safely, while guiding your aircraft to a point where you yourself could eject safely and have the aircraft come down in an area where no one would be hurt and wartime operations could be maintained on the airfield. These gentlemen told an extraordinary tale."

The president then addressed the Old Man and the generals, "Gentlemen, you've all read the accounts of the crew on the airplane ride up here and heard Lieutenant Lawless explain his side of things. The results obtained from the Pale Horse strike speak for themselves. Crew R-13 put out a very big fire for us, literally and figuratively. We can handle the required paperwork, later, as circumstances dictate.

"Lieutenant Colonel Spraggins, do you support the recommendations of these officers and Sergeant Stokes, regarding Lieutenant Lawless being awarded the Medal of Honor? Frankly, they all agree that the mission couldn't have been done and they wouldn't be alive, today, if it hadn't been for his piloting skills and leadership."

"Yes, sir, Mr. President. Consider my recommendation forwarded to General Lupold at 8th Air Force for his endorsement, in the absence of a wing commander, right now."

"Very well. General Hubbard?"

"I concur, Mr. President. Consider my recommendation forwarded to CINCSAC for his approval."

"We're in agreement," said General Hatcher, speaking for both himself and the Chief of Staff of the Air Force, who merely nodded his concurrence.

President Harvey looked to General Hubbard, who said, "Consider him endorsed, Mr. President."

Turning to look again at Outlaw, the president added, "Son, in the whole history of our great nation, you have just set some sort of speed record for the approval of an award of the Medal of Honor. Congratulations, Lieutenant, and congratulations to you, Captain Stumpfegger, Captain Chinchilla, and Staff Sergeant Stokes."

Outlaw was initially stunned into silence, but managed a shaky, mumbled reply, "You can actually do that, Mr. President?"

The president replied, "Indeed I can, Lieutenant. Extraordinary circumstances necessitate extraordinary actions. In your case, this information is classified and the fewer people who get wind of it in the short term, the better. So, it's my call.

"As we're doing this on the fly, your medals will be here shortly. The wing awards and decorations officer is working feverishly, as we speak, to get the citations done and redacted. He found someone in his realm of endeavor with the equipment and talent to engrave the medals.

"Oh, I almost forgot. Each of you gentlemen will be given the duty assignment of your choice, when your time here is up, or even right now, if you so choose. No need to make an immediate decision, however."

"May I speak, Mr. President?" Outlaw asked.

"Yes, by all means, Lieutenant. You want to move to the head of line on the pilot upgrade list, around here?"

"No, sir. There are two captains and six first lieutenants in line ahead of me. I wouldn't want any of 'em to feel slighted, just because I drew the short straw and had to fly the nuke strike. In a way, sir, I wish somebody else *had* flown it.

"I'd really like to go back to Garriott as an IP in the T-38, Mr. President. When I'm done there, I can come back into SAC as an aircraft commander in the BUFF, or maybe even the B-1, as it becomes operational. I'll be truly ready, then, and won't run the risk of steppin' on anybody's toes."

"You don't want that F-16? It's yours, if you still want it. I'll make sure the TAC and SAC brass are both on board with it. I'm now *the* shot-caller, after all."

"Thank you, sir, but I'll decline. I think I've earned the right to call myself a 'crew dog.' But, I think I've got some things to pass along to the student pilots still in the pipeline."

"Then, we'll make it happen, Lieutenant. Gentlemen, I guess all that's left for us to do is wait for those decorations to get here," said the president with a smile.

The medals arrived a half-hour later, after coffee and small talk, and were duly presented to the four surviving Pale Horse crew members. The meeting was then then dismissed by President Harvey.

As Outlaw limped along on his knee brace out the door, Major McClellan clapped him on the back and said, "Outlaw, after a session like that, you're gonna have to buy me one of those Perriers at the O'Club."

Outlaw chuckled at his candor and said, "Some other time, Major. Can ya give me a rain check? I gotta get home, count the grey hairs I'm sure I've started sproutin', and get some sleep in my own bed. Then, I think I'm gonna go home on convalescent leave for a few weeks and visit my folks."

President Harvey offered his hand to Outlaw. He held the grip and added, "Well, Lieutenant...er, *Outlaw,* as I understand everyone calls you, I need to get back to Washington. Take some leave and get back in the cockpit, soon. We need you in the air, son."

With that, the president saluted him, turned, and then left with his Secret Service detail. Outlaw was a bit stunned, just having been saluted by the President of the United States, but understood that it came with wearing "the Medal."

46. "Another One of Those Talks"

Spurlin Air Force Base
Wing Headquarters Building Parking Lot
December 10, 1982

When Outlaw limped outside into the clear, cold Maine afternoon, the day was already clinging to him and weighing heavily on his shoulders, despite the enormous, albeit guilt-tinged relief coursing through his veins. He squinted against a brilliant sun and saw Bergen leaning against her silver Chevy pickup truck with her arms folded, her cheeks and nose pink from the cold, obviously waiting for him. Her presence in the conference room had been commanding and telegraphed to everyone present that she would be moving up the OSI hierarchy or successful in any law enforcement agency for which she might choose to work, should she choose to leave the Air Force. That countenance had softened, now, back into the Bergen he'd always known, as her breath condensed in the frigid air.

He smiled and said the only thing that came to his mind, "Thanks, Berg. You really saved my ass, in there."

"Hey, I'm not gonna let anybody mess with my man," she said with an unconcerned air, and then lit a cigarette, drawing deeply on it, and avoiding eye contact.

"*Your* man?" he asked.

"Yeah, *my* man," she said, turning her gaze on him.

"I guess we're gonna need to have another one of those talks," he answered, "but first, there's something new you need to know about your man."

With his one good arm, he opened his overcoat and removed the gray wool scarf from around his neck, revealing the powder-blue, star-spangled ribbon with its dangling medal.

"Wow," was all she could manage to reply, overcome as she was by sadness and joy; joy at the fact he was back home and healing and sadness in the knowledge of what he might have had to endure to earn that medal, as well as what demons he might have to fight for the rest of his life.

"Like I've told you all along, Dillon, you're a very special man."

She didn't call him "Dilly" this time.

"That medal bears testament to it," she continued, "and yes, we'll have that talk. We have some catching up to do and I have a great deal of apologizing to do. I want to grow old with you and I can't imagine you not being a part of my life."

An awkward silence filled the distance between them for an instant, before she spoke, again.

"Need a ride home, handsome?" she asked with a wisp of a smile on her lips.

"I sure do, but we've gotta stop havin' these stops and starts, Berg. They're kinda rough on a heart."

"I know," she said. "No more stops, Dillon. I love you."

"I've always hoped you would," he said. "And, just so I know I'm reading' this situation right, like the last time you gave me a ride home, I'm hurtin', but I've got a great girl to see me through. That right?"

"That's affirmative, Flyboy."

THE END

Glossary of Terms

AC – Aircraft-commander; in the B-52 he (women did not fly the B-52 in 1982) sat in the left pilot-seat and served as both mission-commander and crew-commander.

ACE – Accelerated Co-Pilot Enrichment Program, in which B-52 and KC-135 co-pilots had the opportunity to fly the T-37 or T-38 trainer aircraft to build flying hours and increase proficiency.

AI – Air-intercept radar (hostile); in the MiG-25 Foxbat, that radar was known to NATO as "High Lark."

ALPHA – Intrabase radio command net code for the Wing Commander ("wing king," in crew-dog slang); also the first letter designator in the international, phonetic alphabet.

AR – Air-refueling.

BANDIT – A confirmed hostile aircraft.

BOGEY – A suspicious aircraft; one that has not yet been positively identified as friendly or hostile.

BUFF – Air Force-wide nickname for the Boeing B-52 Stratofortress; Big, Ugly, Fat Fucker.

CHAFF – An electronic counter-measure developed during World War II and originally called, "Window." Chaff consists of thin strips of aluminum cut to specific frequency lengths, that, when released from an aircraft, will clutter hostile radar screens. In the B-52G, chaff bundles were stored in the ventral side of the wings between the inboard and outboard flap sections.

CHARLIE – Intrabase radio command net code for the Wing Deputy Commander for Operations (DO); also the third letter in the international, phonetic alphabet.

CIA – U.S. Central Intelligence Agency.

CINCLANT – Commander-in-Chief, Atlantic Command.

CINCSAC – Commander-in-Chief, Strategic Air Command.

DASH-1 – Slang term for any aircraft flight manual in the Air Force inventory; in the case of the B-52G, the technical-order was entitled *T.O. 1B-52G-1*.

DEW – Distant Early Warning; this string of radar installations stretched from the Alaskan Aleutian Islands across Arctic Canada, all the way to Greenland and Iceland. The main function of the "DEW Line" was to watch for the approach of Soviet bombers and missiles aimed at North America.

DIA – U.S. Defense Intelligence Agency.

DO – Deputy-Commander for Operations; "Charlie" in intranasal radio command net parlance.

ECM – Electronic counter-measures, consisting of the ability to jam hostile radar emissions, communications, and/or the dispensing of "chaff" and heat-emitting flares from an aircraft.

FCI – Flight Command Indicator. An instrument controlled by the Radar Navigator on the bomb-run that ensures accuracy on the drop. Once told, the pilot must center the needle in that particular instrument to ensure the proper ground-track to the aiming-point is flown.

FLARES – heat emitting devices designed to confuse the infrared seeker heads on air-to-air or surface-to-air missiles. In the B-52, flares were loaded in the ventral side of the horizontal stabilizers.

GCI – Hostile ground-controlled intercept radar.

GREMLINS – A tongue-in-cheek superstition among Air Force aircrews of mythical creatures running about in aircraft bent on causing mischief and systems malfunctions.

GRU – Soviet Military Intelligence.

HUMINT – Human intelligence; information gleaned from individual sources.

ILS – An airfield-based navigational aid that sends signals for pilots to have course and glide-slope information on final-approach to the airfield. Used mainly for instrument approaches in diminished visibility conditions.

KGB – Soviet Committee for State Security; the Soviet equivalent of the American CIA.

ORI – Operational Readiness Inspection; period inspection of Air Force units to determine combat-readiness.

EW – Electronic Warfare Officer; EWs are also rated navigators.

EWO – Emergency War Orders; orders which result in nuclear-strikes.

FOXBAT – NATO code-name for the Soviet MiG-25 fighter-interceptor aircraft.

IN – Instructor Navigator.

IP – Instructor Pilot; also, the "Initial Point" on a bomb-run (last chance for proper bomb-aiming).

"IVAN" – U.S. military slang for Russia or Russians.

MiG – Soviet aircraft built by the Mikoyan-Gurevich Design Bureau; sometimes used as jargon for any Soviet-built fighter aircraft.

NATO – North Atlantic Treaty Organization; the U.S. and its European allies.

NSA – National Security Agency.

OSI – Office of Special Investigations; the U.S. Air Force's criminal investigative branch.

PRP – Personnel Reliability Program; and evaluation process within the Strategic Air Command the determined an individual's suitability to deal with the handling and/or release of nuclear-weapons.

REFORGER – An annual exercise conducted by the U.S. and its NATO allies that forces could be quickly deployed to West Germany (Return of Forces to Germany). In the event of war, it would not be termed *Exercise* REFORGER, but rather *Operation* REFORGER.

ROTC – Reserve Officer Training Corps.

SAC – Strategic Air Command; the main nuclear war-fighting entity of the U.S. with manned bombers and Intercontinental Ballistic Missiles (ICBMs).

SAM – Surface-to-air missile or missile-system.

SCATANA – Security Control of Air Traffic and Navigational Aids; wartime control measure to selectively activate U.S. navigational aids to deny enemy use of them and established FAA airways within the United States.

SIGINT – Signals intelligence; information gleaned from monitoring enemy communications.

SIOP – Single Integrated Operational Plan; the U.S. "blueprint" for nuclear war, involving the U.S. Air Force and Navy.

SPETSNAZ – Soviet/Russian special operations forces; still extant within the Russian army and navy.

TAC – Tactical Air Command; the Air Force's main tactical (fighter) command.

TDY – Temporary Duty; usually off-station for 180 days or less.

TWEET – The T-37B jet trainer aircraft.

UNT – USAF Undergraduate Navigator Training.

UPT – USAF Undergraduate Pilot Training.

USAFE – United States Air Forces in Europe.

WILD WEASEL – USAF tactical fighter aircraft equipped with detection-gear and weaponry to destroy surface-to-air missile (SAM) batteries and/or conventional anti-aircraft defenses. In 1982, those aircraft were the F-105G Thunderchief and the F-4G Phantom.

WINCHESTER – A status advisory that a USAF aircraft has expended all of its ordinance.

CPSIA information can be obtained
at www.ICGtesting.com
Printed in the USA
LVHW080755120721
692417LV00011B/34